EMBERS OF PASSION

Anna woke up in the middle of the night. It was completely dark, and only embers from the fire gave a slight glow in the dark cave.

She moved closer to Nathan, and his arm automatically tightened around her.

She ran her hand up to his face, running her fingers along his jaw and cheek. She loved his face. She had loved it the first moment she had seen him. Her body jumped as she heard the cry of the mountain cat again, and she moved still closer to Nathan.

Suddenly his arms were around her, pulling her up to him, his mouth covering hers with an urgency she never before knew existed.

"Anna." She heard him say her name, and it excited her more than she thought possible. His lips again sought hers in the darkness, and she felt his hands moving down the length of her body, feeling, exploring.

He stopped suddenly, his hands cupping her face.

"Are you sure you want to do this?"

"Yes," she said without hesitation. . . .

SWEET MEDICINE'S PROPHECY
by Karen A. Bale

#1: SUNDANCER'S PASSION   (1778, $3.95)

Stalking Horse was the strongest and most desirable of the
tribe, and Sun Dancer surrounded him with her spell-bind-
ing radiance. But the innocence of their love gave way to
passion—and passion, to betrayal. Would their relationship ever survive the ultimate sin?

#2: LITTLE FLOWER'S DESIRE   (1779, $3.95)

Taken captive by savage Crows, Little Flower fell in love
with the enemy, handsome brave Young Eagle. Though
their hearts spoke what they could not say, they could only
dream of what could never be. . . .

#3: WINTER'S LOVE SONG   (1780, $3.95)

The dark, willowy Anaeva had always desired just one
man: the half-breed Trenton Hawkins. But Trenton belonged to two worlds—and was torn between two women.
She had never failed on the fields of war; now she was determined to win on the battleground of love!

#4: SAVAGE FURY   (1768, $3.95)

Aeneva's rage knew no bounds when her handsome mate
Trent commanded her to tend their tepee as he rode into
danger. But under cover of night, she stole away to be with
Trent and share whatever perils fate dealt them.

*Available wherever paperbacks are sold, or order direct from the
Publisher. Send cover price plus 50¢ per copy for mailing and
handling to Zebra Books, Dept. 1878, 475 Park Avenue South,
New York, N.Y. 10016. Residents of New York, New Jersey and
Pennsylvania must include sales tax. DO NOT SEND CASH.*

SWEET
MEDICINE'S
PROPHECY
#5

SUN DANCER'S LEGACY

BY KAREN A. BALE

ZEBRA BOOKS
KENSINGTON PUBLISHING CORP.

ZEBRA BOOKS

are published by

Kensington Publishing Corp.
475 Park Avenue South
New York, NY 10016

First printing: August 1986

Printed in the United States of America

This book is dedicated to the memory of Bob Fore.

Chapter I

Aeneva sat astride her horse, looking out over the land below her. It was so unlike the land where she had been born and had grown up, but she had grown to love this place nevertheless. It had taken her awhile to realize that she didn't have to live on Cheyenne land to be a true Cheyenne.

She heard horses behind her and turned to see her husband and sons riding toward her. Her sons. Nathan was almost sixteen years old, sitting tall in the saddle, his long blond hair shining next to his dark skin. Nathan was not her blood child but the child of her husband and a white woman. But it didn't matter. Nathan was as much hers as if she had borne him herself.

"*Haahe*, Mother." Nathan used the traditional Cheyenne greeting as he approached Aeneva.

Aeneva smiled at him, lifting her hand in greeting. She looked past him to the two riders who were lagging behind. She cocked her head to one side in mock disapproval. "Can you never let your brother or father win a race?"

"That would not be honorable, Mother, to let them think that they could beat me. And we

Cheyennes are always honorable, are we not?"

Aeneva looked at Nathan's sparkling blue eyes and flashing smile, and she felt a stabbing pain in her heart. Looking at him was like looking into the past. He was the image of Trenton, his father, her husband, the man whom she had always loved.

"Are you all right, Mother?" Nathan's voice sounded anxious.

Aeneva nodded. "I am fine. It just seems that you have grown up so fast. When I first saw you, you were but a tiny boy, now you are almost a man. Soon I will lose you."

Nathan reached out and touched his mother's arm. "You will never lose me, Mother, just as you'll never lose Roberto."

"You cheated, Nathan!" a voice yelled out. A dark-haired boy on a horse reined in next to Aeneva and Nathan. "You always take that shortcut. It's not fair."

"Come on, Berto. I told you we race up here any way we can. I just happen to know a shorter way, that's all." Nathan laughed wickedly, stopping abruptly when he saw his father ride up on his magnificent Appaloosa. The horse shifted his weight, snorting impatiently.

"You cheated, Nathan," Trenton Hawkins stated evenly, staring at his oldest son.

"I didn't cheat, Pa, I just took a shortcut. Berto always goes the long way. I took my own way. That doesn't mean I cheated."

"Well, if you're such a good horseman, it seems to me you could give your little brother a head start instead of using a shortcut to make sure you beat him every time. It's all right to lose once in a while, Nate."

"I know that, Pa." Nathan lowered his head in contrition, then quickly lifted it in a nod toward

Roberto. "I'll give you a ten second head start on the way down, Berto, but you better ride hard."

"No shortcuts, Nathan."

"No shortcuts."

"Well, now that we have the family dispute settled, have we decided when we are going to San Francisco to visit Joe and Larissa?"

"Tomorrow!" Nathan exclaimed loudly.

"Yes, I want to see Uncle Joe and Aunt Larissa," Roberto chimed in.

"And what about the ranch?" Trenton asked.

"The ranch will be fine without you for awhile, Pa. We've never gone anywhere since we moved here. I think we should go."

"So do I," Aeneva answered quietly.

Aeneva, Nathan, and Roberto all looked at Trenton, awaiting his reply.

"I don't suppose I have a choice in this. I think I'm outnumbered."

"It'll be fun, Pa. I've always wanted to see California. I hear there are real pretty girls there."

Aeneva and Trenton exchanged amused glances before Aeneva spoke. "I do not know much about the young women there, Nathan, but we are going to California to see your aunt and uncle. Wouldn't it be wise to wait until we get there before you start worrying about the young women?"

"Yes, Mother," Nathan answered, slightly embarrassed by his overzealousness.

"What about Clare? Huh, Nate?"

"Shut up, Berto."

"What's wrong, Nate? You too embarrassed to tell us about Clare?"

"I swear, Berto—" Nathan leaned across his horse but Aeneva held out her arm to stop him.

"So, Trenton, when do we leave?"

9

"We can leave in a week if I can tie up things around here. Jake should be able to take care of things around here, keep everyone in line."

"Yahoo!" Nathan exclaimed wildly. "Let's go back down, Berto. You've got a ten second lead."

When the two boys had ridden off, Aeneva dismounted and walked to the edge of the grassy bluff. Trenton followed, wrapping his arms around her from behind.

"I have grown to love it here, Trenton. I never thought I would grow to love another place as much as I loved my home, but I think of this as my home now."

"It is beautiful, isn't it?" Trenton looked down on the green valley below them, and the rolling hills beyond. Three hundred acres and they were his. Thanks to the money Joe had loaned him, he and Aeneva were able to buy the land and build a small house. Over the years, raising cattle proved to be productive and the ranch flourished. Trenton and Aeneva raised prime beef and in the fall and spring drove the herds south to Phoenix. From there they were herded northward to Cheyenne and loaded onto cattle cars and sent to Chicago for slaughter. Not only was Trenton able to repay most of Joe's money, but he was able to build the ranch into a viable power in the region.

"Are you really happy here, Aeneva? I've always wondered if you were happy leaving your people. Living in a big ranch house is not the same as living on the open prairie."

"There are times when I miss the land, especially in the spring when everything is so fresh and new. But mostly I miss my brothers."

"We could go back."

"No, I told you when we left that I would never go

back. It would not be the same. I will always carry my memories of my brothers and my family with me. I will always have those." Aeneva stared down at the valley below, thinking how far she had come from the lodge where she had been born in the snow so many winters ago. She wondered if her grandparents and parents saw how she lived and she wondered if they approved. She did miss her people, and not a day went by that she didn't think about her brothers, but she was convinced that her decision to go west with Trenton was the right one. She had been happy with him and her sons.

"Ready to go home now?"

Aeneva slowly shook her head. "No, I think I could stay here forever."

"Sometimes I think I've made a mistake. I'm afraid I've lost sight of everything that ever truly mattered to me."

Aeneva turned around in Trenton's arms, placing her hands on his chest. "You have made the right decision. You have built something of value which you can leave to your sons. This is a wonderful land, Trenton. It is yours and it will be your sons'. We could not say that about the Cheyenne land. Already it is as my grandfather predicted; already the white man has moved in and taken over much of the land." She nodded her head. "You have done the right thing, my husband."

Trenton smiled, staring down into his wife's face. She was still so beautiful, even after all these years. He couldn't imagine growing old without her. "We should probably be getting back to the ranch. The boys are probably already packing for San Francisco."

"Yes, and they probably have all of the wrong things."

They rode down the hill that led into the valley,

crossing the stream that gurgled past. The plump cattle grazed aimlessly on the tall spring grass, moving lazily from one spot to another. Aeneva and Trenton galloped toward the ranch, each enjoying the freedom of the ride. The ranch loomed in the distance, its two-story structure standing out of the dirt. Flowerpots surrounded the ranch house, while tall flowering shrubs grew in colorful rows around the garden. Two large trees grew on either side of the house, standing as silent sentries. The barn and corrals were built away from the house, and when Trenton and Aeneva dismounted, one of their workers took their horses.

Aeneva nodded and smiled toward the man. *"Como esta,* Alfonso?"

"Bien gracias, señora. *Y Usted?"*

"Muy bien. Y Rosalia?"

"Mas mejor, señora. *Gracias."*

"Bueno," Aeneva replied softly, lowering her head and putting her arm through Trenton's. "I will never get used to this."

"We've been over this a hundred times, Aeneva."

"But it is still hard for me to accept. I come from a land where people do not work for other people, and the only possessions you own are the ones you can throw on your horse."

Trenton stopped, placing his hands on Aeneva's shoulders. "I come from the same land, Aeneva. But didn't you just tell me that I've done the right thing?"

Aeneva nodded. "Yes, yes you have. But it is still difficult for me to see myself as a señora."

"Don't worry, you'll never change. You take care of all of the people on this ranch. You make clothes for the boys and me. You cook for everyone. You try to do everything for everyone. Even in San Francisco you'll be mixing some strange medicines and

12

handing them out to people."

"Do not make fun of my strange medicines. They have saved many people."

"I know that. I'm proud of you. I just want to know that you're happy here."

Aeneva smiled and kissed Trenton. "I am happy as long as I am with you." She rested her head on his chest.

"So what's wrong?"

"Nothing is wrong."

Trenton pulled away, lifting up Aeneva's face. "You forget that I've known you almost all of your life, Aeneva. You can't lie to me. What's the matter?"

Aeneva stared past Trenton, shrugging her shoulders. "I just wish I had been able to give you a child. That is my one sorrow and my one regret."

"Aeneva, I have never once thought of our family as incomplete. We have Nathan and Roberto. What more could we ask for?"

Aeneva's dark eyes met Trenton's light ones. "Nathan is your blood son and Roberto is mine, and they are both equal in my heart. But I had always dreamed of having *your* child, Trenton. Your son or daughter."

Trenton put his arms around Aeneva, pulling her close. "I've dreamed of it, too, but I know how lucky we are. We have each other and we have our sons. We cannot ask for more."

"Yes, I know that you are right but—"

"Don't argue with me. I can be as stubborn as you." Trenton took her elbow and led her up the steps to the ranch house. He smiled to himself as he heard Aeneva's boots thud on the wood of the porch. It still amazed him that she wore boots when she rode; she had hated the feeling of them at first. But she had grown used to them just as she had grown

13

used to so many other things in her new life with him. But her moccasins were still close at hand. She wore nothing but them inside the ranch house.

Aeneva and Trenton walked up the polished wooden stairs to the bedrooms, the sounds of laughter coming from Nathan's room. They walked to the doorway, looking in at their two sons. Nathan was steadfastly picking out clothes, while Roberto was pretending to dance around with one of the jackets.

"Oh, you're so handsome, Nathan," Roberto said in a mocking girl's voice to the jacket, "I am so glad you came to San Francisco. Whatever will I do when you leave?"

Nathan responded with a pillow to Roberto's head, knocking the younger boy off his feet. They both laughed loudly, turning when they realized their parents were standing at the doorway. Quickly Roberto stood up next to Nathan. Both of them laughed in amusement, trying to act serious but unable to accomplish that feat.

Trenton stepped forward, eyeing the two boys for a moment. His own son was the image of himself, he knew, but it was Roberto who startled him. The older the boy got, the more he grew to look like his father, Ladro. Ladro. Trenton shook his head. He had hated the man for stealing Aeneva away from him, but he had grown to admire and respect him in the end. Ladro had saved his life and, in return, he had promised to raise his son as if he were Trenton's very own. And he had done that. Looking at the two boys standing next to each other was like looking at him and Ladro.

"You all right, Pa?" Nathan asked anxiously.

Trenton nodded, narrowing his gaze at the two boys. "I suggest you two stop fooling around and start packing. And when you're done, there are chores that need to be finished."

"Oh, Pa," Roberto whined but Nathan nudged him with his shoulder.

"Okay, Pa. We'll get to the chores as soon as we're done here."

"Good. Oh, and Roberto, you better take some lessons before you ask a girl to dance."

Trenton smiled at Aeneva as they walked out, hearing the laughter of the boys as they walked back down the stairs. "God, I'm glad they get along as well as they do."

"Yes, they are as much brothers as if they were blood. Much like you were to my brothers."

"Yes," Trenton said nodding. He stopped when they reached the bottom of the stairway. "I wish Roberto could have known Ladro. He was a good man."

"He will know him through us." Aeneva reached up and touched Trenton's face, a loving gesture done hundreds of times, but one that always signified her depth of feeling for him. "When will you stop feeling guilty for Ladro's death? It was not your fault. He knew what he was doing when he ran in front of you. I think he wanted it that way."

Trenton clenched his jaw. "It all would've been so different if Ladro hadn't been killed. Maybe you would've stayed with him and I would've come back here for Nathan. Maybe we would have had separate lives."

"I do not think so, my husband. I am as bound to you as the wind is to the eagle. Nothing could have ever kept us apart."

Trenton looked at his wife and nodded. "I know that but I just wanted to hear you say it again." He put his arms around Aeneva. "I do love you,

15

Aeneva." His mouth touched hers and as always, her kiss reassured him that together they would always be strong.

"Oh, Nathan. Nathan." The girl's moan resounded in the old barn.

Nathan opened his eyes for a second to see if anyone was around and he closed them again. He tried to pull the girl's bloomers down but they were stuck. "Could you help me, Clare?"

Clare sighed heavily and stood up, pushing down her bloomers. She unbuttoned the bodice to her dress and pulled at the tiny ribbons that held her chemise. Nathan watched in fascination as her small, round breasts broke free of the material.

"Is that better?" Clare fell on top of Nathan, pulling his head to her breasts. Her moans filled the wooden barn.

Nathan had never experienced anything like this. Clare smelled so fresh and sweet, and her breasts were young and firm. He felt himself harden with desire and became suddenly alarmed at the touch of Clare's hand on his pants. Quickly he fumbled with his pants and his long underwear, and before he knew it he was on top of Clare, her legs spread, his body entering hers. Suddenly Clare began to scream, and he felt himself lose control. He covered Clare's mouth with his own as their bodies moved furiously against each other. When it was over, Nathan fell to the side, exhausted yet exhilarated. He was finally a man. He felt Clare as she moved next to him.

"Do you love me, Nathan?"

"Yeah," Nathan said quickly, then realized he was lying.

16

"And you won't forget me when you go to California?"

"I'll never forget you, Clare." Nathan put his arm around Clare but he realized that there was something missing. Although he had just found out what it was like to be a man, he did not know what it felt like to be in love. He hoped that he would find out what that was like someday.

Trenton kept looking back at the ranch as they rode away. Roberto and Nathan had ridden far ahead of their parents.

"Trenton, will you stop worrying? Everything will be fine. Jake is a good man and with Alfonso's help, they won't even miss us. Please, we need this. The boys need this."

Trenton nodded cursorily. "I know, but what if something comes up? What if the cattle get sick? What if—"

"That is enough. Whatever happens will happen whether we are here or not. I do not want to hear anymore about the ranch. I haven't seen Joe for five years, not since he stayed with us. I want to enjoy being with him and Larissa. Besides, you do want to give him the rest of his money in person, don't you?"

"Yeah, I do. I can't wait to see his face. Are you excited about the trip?"

Aeneva nodded enthusiastically. "Yes, I have never ridden in a stagecoach."

"It's not all that comfortable but it'll get us there in about three weeks. Quicker than if we were to ride."

They rode through the grassy valley, the mountains behind them an ever-present reminder of the land they were leaving. Soon they would be getting to the

17

more arid climate of Phoenix and Yuma. It would be desert from there until they reached San Diego. They camped in the foothills, watching the sunset as they ate their dinner. Trenton and Aeneva retold stories of their childhood and their lives with the Cheyennes. As they spoke, it became obvious to each of them that Roberto became more and more curious about his father while Nathan showed no interest whatsoever in his mother.

"Your father was a good man, Roberto. Very brave. He saved my life," Trenton said.

"You're sitting by your *real* father, Berto," Nathan said angrily.

Roberto ignored Nathan's angry remark. "Do I look very much like him, Mother?"

"You look more and more like him all of the time," Aeneva responded proudly.

"Does Nate look like his real mother?"

"Aeneva is my real mother!" Nathan responded angrily before anyone could speak. "That white woman never wanted me."

"Nathan," Aeneva said gently, surprised by the boy's sudden outburst. "How do you know that? She died giving you life. She loved you very much."

"I don't believe it!" Nathan said angrily, stomping away from the fireside.

Aeneva looked at Trenton. "Go after him. Talk to him. It is unnatural that he feels this way about his blood mother."

"But what do I tell him? That she tricked me into marrying her by getting pregnant? That she really didn't want him?"

"But she did want him in the end, Trenton. That's why she tried so hard to live so that she could give him life."

"All right. I'll go talk to him." Trenton stood up

18

and walked past Roberto, mussing his hair as he did so. He found Nathan perched on a rock looking out over the stark but stunning Arizona landscape. "You all right, Nate?" Trenton asked casually, knowing how much alike he and his son were. He knew he had to tread easily.

"Yeah."

"It's not like you to brood, Nate. What's really eatin' at you?"

"Nothing, Pa. I told you."

"But you're not telling me the truth."

"It's pretty out here, isn't it? I'm glad you and Mother came out here. I feel like I really belong here."

Trenton pressed Nathan's shoulder tightly. "Nate, what is it?"

Nathan shook his head slowly, staring out into the fiery sky. "I don't know, Pa. I guess I'm just feeling a little sorry for myself. I don't know why."

"I think I do." Trenton sat down on the rock next to his son. "I never have told you much about your real mother. That's my fault."

"No, it's not. I never wanted to hear."

"Well, I think it's time you heard now." Trenton cleared his throat. "I met Lydia while I was scouting for the army. She was bright and pretty and I liked her but didn't love her. She mistook my interest in her for love. But I had never forgotten about Aeneva. I knew that someday I would go back and marry her. But I made the mistake of being with Lydia a few times, and she got pregnant."

"You didn't have to marry her. You could've left her."

"No, I couldn't. Her father had me locked up, and I was forced to marry her. We went to live in St. Louis. I worked on the docks." He stopped and smiled for a moment. "That's where I met Joe. I was young, not much older than you are now, and not too wise about the ways of the world, and here I was married and with a child on the way. Anyway, I was determined to get out of that place so I worked and I gambled and I saved some money."

"So you and my mother left?"

"No, she never left St. Louis. I had an enemy who was out to get me. One night while I was out with Joe, this man came and took your mother. She was very pregnant with you at the time. Joe and I went after her, but she had already escaped and swum across the river. When she reached the other side she was exhausted and ready to deliver you. By the time I got to her, she was dying. She made me promise to take care of you. She's the one who named you Nathan."

"She named me?"

"Yes, after her grandfather."

"Did you care for her at all, Pa?"

"Yes, I did, especially at the end. She showed such strength and courage before she died."

"I wonder if she would've wanted me if she'd lived."

"She'd have wanted you and she'd have loved you as much as Aeneva and I do. You were the only thing she cared about at the end."

"And what about you, Pa? You said it was a mistake to ever get involved with her. Do you regret that I was ever born?"

"Oh, Nate," Trenton replied unevenly, trying to control the emotion that filled his voice. "You were what kept me going in the beginning. You gave me a reason to go on and to be strong. You were always so bright and happy. When I thought I had lost Aeneva both times, the thing that kept me going was know-

20

ing that I had you to go back to." He clasped his son tightly to him. "I love you, Nate, maybe more than I can ever tell you. But don't ever forget it." Trenton was surprised that Nathan would let him hold him. How long had he been feeling this doubt? "You all right now?"

Nathan pulled away, suddenly uneasy at this open display of affection. "Sure, I guess I just needed to know how you really felt."

"What about Aeneva? Do you doubt how she feels about you?"

Nathan smiled broadly. "I have never doubted how she feels about me. She and I have something real special."

"So did you and her grandmother."

"Sun Dancer?"

Trenton nodded. "You think your mother was beautiful, you should have seen Sun Dancer. Your grandfather, my father, saw her once when she was very young. He said she almost took his breath away. He never forgot about her." Trenton smiled. "And she spoiled the hell out of you. You couldn't do anything wrong as far as Sun Dancer was concerned."

"I wish she was still alive."

"So do I. She was quite a woman." Trenton stood up. "We should get back. Your mother will wonder if we're still alive." Trenton stood up and started toward camp but Nathan's hand on his shoulder stopped him.

"Pa."

"What?"

"Thanks."

"For what?"

"For telling me what I already knew."

Trenton nodded and held out his arm, placing it around Nathan's shoulder as they walked back to

21

camp. Nathan was a son that any man could be proud of, and Trenton didn't ever want to let him forget it.

Trenton reined in his horse, looking down at the ground in front of him. "There's a wagon train ahead of us. Look at the tracks. Maybe we can catch up with them and travel with them for a time."

"Yeah, maybe there're some girls on it, Nate," Roberto chided his older brother.

"How would you know, Berto, you don't know the difference between a girl and a—"

"That's enough." Trenton held up his hand. "Why don't you two try to act civilized. You might like it."

"Yes, when we are in San Francisco, Joe and Larissa will expect you two to act like young gentlemen, not hooligans."

"Hooligans?" Nathan asked in bemusement.

"Yes, it is a word I learned. Your father and Joe were hooligans at one time."

"Joe and I were a lot of things but we were never hooligans," Trenton laughed.

"Pa, can I ride on ahead? I want to see if I can find those wagons."

"I don't want you riding by yourself out here, Berto. Nate, go with him."

"Be back soon, Pa."

The boys rode off in a cloud of dust. Aeneva and Trenton rode in a companionable silence for some time until they heard the sounds of horses. Nathan and Roberto came galloping back, abruptly reining in their horses.

"What's the matter with you two? You look like you've seen a ghost."

22

"Trouble, Pa."

Trenton pulled up. "What's wrong?"

Nathan pointed back in the direction from which they had just ridden. "There are some wagons up ahead. The horses are gone but there are people still there."

"How do you know?"

"When we tried to get close enough someone pointed a rifle at us. He told us to keep away. It's cholera, Pa."

"You boys stay here. We're going to see if we can help them."

"Will you be all right?" Berto asked anxiously.

"We'll be fine."

"Hand me the water bag, Nathan," Aeneva ordered. She was already sorting through her medicine bags.

"You can't go in there, Mother. You might get it, too."

"Perhaps I can help these people, Nathan. Just hand me the water bag and do as your father and I tell you." At the worried look on Nathan's face she smiled. "I have been around this disease before. Many of my people had it. I did not get it, Nathan. I will be fine."

"You're going to stay there and help those people, aren't you?"

"If they need me, I will stay."

Nathan nodded his head in resignation. "I want to help, too."

"No, I will not have you endanger yourself. If I must stay here for awhile, I want you and Berto to go on to San Francisco with your father. I will follow later."

"Mother—"

"Do not argue with me, Berto. Your brother has

23

already learned that it will do him no good to argue with me." She smiled at the boys. "Take care of your father. He is helpless without me."

"You boys stay here until I come back for you. If you follow us, I'll tan your hides until you can't ride for a week."

Aeneva and Trenton galloped toward the wagons. There were three of them, strung out in a semicircle. They approached cautiously, awaiting a rifle shot warning. The shot came as they neared the rear wagon.

"Stay away, folks. We got cholera here. Unless you be wantin' to die, you better leave us alone."

"We want to help you," Aeneva said gently.

"You can't help us."

"My wife has a lot of medicines that might be able to help you."

"And what would she be knowin' about cholera?"

"The disease hit my tribe many years ago. I worked with my grandmother to help the people. Many people died but we were able to save some."

There was an awkward silence while Aeneva and Trenton waited on their horses. "I don't think they want your help, Aeneva."

"They want my help. They are just scared."

"I agree with the boys. I don't want you going in there. I don't want to lose you again."

"You won't lose me. You know I must help these people, Trenton."

"I know. I'll send the boys back and stay here with you."

"No. I will stay. You take the boys on to San Francisco and come back here." At the angry scowl which suddenly appeared on her husband's face, her voice softened. "Please, Trenton. The boys are looking forward to this trip, and they will be safe away from here. By the time you get back, it should be safe."

"What about you? What if you do get it this time? What do I do then?"

"You worry too much, Trenton. I will not get this disease."

"Why not? Do you think your grandmother will be at your side, looking out for you?"

"Yes." Aeneva responded immediately. "I will be safe, Trenton."

"All right, I'll take the boys on to San Francisco, but only after I'm sure there's something you can do here. They might all be past your help, Aeneva."

"All right. We will wait then."

"You people. You still want to help us?" The strained voice of the man came from one of the wagons.

"Yes," Aeneva replied. She started forward, but Trenton caught her arm and she reined in her horse.

"I'm not going until I know exactly how many people there are and if any of them can use your help."

Aeneva nodded, leaning toward her husband. Their lips touched, and she felt his hand go behind her head. "Do not worry, Trenton. I will be all right."

"I'll believe that when I'm holding you in my arms again." He pressed his mouth to hers one last time and then watched her as she rode to the wagons, knowing that she might very well be riding to her own death.

The man held out his hand to Aeneva, helping her up into the wagon. "The name's O'Leary, ma'am. Patrick O'Leary."

"Happy to meet you, Mr. O'Leary," Aeneva said as she climbed up into the wagon. "My name is Aeneva."

"It's a Cheyenne name, isn't it? Means winter."

"Yes, how did you know that?"

"I, myself, was married to a Cheyenne. Fine woman she was." He bent over suddenly, grasping at his stomach. "Are you sure you be wantin' to do this, ma'am? It's a terrible thing this cholera."

"I am not worried, Mr. O'Leary." She stepped forward to look at the man but he held up his hand.

"No, please don't come near me. This wagon has a foul smell to it because of the dysentery. I try to clean it when I can, but I haven't much strength left in me."

"I am not worried about the smell, Mr. O'Leary. I am here to help you. If you say you were married to a Cheyenne, then you know that the smell around some of the camps was terrible. This is nothing."

O'Leary threw back his head and laughed. "A woman with a sense of humor. I like that." He bent over again, rubbing his legs. "It's these damned cramps in my legs. They're gettin' worse all the time."

Aeneva walked over to O'Leary, ignoring his protests. She felt his head with her hand then bent over and slowly began rubbing his legs. "I want you to relax, Mr. O'Leary, or the cramps will get worse."

"Don't be worryin' yourself none about me, ma'am. We both know that I'm dyin'. There's nothing you can do for me now."

"I will do whatever I can for you, Mr. O'Leary. I did not think you Irish gave up so easily."

"Oh, I like you, ma'am. If I weren't so sick I'd probably be fallin' in love with you right now."

"It wouldn't do you any good. I am a happily

married woman.''

"Is he Irish?"

"No."

"Well, then, how do you know if you're happy if you've never been married to an Irishman?'' O'Leary laughed loudly, his face wincing in pain.

"I have known many men, Mr. O'Leary, and all of them have thought they were the best. You are no different.'' She knelt down next to him.

"Oh, and a hard woman you are, too.''

"Probably not hard enough for you, Mr. O'Leary.'' She put her water bag to his lips. "Drink. How long has it been since you've had fresh water?''

"I don't know but I do know that it's the water that gave us the dread disease. People were dropping like flies for awhile. Those who didn't get sick went on without us. Took our horses, too. Guess I'd have done the same.''

"I somehow doubt that.'' Aeneva looked around the wagon. "You lost your wife? Have you no family left?''

"I lost my wife long before the cholera hit, ma'am. When Anna was just a wee one. It's just me and her left now.''

"Who?''

O'Leary nodded to the corner of the wagon. "Come out from behind the bureau, Anna. Don't be afraid now.''

Aeneva watched as a young girl slowly appeared from behind the bureau. She had long, tangled dark hair, and her large round eyes appeared curious and frightened as she moved toward her father. She seemed small and frail but Aeneva sensed a strength as the girl put her arm possessively through her father's. "Hello, Anna.''

"Go on, Anna. Say hello to the nice lady. She's

27

come to help us."

The little girl stepped forward and curtsied. "Hello, ma'am," she said in a small voice.

Aeneva smiled and reached into her bag. "I bet you are hungry, aren't you, Anna?"

The little girl looked at her father and then back at Aeneva. "Yes, ma'am."

Aeneva handed the girl some fresh fruit they had packed for their trip. "Here, Anna, have an orange. It will be good for you." Aeneva looked at O'Leary, then back at Anna. "And why don't you go outside and get some fresh air. It will do you good." She smiled evenly and handed the water bag to the girl. "Have a drink and go outside. Your father will be fine. I will take care of him."

Anna looked doubtfully at O'Leary but with a nudge from him she jumped out the back of the wagon.

"Why did you let her drink out of my water bag?"

"She has already had the disease, has she not?"

"Yes. How could you tell?"

"She shows some of the signs but she is already beginning to get well. I do not think drinking out of the same water bag will hurt her." Aeneva put her arms under one of O'Leary's. "Can you move to the other side of the wagon. I want to clean this up. No wonder you are ill. You are a messy man. Mr. O'Leary."

"Just what both my wives used to tell me."

"Both?"

"Yes, before I was married to my Cheyenne wife, I was married once before. Lived in San Francisco, I did. Had myself a good job. But—" He shrugged his shoulders as he sat down against the other side of the wagon. "It was the drink, you know. It got the better of me. It always gets the better of us Irish."

"I do not believe that. You seem much too strong a man to let drink control your life."

"That's where you're wrong, ma'am. I thought I was strong but I wasn't. The bottle gave me strength." He looked around. "Speaking of that . . ."

Aeneva cleared the dirty linen, throwing it out the back of the wagon. "Forget about the bottle, Mr. O'Leary. You will not be needing it. You will be drinking something else from now on."

O'Leary sat straight up. "What do you mean I'll be drinkin' something else. You are a hard woman, ma'am. Here I thought you'd come to help me."

"I have." Aeneva walked over and stood in front of O'Leary. "Take your clothes off, Mr. O'Leary."

"What? Why I've never had a woman tell *me* to take *my* clothes off before."

"Well, I am telling you now. Take them off and throw them out the back of the wagon. Tell me about the others."

O'Leary shrugged. "I don't even know if anyone is still alive in the other wagons. The Williamsons are in the wagon in front of us. He is dead, along with three of his children. Last time I knew, the missus and two of the children were barely alive. The Skovmands are in the front wagon. Just him and her left. Not too good last time I checked on them."

"Have you been taking care of them all, Mr. O'Leary? And here I thought you were such an awful man, what with your drinking and all."

O'Leary shook his head in wonder. "I never knew a Cheyenne woman who could sound so Irish."

"It's all in the listening, Mr. O'Leary. I was speaking French and English when I was smaller than your daughter. You understand?" she asked in Cheyenne.

29

O'Leary laughed. "I'm sorry I'm to be dying. I'd like to be gettin' to know you better, ma'am."

"You will if you'll let me help you." She climbed out the back of the wagon, her voice carrying back in. "I am going to burn your clothes and your linens, Mr. O'Leary, so you should find something clean to put on before I come back in here." Aeneva smiled to herself as she heard O'Leary cussing out loud. She swung up on her horse and rode out of the small camp. She saw Trenton waiting in the same place. She stopped her horse before getting too close to her husband.

"I am going to stay, Trenton. There are people who need my help." Trenton started to ride closer but Aeneva held up her hand. "I don't want to get close to you. There is a chance I could catch the disease again. I am going to need a lot of water, fresh linens, and food. Just leave them here."

"Damn it, Aeneva! Why did you have to do this?"

"You know why I had to do it. Do not be angry, Trenton. Take the boys to San Francisco and come back for me."

Trenton nodded, his anger fading to resignation. "Please take care of yourself. I love you."

"And I you. Have a safe trip. Tell the boys I love them." Aeneva reined her horse around and rode back to the wagons. She dismounted and hurriedly built a fire, burning all of the things from O'Leary's wagon. Then she took one of O'Leary's pots, scrubbed it with sand and rocks, filled it with water, and placed it over the fire. She mixed some of her medicine and put it into the water. While the medicine boiled, she went to the second wagon. She looked in the rear of the wagon, turning her face away because of the foul odor. She held her breath and turned back to the wagon. "Mrs. Williamson, are

30

you all right?'' Aeneva called out the woman's name but there was no answer. She stepped up into the wagon, covering her nose with the hem of her skirt. She shook her head as she looked around her. Mrs. Williamson lay dead, her two children next to her. Aeneva bent down to examine the children more closely. Tears stung her eyes. They, too, were dead. She climbed out of the wagon and walked to the front wagon. She steeled herself for what was to come. She looked into the back of the wagon. She could tell without looking closer that the Skovmands were also dead. She shook her head and walked back to the fire. She sat down, stirring the tea with a stick. A noise behind her made her turn, and she saw Anna standing, staring at her. Aeneva smiled.

"Hello, Anna."

"Hello, ma'am."

"Are you playing?"

"Yes, ma'am."

Aeneva held out her hand to the girl. "Would you come here, Anna? I want to talk to you about your father."

Anna kicked her foot in the dirt for a second before deciding to go forward. She stood next to Aeneva, looking into the pot. "Is it soup?"

"No, it is tea, good tea. It will help your father and you."

"I don't like tea." Anna crinkled her little nose at the thought.

"Has your stomach been hurting you, Anna? Have you had big pains?" Anna nodded. "This tea will help take the pain away. And we must make your father drink it. He must not drink from his bottle. That will not help him but this tea will. Do you understand, Anna?"

"Yes, ma'am."

31

"Good. When it is brewed I will give you a cup, and you will drink it right in front of him. You can tell him how good it is."

"Is it good?"

Aeneva shook her head. "No, it tastes terrible but we must tell your father that it is good. He will believe you. It will be a little game."

The girl smiled for the first time. "I like games. Papa is always playing games with me."

"Good. Why don't you give me your clothes, Anna? I am going to burn them."

Anna put her arms possessively to her skirt. "No, this is my favorite skirt. I don't want you to burn it."

Aeneva got onto her knees, putting her hands on the girl's small shoulders. "Anna, do you remember how sick you were a few days ago? You had a fever, a stomachache, and your legs hurt. Do you remember?"

"Yes, ma'am."

"Do you want to be sick like that again?"

"No, ma'am." Anna answered with large, round eyes.

"Then I must burn your clothes. The disease is spread through your clothes and all of the things in your wagon. We will have to burn everything. Even the wagon."

"No!" Anna started to run toward the wagon but Aeneva grabbed her and pulled her back. "It's all right, Anna. You will be all right. If you will help me, I will try to make your father well. She brushed the girl's dark hair from her face and for the first time noticed what a deep blue her eyes were. "I will make you a promise."

"What?" Anna asked suspiciously.

"If you help me gather up all the things and burn the wagons, when we get your father well, I will make you many new clothes. Would you like that?"

Anna's face lit up. "Oh, yes, ma'am. I would like that." She looked down at her beloved, bedraggled red skirt. "Could you make me a red skirt just like this one?"

"Yes, I know I could. I will make you anything you want." Aeneva pulled the frail child to her and felt a rush of emotion for her. She had no mother and there was a good chance she would also lose her father. Aeneva pulled away, smiling at Anna. "Why don't you see if your father needs help getting dressed. We won't burn your clothes yet. I will be in soon with the tea."

"Yes, ma'am." Anna ran off in the direction of the wagon.

Aeneva watched her go, a torrent of emotion welling up inside of her. She had a strange feeling that if she and Trenton had had a daughter together she would have looked like Anna. She let herself dream what it would be like to have a daughter but she would not let herself feel. Anna already had a father, and it was up to Aeneva to save him. She dipped a bowl into the tea and started toward the wagon.

"I am coming in, Mr. O'Leary."

"I don't ever want you comin' in here again, woman. You've already turned me own daughter against me."

Aeneva held onto the side of the wagon and climbed in, holding the steaming bowl of tea. She offered it to Anna. "Would you like some tea, Anna?"

Anna nodded her head and came forward. She sipped from the bowl, blowing as she sipped. She turned to her father. "It's good, Papa. You should have some."

"Ah!" O'Leary threw his hands up in the air. "Trying to poison me now, woman, are you? I'll be

33

needing nothing but me bottle. If you'll kindly get me that—"

Aeneva walked over to O'Leary, sitting down next to him. "You listen to me, Mr. O'Leary. If you have already decided that you want to die, then you better tell me so that I can leave. But I think that you are more afraid of living than you are of dying."

"And just what do you be knowing about living, a woman like you?"

"I bet you that I know more about living than you'll ever know, Mr. O'Leary. And I would probably win the bet, too."

O'Leary eyed Aeneva. "Why are you so all-fire determined to save my life? I've not added much during my time here on this earth."

"You are wrong, Mr. O'Leary." Aeneva pulled Anna away from O'Leary so he could see her. "Have you looked at this beautiful child lately? Has it occurred to you that if you die, she will have no one? Is that what you want?"

O'Leary's eyes doggedly met Aeneva's but turned to his daughter. Aeneva could see the love in his eyes as he looked at the child. He held his arms out to her and she went to him.

"Ah, Anna, my girl. What would I have ever done without you?"

"Will you drink your tea now, Papa? It will make your stomach better."

O'Leary nodded wearily. "Yes, I'll be drinking the tea. For now." He took the bowl from Aeneva and placed it to his mouth, turning his nose away before he could drink it. "What do you have in this? This smells like—"

"Just drink it, Mr. O'Leary. I know what it smells like."

After a few dramatic gestures, O'Leary drank the

34

bowl of tea, smiling at Anna when he finished. "There now, I've been a good boy. How about gettin' your old dad a bottle."

"I can't, Papa. It would be bad for your stomach."

O'Leary looked over at Aeneva again. "Have you been fillin' this child's head full of lies? It's the bottle that keeps me alive, damn you!"

Aeneva stood up, walking toward the rear of the wagon. "It is good to hear you talk like that, Mr. O'Leary. It means you still have some fight left in you."

"Damn you to hell and back, woman!" O'Leary yelled as Aeneva climbed down the back of the wagon.

Aeneva smiled to herself. Perhaps O'Leary would make it after all.

Chapter II

Aeneva watched as the three wagons went up in flames. She had made a bed for O'Leary outside with the supplies Trenton had brought from the ranch. She had made stew for Anna and had made her eat more fresh fruit. The girl held onto Aeneva's hand as the flames went high into the air.

"Are they in heaven now, ma'am?" Anna asked in a small voice.

"Yes, Anna, they are in heaven now. They are happy and smiling." Aeneva turned around and walked back to the small camp, squatting down to dip a bowl into the tea. She walked toward O'Leary.

"Don't you be bringin' that poisonous stuff near me. I'd sooner be dyin' of the cholera than be drinkin' that rot again."

"You will be dying of the cholera if you don't drink some more of this tea." Aeneva shook her head in disgust. "If you like, I will take your daughter and leave. You can die all by yourself."

"What do you mean you'll be takin' my daughter?" O'Leary sat up.

"You don't think I will leave her here with you, do you? You will be dead soon and she will be all alone.

37

She will have a home with me."

O'Leary narrowed his eyes. "You'd be takin' my own flesh and blood away from me? You are a hard woman, Mrs. Hawkins."

"My name is Aeneva, not Mrs. Hawkins."

O'Leary shrugged his shoulders in disgust. "I never want to be gettin' to know you well enough to be callin' you by your Christian name."

"That's fine with me, Mr. O'Leary." She squatted next to him. "Drink!"

O'Leary took the bowl from Aeneva, turning up his nose in disgust. "I don't think I be likin' you much, Mrs. Hawkins. And I always thought Cheyenne women were such kind, gentle souls."

"Whoever told you that did not know Cheyenne women very well, Mr. O'Leary. Finish the tea."

"I cannot believe this. I'm bein' ordered around by some savage; by some cruel-hearted woman. I don't want to be hurtin' anyone, Mrs. Hawkins. All I want is my bottle."

"Well, you will not be getting it from me. All of your bottles are burned."

"What? Do you mean you didn't save any of me bottles?"

"Not a one. Water, tea, and soup are the only liquids you will be having for quite some time."

"You'll regret ever having done this to me, Mrs. Hawkins. Someday when I'm dead and buried, I'll be comin' back to haunt you. I won't let you rest. You'll die of fright."

Aeneva shook her head. "I would welcome a ghost in my life, Mr. O'Leary, especially an Irish one."

O'Leary eyed Aeneva suspiciously. "I know you are lying. All Indians are afraid of spirits."

"I am not afraid of spirits, Mr. O'Leary, *especially* Irish ones." She pushed the bowl to his mouth,

38

forcing him to finish the tea. "How are the cramps in your legs? Any better?"

"They are still there. Did you think that tea of yours was going to take them away?"

Aeneva sat in front of O'Leary, pushing his pants up his legs. She took one of his legs and began rubbing. "It does not surprise me that you have been married twice, Mr. O'Leary. I am just surprised that either woman was foolish enough to marry you in the first place."

"Ah, Mrs. Hawkins," O'Leary laughed weakly, "you are the most fun I've had meself in years. You know how to stand up for yourself. I like that."

"I learned at a very young age how to stand up for myself." Aeneva massaged O'Leary's other leg. "There, how does that feel?"

O'Leary pushed down his pants' legs, stretching his legs out as far as he could. "I have to admit, they be feelin' pretty good." O'Leary stared at Aeneva for a long moment. "Why did you do it, Mrs. Hawkins?"

"Do what?"

"Why did you come here to help us? You could have just ridden on by."

"I am a healer, Mr. O'Leary, and sometimes I am able to help people. I promised my grandmother that I would use all of the knowledge that she passed on to me. That is why I stopped."

"And are you not afraid that you'll be catching the dread disease?"

"I will not worry about it. It will happen if it is meant to be so."

"Have you ever heard of the Chinese, Mrs. Hawkins?"

"Yes, I have heard a little. We have a friend who lives in San Francisco. He tells us that the Chinese are very wise people. He says they know many things

39

but they are not treated well."

"No, they aren't treated well. They are treated much like the slaves in the South were before the war."

"Perhaps that is why my friend likes the Chinese. He is a freed slave."

"I see. He understands well what the Chinese have been through. Have you ever noticed, Mrs. Hawkins, how people with fair skin seem to think they are directly related to God?"

Aeneva laughed loudly. "You remind me of someone, Mr. O'Leary."

"Someone good, I hope."

"Yes, someone very good. He was my uncle."

"Cheyenne he was?"

"No, he was a French trapper. He wasn't really related to me by blood but he was more of an uncle to me than any blood uncle." Aeneva smiled as she recalled her dear, beloved Uncle Jean. "He was a blood brother to my grandfather. I have never seen two men who were so full of—"

"I get your meaning, Mrs. Hawkins. They sound like they were my kind of men./"

"Yes, I believe that they were."

"You wouldn't happen to have any more of that tea, would you now?"

"You know there is lots of tea." Aeneva gave O'Leary another bowl. "You look better. I think you're going to make it, Mr. O'Leary."

"If I do, it'll be because of you, Mrs. Hawkins. I think this awful tea of yours cured me, as much as I hate to admit it."

"Well, as much as I hate to admit it, I think you would have gotten well without me or my tea. You're a strong man, Mr. O'Leary, even without your bottle."

"I'll not be forgivin' you that soon, Mrs. Hawkins, but since you saved my life and took such good care of my little girl, I'll consider goin' easy on you."

"That's very kind of you." Aeneva checked on Anna to make sure she was warm. She turned back to O'Leary. "Where will you go after you are well enough to travel?"

"Don't know really. We were on our way to San Francisco but I had no definite plans. I was going to see a friend but he might not be happy to see me after all these years."

"Friends are always happy to see friends, no matter how much time has passed."

"Well, let's just say that when I left Frisco, I left in a bit of a hurry. Didn't have much time to say me good-byes."

"So you and Anna really don't have a place to go?"

"Not really, but I'm sure we'll find a place once we get there."

"Why don't you stay with us, Mr. O'Leary?"

O'Leary spit out the water that was in his mouth. "Are you out of your mind, woman?"

"No, I am of very sound mind, Mr. O'Leary."

"If that's so, why would you even suggest something like that?"

"You and your daughter need a place to stay until you are completely well. We have a large ranch house, large enough for you and your daughter. You'll like it there. It is a beautiful place."

O'Leary shook his head. "You're a strange woman, Mrs. Hawkins. I can't quite figure you."

"You do not have to figure me. I have offered you and your daughter a place to stay until you are recovered. What is your answer?"

O'Leary started to blurt out an answer but stopped. He looked over at Anna, who was sleeping peace-

41

fully. "I know what would be best for her."

"Then why don't you do it?"

"What about your husband? What would he think?"

"He won't think anything. He will welcome you into our home just as I have welcomed you."

"Seems a might strange to me, me bein' a complete stranger and all."

"Do what you will. I won't beg you." Aeneva stretched out on her bedroll and pulled the blanket up over her. She thought of Trenton and the boys and wondered how they were doing. She missed them. She had never been separated from all three of them before.

"Well, I've been thinkin' it over and I've decided to take you up on your kind offer, Mrs. Hawkins. Anna and I won't be stayin' long but it would be good for her to be around some good, gentle folks for a change."

Aeneva smiled, raising herself up on her elbow. "Why thank you, Mr. O'Leary. I do imagine that's as close as I'll ever get to a compliment from you."

"And you'd be right, Mrs. Hawkins."

"So, it's settled then. As soon as you are well enough to ride, you and Anna will come back to the ranch with me. You won't regret it, Mr. O'Leary."

"I never thought I would, Mrs. Hawkins."

"You all right, Pa?"

Trenton looked up at Nathan. The fire had burned down, and he hadn't even noticed it. "You should be asleep, Nate. Got a long day's journey ahead of us tomorrow."

Nathan sat down next to his father. "I can't sleep either, Pa. I'm as worried about Mother as you are. I think we should go back, Pa."

"I keep thinking she's going to get the disease and I won't be there to help her."

"We have to go back, Pa. She needs us."

Trenton looked at his son in the firelight, realizing for the first time how grown up he had become. "No, I promised your mother that I would take you to Joe's. I can't break that promise."

"Let her get mad at me, Pa, I don't care, but I'm going back tomorrow."

"You're as stubborn as she is, you know?"

"Where do you think I got it from?"

Trenton laughed. "Yes, but I'm her husband, and she'll take it out on me if I don't get you two safely to Joe's."

"You don't have to make the trip at all, Pa."

"What?"

"I can get Berto and me to San Francisco safely. Don't look at me that way. I'm not a kid anymore. I'm sixteen years old, and even you said I'm as good a tracker as you."

"Are you crazy? Do you know what your mother would do to me if I told her I'd let you two go on to California alone?" He shook his head. "She'd probably poison me with one of her strange teas."

"By the time you get back to her we'll be safe in San Francisco, sitting in Joe and Larissa's fancy house. She'll be glad you're back with her. Besides, all we do is ride to Yuma and get on the stagecoach."

Trenton shook his head, a look of determination on his face. "No, Nathan, I can't let the two of you go on alone. Go to sleep now. We've got a lot of traveling ahead of us."

"But, Pa—"

"Don't argue with me, Nathan." Trenton watched his son as he angrily walked across the camp to his bedroll. Trenton trusted Nathan; he had never doubted the boy's ability as a tracker. But he was more afraid of what was awaiting two unsuspecting boys on the trail. They would never be prepared to defend themselves. No, he could never let them go on alone.

"Have you ever seen the Sierra Nevadas, Pa? I hear they're quite a sight."

"No, I've never seen them, Nate. Joe says they're something to behold."

"Just imagine what it was like when the first tracker found California, Pa. It must've been unspoiled and beautiful."

"Kit Carson was here a lot of years ago. I read somewhere that he said it was one of the most beautiful places he'd ever seen."

"I wish I'd been with him when he discovered it."

"How long is it to San Francisco?" Roberto asked, his voice betraying his impatience.

Trenton and Nathan exchanged amused glances. "We have to get to Yuma first, son. Then about three weeks on the stage."

"Three weeks! I don't want to ride for three more weeks."

"You won't have to ride for three weeks. Once we get to Yuma, we'll take the stagecoach. You'll like that."

Trenton kept up a hurried pace, all the while ignoring Roberto's pleas that they stop and rest. After they had eaten that night, Nathan went to his father.

"Pa, I think you should go back."

"We've already discussed this, Nate."

"Pa, listen. Berto can't keep up this pace, and he'll

drive us crazy with his whining if we don't slow it down. I can get Berto and me to Yuma. When we get there, we'll take the stage to San Francisco." He shrugged his shoulders. "It's simple."

"And what about bandits or Indians? How do two young boys defend themselves against a group of grown men?"

"How do two young boys and their father defend themselves against a group of grown men?"

Trenton regarded his son for a moment, biting his bottom lip as he thought. "You think you have me all figured out, don't you?"

"I never said that, Pa."

"But you're thinking it." He walked to the fire and picked up the pot. He poured himself some coffee. "It wasn't so long ago that I was your age, Nate. I haven't forgotten."

"I never thought you had, Pa."

"I remember thinking that nothing could ever hurt me because I was young and strong and I knew more than anybody in the world." He squatted down next to Nathan. "Is that about right?"

Nathan looked down at the ground. "I just think I can handle it, that's all. I never said I was smarter than you."

"I know you didn't but all kids think they're smarter than their parents. That's part of growing up."

"Did you think you were smarter than your pa?"

Trenton sipped from the coffee cup and nodded. "There was a point when I was convinced that my father couldn't even track anymore. I felt sorry for him because I had gotten older, stronger, and smarter. I didn't want to hurt his feelings but—" Trenton shrugged his shoulders. "That's the way of the world. I knew it was time to tell him that he was not as keen as he'd been before. You see, my dad was one of the best. He never missed a sign, never a track, never a trail. But for a while it seemed like he missed everything and I noticed everything." Trenton laughed loudly, clearly enjoying the memory. "But you see, I was too young and too stupid to realize that my dad was missing the signs on purpose. He wanted me to learn how to track on my own, and the only way to do that was for me to notice things without him pointing things out."

"Bet you felt real stupid, huh, Pa?"

"I felt more than stupid, Nate. I felt embarrassed by my own boastfulness—that I would think that I was better than my own father. But he never rubbed it in, never made fun of me. He just taught me."

"I'm sorry, Pa. I feel kinda like you did. But I don't doubt you—you are the best tracker I've ever seen."

"Not as good as you're going to be someday." Trenton drank the rest of his coffee. "All right, Nate, I'll let you and Berto go on alone."

"You mean it? You'll let us go to San Francisco alone?"

"Yes."

"Yahoo!" Nathan yelled, clapping his father on the shoulder. "You won't regret it, Pa. I'll take real good care of Berto. I'll get us there safely."

"I'm going to give you the money I owe Joe. Can you handle it?"

"Sure, Pa. Don't you trust me?"

"I trust you, Nate, it's just other people I don't trust. You have your knife?"

"It's tucked into my boot."

"If you meet up with any strangers who want to ride along with you and you don't like the looks of them, ride away. Don't camp out in the open, be sure—"

46

"Pa, you taught me all this stuff when I was a kid."

Trenton nodded absently. "I know but I just want to make sure you remember everything. What about Indians? You might meet up with some Indians along the way."

"I'll use sign and give them gifts. If they look hostile we'll try to get away."

"If you can't get away?"

"I'll tell them I have Arapaho blood in me. It should pull some weight, shouldn't it?"

"Not out here, I'm afraid," Trenton replied more easily. "Make sure Berto doesn't do anything foolish. You know how he is. Make sure he stays by you at all times, especially when you get to the city." Trenton shook his head and ran his hand through his hair. "I shouldn't be doing this. Your mother will kill me."

"She won't kill you, Pa. She'll be glad to see you."

"I can't wait to see her."

"See, this will work out best for everyone. Don't worry, Pa. Berto and I will be in San Francisco before you can spit."

"You hear that, Nate?" Roberto whispered in the cool night air.

"Hear what?"

"Those noises."

"There are lots of noises, Berto. Go to sleep."

"But I heard a mountain lion. I know I did."

"Why would a mountain lion want to eat a scrawny kid like you?"

"That's not funny, Nate. I really did hear something."

"You've said that every night since we've been away from Pa. Don't you think I can take care of you?"

47

"I don't know. I guess I just miss Pa."

"I know. I miss him, too. But Mother needed him. Don't worry, Berto. We'll be okay."

"Are you sure you didn't hear a mountain lion?"

"I didn't hear a mountain lion, Berto. A wolf maybe, but not a mountain lion."

"That's not funny, Nathan!" Roberto pulled the blanket up over his head.

"Go to sleep, Berto, Everything's all right."

Once they reached Yuma, Roberto seemed his old self again. Nathan stabled the horses and bought tickets on the stagecoach to San Francisco. The stage would leave the next morning. They rented a room for the night and were up at dawn, breakfasted and ready to board the stage.

Roberto was excited and, as usual, couldn't contain his enthusiasm. He talked constantly, questioning the driver until Nathan pulled him back.

"Leave him alone, Berto. You're getting in his way."

"This here's a Concord coach, Nate. Did you know that?"

"Where'd you find that out?"

"The driver told me. He says maybe I can ride on top."

"Not a chance. The way you move around, you'd fall off before we were five miles out of town."

A matronly woman passenger in gray gingham turned to look at Nathan, a smile of understanding on her face. The driver opened the coach door.

"Let's go, folks."

As the woman and her husband climbed into the stage, Roberto nudged Nathan.

"Look at that, Nate! Doesn't she look like Clare?"

48

"Who?"

"Her, there on the door."

Nathan noticed the painting of the lovely, fair-haired woman on the inside of the stagecoach door. "I don't know. I guess so."

"I wonder why they paint women on the doors?"

The woman in front of them turned, smiling again. "They do that on all the coaches, dear. I think it's supposed to make you forget about the dust."

Nathan tilted his hat. "Thank you, ma'am." He started Roberto up the steps behind the woman. The trip to San Francisco had begun.

At first Nathan almost grew impatient with the matronly woman's unceasing conversation, but he soon became grateful for it as the days wore on. Roberto could not sit still and be silent at the same time. When he was talking to the woman, Nathan was left alone with his own thoughts for awhile.

The dusty small towns that had marked the seemingly endless desert soon gave way to oak-shaded watering stations as they neared San Diego. During the overnight stay, Nathan took Roberto down to the ocean. Roberto raced the surf, his pants rolled up above his knees, while Nathan stood quietly, trying to absorb the immensity of the sea.

The next day Roberto sat more quietly in the stage, and his impatience soon mounted. "When will we be there, Nate?" he asked for the hundredth time.

"Just be quiet. We'll be there soon enough," Nathan replied, wishing that the talkative woman hadn't gotten off in Santa Barbara.

As the stagecoach rolled and bounced up the coastline, Nathan dreamed. He studied the rich, new land called California, and he fell in love with its immense natural beauty. It had changed from arid desert to grassland and then to rich, fertile coastline. The possibilities for a good life in California were limitless, he thought.

They reached San Francisco in three weeks, two days, none too soon for Nathan and the other passengers who had grown weary of Roberto's incessant complaining. As the two boys stepped off of the stage their eyes grew wide with eagerness and anticipation. San Francisco. Carriages and horses were everywhere, and strange conveyances that resembled stagecoaches but carried more people went up and down the hilly streets.

Nathan heaved their trunk onto his shoulder. "Let's get a ride on one of those things and get to Joe's. He'll be waiting for us." He fumbled through his pocket. "I have the directions somewhere."

Roberto put his hand on Nathan's arm. "Wait, Nate. Can't we look around first? We won't be able to look around on our own once we get to Joe's."

"No, I promised Pa I'd get you right to Joe's."

"Oh, come on, Nate. I thought you were adventurous. At least, that's what you've always told me."

"I'm a lot more adventurous when you're not around. Besides it's almost dark."

"Let's just look around for awhile. It can't hurt. Joe doesn't even know we're here yet."

Nathan thought for a moment. "All right, I guess it can't hurt to look around for awhile. I don't want to carry this thing around with me. Let's check it in at the station."

The boys walked up and down the streets, pointing out things to each other and smiling as they noticed something new for the first time. The clang of a bell attracted Roberto's attention and he ran toward it.

"Come on, Nate."

Roberto stepped up onto a long car that was pulled by two horses.

"Wait up, Berto." Nathan followed Roberto onto the horse-drawn trolley.

"That'll be ten cents a piece, son."

Nathan reached into his pocket and handed the driver twenty cents.

Nathan and Berto sat down. Nathan smiled as he saw the enthusiasm on Berto's face. The horses started moving when the car was filled up with people. Berto hung his head out the side, watching as carriages, omnibuses, and people on horseback rode through the bustling city. He stretched his head out as far as he could to watch as the car went down one of many steep hills. The sights and sounds of the city were all-pervasive. Berto popped his head back into the car.

"What're you smiling at?"

"I don't know. It just feels good to be here."

"Yeah, it's sure a lot livelier than the ranch."

Nathan nodded in agreement, feeling indescribable guilt as he did so. He knew everything his parents had been through and how hard they had worked to make a good life for their sons.

"Chinatown!" the driver called out.

"Let's go, Nate." Roberto jumped off the trolley before Nathan could stop him.

"Damn you, Berto!" Nathan yelled as he followed his brother. He ran after him, grabbing him by the collar of the shirt. "If you do that again I'll smash your face in."

"Come on, Nate. This is San Francisco. You're the one who's told me for so long how you want to come here and live someday. Well, here we are. Let's explore it for awhile. Just you and me."

Nathan rumpled his brother's hair. "All right, let's go."

Chinatown was unlike anything they had ever

seen. There were people everywhere, their singsong language, long pigtails, and black silk tunics seeming totally foreign to the boys. There was a variety of stores and laundries on every corner. Pharmacies advertised the latest medicines, and exotic smells came from several restaurants. People delivering laundry walked down the crowded streets while balancing bamboo poles across their shoulders from which hung baskets filled with clothes. It was bustling and noisy. There was calligraphy painted everywhere, and colored decorations and fluttering ribbons seemed to hang from every storefront.

They walked up and down the narrow streets, intrigued by all of the different shops and wares that were being sold. Plucked chickens hung from the front of one store, while another advertised tattoos. Several Chinamen came up to the boys as they walked along, promising them delights beyond belief.

"What do they mean?" Roberto asked Nathan.

"Never mind." Nathan pushed Roberto along, himself wondering what kinds of delights were being offered.

There was jewelry, clothing, shoes, porcelain, glassware, and utensils. There were rugs from China and Persia, ivory from Africa, furniture from Spain. Everywhere the boys looked, there was something to keep them fascinated. They bought some kind of sweet drink from a vendor, and Roberto bought a fan for their mother. Nathan stopped to look at a necklace for their mother.

"What do you think, Berto?" Nathan turned around to look for his brother but he wasn't there. "Berto? Berto?" Nathan ran out into the street, trying to see some sign of his brother. He looked up the street and saw a boy who resembled Roberto and he followed him. The boy went into a coin shop but when Nathan went inside the boy was gone.

"Have you see a boy about this size with dark hair? Did he just come in here?" he asked the wizened old man who owned the shop.

The man just stared blankly at Nathan.

"Damn it! Where did he go?" Nathan ran back out onto the street and looked both ways. No Roberto. The sound of Roberto's voice transformed his frantic worry into anger.

"Nate, over here. You gotta see this."

Nathan turned around and saw Roberto across the street in front of a tattoo shop. "I ought to kill you right now," Nathan yelled angrily, grabbing his brother by the arm. "Where were you?"

"I was just lookin' around. Can you believe this? Look! This guy has a dragon all the way down his arm!" Nathan tapped his foot impatiently while Berto watched for a few more minutes, then followed as Berto darted away. Nathan followed him down an alley and through a door. A sickeningly sweet smell assaulted him. He grasped his brother's shoulder.

"Come on, Berto."

"What is this place, Nate? God, the smell makes me sick to my stomach."

A Chinese man walked toward them. "You want to smoke the poppy? You have money?"

Nathan grabbed Roberto, shaking his head. "No, no thanks." He pulled Roberto down the alley behind him. He stopped at the end of the alley. "Do you know what that place was, Berto? That was an opium den. I've heard Joe talk about those places before."

"I'm sorry, Nate. I didn't know."

"Just stick by me, okay?"

"All right."

The boys continued walking down the dark streets, looking at all the unfamiliar sights when again Berto sprinted ahead. He ran to a group of men who were gesturing and talking loudly.

"Damn it, Berto. What in hell are you doing?" Nathan quickly caught up.

"Come on, Nate. They're talking about a cockfight."

"How do you know? Do you understand Chinese now?"

"I heard 'em, plain as day. Come on, Nate. Let's go watch."

"Are you crazy? You're eleven years old. You think they're going to let an eleven-year-old kid go in there?"

"Sure, why not?" Before Nathan could stop him, Berto started after the group of men who went into a butcher shop.

"Berto!" Nathan walked after his brother, angry but at the same time intrigued. They followed the men into the butcher shop. A Chinaman held up his hand to stop them.

"Can we go in?" Berto asked.

"You have one dollar?" The man asked in English, scrutinizing the two boys calmly.

"Sure," Berto reached into his pocket and came out with a coin. "Here."

Nathan covered Roberto's hand with his. "Wait, Berto." Nathan eyed the Chinaman suspiciously. "You have better things to spend your dollar on."

"Ah, Nate. Please. Just this one thing. I won't ask for any more."

"I've heard that before."

"Please, Nate. I've always wanted to see a cockfight."

Nathan looked at his brother, nodding his head

indulgently. It was hard to refuse Berto anything. "All right. But after this we go straight to Joe's."

"Whatever you say, Nate." Berto handed the coin to the Chinaman. The Chinaman nodded his head and led the boys through his shop to a door in the rear.

"I'm gonna string you up like one of those dead chickens if something goes wrong. I swear I will."

"Nothing's gonna happen, Nate. It'll be exciting."

They followed the Chinaman down some dimly lit stairs through another door. Nathan hesitated putting a protective hand on Roberto's shoulder. The Chinaman stood in the shadows, waiting silently.

"I don't like this, Berto. I've heard all kinds of things about these places. Let's get out of here."

"Oh, heck, Nate, you're such a chicken I can't believe it. Here we are away from our parents for the first time and you're afraid of your own shadow."

"Don't push me, Berto. I'm still a lot bigger than you, and I'd love nothing better right now than an excuse to beat the hell out of you."

"All right, Nate. Sorry. I'm just excited. I've never done anything like this in my life. Just think, it's something we can talk about when we're old."

Nathan couldn't keep from smiling to himself. Roberto always had that effect on him. "All right, but you just keep quiet. We don't want to attract any attention to us. We're just kids. They might not take kindly to kids going in there."

"Okay, Nate, whatever you say."

Abruptly, the Chinaman stepped in front of them and led the way. Cautiously Nathan followed the Chinaman into the smoke-filled, dimly lit room. The sound from within was furious and loud. Men were shouting and pushing each other. Nathan held onto Roberto and looked around. Feathers littered the filthy floor, and the pungent smell of sawdust and sweat filled the air. But the worst smell of all was the dank smell of blood. Nathan recognized it immediately.

Nathan pressed his back to the wall, holding onto Roberto. The crowd shifted while the Chinaman pushed his way through, collecting bets and paying off the winners. Angry Chinese voices filled the room along with boisterous American curses.

Nathan tried to pick out the Americans, clutching to the familiarity of the language in the sea of Chinese. But suddenly the roar from the crowd swelled, and he was too far away to see. He heard the frantic beating of wings and a single shriek of pain before the shouting drowned out the sounds of the cockfight. The Chinaman bustled to pay off bets.

"Who fights next?" A man in a gray brocade suit asked.

"Jade Glory and Fool's Gold," the Chinaman said softly.

"Jade Glory and Fool's Gold," the man repeated loudly. He reached into the inside pocket of his jacket and took out a sizable amount of cash, flashing it in the face of the Chinaman. "Five hundred dollars on Jade Glory. That big, white cock never loses a fight." He tipped his head back drinking from a silver flask, and wiped his mouth with the back of his hand.

The crowd had grown still while the man in the gray brocade suit spoke. Now, eager voices rang out as bets were placed and the birds were brought in.

For the first time, Nathan noticed tiers of bamboo cages draped with dark cloth against the far wall. Chinese handlers carried the two birds forward, pinning their wings flat against their bodies. Enraged crowing carried over the noise of the crowd. As the handlers stepped into the bamboo ring and bent

56

down, Nathan lost sight of them. He leaned forward to say something to Berto. The boy was gone.

Nathan shouldered forward through the crowd, calling Berto's name. The birds were going at each other with a vengeance, and their screeches resounded throughout the room. Stopped by the bamboo barrier, Nathan gripped it with both hands, scanning the faces around the ring. The birds rose, clashing in midair. A glint of silver caught Nathan's eye, and he watched in grim astonishment as the large white bird thrust a silver spur into the face of the gold bird. Blood spattered the sawdust. The crowd cheered.

Nathan swallowed hard, searching again for Roberto's face. A shout drew his eyes across the ring. The man in the gray suit was going wild as he elbowed forward, trying to get a better look. Sickened with worry, Nathan saw Roberto trapped against the bamboo barrier, a look of panic on his young face. Helplessly, Nathan watched as Berto tried to push his way free but was held against the ring by the relentless crush of the crowd. Almost directly in front of him, the bloodied birds circled and feinted, their silver spurs now stained dark red. Behind Roberto, the man in the gray suit shoved his way forward, knocking Roberto to one side. Ashen-faced, Roberto clutched at the man's sleeve.

"Get outta here, kid!" The man angrily shook him off.

Roberto lost his balance and fell into the ring. Under his weight, the bamboo barrier collapsed, pinning the large white bird for an instant. Nathan screamed his brother's name as the boy scrambled to his feet. Inside the ring, the golden cock saw his advantage and took it. He rose and drove downward with all his weight, driving his spur into Jade Glory's skull. The crowd went silent.

57

"You stupid kid! You idiot!" The man in the gray suit yanked Roberto around to face him. "I ought to break your worthless little neck. You just cost me five hundred dollars, you little shit!" The man hit Roberto hard across the face, knocking him to the ground. He picked him up again, putting his hands around his throat and squeezing tightly. "You're going to pay for this."

Nathan jumped the barrier. "That's enough, mister. Leave the boy alone." Nathan tried to ignore the two men who stood on either side of the man.

The man turned around, a leer on his face. "What's this? Another boy? When you start letting boys in here, Chin?" The man let go of Roberto and confronted Nathan. "So, you think you can take me on, do you?"

"I never said that. I just told you to leave my brother alone."

The man shoved Nathan backward. "What's the matter, boy, afraid?"

Nathan ignored the man's taunts. "Come on, Roberto." Roberto walked past Nathan. "Keep walking, Berto."

The man shoved Nathan again. "Look, kid, if you're going to come into a man's place, you ought to be able to fight like a man." He looked around the room. "Don't you think so, men?"

A murmur went through the crowd and swelled to a cheer.

"I don't have any fight with you, mister. I'll just be going." Nathan started to walk away but a shove from behind sent him sprawling. He turned over and jumped up, prepared to fight. He knew the man wouldn't let him go without one. "I don't want to fight you, mister."

"Well, that's too bad, sonny, because you don't

have a choice. I have five hundred dollars here that says I can beat the tar out of you."

"I don't have any money to bet with."

"That's all right. If you lose, I get to kill you. If you win, you get the five hundred dollars. That's fair, isn't it?"

Nathan backed around in a circle, facing the man and sizing him up. He was tall, not as tall as Nathan but he probably outweighed him by fifty pounds. He was a big man, and there were his two bodyguards to consider. "You sure you want to do this, mister? I don't want to hurt you."

The man laughed loudly, taking out his flask and drinking greedily from it. "I'm not worried, sonny." He threw the flask on the ground and ran straight at Nathan, tackling him. Nathan was pinned to the ground held by the man's weight. Through the pain Nathan tried to remember what his pa had taught him. He braced one arm in the sawdust and heaved, using the man's weight against him. He punched at the man's face as they rolled, striking again and again until a choking sound came from the man's throat.

Nathan stood up and backed away, warily eyeing the circle of men. He saw Roberto at the door and started toward him. But he stopped, unable to catch his breath. There was an ice-hot pain in his shoulder that quickly spread to his chest. He fell to his knees. He saw the shiny boots of the man as he stood in front of him.

"You should have let me win, sonny. I don't like to lose."

Nathan looked up at the man as he walked away, ingraining the face in his memory for all time.

"You bastard!"

Nathan heard Roberto's voice and looked up. The

boy was throwing himself at the man, pummeling him with his small fists. The man picked Roberto up and threw him against the wall, kicking him over and over again. Nathan pulled his knife from his boot and stumbled to his feet, walking toward his brother.

"That's it, mister."

The man turned around smiling. "Even if you know how to throw that knife, this kid will be dead before you can do it."

A glint of steel flashed in the man's right hand. He was pointing a gun at Roberto. Nathan's hand began to shake and sweat poured down his face. He could barely breathe, and the pain in his back and chest was almost unbearable. He dropped the knife. "All right, mister. Just let him go."

Suddenly from out of the crowd the Chinaman appeared. "Driscoll, leave boy alone. He has done you no harm."

Driscoll pushed the Chinaman away but he grabbed Driscoll's arm again. "Get away from me, chink!" He aimed his gun at the Chinaman.

Nathan seized the opportunity and flew forward, throwing himself at Driscoll, but he was already too weak. The larger man easily shoved him away and fired. A pain exploded in Nathan's chest. He fell, fighting the darkness that was quickly engulfing him.

"Nathan!" Berto screamed lunging forward. But Driscoll fired again. Roberto fell at Driscoll's feet, next to his brother.

Driscoll replaced the gun and bent down next to Nathan, pulling his knife free. He wiped the blood on Nathan's coat. Then he searched Nathan and whistled softly when he found the money belt. "Well, well." He smiled and stood up. "Of course none of you saw anything here. Not one thing." There was silence in the room as Driscoll looked from face to face. He looked at his bodyguards. "Get rid of these bodies." He walked to the door. "And don't allow kids in here anymore, Chin. Messes up the whole place."

Nathan watched helplessly as Driscoll left, swearing that if he lived, Driscoll would die.

Chapter III

Nathan saw lights, tiny beams of flashing colors that raced across his brain. He felt the fog he was in, tried to wake up but could not. He heard voices in the background but they were foreign to him. He couldn't make sense of anything. He tried to move but pain raced throughout his body. Where was he?

"How you feel, boy?"

Nathan heard the singsong voice, the strange accent, and he forced himself to open his eyes. He blinked several times, trying to make the fog go away. A Chinaman stood in front of him, his hands clasped together in front of him. He looked steadily at Nathan. Nathan thought he looked familiar. "Who are you?"

The man bowed slightly. "I am called Chin."

Nathan looked around him. The room was small and dimly lit. He still couldn't see much. "Where am I?"

"You are here with Chin," the Chinaman answered logically.

Nathan tried to sit up but the pain prevented him from doing so. "Why am I here?"

"You were almost killed, boy. Do you not remember it?"

63

"Killed?" Nathan shook his head. "I remember walking around Chinatown with my brother and—" Nathan's eyes darted around the room. "Berto, where is my brother?"

Chin put his hands on Nathan's shoulders, pressing him back onto the mat. "You must rest, boy. It is the only way you will get well."

"No, I have to find my brother. He's just a boy." In spite of the pain, Nathan sat up.

"You will not find your brother."

"What do you mean?" Nathan looked wild-eyed.

"Your brother is no longer here."

"What the hell do you mean? Would you speak English!"

"Your brother is dead."

"Berto, dead? No, it can't be." Nathan shook his head. "I have to find him. You have to help me find him."

"Do you remember the fight you had with the man in the gray suit? The man called Driscoll?"

Nathan thought for a minute, and it started coming back to him. He remembered the fight, and he remembered what the man had done. "He shot Berto."

"Yes, and he ordered two men to dispose of the body immediately."

"Oh, God." Nathan closed his eyes, not wanting to imagine what his parents would do when they found out. He tried not to think of Berto's young face, but he couldn't get it out of his mind. Berto had trusted him and he had let him down. Tears stung his eyes but he quickly wiped them away. "How did you get me out of there?"

"While Driscoll's men were dragging your brother away, I and my friends dragged you away. He thinks you are dead also."

"Why did you even bother helping me?"

"Because you were very brave. You save my life. I have never seen anyone stand up to Driscoll like that."

"For all the good it did me," Nathan muttered. Pictures of Roberto floated through his mind. He could hear his voice and see his smile. He wanted to touch him but he could not. He heard Chin move around the room but he had no desire to see what he was doing. He didn't want to do anything anymore. He felt a hand on his arm.

"Drink this, boy. It will help you sleep."

"I don't want to sleep." Nathan yanked his arm away from Chin. "How could anyone kill a boy in cold blood? I don't understand."

"I will explain to you about Driscoll if you will drink the tea."

Nathan looked at the cup the man was holding and watched the steam rise from the liquid. How many times had he drank one of his mother's teas for an ailment. How many times had she given her tea to Berto? Nathan lifted his head and sipped at the hot liquid, letting its warmth seep throughout his body. Chin held his head as he finished the tea and soon he felt his body relax. He felt the pain but it was far away from him now. It wasn't quite so real. He dreamed about his parents and Berto, and he felt comforted. He felt as if Berto were close to him. He heard a noise and opened his eyes.

"You sleep for long time. That is good."

Nathan looked around the small room again. He wasn't dreaming. "Berto, my brother?"

"I think you know the answer to that."

Nathan nodded silently. "You have any more of that tea?"

"I don't think you need that tea. It is time to face

your demons."

"What does that mean?" Nathan winced as he tried to sit up.

"It means you must decide it is time to live."

Nathan nodded. "All right, tell me about this man Driscoll. Is he rich?"

"He have much money and he spend much of it on gambling. He like to come here and be a big man."

"Why do you allow it? It's your place."

"He very powerful man in this city. He could bring big trouble for Chinatown if I tell him to stay away."

"Aren't there people here in your town who could make him stay away?"

"Yes, there are such people but it is best as it is. If something happened to an important man like Driscoll, many powerful men would be down here investigating. You understand?"

"So, he's real rich, huh? Does he have any children?"

"Yes, he has one daughter."

"Does he care about her?"

Chin looked puzzled. "Why you care about Driscoll's daughter?"

"Just tell me, Chin."

"Yes, I have heard he gives her everything. Right now she is in school in the East."

"How old is she and what is her name?"

"I do not know such things about the man."

"I think you know everything about the man, Chin. You hate him as much as I do."

"I did not realize you knew so much about me, boy."

"I don't know a lot about you, Chin, except that you are a man of honor. A man of honor does not like to be treated the way Driscoll treats people."

"Why do you think I am a man of honor?"

"Because you saved my life. Driscoll could have shot you when you pushed him, but you did it anyway. You could've dumped my body into the bay but you didn't. You brought me here and you are taking care of me. What would you call it if it isn't honor?"

Chin regarded the boy in front of him. "How is it a boy your age knows of honor?"

"I have had very good teachers."

"Your mother and father?"

"Yes, my mother and father." Nathan's voice broke as he spoke. How could he tell his parents that Roberto was dead? He had promised his father that he would get Roberto safely to San Francisco, had boasted about it. He closed his eyes, feeling the tears begin to rise again.

"Do not blame yourself for your brother's death. You fulfilled your honorable obligation. It was his time, not yours."

"I didn't do enough." Nathan closed his eyes. He wasn't ready to live yet. He didn't want to face the fact that he was responsible for his brother's death. There was no honor in that.

Nathan sat up against the wall. The pain was less, and he was beginning to feel stronger. He watched as Chin moved quietly around the small room making tea and steaming rice. He had learned quite a bit about Chin since he had been here. Chin had come to San Francisco ten years earlier to find his sister. She had been sold into prostitution, and Chin followed her to America. He never did find her but he decided to stay. He found there were many opportunities for an industrious man in Chinatown. He opened a butcher shop, a jewelry shop, and a small restaurant, but he made most of his money from cockfighting. He was a smart man and probably a rich one, Nathan guessed. He would continue to play the dumb Chinaman to the boorish, rude and wealthy white men who patronized his games, and he would continue to take money from them until there was no longer a need to do so.

"What is her name, Chin?" Nathan asked suddenly.

"You talking to me, boy?" Chin turned away from the pot.

"I can find out for myself. I'm not going to hurt her. I just want to know everything there is to know about Driscoll."

Chin kept to his cooking, ignoring Nathan completely.

"Well, if you won't help me, I'll find out what I need to know alone." Nathan pushed the blanket from him and started to stand up, bringing Chin running from across the room to help him back down to the mat.

Chin shook his finger furiously at Nathan. "Do you know what I do not like about you people? You are all bullies. You all think you can get whatever you want by pushing people around." He put his finger to his head. "You do not use your heads enough. Does not the water wear down the stones?"

"There you go, speaking in those strange phrases again."

"Would it not be better to wait until you are stronger to get back at Driscoll? And while you wait, you can find out everything there is to know about him, his likes and dislikes, his strengths and weaknesses. Know your enemy before you confront him, boy."

Nathan studied Chin, realizing that the man was

absolutely right. "You're telling me Driscoll's too powerful for me to mess with right now."

Chin nodded slightly. "It would be dangerous to tempt fate now. Driscoll is powerful and rich but if we wait long enough we can find a way to the man." Chin looked at Nathan, tilting his head slightly. "You are good-looking, boy, the kind a young girl would find attractive."

"What are you talking about?"

"His daughter's name is Rebecca. She goes to school in the East but she comes home every summer."

"What are you thinking, Chin?"

"I was not thinking anything except that what better way to get to know your enemy than through his daughter?"

"How old is she?"

"She is only ten years old now but she will be of marriageable age one day."

"And you think Driscoll would just let me walk right up and take out his daughter when the time comes?"

"You must use cunning, boy. You are not using your head."

"All right, you tell me how to do it."

"You find out where they are going to be, and you arrange to be there. We make up a name for you, buy you new clothes, and as long as Driscoll does not see you, you make his daughter fall in love with you."

"I'd have to wait at least six years before I could even court her."

"Six years is not long if you stay busy. Have you finished the letter to your parents?"

"Yes." Nathan picked up the envelope addressed to his parents and held it a moment." I hope they answer this one. I don't know what I'll do if they

69

don't want me back."

"Do not worry. I will see that it is mailed."

"Chin, would you forgive me if you were my parents?"

Chin's slanted eyes studied Nathan for a moment. "If I were your parents, there would be nothing to forgive."

Nathan smiled, nodding his thanks to Chin.

Weeks went by, but still Nathan didn't receive a reply to his letters. He was convinced his parents couldn't forgive him. He tried to keep busy with the newspapers and books Chin brought him but all he could think about were his parents and Berto. He felt as if a part of him had been taken away when Berto was murdered.

He stood at the window that overlooked the bay. It was a dark, overcast day, and the gloom all but encompassed him. He missed his family and he missed the bright sun of Arizona.

"You all right boy?"

"Why haven't I heard from my folks, Chin? I can't believe they haven't written."

"Perhaps they did not receive letter."

"But I wrote two. You did mail them, didn't you?"

"Yes, I mail."

"Maybe they can't forgive me."

"Why not go see them. Explain."

"No, if they haven't written back they don't want to see me."

"You don't know that. You not giving your parents a chance. Go to them."

"I can't, Chin. I can't go back until I've avenged Berto's death and gotten back Pa's money." He stared out the window again. "Doesn't this fog ever get to you, Chin?"

Chin padded across the room and stood next to Nathan. He barely reached Nathan's shoulder. "Sometimes it make me sad but then I think it could be worse. I could be in jail somewhere and never see the light of day."

Nathan turned and looked at Chin, a quizzical expression on his face. "You're a funny guy, Chin. You don't let much bother you."

"Don't have time to worry about things I have no control over. I control the things I know I can control and then I do not worry."

"You still think I ought to go home to my parents, don't you?"

"Is for you to decide."

"Then help me."

"It is difficult decision, boy. Driscoll is very powerful man. Even if you make much money and grow powerful yourself, it does not mean you can get back at him."

Nathan watched as the dark clouds skirted quickly past. "I know what my mother would say."

"What is that?"

"She would tell me to give up this idea of revenge and go home."

"And your father?"

Nathan shook his head. "I don't know. My mother told me once that when Pa was about my age he set out to find the man who was responsible for his father's death."

"Did he find him?"

"Yes."

"Did he kill him?"

"No."

"But is that not what you want to do to Driscoll? Do you not want him to suffer and then die?"

"Yes, damn it! He murdered my little brother for no good reason. He had no right, Chin. He had no right." Nathan turned away from the window and walked to the chair that sat in front of the small iron stove. He sat down and warmed his hands by it. "He was just a boy."

Chin walked to the stove, holding his hands over it. "You must do what you think is right, boy. I will help you no matter what you decide to do."

"Why? Why would you do that?"

"I like you."

"Is that all?"

"You are smart, too, like I was at your age." Chin rubbed his hands together. "And I hate Driscoll as much as you do."

Nathan pulled his chair closer to the stove. "I understand why you hate him. He treats you and your people like dirt."

"That is not the reason I hate Driscoll so much," Chin said, his tone becoming quietly angry. "I told you I had come here to look for my sister. May Ling was a beautiful girl, very delicate, easily frightened. I told you I looked everywhere for her but couldn't find her. I knew she was here in San Francisco because I had received some letters from her. I searched for many months and finally found some prostitutes who had known her. They were scared and did not want to talk to me. But one of them finally told me that May Ling had been murdered by one of her customers. A white man."

Nathan sat up straight. "Driscoll?"

"Yes, our friend Driscoll had murdered my little sister. She was only nineteen years old. A beautiful, bright girl murdered by that dog."

"But that was a long time ago, Chin. Why haven't you done anything about it?"

"I decided to wait and to study the man. I heard that he liked to gamble so I opened up my place. He has been here every week, sometimes two and three times a week for the last seven years."

"So what are you waiting for?"

"Driscoll is getting even more powerful. It is said that he may be the next senator of our state."

"Then he'll be too powerful to touch."

"On the contrary, boy. He will be that much more vulnerable because he will have that much more to lose."

"But how can you be so patient? How can you let him abuse you the way you do and not get angry?"

"My anger guides me, it does not consume me." Chin took the kettle from the stove and poured them some hot tea.

Nathan nodded and cradled the cup in his hands. "I'm staying here with you, Chin. Nothing's going to keep me from getting Driscoll."

Joe stared into the black cup of coffee, watching the steam rise in a circular pattern.

Larissa put her hand on his shoulder. "Joe, maybe you should go up and get some rest. You've been sitting here for a long time."

Joe shook his head. "I don't need to rest. I need to know what happened to Nate and Berto." He looked over at Charley, their Chinese cook. He had come running home to them with a story about two boys getting murdered at the cockfights. Joe had thought it sad enough until Charley had described the boys to him. There was no doubt in his mind that they were Nate and Berto.

"You all right, Mister Joe? I no like seeing you so unhappy. I so sorry to bring you such bad news."

73

"Tell me again, Charley. The boys did nothing to provoke this man? He just got angry and started after the smaller one?"

"Yes, the small one. He almost fall into the bamboo, and he grab onto man for support. The man throw him down. When he land on bamboo, one of the birds kill the other. The man blame the boy for this and start beating on him. Suddenly, another boy, a bigger boy, comes from across the ring to help the smaller boy. They get in fight and when boy starts to walk away, the man throws knife at him. Then he goes after small boy again. Older boy gets up one more time to try to help but man shoots him and then shoots younger boy."

"You're sure they were dead?"

"I saw the bodies dragged out of there, Mister Joe. They were dead."

"Have you ever seen him there before?"

"Yes, plenty times. He dress in fancy clothes and drink out of silver container. He flash money around every time he make bet."

"What does he look like?"

"He have brownish-red hair and very white skin. He not as tall as you, Mister Joe, but he pretty tall. He very big here." Charley made a circle around his stomach with his arms.

"He's big in the belly?"

"Yes, too much rich food and alcohol. And his face is puffy."

"Did you hear a name, Charley?"

"Chin called him something but I could not hear."

"Who is Chin?"

"He is owner. He tried to stop this man but he push Chin away."

Joe slammed the cup of coffee down on the table. "Tell me where Chin lives, Charley. I want to talk to him."

"I cannot do that, Mister Joe."

"What do you mean you can't do that? Do you realize that these boys were almost blood to me?"

"I understand, but you must also understand that I cannot tell on my own." Charley lowered his eyes.

Joe made a long sweep with his arm and knocked the coffee cup to the floor. The sound echoed in the kitchen. "I'll find this Chin with or without your help, Charley." He stood up, ignoring Larissa's concerned expression.

"There many Chins in Chinatown, Mister Joe."

"I don't give a damn if there are one thousand Chins in Chinatown. I'm gonna find your friend and I'm gonna find out who murdered those boys!"

Joe looked up and down the busy street, squinting at the singsong sound of the Chinese language that continued to assault his senses. This was the second week in a row he had come here looking for Charley's friend but he had found no sign of him. He had located a number of Chins, all of whom refused to tell him anything. "Goddamned Chinese!" he muttered to himself, not really cursing the people but their secretive ways. He had been familiar with the Chinese ever since he and Larissa had come to San Francisco almost ten years ago, making a name and place for themselves on the gambling money he had saved and buried on Cheyenne land. He figured it was a good place for him and Larissa to start a new life together. He smiled broadly when he recalled how astounded Larissa was when she finally realized what kind of life Joe really had mapped out for them. It was to be a full, rich life, rich in material things but rich in other things that counted as well.

There had been people in the city who had publicly rebuked him because of his color but Joe didn't care. He had expected that. He knew that money was the great equalizer. So, when he had made several large deposits in several different banks, people were suddenly interested in this rich black man. As Joe pushed his way into society he couldn't help but laugh. If only the people knew he was an ex-slave and Larissa was an ex-prostitute, but still he felt as good as any of the people in San Francisco. Joe then searched the city for people who needed work, and he hired them to work in their mansion. He loved giving of his time and money, and soon San Francisco women were overcome by his charm, wit, and benevolence. But Joe wasn't fooled. He knew that most of them liked having him around because it was fashionable.

"You like, mister?" A Chinese man bumped Joe's shoulder and showed him some obviously fake jewels.

Joe shook his head and walked away, heading toward the next Chin on his list. He strode into the butcher shop, looking around as if he were interested in the meat that lay on the open counters.

"You want something, mister?"

Joe turned around, sizing up the man in front of him. "Your name Chin?"

"I am Chin. You want meat?"

"No, no thanks." Joe looked around. "I heard you have games here."

"Games?"

Joe leaned closer and whispered. "Cockfights."

"Yes, it is true. I have them every night. You want come?"

"I'm kinda interested in them. You see, I'm from the South, and my daddy raised good fightin' cocks."

"I see." Chin looked at the tall black man in front

of him and knew immediately that he was not what he seemed. "You come back this night after dark."

"I heard you have all kinds of people who come here."

Chin walked away from Joe and walked back to the counter where he picked up a cleaver and began adroitly cutting meat. "You come back tonight."

Joe nodded absently, looking around the room again. He left the store and walked briskly up the street. He knew that this man was hiding something as surely as he knew Nathan was alive. "That's all right, I'll play his game," Joe muttered to himself. "One way or another he'll tell me what he knows."

"No! I forbid it. You will ruin everything."

"What's the matter with you, Chin? All I want to do is go down to the cockfights tonight. I've been cooped up in this place for too long now. I've got to get out."

"But that is not the place to go. Too many people."

"I'll wear a hat. No one will even notice me."

"Like no one noticed you the last time?"

"I want to go, Chin."

"What if Driscoll is there and recognizes you?" Chin shook his head adamantly. "No, if you go tonight and you are recognized by Driscoll, there will be no more lives for you. He will make sure of it."

"What the hell am I supposed to do all the time? I'm used to being out in the open, riding my horse on the open land. I can't take it in this little place anymore."

"Then go back to your family. That is where you belong."

Nathan was sure there was a note of disdain in Chin's voice. He realized how ungrateful he sounded.

77

He had to take it slow; he had to be patient. "All right, I'll stay here."

"For once you see reason." Chin lowered the paper he was reading closer to the lamp, squinting at the print. "I buy English newspaper and English book for you to read." He raised his head slightly. "You do know how to read?"

"Very funny."

"You read tonight and you stay busy. Tomorrow we sit down and plan."

"What do you mean?"

"It is time. We must make plans." He lifted his eyes from the paper and looked at Nathan. "You must decide if this is what you really want to do. There is no shame in going back to your family."

"I know that but I can't go back until I get Driscoll."

Chin nodded. "All right. Tomorrow we sew the seeds that we will harvest in the future."

Joe hadn't been to a cockfight since he was a kid, and he was surprised that the atmosphere was almost the same, except that most of the people spoke a different language. The dank smell was still the same, the cloying smell of sawdust, blood, and sweat. Bamboo cages were lined up along the walls, and the cocks that were waiting to fight were squawking and fluttering their wings under their covered cages. He walked around the circle, keeping his eye on every well-dressed man who came into the room, but no one fit the description of the man Charley had described.

Joe placed a bet on a black cock, fit as any bird he'd ever seen, and he won two hundred dollars. He smiled to himself as he pocketed the money. He still hadn't lost the touch. He pretended to watch the birds but he was really watching the crowd. He looked for Chin but he couldn't find him. He knew it was too dangerous to ask questions in a place like this so he just listened.

Hours had passed, and while Joe had won three hundred more dollars, he was none the richer in information. Just as he was about to give up and go home, Chin arrived. Joe watched as Chin talked to two of his men. One of them nodded and left, the other walked around the room collecting bets. Chin just stood watching everyone.

Joe decided to place another bet, all five hundred dollars he had won that night. He bet on a bird that he really wasn't keen on, but he needed an excuse to talk to Chin whether the bird won or lost. After the fight, as Joe was collecting his five hundred extra dollars, he approached Chin, a big smile on his face.

"Hey, Chin, remember me? I was in your place this afternoon." Joe quickly counted his winnings. "Woo-wee! I am lucky tonight!"

"So, you have done well, I see."

"Hell, I've done more than well, Chin."

"If you feel so lucky, why not bet more?"

"No siree. I'm stoppin' while I'm ahead. Hell, I could buy myself a farm with this kinda money."

"Sound like good idea."

Joe realized that Chin had terminated the conversation, and he watched as the man walked around the room, looking at the people, then he left by a side door. Joe looked around him and followed Chin, making sure that no one was watching him. He opened the door and slipped through but was stopped by a silent but knowing Chin.

"What is it you want?"

Joe closed the door behind him and looked at Chin

in the dimly lit hallway. "I want some information."

"Why should I give you information?"

"You don't have to give me anything but I'll find out what I want to know with or without your help." He regarded Chin silently for a moment. "Tell me about the night Driscoll was here, Chin."

"Who?"

"Don't play games with me, man. It's just you and me here. I want to know about the night Driscoll killed the two kids."

"Why is it important to you?"

"It's important because I knew them both. One was like a son to me."

"I am sorry. I did not realize." Chin turned, his hands tucked inside his wide sleeves. "Follow me." Chin led Joe up the stairs to a small room. The smell of strong tea saturated the room. Chin nodded to a chair. "Sit down, please."

Joe sat down, waiting patiently as Chin brought a pot and two cups to the small table. After he had poured Joe a cup he sat down. "Tell me of these boys," Chin asked.

"There were two of them. One was white, blond hair, blue eyes, about sixteen. The other was Mexican, dark hair and eyes, about eleven. I heard they were both shot in your place by Driscoll and I want to know why." Joe picked up the steaming cup of tea. He looked at Chin over the rim as he sipped.

"There is no reason why men like Driscoll shoot people."

"Let's get something straight, Chin. These boys weren't just people to me, they were like kin."

"How is it you know these boys?"

"Their father is my best friend. The oldest one, Nathan, hell, I practically helped to raise him. I was there when he uttered his first sound." His black eyes sought out Chin's. "I love that boy, Chin."

"I am sorry. It is difficult to lose loved ones. I, too, am familiar with that kind of loss."

"So, tell me about Driscoll. Driscoll *was* the man who shot them, wasn't he?"

"Yes, it was Driscoll. How did you come by this information?"

"I, too, have my sources."

"So you want to know about Driscoll. That is easy enough. He is a man of great power and influence in this city. He married into the money but he controls it. His wife is from an old San Francisco family."

"What kind of a relationship does he have with his wife?"

"It is like many in that class of society. They tolerate each other but he has other women. It is said he likes Oriental women."

"Which he can get easy enough down here."

Chin nodded, pouring them both more tea. "I would offer you some advice, friend."

Joe picked up the cup of hot tea. "And what would that be?"

"Do not try to get at Driscoll. He is a dangerous man. He will eliminate you from the face of the earth without a second thought."

"I'm not stupid enough to walk right up to him."

"That is wise for he always has at least two bodyguards with him."

Joe leaned forward, his elbows resting on the table, his eyes searching Chin's in the dim light. "You seem like a decent man, Chin. Why do you tolerate men like Driscoll?"

"It is what I have been taught to do. I know no other way. I lower my eyes and make him think he is better than I."

"But how can you do it? Don't it drive you crazy?"

81

Chin's eyes glowed black in the lamplight. "You should know the answer to that better than I, black man. Can it be that you or your parents were slaves and that every time your master walked past you you had to lower your eyes? It is no different except that I choose to do this."

"Why? Why would you choose to do something like this?"

"Perhaps it is because I delight in taking money from the boastful white men, or perhaps it is because I know no other way."

"Yeah, but it's different for you. Me and my family weren't free. We were forced into slavery."

"And what do you think many of my people are doing on the white man's railroads? They are forced to work long days for little money, and they are treated like dogs."

Joe nodded, lifting the tea to his mouth but stopping. "You have anything stronger than this?"

"You mean alcohol?"

"Yeah, I could go for a drink right now. All this talk of slavery's got my throat real dry."

Chin got up and padded across the room to a cupboard. He came back with a bottle and two small cups. "This is plum wine. Very good. Very strong."

"That's fine with me. Long as it's got alcohol in it. So, tell me why Driscoll got mad at the boys."

Chin poured the wine and sat down. "The young one wanted to see the birds better and he moved closer to the ring. But the men closed in on him. He fell backward into the ring, onto one of the birds. It was the bird that was winning, the one Driscoll was betting on. The bird lost and Driscoll went crazy."

"No one tried to help?"

"Everyone else was as angry as Driscoll. The boy ruined a good bet for everyone."

"So what happened then?"

"Driscoll started pushing the boy around and his big brother told Driscoll to stop it. Driscoll wouldn't listen and began pushing the older boy around, too. The boy didn't want to fight. He tried to get his brother and leave but Driscoll wouldn't let him. He stabbed him in the back."

Joe slammed the cup down on the table. "He stabbed Nathan in the back? Good Christ!" Joe said angrily. "What about the young one? What happened to him?"

Chin poured Joe more wine. "Drink, it is not a nice story." Chin waited until Joe had drunk and then he continued. "The young one came at Driscoll like a young tiger with his claws bared. Driscoll is a big man; he had no trouble with the boy. He threw him against the wall and kicked him over and over again. The older one crawled toward Driscoll, a knife in his hand, but Driscoll had already pulled his gun and had it aimed at the young one."

"That's when you tried to stop Driscoll?"

Chin showed mild surprise. "How do you know this?"

"Like I said, I have my sources."

"Yes, I tried to stop him but he pushed me aside. He shot both of the boys. I tried to get to the boys to see if they were still alive but Driscoll's men removed them immediately. Driscoll did not want to leave any evidence."

"Evidence," Joe muttered, this time pouring the wine for himself. "They were nothing but 'evidence' to him in the end. The dirty bastard!"

"Perhaps you should go now. I do not even know your name."

"Joe. My friends call me Joe."

"Perhaps you should go now, Joe. Sometimes the

83

wine is not good for a man when he is trying to forget. Sometimes it makes remembering all too clear."

Joe nodded. "Yeah, maybe you're right." Joe leaned his elbows on the table, his chin resting on his clenched fists. "Just tell me one thing, Chin. Why is it someone I know saw a blond kid fitting Nathan's description in here not more than a week ago?"

Nathan paced around the room, throwing the paperback down on the floor. He shook his head. *A Woman's Almanac* was not his idea of exciting reading. He walked over to the door and opened it slightly. He could hear the noise from the crowd down below. He wanted to go back down and see the fights, but more honestly, he wanted to see if Driscoll showed up. Chin would never even know if he sneaked out for awhile. He slipped on the heavy dark seaman's jacket and the knit cap that Chin had obtained for him. He opened the door and looked in the hall. The only other room on this floor was an empty one that Chin sometimes rented out. He walked quietly down the hall but stopped when he heard voices in the room. He thought he heard Chin's voice so he hurried to the wooden stairs that led downstairs to the cockfighting. He hurriedly descended the stairs and walked in the dimly lit hall-way to the door which he and Roberto had first approached together on that day more than two months ago. He put his hand on the knob and sud-denly he felt his heart race. His ears rang and he felt as if his legs would give way from under him. Two months ago he had a brother—now he had none. And it was because of this place.

He opened the door slightly, and the sound of the

men's frenzied voices carried out to him. The thought suddenly occurred to him that Driscoll could be in the room and if he were, what could he do about it? He had no weapon and even if he did, Driscoll's bodyguards would see to it that he was finished off for good this time. But he had to see—he had to see if Driscoll was in the room.

He opened the door and quickly closed it, moving easily into the crowd. He attracted no attention without Roberto. The glances he received were from men who thought he was a young seaman touring Chinatown. Nathan walked through the crowd, looking nonchalantly at people, trying to find Driscoll. He stood in the back of the room, ignoring the squawks and cries of the birds as they fought to their deaths and the yells of the men who egged them on. His eyes perused the room, stopping at each man who looked even remotely familiar. He waited for awhile until another pair of birds had begun to fight, and then he decided to leave. But as he started for the side door the rear door opened and in walked two of Driscoll's bodyguards, followed by Driscoll and another guard. Nathan pulled the knit cap further over his eyes, pulling the collar of the coat up to hide his light hair. He looked straight ahead at the birds, trying to ignore Driscoll, but it was hard to ignore the man. As soon as he entered a room he took control. He blustered up to the front of the crowd and screamed at the men for not betting more. The poor birds, after all, he said, were risking their lives. The hatred in Nathan rose so steadily and unannounced that Nathan was surprised by its deadly presence. He hated the man and he wanted to kill him. He moved into the crowd, getting closer to Driscoll. He stopped when he saw one of his men turn and glance at him. He watched Driscoll as the man boasted and cajoled his way into bets, and he watched as he belittled the Chinese men who ran the games in Chin's absence. It made Nathan's stomach turn. He knew what he had to do. Chin had put his gun away in the cupboard with some shells. Nathan was going to get the gun. He walked slowly to the side door but was stopped by one of Driscoll's men. The man walked toward him.

"Where've I seen you before, kid?"

Nathan looked at the man and shook his head. "Don't know. Only been here a day. Came in on a ship."

"Where from?"

"Up from Panama." Nathan turned back to the fights, trying to get the man interested in something else. "Ain't never seen myself one of these before."

"That a fact?"

The man seemed to consider what Nathan had said but before he could do anything, Lee, one of Chin's assistants, came up to Nathan. "We have what you asked for, sir. Will you follow me, please."

Nathan smiled and turned to follow Lee but a hand on his arm stopped him. He looked at Driscoll's guard. "What's wrong, mister?"

"I know I've seen you someplace before but I can't remember where." He squeezed Nathan's arm tightly. "I'd like you to stay around here until I do remember."

"Sure, mister, but hurry up. I got me a woman waitin' for me." Nathan watched as Lee hurried out the side door. He silently prayed to himself that he was able to find Chin.

Just as Joe was about to get up, Lee burst into the room, speaking in rapid Chinese. Chin waived him away and turned to Joe.

"My men are in need of my assistance, Joe. You will excuse me?"

"Sure, what is it?"

"Just a small matter concerning money. Goodbye."

Chin quickly padded down the hall to his room and recovered the gun and shells he had hidden in the cupboard. He hurried downstairs and entered through the side door. He walked slowly over to the ring, taking his normal place. He took the money from his assistant and stood, watching the crowd with fixed eyes. He spotted Nathan immediately and the man behind him. He walked over to them. "Pardon, sir, but I have business with this young man."

"What business you got with this kid, chink?"

Chin looked from Nathan to the man. "Young man request I find him a woman. He say he never have woman before. You understand?"

The bodyguard laughed loudly, slapping Nathan on the back. "I thought you looked young, kid. Go ahead, have your woman. Have fun for me, too."

Nathan smiled sheepishly and followed Chin out the side door and up the stairs.

"Why you be so stupid? Driscoll came this close to seeing you." Chin padded across the room. "If you are not going back to your family then you can't stay here. Is too dangerous."

"But Chin—"

"Do not argue. If you want to stay alive, you must leave here."

Chapter IV

"There, how's that?" Aeneva brushed the red skirt and watched as Anna looked at herself in the mirror.

"It's beautiful, ma'am. I never had meself such a lovely thing before."

"I can make you lots of beautiful clothes, Anna. I've never had a daughter. I would like very much to make some things for you if you'd let me."

"I'd like that very much, ma'am." She sat down in the chair opposite Aeneva. "Where are your sons now? Will they be in San Francisco by now?"

"Yes, and we should have had word from them by now. I don't understand."

"I'm sure everything's all right, ma'am." Anna smiled lightly.

"Do you like it here, Anna?"

"Oh, yes, ma'am, very much. It's the most beautiful place I've ever seen."

"Would you like to stay for awhile if you could?"

"Oh, yes, I'd be likin' that very much but I don't know if me father would be likin' it much. He likes the city life, he does."

"And what about you, Anna. What do you like?"

The girl shrugged her shoulders. "I like the peace

and quiet. It seems that most of me life I've been to noisy places. That's why I like it here so much." Anna got up and walked to the window. "I've never seen a place where you could look forever and not see another thing."

Aeneva got up and stood next to the girl. "You should have seen the land I grew up on, the land your mother came from. It was like this, only tall prairie grass grew everywhere and buffalo grazed for as far as you could see. In the spring after the snow and rains they would roll in their wallows, and you could hear them all across the prairie. And where they wallowed wildflowers bloomed."

"Why did you leave it if you loved it so much?"

"I left it for something I loved more. My husband."

"That is what my mother did for my father but I do not think she was happy in the white world. People always stared at her and made fun of her. She didn't speak good English like you."

"You remember your mother then?"

"Yes. She was a nice lady who never got angry with me father. I don't know why she stayed with him. She wasn't happy."

Aeneva put her arms around the girl, pulling her close. "She stayed because of you, Anna. It sounds like she was a good mother and she loved you very much."

Anna pointed. "Here they come."

"It's about time. Come, you can help me with the supper." Aeneva led Anna into the large area which served as dining room and kitchen. Aeneva pulled a pan from the hollowed-out adobe oven and looked inside. The meat was sizzling, it's juices spitting as Aeneva stabbed it with a fork. "What do you think?" she asked Anna, seeing the girl's curiosity.

Anna peeked into the pan, taking a deep sniff. "It

90

smells wonderful to me, ma'am.''

"Good. Let's check those biscuits. Why don't you get out the butter and I'll set the table.''

"No, please let me do that, ma'am. I've been watching you and I think I can do it.''

"All right.'' Aeneva turned the pan of biscuits into the basket and covered it with a towel. She watched Anna with delight. The girl had blossomed in the few weeks she had been with them. She had gained some weight, and her cheeks were a healthy rosy color. Her deep blue eyes twinkled when she laughed, and Aeneva was overcome with a feeling she hadn't felt in years. It was something close to wanting another child.

The door slammed open and in walked Trenton and O'Leary. Trenton walked over to Aeneva and kissed her on the cheek and smiled at Anna. "That's a beautiful table, Anna.''

"Thank you, sir.''

"Aye, you be learnin' useful things, girl.'' O'Leary sniffed at the air. "I hope you can learn how to cook like Mrs. Hawkins, girl. Keep your old dad healthy.''

"Don't you think a nine-year-old girl has better things to do than take care of her father, Mr. O'Leary?'' Aeneva asked in a haughty tone, plunking the heavy roasting pan onto the table.

"And what business, may I ask, is it of yours, Mrs. Hawkins?''

"It is my business as long as you are staying in my home.''

"Well, if ye be makin' threats, my daughter and I'll be a leavin' in the mornin'.''

"I sincerely doubt it, Mr. O'Leary,'' Aeneva stood with her hands on her hips, confronting the Irishman. "You would die without my cooking.''

"Aye, and it's the truth you be tellin'. I've not

91

tasted anything quite so good since I left Ireland and me own mother's cookin'."

"So stop threatening me and sit down and eat." She looked softly at Anna. "Anna, don't worry. Your father and I just like to argue. It does not mean we don't like each other."

"To the contrary, me darlin', it means we like each other a lot."

Trenton hung his hat up and sat down at the table. "I do have to say, O'Leary, things haven't quite been the same since you've been here."

"See there, without me you'd have been missin' your two boys something fierce. But instead you have something to keep you occupied."

"Shouldn't we pray now, Papa?" Anna asked in a quiet voice.

Trenton and Aeneva exchanged amused glances. They knew that O'Leary hated to pray but did so for the sake of his daughter.

"Aye, I'd hate to be forgettin' the grace now." They folded their hands. "Heavenly Father, grant that this food be blessed and that the people who give it so freely be equally blessed. Amen."

Aeneva looked at O'Leary. "Why, Mr. O'Leary, that was very nice."

"You'd be kickin' me out of house and home if I was to say anything else." O'Leary piled large quantities of food on his plate and began eating with a vengeance, something he had been doing ever since he'd recovered from the cholera. "So, when are we to be meetin' those two boys of yours?"

"I was just thinking if we don't hear from Joe soon I'm going to send a telegram. We should've heard something by now."

"Don't worry, Trenton. I'm sure Joe would have let us know if something was wrong."

"I just still feel uneasy about the two of them traveling the rest of the way alone."

"How old did you say your oldest son was?"

"Sixteen."

"Ah, when I was his age, I was on a boat sailing to America. He's a man. You have nothin' to be worryin' about."

"Yes, but Berto is only eleven. What if—"

"You worry too much, Mrs. Hawkins, that's your problem." He winked at Aeneva conspiratorially. "You should learn to drink whiskey. It teaches you to relax."

"I don't want to relax. I just want to hear from my sons."

"It's a good dinner, ma'am."

Aeneva looked at Anna, realizing that the child was trying to dispel her fears. The girl was very adept at reading a situation and avoiding confrontations. She had probably learned that from traveling with her father. "Thank you, Anna. Why don't you have another biscuit."

"Thank you, ma'am."

"Anna, what did you think of that mare you rode today? Did you like her?"

Anna looked at Trenton. "Yes, very much, sir. She is beautiful and she minds well."

Trenton smiled at Aeneva. "I'd like her to be yours, Anna. She seemed to take quite a liking to you. I'm not sure she'd let anyone else ride her."

"Oh, no, sir, I couldn't be doin' that. She's your mare."

"No, she's your mare, Anna." Trenton narrowed his eyes at O'Leary. "That is if your father says it's all right."

O'Leary chewed on his food, seeming to consider the request. "Well, I think it would be all right. If the

93

mare likes you that much we'd hate to disappoint her now, wouldn't we."

"Oh, thank you, sir." Anna jumped up and ran around the table, throwing her arms around Trenton and kissing him on the cheek. Instantly she was embarrassed and pulled away.

Trenton gently pulled her back. "You are very welcome, Anna. But please do me a favor. Don't call me 'sir.' My name is Trenton."

"Oh, I couldn't be callin' you that, sir."

"Then call me Mr. Hawkins but don't call me 'sir.' You make me feel old when you call me that."

Anna smiled. "If it would be pleasin' you then, that's what I'll be callin' you, Mr. Hawkins."

"And I don't want to be called ma'am anymore, Anna. If you won't call me Aeneva, call me Mrs. Hawkins."

"Yes, ma'am."

"You people are enough to drive a man crazy. Don't you be havin' any bad habits?"

"What did you have in mind, O'Leary?" Trenton leveled his gaze at his guest.

"You don't drink, you don't gamble and your wife is the only woman I've seen around here. Where does a man go for some fun?"

Trenton shook his head, pushing his plate away and propping his elbows up on the table. "Were you planning on taking Anna with you?"

O'Leary stopped in mid-bite, putting his fork down on the table. "Now I can see where your wife gets her sharp tongue from."

"My wife had a sharp tongue when I met her. Don't blame it on me."

O'Leary laughed and pounded the table with his fist. "I like you, Hawkins."

"I do not like being talked about as if I am not in

94

the room." Aeneva stood up, noisily stacking plates. She walked to O'Leary and took his plate away from him while he was still eating. "If you find the company here so unbearable, Mr. O'Leary, you can leave anytime you wish." She walked to the counter, followed by Anna who had quickly picked up some things to help Aeneva.

"She has a temper, that one." O'Leary looked at Aeneva. "Aye, but she's a good woman. Not many would've stuck by me and me girl like she did. I owe her a lot, I do." He watched Aeneva and Anna as they talked. He noticed the way Anna looked at Aeneva. "My little Anna seems to be very taken with your wife, Hawkins."

"She's an easy person to be taken with," Trenton replied.

"I've not seen Anna this happy since her mother was alive. She likes it here."

"We like having her here. She's a lovely girl. We don't miss the boys quite as much with her here." Trenton stood up. "Let's go into the living room. I have some good scotch I've been saving."

O'Leary made a choking sound. "Scotch? My God, man, do you want me to die of poisoning? I'd rather be drinkin' straight alcohol!"

"Whatever you wish, O'Leary." Trenton walked into the big room to one of the wooden cabinets. He pulled out a bottle of scotch and two glasses. "A friend gave this to me five years ago, and he told me it was at least ten years old."

"That old?" O'Leary was suddenly interested. He walked toward Trenton. "Well, couldn't hurt to have a small taste of the stuff."

Trenton poured them each a glass and walked to a chair and sat down. "What do you think?"

O'Leary followed Trenton, sitting down in a chair

opposite him. "It's not Irish whiskey but I've tasted worse."

"Have you given any thought to what you want to do, O'Leary?"

"What do you mean?"

"Are you still going west from here?"

"West it is to find me fortune."

"And where do you plan to find this fortune?"

"In the gold mines, of course."

"Most of the streams are panned out, and the men who are hard rock mining have been there for years. They're not going to let you come right on in."

"I'll find meself a way to get in there. Don't you be worryin' yourself on my account."

"What about Anna? Do you intend to take her there? Do you think that's a safe place for a little girl?"

O'Leary downed the rest of the scotch and eyed Trenton warily. "You and the missus have taken a keen interest in Anna since we've been here. She's my little girl, not yours."

"I know that, O'Leary. I just wonder if you've ever considered what she's been through."

"I've considered it more than you, Hawkins, you can be sure of that."

"But why? Why would you drag a little girl all around the country just because of your dreams?"

O'Leary stood up, slamming his fist on the table. "It's me dreams that've been keepin' me going all of me life, Hawkins. They're what kept me goin' in Ireland when me family was starvin' because we couldn't even grow potatoes in the soil. They're what kept me goin' when I came to this country dirt poor and ignorant of the ways here. But I kept going because I had me dreams." O'Leary walked around the room, appreciating the fine wood and the stone fireplace. "I bet you had dreams, too, Hawkins. You've come quite a ways for a man who was born to an Indian."

Trenton grabbed the bottle and poured them both some more scotch. "I'm sorry, O'Leary, I'm the last person in the world who should be criticizing any man. I've made lots of mistakes in my life."

O'Leary walked back to the table and picked up the glass. "I understand your concern for me little girl but I can take care of her. I always have."

"All right. I won't say any more about it."

"Tell me, Hawkins, what would you do if you did have yourself a little girl around here?"

"What would I do if I had a daughter?" Trenton smiled, staring across the room. "I'd probably spoil her rotten, give her anything she wanted. I'd want her to be like her mother."

"And why is that?"

"Because Aeneva is a strong yet gentle woman. She is a very able woman. Did you know when she was very young she was known as 'Woman Warrior'?"

"Doesn't surprise me a bit. I'm glad I didn't have to face her."

Trenton laughed. "When we were kids she was a tough little thing. She'd fight anyone, boy or girl, it didn't matter. She had no fear."

"And you'd like your daughter to be like that, would you?"

"I'd like her to have that kind of confidence and Aeneva's sense of honor as well."

"Aye, it's very apparent to me that the woman possesses a fine sense of honor. I'd bet me life on it that she's a fine mother as well."

"She's patient and fair, and she has a sense of humor, too. She and the boys are always laughing about something."

"And your sons, fine lads I bet they are."

"I think they are. They drive each other and us crazy. They argue about everything."

"And you and the missus love it, don't you?"

"Yes, we do." Trenton was quiet a moment, staring across the room. "I'm riding into town tomorrow, O'Leary. Want to come with me?"

"Mother Mary of God, me prayers have been answered. I thought I'd die if I had to stay out here one more day."

"I take it that's 'yes.'"

"That's yes, man. Do you be needin' supplies?"

"I need to find out why I haven't heard from my boys. I'm going to send a telegram to San Francisco."

"I don't care what you have to go there for, man. Just get me to a town so I can get something decent to drink."

Trenton started to speak but stopped as Aeneva and Anna came into the room. He looked at Aeneva. He thought she grew more lovely with age. He could see how happy it made her to be around Anna.

"Anna and I have prepared dessert. Would you care for some, Mr. O'Leary?"

"Dessert? Now what would I be wantin' with dessert?" He reached over and grabbed the bottle. "I have just what I need right here."

"You might regret it, Mr. O'Leary. We made blueberry pie. We picked the blueberries fresh this afternoon."

"Mrs. Hawkins—"

"I insist, Mr. O'Leary," Aeneva said firmly, walking over and taking the bottle out of O'Leary's hand. "Anna, dear, why don't you go bring the tray in here." She turned back to O'Leary, bending over the table so her eyes were even with his. "I suggest you have some of the pie we made, Mr. O'Leary, or I will

98

personally see to it that you are thrown off this ranch and never allowed on it again."

"Now, Mrs. Hawkins, you wouldn't be doin' that to me sweet daughter, would you?"

"I did not say I would do it to her, Mr. O'Leary." She continued staring at him, her dark eyes hard. "I will not tolerate the way you treat that child. I suggest you treat her more civilly or I will make sure you're making your bed out in the hills somewhere."

"Now don't get melodramatic, Mrs. Hawkins. I was just—"

"I don't care what you were doing, Mr. O'Leary. Just trust what I say is true." Aeneva straightened up, smiling as Anna came back into the room, struggling to carry the heavy tray. Trenton jumped up to help her. "Thank you, dear. Guess what? Your father decided to have some pie after all. Didn't you, Mr. O'Leary?"

"Why yes, I'd like nothin' better than to have me a piece of that lovely blueberry pie."

"You'll like the pie, Papa. I picked the berries meself." Anna handed her father a plate with a slice of pie on it. "Here, Papa."

"Thank you, me girl." O'Leary made a great show of tasting the pie and rolling his eyes. "Surely it's the best bit of bakin' I've tasted since I had me own dear mother's."

"It looks like Anna is taking after her dear grandmother then, doesn't it, Mr. O'Leary? That is fortunate," she added dryly.

O'Leary ignored Aeneva. "Anna, me girl, would you like to be stayin' with Mrs. Hawkins tomorrow while I go into town with Mr. Hawkins?"

"Oh, yes, Papa, I'd like that very much."

He put his fork down on his plate. "I won't be puttin' you to too much trouble watching me little

99

girl now will I, Mrs. Hawkins?"

"No, I will gladly watch Anna. We can find many things to do. Can't we, Anna?"

"Oh, yes, ma'am." She stood up, starting to clear the plates. "I'll be clearing up now, ma'am, if you don't mind. I'd like to get to bed early. I want to be good and rested for tomorrow."

Aeneva reached over and took Anna's hand. "Leave the plates, Anna. I will get them."

"Are you sure, ma'am?"

"Yes, I am sure, Anna. You run off to bed now."

Anna kissed her father goodnight, then tentatively went and kissed Trenton on the cheek. "Thank you for the mare, Mr. Hawkins. I'll take good care of her."

"You're welcome, Anna."

Anna walked around the table to Aeneva and she smiled warmly, putting her arms around the woman's neck. "Thank you for the beautiful clothes and the wonderful red skirt. I've never had such beautiful things before. You make me feel like a princess, ma'am."

Aeneva looked at the tiny face and took it in her hands, kissing Anna gently on the cheek. "You are a princess, Anna. Goodnight."

"Goodnight, ma'am."

Aeneva watched as the girl left the room. "I feel I owe you an apology, Mr. O'Leary."

"And why is that, Mrs. Hawkins?"

"You have raised a lovely daughter. She is a fine girl, and she has been taught how to respect people. She could only have learned that from you. I am sorry."

O'Leary was uncharacteristically silent before he spoke. "I fear I can't be takin' the credit for it, Mrs. Hawkins." He looked up at Aeneva. "But I do appreciate the gesture of apology. You see, Anna was a good child from the time she was born. She is what she is because of the way she is inside and because of her mother. I can take none of the credit.''

"I don't believe you.''

"A little while ago you told me you'd have me thrown off your ranch if I didn't change my ways. Now, suddenly, you think me a saint.''

"I never said I thought you were a saint, Mr. O'Leary, but I do know that you have a lot of good in you.''

"You don't know me at all, Mrs. Hawkins. You're mistakin' me for someone else in your past, someone who was decent and good.''

"I'm not making any mistake, Mr. O'Leary. I know what I saw when I got to those wagons. Those people wouldn't have lived as long as they had if it weren't for you. And Anna told me how you took care of her, even when you got sick.'' Aeneva stood up, clearing the plates. "This is one time I won't argue with you.''

"Well, I should be thankin' the good Lord for that then.'' O'Leary stood up, looking at Trenton and Aeneva. "I want to say somethin' to you both while I've got me right mind about me. You've both done a decent thing by taking me and me little girl in. I'm not sure I'll ever be able to repay you for what you've done.'' He drummed his fingers along the edge of the table for a minute, appearing to be somewhat nervous. "I know I may not show it but I do love me little girl, Mrs. Hawkins. She is everything to me. She has kept me going when all I wanted to do was drink meself to death. You are right—Anna is a fine person, and she deserves better than me. I just want you both to know that I will do right by her.'' O'Leary started away from the table but stopped, looking at Aeneva.

"I don't think I ever thanked you properly for savin' me life, Mrs. Hawkins. I know I can be a might tryin' at times but I do thank you. You made me so damned mad when you burned my whiskey bottles that I knew I had to get well just so I could make you pay." He laughed and shook his head, suddenly serious. "But I don't feel that way anymore. You're a fine woman, Mrs. Hawkins. Anna would do well to learn from you. I would be proud if my daughter was to grow up into a fine woman like yourself." O'Leary walked out of the room and up the stairs.

Aeneva watched him and looked over at Trenton. "I don't understand him."

"I think he's real easy to figure out."

"Then please explain him to me."

Trenton held out his hand, and Aeneva stood up and walked over to him, sitting down on his lap. "I think Mr. O'Leary was trying to tell you that he wished he'd married a woman like you." He kissed her softly. "I think he's in love with you in his own way."

Aeneva pulled away from Trenton. "You aren't thinking clearly. You've had too much to drink."

"I'm thinking very clearly, and I hardly had anything to drink. The man is in love with you."

"Trenton—" Aeneva was clearly nonplussed, unable to understand what Trenton had just told her.

"It may not be the kind of passionate, enduring love that I feel for you, but he feels a kind of love for you. I can see it when he looks at you and Anna together."

"He watches us together?"

"Constantly. He'd like for us to believe that he's always drunk but he isn't. He hides behind that. It's his way of hiding from the world."

"But why would he do that? He is a good man, and

he could give so much. I wonder what happened to him to make him do this."

"Maybe nothing happened, maybe he's always felt the need to hide away. Some people do."

Aeneva put her arms around Trenton's neck and hugged him tightly. "I feel so sorry for him, Trenton. I feel as though I've been terrible to him."

"Are you kidding? He looks forward to fighting with you. He eggs you on."

"But I should be more forgiving of the man. I should—"

Trenton touched his finger to Aeneva's mouth. "Enough. You are perfect just the way you are." He kissed her deeply. "I know O'Leary thinks so. So do I." He kissed her again, pulling her closer. "Let's go up now. I'm going to ride into town tomorrow."

"Let me know as soon as you hear something."

"Don't worry, everything's all right. We're probably going to feel foolish for ever having done this."

"I don't mind feeling foolish as long as my boys are safe."

"Everything will be just fine. You wait and see."

Trenton sent the wire and went across the street to the restaurant to eat. He knew it would be a while before he'd hear anything from San Francisco. He just hoped Joe would respond immediately. As he sipped at his coffee, he thought about O'Leary. He said he'd meet him here for lunch but Trenton could guess where he was—down the street at the Silver Dollar Saloon. The Silver Dollar had good whiskey and mean women, a combination O'Leary couldn't resist.

As Trenton watched the people coming in and out of the restaurant, he couldn't help but remember all of the times he had eaten here with the boys. They had always ordered the same thing: stack of hot cakes, eggs, ham, biscuits, butter, jam, milk, and coffee. The waitresses always loved to wait on the boys because they enjoyed the food so. He smiled to himself as he thought about Nathan and Roberto and realized how much he missed them both.

Trenton ate his breakfast at a leisurely pace, reading the newspaper he had picked up that morning. He thumbed quickly through the paper, feeling strangely uneasy. He stood up and paid for the breakfast, deciding to track down O'Leary. He walked out onto the sidewalk and headed on down the street to the Silver Dollar.

"Mr. Hawkins, Mr. Hawkins, sir."

Trenton turned. He saw the boy from the telegraph office. "Yes. Do you have a reply to my wire already?"

"Yes, sir, Mr. Bondey says to come right away."

"All right." Trenton followed the boy across the street, waiting as a buckboard drove by. He stepped up onto the wooden sidewalk and walked down to the telegraph office. He opened the door. "You have an answer for me, Mr. Bondey?" Trenton let go of the door immediately. Bondey's face was white. His wire-rimmed glasses seemed to stand out on his thin face.

"I'm awful sorry, Mr. Hawkins."

Trenton strode forward, yanking the piece of paper out of Bondey's hand. Trenton read the words but still he wasn't sure of what he had read. He stumbled slightly, reaching back to find something to lean on for balance. From out of nowhere, Mr. Bondey pushed a chair behind him. Trenton slid down into the chair and read the wire again. "Trenton. Both boys missing and presumed dead. Accident in Chinatown. I am doing all I can to find out details. I'll be in touch. I'm sorry. Joe." Trenton's hand began to shake uncontrollably, and his eyes teared up suddenly. He stood up, walking to the door. "Thank you, Mr. Bondey."

"Any reply, Mr. Hawkins?"

Trenton walked out the door, unable to see anything through tears that blinded him. It couldn't be true—nothing could happen to his boys. He started to cross the street, barely missing a stage-coach. He walked down to the Silver Dollar and up to the bar.

"Can I help you, Mr. Hawkins?"

Trenton had known Zeb, the bartender, for years but right now he didn't feel like small talk. "Just give me a bottle, Zeb."

Zeb nodded and handed a glass and a bottle to Trenton. "There's a table over in the corner, Mr. Hawkins. You can be alone there if you like."

Trenton nodded and walked over to the table, sitting down as if the weight of the world were on his shoulders. He put the piece of paper in his pocket. After uncorking the bottle, he poured himself a glass, downed it quickly, then poured himself another. He drank it down just as quickly. He had never been one given to drink but he did have to agree with O'Leary on one point: It did help to dull the pain of life some-times. Trenton deliberately forced thoughts of his boys out of his mind, fearing that he would lose all control if he thought of them. He poured another drink, then another, until his mind was like a fog. He leaned back in the chair, watching as the women worked their way around the room. One of them had dark hair and eyes, and she smiled at him. A picture of Aeneva came to his mind, and his gut felt as if it were being ripped from him. How could he tell Aeneva that their boys were dead? How could he? He kept drinking until the liquid in the bottle was gone. He started to get up to ask for more but his legs wouldn't hold him. He collapsed back in the chair, wondering how he was going to make it to the bar to ask for another bottle. He was vaguely aware of laughter and piano music in the background, but the sounds never fully reached him.

"Well, well, if it ain't me old friend Mr. Hawkins. And drinkin' whiskey he is, too."

Trenton looked up at O'Leary. "I was hoping I'd never have to look at you again. Thought you might've run off with one of these whores."

"Oh, and ye got a bit of a nasty tongue when you drinks." O'Leary pulled out a chair. "You won't be mindin' if I sit a spell, will you?"

"I don't want you here, O'Leary. Not now."

O'Leary pulled out the chair and sat down. "Why don't you want me here now? You look like you could use a little cheerin' up. Hey, what is it, man? You look as though you seen a bloody ghost."

Trenton took the paper from his pocket and dropped it on the table in front of O'Leary. He watched O'Leary as he read it, puzzled by the expression that came over O'Leary's face. "What's the matter? Cat got your tongue? Don't you have something witty to say now, Mr. O'Leary?" Trenton stuffed the paper back into his pocket.

O'Leary got up and walked to the bar, returning with a full bottle of whiskey. He grabbed Trenton's arm and yanked him to his feet. "Come on, man, I've rented meself a room for the day. I might as well avail myself of it." O'Leary waved to Zeb for help, and together they took Trenton up the stairs to O'Leary's room. Trenton sat down on the bed, staring blankly ahead of him.

"Can I have a drink, O'Leary?"

"Of course you can, man." O'Leary quickly poured them each a drink and handed a glass to Trenton. "I don't quite know what to say, Hawkins. I know how much you and the missus loved those boys. I know how I'd feel if anything happened to my little girl." O'Leary took a swig of the whiskey, clearing his throat. "Is there anything I can do for you?"

Trenton slowly brought the glass to his lips but stopped. His hand began to tremble and soon his entire body was shaking. He stood up slowly, staring across the room, then suddenly he threw the glass against the wall. Calmly he walked across the room and picked up a piece of the broken glass and, holding it to his arm, he stared at it for a long, thoughtful moment. Then with a swift movement he ran the jagged piece of glass lengthwise down his left arm. He uttered not a sound.

"Holy God, man, what are you tryin' to do, kill yourself?" O'Leary quickly untied the bandana from around Trenton's neck and tied it around his bleeding arm. "We've got to be gettin' you to a doctor or you'll bleed to death." O'Leary winced at the sight of the blood. "Holy Christ, I've not seen anything so crazy since me grandmother used a knife on her own foot to cut out some infection."

"It's custom," Trenton said softly, still staring at the space in front of him.

O'Leary grabbed at Trenton's arm but Trenton shook him off. "Come on, man. If we don't get you to a doctor soon, your blood will be all over this room."

"I won't bleed to death, O'Leary. I haven't severed anything vital."

"Then why did you do it? It was a crazy thing to do, man."

"It's custom."

"That's the second time you've said that. What

107

do you mean?"

"My mother's people are Arapaho. When someone, a loved one dies, it is custom to inflict pain on yourself in some way in order to feel closer to the person who died." He looked at O'Leary. "You should have known about the custom from your wife."

"Aye, I do recall seeing some of the women screaming and wailing and a tearin' their clothes apart, but never did I see anyone do what you just did."

Trenton walked to the door. "I have to go."

"But where're you goin'? You can't be ridin' home in that condition."

"I need to get out of town. I need to be in the hills." Trenton looked straight at O'Leary. "I need to mourn."

"I understand." O'Leary grabbed the whiskey bottle. "I'll be comin' with you."

Trenton strode out of the room and down the stairs, attracting the attention of everyone as he held onto his bloody arm. He was shadowed by the much shorter O'Leary, who held onto his whiskey bottle as tightly as Trenton held onto his arm. Trenton walked down the street and unhitched his horse, swinging up and galloping out of the town. O'Leary followed close behind, mumbling and cursing to himself in Irish.

Trenton rode for miles, not knowing where he was going but knowing he'd feel when to stop. Ignoring O'Leary's protests, he kept riding until he found a suitable place. He reined in his horse and dismounted. He looked up at the hills in front of him, illuminated by the moon. Evergreens and brush threw ominous shadows all around, and coyotes sounded their howls to each other in the lonely night. These were the hills where the boys had always hunted and played. These were their hills. Trenton began to climb.

"Are you crazy man? What are you doin'? You're going to kill yourself for sure this time. You can't go climbing mountains at night. You'll break your neck, and your wife will never forgive me."

Trenton ignored O'Leary's rantings and kept climbing. His arm throbbed, and the pain was his guide. He kept going higher, slipping and falling, but always climbing back up. He stopped when he found a large rock that suited him. He climbed up on top of it and stood there, facing the stars and the sky and earth, and the God who had killed his sons. He unbuttoned his shirt and took it off, throwing his hat off after it. He unwrapped the arm and pressed it, forcing the blood to come faster. He stuck the fingers of his right hand into the blood and drew lines across his cheeks and his chest, then he held his arms out to the sky.

"Oh, Great Spirit, how could you do this to two innocent boys? They have done nothing to hurt you. You are punishing me for wrongs I have committed. I understand. But punish me. *Me!* Let my boys live. Let my boys live and I will give my life to you." Trenton was quiet a moment and then he began to chant, an old Arapaho chant his mother had taught him as a boy. It was a chant to chase evil spirits away.

He stared out into the blackness and heard the voices of the ancients. They knew his sorrow and they chanted with him, their voices rising to a fevered pitch. Trenton could not see them in the darkness but he could hear them. They were all here with him.

He chanted until no sound would come from his throat; then he stood, still as the night, reaching into the darkness for an answer. He dropped to his knees, exhausted, and he pressed his face against the cold rock. "No!" he screamed, the anguish in his voice echoing throughout the hills. He cried for what he had had and for what he had lost. And he cried for the emptiness that he knew would exist in him forever without his sons.

O'Leary grabbed his chest, gasping for breath. He looked down at the ground below and quickly turned away, grabbing onto the rock for support. "Mary Mother of God," he exclaimed, "the man's either a fool or he's got the footing of a deer." He looked down below him again. "I can barely make it in daylight. How in God's name did he do it in the dark?" O'Leary continued to talk to himself until he found Trenton, then he abruptly stopped. Trenton was lying perilously close to the edge of an overhanging rock that was some two hundred feet above where O'Leary left the horses. Trenton's face and chest were covered with streaks of blood, and his left arm had congealed and stopped bleeding. O'Leary took a deep breath and climbed up onto the rock, grabbing Trenton's good arm. He pulled but Trenton didn't move. "Damn you, man. You feel like a ton of bricks." O'Leary pulled again and Trenton moved slightly. O'Leary pulled until he had Trenton close to the other side of the rock. He slapped him hard in the face. "Time to wake up, Hawkins. God what a sight you are this mornin'."

Trenton mumbled something but didn't open his eyes. Anticipating this reaction from years of his own experience, O'Leary unscrewed the top to the canteen on his shoulder and poured the water over Trenton's head. Trenton's body jumped and he shook his head. O'Leary poured more water on him.

"That's enough!" Trenton tried to sit up but lost

his footing and fell off the rock at O'Leary's feet. "Damn," he said angrily and managed to pull himself to a standing position. "Where the hell are we anyway?"

"You tell me. You brought us here last night."

"Last night." He brought his left hand up to rub his head and winced. He looked at the gash in his arm. "What the hell happened?" He looked at the blood on his chest. He turned back to the rock, climbing back up to retrieve his shirt. He reached into his pocket and pulled out the piece of paper and shook his head. "It's true." He closed his eyes. "I thought it was a nightmare."

"I wish it were, man. I wish it were." O'Leary grabbed Trenton's arm. "Come on now, it's time to be getting down. I can't breathe up here."

"Wait a minute." Trenton shook his arm free, staring out at the land beneath him and the mountains beyond. "Indians, most all Indians, believe that when you die you become one with the land so that you don't really die at all. I remember thinking when I was growing up what a wonderful thing that was to believe in, what a life-sustaining belief. But I don't believe that anymore. I'd like to think my boys are part of those majestic mountains out there but I can't really make myself believe it."

O'Leary climbed up onto the rock and sat down next to Trenton. "I lost me first child, a little girl she was. She was everything to me, everything that mattered. When she died I really took to the bottle. Then me wife left me." O'Leary shook his head. "I had no such spiritual thoughts as you were just speaking when my little Rosie died. All I could think of was how cruel God was for takin' me little darlin' away from me. I hated everyone, even my other daughter."

"You mean Anna?"

111

"No, I mean Megan. I don't believe I ever said a kind word to the poor darlin' after Rosie died. I hated her for bein' alive but I hated meself more than anything. I blamed meself for Rosie's death. I still do."

Trenton took his shirt from O'Leary and slipped it on. "Do you ever get over blaming yourself?"

O'Leary shook his head slowly. "I've never got over blamin' meself because it was my fault." He took a swig from the whiskey bottle, sighing deeply after he did so. "It was the Christmas when Rosie was five years old. She'd been sick for a time, prone to the pneumonia she was. She wanted with all her heart to see the Christmas lights they put up in the windows of the fancy houses. My wife said no because she had been so sick. Well, one night when me wife was out to one of her society functions, I stayed home and took care of Rosie and Megan. Megan was only a baby, and she was already asleep in her crib. Rose asked me to tell her a story—she didn't like the nanny me wife had hired to care for her—so I told the nanny we didn't need her. I sat on Rosie's bed, cradling her in me arms like a little doll, regaling her with tales of Ireland and leprechauns. I carried her to the window and she looked out on the lit city and said, 'Papa, please show me the Christmas lights.' I told her we couldn't because she had been so sick. But she said that didn't matter. She told me that she didn't want to live if she couldn't see the lights." O'Leary raised the bottle and drank liberally. "So I took me little girl to see the Christmas lights of the city. I wrapped her up and put her in the carriage and we went out. It was a cold night but oh, you should've seen her little face, Hawkins. We saw an angel all lit up in one big house, and she began to cry. She said, 'I love you, Papa. You've made me very happy.' She died two weeks later."

The silence was deafening, broken only by an occasional whinny from one of the horses down below.

Trenton ran his hands through his hair, shaking his head. "I'm sorry, O'Leary. I didn't know."

"How could you? I've never told anyone about it. But I want to tell you something, Hawkins, and I want you to listen well. Guilt is a nasty thing. It eats away at you. It eats you up inside, and it makes you wish you'd never been alive. And it makes you wish you never had the capacity to remember anything. God, how many times I wish I could quit remembering." He downed the rest of the bottle and sent it crashing to the rocks below. "Don't be like me, Hawkins. Don't let the guilt eat away at you. It does no good. It serves no purpose. You've got yourself a fine woman. Together you can go on. But don't be drivin' yourself crazy over the 'what-ifs.' You can't go back."

"But I shouldn't have let them go on alone."

"Your boys wanted to go on alone, and you gave them a chance to believe in themselves. You must remember that, man."

Trenton's eyes teared up at the mention of the boys. He could think of them only in terms of if: If he hadn't let them go on alone, they'd still be alive. If they'd never taken the trip, nothing would have happened. If . . . O'Leary was right. The 'what-ifs' could make you crazy. And he knew the man was right about something else, too: Guilt would do nothing but destroy him. He glanced over at O'Leary. The man sat perfectly still, staring out at the mountains. Trenton knew what it must have taken for O'Leary to have told him about his daughter, and he knew why he had done it. He touched O'Leary's shoulder.

"Is there a possibility your daughter would have died even if you hadn't taken her out that night?"

113

O'Leary shrugged his shoulders. "A fragile little thing she was, as delicate as a butterfly. The doctors said she would always be a sickly child but she grew worse as she got older." He shook his head. "I don't know but I think she knew."

"She knew she was going to die and that's why she wanted you to take her to see the lights?" O'Leary nodded, and Trenton could see tears streaming down the man's cheeks. He put his arm around his shoulders. "Then you shouldn't feel guilty, O'Leary. You should feel proud. You gave your daughter what she wanted most in the world, and she probably died happy because of it."

O'Leary looked down, wiping his face with the back of a hand. "Her last words to me were, 'Do you remember the lights, Papa?' It tore me heart out that there was nothing I could do for me little girl." O'Leary broke, his sobs coming in great waves. He covered his face with his hands, and the sound of his anguish echoed down the rocks. Trenton kept his arm around O'Leary, feeling his anguish and knowing how truly painful it was.

"You did do something for her, O'Leary, don't you see? She remembered the lights even before she died. You gave her that. No one else but you gave her that gift."

O'Leary breathed deeply, wiping his face with his hands. He looked over at Trenton and smiled. "Strange way for two men to become friends, don't you think?"

"I don't think it's so strange. There's a reason for everything."

"There you go, gettin' spiritual on me again."

"I'm not getting spiritual. I just think it's a good thing that you and Anna are going to be around for awhile. Aeneva is going to need you both when she finds out about the boys."

O'Leary pursed his lips and shook his head. "'Tis a rotten shame, a fine woman like that to lose her sons. Something's not right in the world."

"O'Leary, will you and Anna stay for awhile? Aeneva cares for Anna a great deal. I think having her around will help her a lot."

"Of course, man, I'll be glad to stay around but I don't know if the missus will like having me around much longer."

"Let's stop with the games. You know she likes you as much as you like her. You both rub each other the wrong way but you care for each other."

"That we do, man, that we do. And I'll do anything I can to help the missus through this. Anything at all."

Aeneva crumpled the note and dropped it on the floor. "I do not believe it. It's not true."

Trenton put his hands on Aeneva's shoulders. "It is true, Aeneva. I waited for and received confirmation from Joe."

"But it says presumed to be dead. That means they could be alive. You thought I was dead and I was alive." She pulled away from Trenton and shook her head adamantly. "No, they are not dead. My boys are not dead."

"Aeneva—"

"Do not touch me!" She screamed at Trenton, the panic beginning to rise in her. She felt as if she were drowning. She was close to the top but she couldn't get air. She paced nervously around their room. "Why didn't he tell us? Why didn't Joe tell us sooner?"

"He was trying to find out everything he could. He

wanted to confirm it if he could."

Aeneva walked to her bureau drawer and opened it. She pulled out a small box and opened it. "Do you remember this?" She held up an acorn necklace. "It was the first necklace Nathan ever made for me. And this, look at this shiny rock Roberto gave me. He loved rocks." She methodically sorted through all of her treasures, smiling as she recalled the memory attached to each one. When she finished going through them she put them back in the box and hugged the box to her chest. "They are not dead to me, Trenton. They will never be dead to me." She stood at the bureau immobile and silent.

Trenton walked up behind her and put his arms around her. As he held onto her he could feel her strength subside until she collapsed in his arms. "Aeneva," he said softly. She was on her knees, rocking back and forth, still hugging the box to her chest. He could hear her saying something, and he knew that she was chanting. He sat with her for what seemed like hours until she finished chanting. Then she looked up at him with her large brown eyes, and she cried as he had never seen her cry in her life, and he cried with her. There was now a void in their lives that could never be filled by anything or anyone again.

Trenton looked over at Aeneva as they rode, and he was relieved. She looked better than she had looked in a month, since they had found out about the boys. Since then, a letter had arrived from Joe explaining in more detail what had happened. While it was still a shock, Aeneva went on with her life, and she still talked about the boys with complete and utter joy in her heart. And there was Anna. Trenton looked at the way the little girl smiled at Aeneva, and he knew that she was part of the reason Aeneva had to go on. The child was so full of life and so loving and thoughtful, Aeneva seldom had time to think of anything but Anna.

They rode back to the ranch and dismounted, walking up to the house. Anna automatically took Aeneva's hand, and she picked her a rose from the rosebush as they walked by. Aeneva laughed and smelled the rose as she did whenever Anna picked her a flower.

O'Leary had been gone for over a week, and Trenton was growing increasingly concerned. Ever since Trenton had received the wire and O'Leary had helped him through that night and day, he had developed a real fondness for the man. He had stuck true to his word and had been wonderful to Aeneva, even telling her about Rosie. But as the days wore on and Aeneva seemed to grow stronger and more attached to Anna, O'Leary seemed to grow more restless. He made more and more frequent trips into town, and Trenton was afraid that this last one had been a fatal one. O'Leary wasn't known for his discretion in either cards or affairs of the heart, and Trenton was afraid he'd gotten himself killed.

But as always, Trenton was again surprised by the wily Irishman. He came back from town that night, dressed in new clothes and looking like a fine gentleman. He brought Trenton a bottle of Irish whiskey, Aeneva a bottle of perfume, and he brought Anna a flowered bonnet.

"So, girl." He looked at Anna. "What do you be thinkin' of your dad's good fortune?"

"I'm happy for you, Papa."

"I'm happy for you, she says. Well, don't you know, girl, I've just won our stake to go to Cali-

117

fornia. We're leaving tomorrow. I have seats on the stagecoach.''

Trenton looked at Aeneva, and he saw the color leave her face. But he knew her and he knew she wouldn't say a word. Anna was O'Leary's daughter, and Aeneva wouldn't try to interfere again.

"But Papa, can't we stay just a little while longer? I like it here. And what about my horse?"

"Now, girl, don't be worryin' yourself about a horse. I can buy you plenty of horses when we get to California."

"But I don't want another horse, Papa. I want this horse. I love this horse. Please, Papa." Anna's eyes filled with tears, and they streamed down her little face.

"Me mind's made up, girl. We leave in the mornin'. We can't be takin' advantage of these fine folks any longer. Go up and start packin'. Go on now.''

Anna looked at her father. She walked to Trenton and hugged him, kissing him on the cheek. She walked to Aeneva and hugged her fiercely, her small body wracked with sobs as she buried her face in Aeneva's chest.

"It's all right, Anna. We will see each other again. I promise you." Aeneva stroked Anna's hair until she quieted down. "Do you want me to help you pack?" Anna nodded and Aeneva took her hand and led her up the stairs.

Trenton looked at O'Leary. "Why is this so sudden, O'Leary? Are you in trouble?"

"I'm not in any trouble at all, my friend. I just won me a lot of money, and I'm anxious to get on with me life."

"And what about Anna's life?"

"What do you mean?"

118

"Are you going to drag her all over the place with you? God, man, think of her for a change. She's just a little girl."

"I think we had this discussion before, and I told you then she's my little girl, not yours. I don't need your advice, Hawkins."

"I think you do. I think you're making a big mistake."

"What do you want me to do? Stay here and live off of you and Aeneva forever?" He shook his head. "Oh, no, I've got me a little pride left."

"Then why not leave Anna here with us until you're settled? Wouldn't that make more sense than dragging her around from camp to camp? Once you've staked your claim and found a place, you can send for her. You know she'll be safe with us."

"I appreciate what you're sayin' to me, Hawkins, I really do, but I can't be leavin' me own flesh and blood with you. She needs me."

"I think it's more like you need her." Trenton stood up, a disgusted look on his face. "I'll wish you luck only because I think Anna will need it. I don't understand you, O'Leary."

"There's nothing to understand, man. She's my little girl, and she goes with me."

Trenton nodded, finally relenting. "Just remember something. If you or she ever need anything, you can always come here. Don't ever hesitate to write us. Whether I like it or not, I guess you're part of the family, O'Leary."

O'Leary stood up. He walked over to Trenton and grabbed him in a bear hug. "You're a good man, Trenton Hawkins. I'll take your word on what you just said. You never know, you may have to take care of one of us sometime. And tell Aeneva that even Anna's own mother was never more loving or dear to the girl. Tell her I think she's a fine woman. Tell her she will be happy again. I promise her that.''

"What do you mean?"

"Oh, nothing. Just tell her for me, will you?" O'Leary patted Trenton on the back. "Go on up, man, I'll be up in just a bit. Goin' to have meself a nightcap."

"All right, O'Leary. I'll see you in the morning before you leave."

"You take care of yourself, man. I'll be thinkin' of you."

Trenton shook his head slightly, thinking it was just like O'Leary to say something strange and unintelligible. But still he had to admit he liked the man and he wished him well. He walked up to his room. His only concern was for Aeneva. She had already lost her two sons. He didn't know how she would take losing Anna. But that was something they would face together. They would have no other choice.

O'Leary folded the letter and put it in the envelope. He placed it next to the whiskey bottle on the desk where he knew they would see it. He started for the stairs and quietly went up them. He opened the door to Anna's room and went inside, walking to her bed. He looked down on her sleeping face and smiled. He brushed the hair back from her face. She was a strong one, this Kathleen Anna O'Leary, and she would be strong even without him. She probably would be even stronger. And she would be loved here, loved in the kind of way that a girl like her should be loved. He knelt down and touched her cheek with the back of his hand. Her skin was as soft as a rose petal and just as fresh. He leaned over and kissed her on the cheek. "I love you, me little darlin' Anna. Be good, be strong and be happy. God bless you, girl." O'Leary kissed his daughter one more time, then stood up and walked out of the room, down the stairs and out of the house. As far as he was concerned, Anna belonged to Aeneva and Trenton now. She was their daughter.

Chapter V

Aeneva came down the stairs, one of Trenton's heavy sweaters wrapped around her. Although it was spring, the mornings were still fairly cool. She went to the kitchen and, filling the coffeepot with water, she put it on the stove to boil. She smiled to herself, remembering the first time Trenton had brought home the stove. She had refused to use it, continuing to cook in a pot over the fireplace. But eventually, logic had worn her down as Trenton showed her all of the things she could do with the oven. Now, she admitted to herself, she did like it.

She got down bowls and got out the fresh things she needed for breakfast. She was going to make blueberry muffins, hotcakes, fried ham, scrambled eggs, and strong black coffee—Mr. O'Leary's favorite breakfast. She was going to miss him, and she had grown to love Anna as if she were her own daughter, but she knew that O'Leary was doing what he thought best. She knew that he would never do anything to hurt his own daughter; he loved her too much.

As she bustled around the kitchen, Aeneva had to admit that she felt better than she had felt in a long time. The ache caused by the deaths of Nathan and Roberto would never disappear, but she knew in her heart that she had to go on. She knew that she had a purpose. Maybe she felt better because of the dream she had had the night before. She pictured herself riding on the prairie all alone and lost. She looked around her and she was afraid. She cried and cried until she couldn't cry anymore, and then out of nowhere, Sun Dancer appeared. She dismounted and ran to her grandmother, throwing her arms around her. Her grandmother soothed her as she had always done, and she told her to be strong. She told her that she had a purpose to serve, and she must never believe that death was final. She told her to keep strong through her love. Aeneva smiled again, this time through her tears. She thought of her boys, and her heart overflowed with pride and love for them. They would never be dead to her.

She went into the dining room and began setting the table. She looked over to the living room and saw glasses sitting on the table. She realized that Trenton and O'Leary must have stayed up late. She walked over and picked up the glasses. Then she saw the whiskey bottle and the envelope. She opened the envelope and sat down on the chair, reading aloud. "To my dear friends, Aeneva and Trenton. By the time you read this I'll be out of your lives for good. And none too fast you say, eh? I know I haven't been the easiest man in the world to have around and I want to thank you both for putting up with me, especially you, Mrs. Hawkins. You're a fine woman, as fine as they come, and my heart aches for you when I think of you losing your boys. That's why I want to do something for you. I've seen how you are with Anna, and I've seen how she adores you. She loves you, she's told me as much. She's happy here and here's where she belongs, with you and Trenton. Now I know she can't take the place of your boys but she can bring you a lot of happiness. I know because she has done that for me. But I'm no good for her and you're both right when you be saying I shouldn't be dragging her around the gold mines. She deserves better than that. I just want you to know and someday I want you to tell Anna for me, that I'm not a kind-hearted person. In fact, I don't often think of anybody else but myself. But I decided this night to do something unselfish. Anna is your daughter now and I won't be talking to either of you again. Everything that I own in the world I left in a trunk in Anna's room. There's also an envelope in there I'd like you to give to her when you feel she's old enough to read what I wrote. I left some money for her, too. If you two need it, feel free to use it. God knows, you spent enough money on me. I guess I'll be going now. I want to thank you for saving my life, Mrs. Hawkins. At first I didn't think it was worth anything at all but now I'm glad I'm alive. It's good to know my little girl will have a good life. Thank you both and God bless you. Patrick Michael O'Leary."

Aeneva refolded the letter. Her hands shook as she tried to put the letter into the envelope. "Oh, Mr. O'Leary," she said softly, her shoulders shaking as she sobbed. "You dear, dear man." She heard footsteps on the stairs and looked up. Trenton was coming down, a look of concern on his face.

"Are you all right?" He put his hands on her shoulders. "What's the matter?"

Aeneva handed him the letter. Trenton sat on the arm of the chair and read the letter, shaking his head in disbelief. "My God, I can't believe it. I can't believe he'd do such a thing."

"I wish I could speak to him again. I wish I could make him understand that I will be all right. I feel as if he left Anna here for me."

"He left Anna here for you and for her. I think he knew it was the best thing for her. He loved her but he couldn't take her to all of the places he was going."

"What about Anna? What will she think? Will she think she's been deserted? I don't want this to be hard for her, Trenton. I want her to be happy. I think she should be with her father."

Trenton put his arms around Aeneva. "You're scared and so am I. We have the responsibility of raising someone else's child. But O'Leary trusted us. He trusted us, Aeneva, or he wouldn't have left Anna with us. We'll do the best we can for her and O'Leary."

Aeneva nodded, leaning her head against Trenton's shoulder. "I've always wanted a daughter. One just like Anna."

"Well, now we have one." Trenton stood up. "What do you say we go up and tell her?"

"All right." Aeneva stood up. "Trenton." Aeneva grabbed Trenton's shirt. "I'm afraid."

"I know, I'm afraid, too. But we'll do fine."

"No, you don't understand." She turned away, closing her eyes as she spoke. "I don't think I could stand to lose another child." She felt his arms go around her and felt the strength flow from him to her.

"We can't be afraid to live, Aeneva. There are always dangers but we must go on. We must." He took her hand and squeezed it tightly. They walked to the stairs and climbed them together.

Aeneva watched Trenton chase Anna under the

126

trees and along the stream. Anna laughed gaily, finally sitting down and taking off her shoes and socks and walking into the water.

"Aren't you coming in, Trenton?" She smiled back.

"No, you go ahead. I'm hungry." Trenton walked back to the oak and sat next to Aeneva. "She's a pretty little thing, isn't she? I swear she's grown since she's been here."

"Yes and she adores you. She can't keep her eyes off of you."

"She has good taste, don't you think?"

Aeneva punched Trenton on the shoulder. "Don't be so smug. You spoil her rotten. Why wouldn't she adore you?"

"Are you sure you aren't just the least bit jealous now that there's another woman vying for my affection?"

"I'm not the least bit jealous. I love it." Aeneva looked at Anna splashing in the stream. "She is a lovely child. She has a good heart. She would have made a good Cheyenne."

"She is half Cheyenne, and she will carry that with her for the rest of her life because of you. You have given her back her heritage."

"She does seem interested to knowing about my people, doesn't she?"

"And the way she follows you around with your medicine basket reminds me of you and your grandmother. Anna might be another healer."

Anna came running back, falling on the ground next to them. "The water felt so good. Why don't you both come in?"

"We're too old for that. We'll just sit here in the sun and rest our weary bones."

"You're not old."

"Thank you, dear." Aeneva reached into the basket and handed Anna a piece of fruit. "There's cake, too. You'd better have some before Trenton eats it all."

Anna laughed. "Trenton sure does like your cake." She laughed again and stopped suddenly, her brows knitting together. "Papa used to say that his mother made the best apple cake he'd ever eaten. I hope he's all right."

"I'm sure he's all right, Anna." Aeneva stroked the girl's long, dark hair. "Do you miss your father much, Anna?"

The girl nodded. "I do miss him. I know Papa wasn't always the nicest person, and sometimes he got downright mean when he drank, but he was a good person inside. He really was a good person."

Trenton pulled Anna close to him, encircling her with his arms. "You don't have to tell us what a good person your father was, Anna. He gave us you, remember? Do you know how hard that must have been for him to do? He loved you very much."

"I know that he did. I don't feel angry with Papa for what he did. He couldn't have left me with two better people, and he knew that."

Trenton hugged Anna tightly, kissing the top of her head. "My one regret is that you couldn't have gotten to know Nathan and Roberto. You would've liked them, Anna. They were full of the devil but they were good boys."

"They would have spoiled you," Aeneva said wistfully. "Nathan always said he wished he'd had a sister."

"It's all right. I'll meet them someday." At the puzzled expressions on Aeneva's and Trenton's faces, she continued. "Do you remember, Aeneva, when you told me about the stars? You said that when people died they went up into the sky and became stars. And the truly bright ones were ones who were very good and very loved. I'm sure Nathan and Roberto are up there right now, or maybe they're around us right now, a part of this very place."

Aeneva looked around her and sighed deeply. She heard the sounds of the buzzing bees and the clicking of the grasshoppers; she heard the sound of the stream as it gurgled by; she felt the gentle breeze as it barely touched her skin, and she wondered if her sons were truly a part of this wondrous earth. She felt the tears rise in her as they so often did but this time she forced them back. She would not mourn their deaths; she would rejoice in their lives and all that they had given her. She would carry them with her wherever she went.

A month had gone by and Nathan had grown stronger. He had never worked so hard in his entire life but his parents had prepared him well for fending for himself. He was not afraid of being on his own but he was lonely. He missed his parents and he missed Berto. He missed being a family.

After the night that Driscoll's bodyguard almost recognized him, Chin decided it was time for Nathan to leave. He sent him farther north, to an isolated place in the mountains. It was a gold mine that had been completely dug out and tunneled by Chin's friend Tong. Chin had long ago decided that this was the place for Nathan to be. Here, he said, Nathan could grow strong, learn and possibly make the money he needed to get Driscoll. But most important of all, he would be safe.

Nathan worked alongside Tong every day. Tong was an old man but he never seemed to grow tired. He had been working in the mine ever since the first bit of gold was discovered in '49. He'd been at it twenty-one years already and had very little to show for it. But Tong was convinced that he had a rich vein, and he wasn't going to give up. And much to Nathan's surprise, Tong did not resist his help.

They were up at dawn and they worked until sundown, with only a break for lunch. Tong looked frail and old but Nathan never ceased to be amazed at the man's strength and endurance.

"Don't you ever get tired, Tong?" Nathan asked one day while they sat under a tree eating their lunch.

"I am always tired, boy, but my mind tells my body that it is not."

"I don't understand."

"Your mind controls everything you do. It is very powerful thing. It can make you feel pain or not feel pain. It can make you strong or not make you strong. Mind can make you do or feel anything. When your body is tired, it is only because you let your mind tell your body you are tired. You must train mind to be strong."

"How come you've done this for so long, Tong? Why haven't you given up?"

"Same reason. My mind does not let body give up. I believe I will find gold and someday I will."

"Haven't people tried to stop you? The men around these parts hate the Chinese."

"It is true but they all left thinking there is no vein here. But I stayed. They think I am crazy but that is better for me."

"Aren't you ever scared, Tong?"

"Fear is eternal darkness. I find strength in the light."

"How come you let me work with you? Some of the men up here would kill an outsider. You welcomed me. Why?"

"I welcome you first because Chin say you need my

help. I welcome you second because I need help now. I am getting close to the gold. I think within a few years I will find it."

"How do you know I won't kill you some night and take your claim? No one will argue with me. They hate the Chinese owning anything."

"I do not worry about such things. If Chin say you are honest then you are honest."

"I won't let you down, Tong. I'll work hard. You teach me what to do, and I'll do the best I can."

"I know that. Now, it is time to rest your mind and body."

"But I'm ready to get back to work."

"No, boy, listen to me. Do not ever neglect your mind. Is the most important thing. You are young now and feel good but someday you will grow older and your body will not be so willing. You must cultivate your mind so that you are able to go on."

Nathan nodded silently, thinking to himself how like the Cheyenne philosophy this was. His mother had always told him to take care of his body and his mind. She had wanted him to have a good education. It had been so very important to her. He closed his eyes and let his body relax. It was so hard for him not to go to his parents. He wanted that more than anything in the world. Even though they hadn't responded to his letters he was sure deep in his heart that they still loved him and that they would welcome him home. But he couldn't go home until he got enough money to repay his father and enough money to buy himself respectability, because that was the only way he could get to Driscoll. And he would get to Driscoll. Nothing would ever keep him from that.

Nathan picked at the side of the cave, staring at the

131

wall. He held the lamp up close to the wall of the cave. Something twinkled. It looked like gold but he wasn't sure. He ran to the back of the cave screaming Tong's name. As was the old man's custom, he came slowly.

"What is it, boy? What have you seen now?"

"Look at this, Tong. What is this?"

Tong lifted up the lantern and held it against the wall, rubbing at the dirt and hitting it gently with his pick.

"What is it, Tong?"

"Have patience, boy." Tong examined the wall closely, again chipping at it with his pick. "This could be a vein. You should work on this for a time. Perhaps it will prove to be real."

"That's it?"

"What did you want me to say, boy? Did you want me to tell you that you found gold after only working here for a few months? Did you really expect it to happen that quickly? I have been here a long time, boy, and I have yet to become rich. I have told you before, this is different from panning and it is different from quartz mining. I do not believe there is any gold left in the streams, and it is too expensive to extract the gold from the quartz. First you must crush it, then wash it, then it must be passed over shelves of mercury, for the gold will stick to the mercury. But we cannot do this because it must be done with machinery that neither of us can afford."

"Then why are you here, Tong?"

"Gold can also appear in loose sand and gravel in hillsides in its pure form. I believe this place was once the bottom of a river and the gold is in the hillsides."

"But you're not sure?"

"No one can be sure of anything, boy."

Nathan watched Tong as he walked to the other end of the cave. He picked up the pick and threw it against the wall, knocking chunks of dirt onto the floor. He looked around him and shook his head. What gave a man the patience to dig down into the earth and chip away at dirt, hoping against all hope that he would someday find gold? He didn't know because he sure didn't possess that kind of patience. He wasn't even sure he could wait long enough to get back at Driscoll. He sat down, emitting a long sigh. What made him think he could even get rich at something like this? He reached for the pick and started to throw it but stopped, instead putting it gently on the ground in front of him. If there was something he had learned from Chin and Tong, it was that patience was usually rewarded. If he waited long enough and worked hard enough perhaps someday he would be able to leave here and go back to San Francisco as a wealthy man, a man who could destroy Franklin Driscoll. He stood up and began picking at the wall, telling himself that it didn't matter how long it took because it was leading him somewhere. From that moment on, Nathan tried to make time immaterial, and he swore to himself that he would someday return to his parents with his head held high.

Nathan hugged Chin to him, twisting his mouth up at the corner. "Sorry, I forgot you people don't like that stuff. What do you have in the bags?"

"Many things." Chin looked around him. "Where is Tong? He is well?"

"Sure, he's out meditating. He likes to go out and watch the sun set."

"And do you not like to watch the sun set also?"

"I don't like to sit around like that, Chin. It bothers me."

"And why does it bother you?"

"I don't know, it just does."

"You are not telling me the truth."

"I don't like to do it because it reminds me of my mother. She used to do that a lot."

"Is it not good to think of your mother?"

"No, because every time I think of my mother I think of Driscoll and the time he robbed me of my brother and my parents."

"Perhaps then it is time for you to return home to your parents. I told you before; you must let your hatred guide you, not consume you."

"And I told you before I'm not going home until I've done what I came here to do."

"And if you never get rich, what will you do then?"

"Then I'll think of another way but I won't give up." Nathan looked at his friend. "Look, Chin, I've never been as alone in my whole life as I've been this last year. I've always had family around me. It just makes me sad sometimes, that's all."

"Then you must be kept busy."

"What do you mean busy? I work twelve hours a day, I work on the exercises you taught me, and I've even learned to meditate a little. What else can I do?"

"You can read and you can learn."

"I've read enough books to last me a lifetime. My mother was always making me read."

"A wise woman, your mother."

"She is. Do you know she can speak three different languages, not to mention Cheyenne, Arapaho, and Crow. She learned to read English when she was just a girl, and she loved to read books. She made Berto and me read at least one book a week. She always wanted me to get a good education since she never had one."

"So, why not do as she would have wished? You can educate yourself through the books that I bring you. Do it for your mother."

"Oh, all right. What did you bring?"

"I just happened to bring books on San Francisco. I thought it would be good for you to learn about its history. I have brought you books on the Chinese also. You need to learn more about the Chinese people. And—"

Nathan got up and looked in Chin's bag. "How many books did you bring?"

"Enough until I come the next time. Then I will bring more."

"I can't read all these books by the time you come back."

"You try. It will help pass the lonely time."

Joe was convinced that Nathan was still alive. Although it had already been over two years since he was reportedly murdered, Joe still had the gut feeling that the boy was still alive. Joe shook his head, settling down in the old apartment he had rented across the street from Chin's place. He had watched the Chinaman's comings and goings for over two years now but he had still been unable to find out about Nathan. He knew that Chin knew about Nathan but for some reason he was not telling him. So Joe had decided that he would find out for himself, no matter how long it took. Larissa, of course, thought he was crazy. It was hard to explain to her the feeling he had, the feeling that Nathan's spirit and body were alive somewhere. Aeneva would have understood his feeling; Trenton would have, too. That was the other thing that puzzled him. If Nathan were alive, why hadn't he contacted his parents? They were so close but for some strange reason Nathan didn't want to be found. But Joe was determined to find him.

Joe was convinced that soon Chin would load up his horse and ride out of town. Joe had tried following him numerous other times but the crafty Chinaman had managed to elude him each time. This time, however, Joe was determined to find out where the man was going.

Joe sat in the room for all of that day and night but his vigilance was rewarded when at sunrise the next morning he saw Chin leave his room and go into the street. His horse was already saddled and ready to go. Joe ran down the stairs and went out through the back of the building, untying his horse. He waited a few minutes and mounted, following in the direction that Chin always rode. He had gone over it in his mind a hundred times. He had always been able to keep up with Chin until the Chinaman got to the hills, then Joe had lost his trail. He had never been able to figure out where the man had gone but he was sure it was somewhere into gold country. Now this time Joe was going to find out exactly where.

Joe followed the trail to the foothills; then he rode ahead on an alternate trail he had checked out earlier. He wanted to find out for sure if Chin was going up to the gold country, and the only way he could do that was to see the man ride past him. Joe waited silently, hoping that the crafty old man hadn't outwitted him again. Joe saw Chin ride up the hill, looking around him as he did so. The Chinaman rode straight up the hill toward the mines. Joe tied his horse to a nearby tree and followed Chin on foot. Chin dismounted and led his horse across a stream. He stopped when he got to the other side, turning to see if there was anyone behind him. Joe quickly ducked behind a tree and watched as Chin continued on. Joe followed Chin to an old mine shaft that looked virtually deserted. There was an old shack built nearby. He watched as Chin unpacked the horse, taking his supplies into the shack. He came back out and unsaddled the horse, letting him graze outside the shack. He went back inside. Joe waited, knowing that whoever was working in the mine wouldn't be out until close to sundown. Joe leaned against a rock and stretched his legs out, waiting patiently. He felt the warm sun on his skin and closed his eyes. He remembered the first time he had ever seen Nathan. He was a brand-new baby. He had helped Trenton care for Nathan and there were times when he felt as if the boy were his own. Skin color had meant nothing to them. He smiled as he recalled the times that he had held Nathan close to him. The bright blond hair had always been such a contrast against his black skin. He had loved that boy and he always would. There had always been a special bond between them. That's why he was sure Nathan was still alive.

He felt the tension leave his body and his head felt heavy. He forced himself to open his eyes, afraid he might miss something. He looked around him, then up at the sky. The sun was starting to go down in the sky. It wouldn't be long before whoever it was in the mine came out.

Joe started to get up and walk toward the shack but decided against it. If Nathan wasn't in the mine, he didn't want to bother Chin more than he already had. He watched patiently as the sun moved toward the horizon, and finally he heard voices coming from the mine shaft. He crouched behind one of the large rocks that surrounded the shack and watched as two men came out of the mine shaft. One was tall, the other one quite short with a long pigtail. Joe squinted his eyes in the twilight, trying to see who the tall man was. He heard a laugh and the sound ripped at his guts. It was a laugh so familiar to him that there was no doubt left in his mind. Joe stood up and walked toward the two men.

"What in hell you think you doing, boy?" Joe watched as Nathan stopped and turned, his expression frozen on his face. "Well, don't you have nothing to say to me?"

"Joe!" Nathan exclaimed loudly, dropping his equipment and striding to the big man. He put his arms around him, holding him tightly. "God, it's good to see you, Joe."

In spite of his anger, Joe hugged the boy to him, relieved that his feeling had been rewarded. He patted Nathan on the back. "I knew you were alive. I felt it inside."

"How did you find me? I didn't want to be found, you know."

"Yeah, I know. It's taken me two years to finally figure out where that Chinaman went to every time he left town. I swear he damn near melted into the countryside."

"Yeah, Chin's good at that. Oh, Joe, I want you to meet my friend Tong."

Joe looked at the small old man and wondered to himself how he ever had the strength to carry his tools, let alone work in the mine. "Pleased to meet you, Tong."

Tong bowed. "How do you do. Please, come into my home and have food with us."

Joe clapped his arm around Nathan's shoulder and followed Tong into the shack. When they entered, the smell of food permeated the entire place. Joe watched Chin for any reaction but there was none. He nodded to Joe, then turned back to the food he was preparing.

"How you doing, Chin?" Nathan went up to his friend. "Did you know that Joe followed you here?"

Chin didn't turn around. "I sensed that I was being followed and that it was the black man. He has been following me everywhere for two years."

Joe walked up to Chin. "Then why didn't you try to lose me? You probably could have thrown me off if you had gone someplace else."

"You would have eventually found the boy. You are a very tenacious man. You would not have given up so easily."

"So, you knew I've been following you all this time. Why didn't you say something to me? You knew how I cared for the boy."

"I cannot break promise I make to boy. It is a matter of honor."

"Honor, honor." Joe shook his head and walked away from Chin. "I'm full up to here with all that bullcrap about honor. I've seen too many people die in the name of that lousy word." He turned to Nathan, anger apparent on his face. "I thought you'd know better, boy. Why the hell didn't you let me know you were alive? Didn't you know I'd be worried?" He walked close to Nathan, pressing his hands into his shoulders. "What about your folks? I don't understand why you did it, Nate."

"I didn't have a choice, Joe. A man murdered my brother and left me for dead. He took all of Pa's money, the money that was to be his last payment to you."

"But that's not your fault. Your Pa would've understood that."

"Pa entrusted Berto's life to me, and I let him down. But most of all, I let Berto down." Nathan strode outside.

Joe followed Nathan past the silent Chinese. He grabbed his shoulder and turned him around. "Why didn't you come to me? I could've helped you."

"I thought about it, Joe, I thought about it a lot."

"Then why didn't you do it?"

"I didn't go to you because this is my responsibility. It's up to me to get Pa's money back and to avenge Berto's death."

"And just how do you plan on doing that?"

"It'll take time but I'll do it."

"Do you know how powerful Franklin Driscoll is, Nate? Hell, his wife's family owns half the city."

"I know that. I also know that Driscoll will eventually run for city office, and probably state office."

"So?"

"By the time I've made enough money to return to Frisco, Driscoll will be even more wealthy and more powerful."

"So, what's your point?"

"My point is that men who are that rich and powerful stand to lose an awful lot if some scandal should be associated with them."

"What kind of scandal you talking about, Nate? I don't like the sound of this."

"Hell, Joe, if you know about Driscoll you know he's involved in everything illegal from prostitution to white slavery. Christ, the man's hands are so dirty I'm surprised he can show his face in public."

"You still haven't told me what you plan to do."

"I'm not even sure myself yet what I'm going to do, except that I'm going to make a lot of money and go back to Frisco a rich man, the kind of man who runs in Driscoll's circles."

"Hell, if it's money you want I can loan you all you want. You can't take Driscoll on alone. I can help."

"No, Joe, I've got to do this myself. Don't you see?"

"Oh, hell." Joe turned around, pacing back and forth. "If you're going to tell me this has to do with honor I'm going to be sick."

"But in a way it does have to do with honor, Joe. Driscoll murdered my brother. Berto didn't have a chance, and I couldn't do anything to help him. This is the only way I can repay Berto. I know I can't bring him back but at least Driscoll will have paid for the terrible thing he did to Berto."

"But why won't you let me help you? I won't interfere."

"I know you love me, Joe, and that's why you want to help but I have to do this all on my own. Listen to me. What if something like this happened to Larissa? Wouldn't you want to do it by yourself?"

Joe shook his head, knowing it was no use arguing with the boy. He sat down on one of the many large rocks and slapped at the dust on his pants. He looked up into the darkening sky. "You remind me so much of your Pa, it's eerie. I remember the first time he went after your mother. Hell, he wasn't much older than you. That old devil Crooked Teeth had stolen her away from the Cheyennes, and your Pa was determined to get her back."

"I bet Pa was great then. I bet he got all fired up over the least little thing."

Joe laughed loudly, slapping his knee. "Yeah, he got fired up over little things, so imagine how he felt when this Crow took your ma! Hell, he would've searched all over the face of the earth for that woman if he had to."

"Yeah, Pa loves her more than anything in the world except for us." Nathan's voice caught as he spoke the last words. "That's why I have to do it, Joe. It's the way Pa would have done it, and you can't tell

141

me any different. I know he would have done what I'm doing."

Joe shrugged his shoulders. "I can see there's no use in arguing with you. But I'll tell you one thing. Now that I know you're alive I'm not gonna just walk right out and pretend I never saw you."

"I wouldn't want you to do that." Nathan touched Joe's shoulder. "You're the only tie I have to Ma and Pa." Nathan was silent for a moment but when he spoke his voice was noticeably shaky. "I want to ask you something, Joe, and I want you to be honest with me. Are you sure Ma and Pa will welcome me back? Are you sure they won't resent my being alive and Berto being dead?"

"What ever gave you such a crazy notion? Don't you know your folks better than that?"

"I thought I did."

"Well, why would you think such a thing then?"

"I wrote them, Joe, right after the accident. I wrote them twice but I never got an answer. I assumed they didn't want to see me again."

"Hell, Nate, they don't even know you're alive. You mean you thought they knew you were alive?"

"I wrote them two letters. They never wrote back. I thought maybe they were angry at me over what happened to Berto, and I can't say as I blame them much."

"Nate, your parents never received those letters. All they know is what I told them over two years ago when you two were attacked. They don't know any different from that."

"Oh, God." Nathan stood up, walking back and forth in the darkness. "So they think I'm dead, too? I just assumed they knew I was alive from my letters."

"Are you sure those letters got mailed?"

"Yeah, I gave them to Chin."

"Are you sure you can trust him?"

"With my life," Nathan responded quickly. "No, it wasn't Chin. It had to be something else."

"Or someone."

"But who? Who would even know that I'm alive?"

"I don't know, boy. Have you made yourself any other enemies besides Driscoll?"

"I haven't even met many people. No, something probably went wrong with the mail."

"It's possible. There was that terrible cholera epidemic then. It's possible no mail got through. Well, hell, that don't matter now. The only thing that's important is that you're alive and well. You can write your folks now. Let them know you're all right."

"No, I can't do that."

"What in hell are you talking about, Nate? These are your parents we're talking about here. How long do you plan on making them suffer?"

"I never meant for them to suffer, Joe, but maybe it's best for now that they don't know."

"What are you talking about? The only thing that would be best for them is to find out you're alive."

"No, not until I've done what I've come here to do."

"Damn you but you're stubborn. Your pa's not gonna stop you from doing what you have to do."

"No, but he might try to interfere, and I don't want him getting hurt. I want him and Ma completely out of this. The other thing is if this plan goes all wrong and Driscoll finds out who I really am, do you plan to tell Pa and Ma that I'm dead? You've already had to do it once. Do you want to have to do it twice?"

"Oh, hell." Joe got up and kicked at the ground. "I wish I'd never laid eyes on you or your father. Would've saved me a lot of heartache." Joe felt

143

Nathan's hand on his shoulder, and he shrugged it off. "Don't think you can talk to me about honor like you can those two in there. Honor starts with your parents, and as far as I'm concerned you're not honoring them right now."

"I'm doing what I think is right, Joe. Can't you understand that?"

"I guess I can't understand it, Nate, 'cause I seen their pain. I've been there, and I've seen how hurt they are thinking you're dead."

"Don't do this."

"Don't do what? Don't make you see the truth?"

"It's your truth, not mine. You can't change my mind, Joe, and you have no right to interfere."

"I have every right in the world, boy." Joe stepped close to Nathan, his face nearly touching the boy's. "I helped raise you. Hell, I even helped change your diapers. I was there when you came into the world. I think that gives me some right to care about you."

"If you care for me, please don't say anything to my parents. Not yet. When the time is right I'll let them know."

"And what if something happens between now and that time, huh? What if something happens to your ma or pa? What if something happens to Driscoll?"

"I'll just have to take that chance. In the meantime, you have to swear to me you won't say anything to my folks. Please, Joe, swear to me."

"Why should I?"

"Because I'm asking you to."

Joe looked at Nathan in the glittering darkness and nodded his head. "I swear."

"That's not good enough."

"What you talking about?"

144

"I want you to swear on my great grandmother's grave."

"She's not buried in a grave, boy."

"Come on, Joe. I want you to swear on Sun Dancer's soul that you won't tell my parents I'm alive until I'm ready to tell them myself."

"You had to bring Sun Dancer into it, didn't you? You know that if I break my promise to you she'll haunt me for the rest of my days. Oh, all right, I swear on Sun Dancer's soul that I won't tell your folks. But you have to make me a promise, boy."

"What's that?"

"I want you to promise me that you'll keep in touch with me. I want to know that you're all right. And when you're ready to come back to the city I'll help you out. You know, I'm not without some influence around there myself."

"I promise I'll be in touch. Thanks, Joe. I'll never forget what you've done."

"Let's just hope it turns out all right, boy. I don't want to see your folks get hurt more than they already have been." Joe thought for a moment. "There's something else I forgot to tell you, boy. You ought to know."

"What is it? Is one of them ill?"

"No, it's nothing like that. You've got yourself a little sister."

"What? You mean they had a baby?"

"No, they found a little girl on that wagon train that had been hit by the cholera. She's been with them ever since."

"A sister," Nathan said quietly, pleased for his parents but somehow quite sad. He felt as if they had already replaced their love for him and Berto with the love of another child. "How old is she?"

"She's almost eleven now and a pretty little thing. You want to know what the funny thing is? She's half Cheyenne Indian. Of course your mother thinks it was a sign."

Nathan couldn't keep from laughing. It was a joke among them all that anything that happened, good or bad, Aeneva always saw a sign. "What's she like, Joe?"

"She's a lot like your mother. She's got herself lots of spirit, and she can ride a horse like a true Cheyenne. She gives your folks so much love they can hardly stand it. She's good for them, Nate."

"I'm glad," Nathan replied too quickly.

"Hey, boy, just because they have her doesn't mean they love you or Berto any less. You know that, don't you?"

"Of course I know that. I was just feeling a little sorry for myself. So, she rides like a true Cheyenne? I bet Ma loves that."

"You should see all the things your Ma has taught her about healing already. The girl's going to grow up knowing a lot of things, Nate."

"Ma and Pa always wanted a daughter. I'm glad now they finally have one."

"They still have a son, too, Nate. Don't you ever forget it."

"I never will, Joe. Sometimes it's the only thing that keeps me going."

"Well, you do what you have to do, boy, then you come back to us all. Hear me?"

"Yeah, Joe, I hear you."

"You hungry? That food Chin's cooked up smells mighty good."

"Sure, let's go back in." Nathan smiled outwardly but inwardly he wondered about his parents and the sister he had never seen. He tried to comfort himself with thoughts that it would soon be over but he knew there was a good chance he might never find the gold he was looking for and therefore never be able to get back at Driscoll. He opened the door to the small shack, and the smell of Chin's food stirred his hunger. But Nathan wasn't hungry for food; he was hungry for revenge. Someday, with or without the gold, he would make Driscoll regret the day he was ever born.

Chapter VI

Anna kneed her mount, galloping as fast as she could. She felt the wind against her face, and she closed her eyes for a moment, letting the feeling completely engulf her. She had never felt anything so wonderful as riding on the open range. When she got to the stream, she pulled up sharply and jumped off, stumbling to the ground as she did so. She laughed loudly, enjoying the pure pleasure of the dirt on her hands. She looked up when she heard the sound of the horse behind her. "Took you long enough," she said to the young man who dismounted from his horse.

"Your father would tan your hide if he saw the way you'd been riding his Appaloosa."

"Oh, Garrett, come on. You're no fun anymore."

"I'm lots of fun. I'm just not crazy like you are."

Anna reached for the boy's hand. "I'm sorry, I didn't mean to make you angry with me. I just can't help it. I told you before, it's in my blood. Once I get on a horse I can't help but ride as fast as I can." She narrowed her eyes. "You better be careful, Garrett, or I'll scalp you when you're not looking."

"Stop it, Anna, I don't deserve that."

"You're right, you don't. I'm sorry." Anna had been referring to some of the neighbors who were overt in their dislike of the fact that Aeneva and Anna were Indians, but Garrett and his family had never been like them. They had always treated Anna and her family with friendship and respect. Anna reached for Garrett's hand. "I truly am sorry, Garrett. I don't know what I would've done without you all these years to stick up for me."

"You don't need me to stick up for you. You do just fine on your own."

"If you're talking about Tommy Leland, he had it coming to him. He's been making fun of me since I first came here. I just couldn't take it anymore."

"Yeah, but did you have to break his nose?"

Anna looked at Garrett and they both burst into laughter. Anna lay down on the ground, looking up at the sky. "I don't know why I have so much anger in me, Garrett. Sometimes I want to hit the whole world."

"Or at least those who say things about your Ma."

Anna rolled over to her side, propping herself up on her elbow. She pulled a piece of wild grass out of the ground and stuck it in her mouth. "She's so good, Garrett. She's the best person I've ever known. I guess I just want everybody else to know it, too."

"The people who count know what kind of a person your mother is, Anna." Garrett took Anna's hand in his. "You're a lot like her, you know."

"No, I'm not. I don't have her patience or her heart."

"Yes, you do. Nobody else sticks up for Albert Perkins the way you do. Nobody has the guts to."

"You do."

"Yeah, but I was just like everybody else until you came here. I was as mean to poor old Albert as everybody else was."

"But you changed and that's what matters."

"Why do you defend Albert, Anna? Why?"

Anna shrugged her slim shoulders as she chewed on the thin blade of grass. "Nobody has the right to humiliate another human being the way those kids humiliate Albert. Just because he's different from them they think they have the right to hurt him in every way possible. But they don't. Nobody has that right."

"So, you'll continue to fight his battles for him and continue to keep getting yourself in trouble for poor old Albert."

"Why not? Somebody has to do it. Besides, as I recall, you were the one who stepped in last time." Anna laughed. "You really gave it to Tim Stimson. He and Tommy Leland are really going to hate us."

"Who cares. You're right, you know. It's our duty to stick up for Albert, at least until he decides to do it for himself."

"Oh, Garrett," Anna said warmly, throwing her arm around the boy's neck. "You are a good friend." Her face was close to Garrett's, and she could feel his warm breath against her cheek. She felt funny inside, funny and afraid. She knew Garrett was going to kiss her but she didn't pull away; she wanted to finally find out for herself what it was like to be kissed by a boy. His lips touched hers gently and she closed her eyes, waiting for more. But Garrett stopped abruptly. Anna opened her eyes. "What's the matter? Did I do something wrong?"

Garrett sat up, absently pulling at the grass in front of him. "No, you didn't do anything wrong."

"Then why did you stop? You were going to kiss me, weren't you, Garrett?"

"Yeah."

"Well, why didn't you?"

"Because you're too young, that's why."

"I am not. I'm almost fourteen years old."

"That's still too young."

"I know lots of girls who have been kissed already. Sally James is younger than I am, and she's already had three boyfriends!"

"Sally James is different from you."

"Why?"

"Because."

"But why?"

"Because she is, that's all!" Garrett replied angrily. He stood up and walked to the stream.

"What is it, Garrett? What have I done wrong? Please tell me."

"You haven't done anything wrong, Anna, I told you."

"Then what is it? It's not like you to keep secrets from me. We've always told each other everything."

"There are some things a man and a girl just can't share."

"What do you mean a man and a girl. I'm talking about you and me, Garrett."

"Look, Anna, I'm fifteen years old. I'm almost two years older than you. Hell, some guys my age are already married with families."

"I still don't understand what you're trying to tell me."

"You're a nice girl, Anna, a good girl. Someday you'll meet someone and settle down and have a family, just like you should do."

"What are you talking about? I thought you and I were both going to wait to get married. Remember? We were going to travel around the world, do exciting things and then get married when we were twenty-seven years old. To each *other*, Garrett, or

152

have you forgotten that?"

"I haven't forgotten." Garrett stared at Anna and gently pulled her chin up. He touched his lips to hers, then slowly pulled away. "There, now you've had your first kiss."

Anna touched her lips with her fingers, and a smile spread across her young face. "It was wonderful, Garrett, I loved it. Wait until I tell Sally James. She won't believe it."

"Anna, wait."

"What?"

"Don't tell Sally about this one. Let's save this one just for us, all right?"

"All right." Anna smiled and put her arm through his. "Garrett," she said, her voice suddenly serious. "Will you promise me something?"

"What?"

"If we do grow up and we don't marry each other, will you promise me that you'll always love me and be my friend? I think I'd die if I didn't have your friendship."

"You don't have to worry about that, Anna." He kissed her again, this time putting his arms around her. "You can share that one with Sally James."

"Really? I can go to California when I finish school?"

"Yes, I don't see why not. It might do you good."

Anna threw her arms around Trenton. "Thank you, Trenton. It's so wonderful. I can't wait to tell Garrett."

"How do you think Garrett will feel about you going away?" Aeneva asked.

"We've already decided that we'll both go to college, get good jobs and then we'll get married."

Aeneva looked at Trenton, a smile showing in her eyes. "So, you have it all planned, do you? Sometimes plans don't always go as we hope, Anna."

"I know that but I refuse to give up. That's what I want to do with my life. I want to share my life with Garrett."

"Honey." Trenton put his arm around Anna. "You're only fourteen years old. A lot can happen between now and then. You might even meet someone else you love more than Garrett."

"That will never happen."

Aeneva walked to Anna, kissing her on the cheek. "Sometimes we can't always tell our hearts what to do. There may come a time someday when your feelings for Garrett change from love to friendship."

Anna sat down on the couch, a sad expression covering her face. "You're both trying to tell me that things don't stay the same forever. I know that. I remember that my father left me here with you two and I was scared but now I think of you two as my parents. But some things don't change, like my feelings for Garrett. You both should understand that. You have loved each other since the time you were kids."

Aeneva sat down next to Anna. "That's true, dear. But something else happened in my life. I fell in love with someone else."

"You mean Roberto's father? You said you had lost your memory. It was natural for you to fall in love with him. He was taking care of you."

"But even after I regained my memory I still cared for him."

"But not in the way you cared for Trenton."

Aeneva smiled at Anna, shaking her head in amusement. "How do you know that?"

"I can tell by the way you look at each other. You

154

still love each other very much."

"You remind me a lot of your father, Anna. You are stubborn, just like he was."

"He was a good man, wasn't he? I know he must have loved me. It's just that sometimes I can't understand why he'd leave his own daughter."

"He did it because he loved you very much, Anna. He knew that he couldn't take you with him to the gold fields or to wherever else he was going. He felt you had been through enough already. He wanted you to have a home. He knew you'd be loved here."

"Do you think that he might write me someday?"

"You never know with Patrick O'Leary, Annie." Trenton sat down on the other side of Anna. "He could come waltzing in here tonight like he's never been gone." Trenton laughed. "He was a strange one but I liked him."

"I would like to see him and know that he's all right, but I don't think I could ever leave you two. You have given me more in these last five years than any girl could possibly ask for. I love you both." Anna kissed Aeneva and Trenton, then she stood up, a very serious expression on her face. "I've also thought that if I don't go to college I could become a writer."

"A writer? What would you write about?"

"There are lots of things I could write about in California. I could go into the gold fields. I could write about the Mexicans and Spanish. I could even write about the Chinese. There are so many interesting things and people there."

"There are lots of interesting places and people everywhere, Anna. Why exactly do you want to go to California?"

Anna shrugged her shoulders. "I don't know. Maybe it's because I've heard about it from the time I

155

was a little girl. That's all Papa could talk about was going back to California and finding his fortune. I hope he has."

"Isn't there something else you're not telling us?" Trenton looked up at Anna.

"What do you mean?"

"Garrett's father told me that their family has land in California, land that Garrett will inherit when he turns eighteen years old."

Anna wrinkled her brows together. "I guess I do remember Garrett saying something about some land in California. But that doesn't have anything to do with my decision to go there."

"Just checking."

"Why are you so determined to keep me apart from Garrett, Trenton? I thought you liked him."

"You know I care for Garrett a great deal, Anna. I just want to make sure you know what you're doing."

"Did you two know what you were doing when you got married?"

Trenton and Aeneva exchanged looks and laughed. "No," they answered simultaneously.

"Well, then, look how well you both turned out. Don't worry about me. I'll be just fine."

Anna walked slowly along, enjoying the sweet smell of the spring flowers. She held onto her mare's reins, letting the horse graze periodically while she bent to pick different kinds of wildflowers. She hummed an old Irish song to herself, a song that her father had taught her when she was a little girl. She wondered why she had never forgotten it. Her mare whinnied and Anna looked up. She ran her hand over the mare's smooth, pink nose. "It's all right, girl. Easy now." Anna listened. She heard sounds coming from over the hill. It sounded like someone was yelling for help. She threw down the flowers and quickly mounted her mare, reining in the direction of the sounds. She had barely gotten over the hill when she saw Tommy Leland and Tim Stimson beating on Albert Perkins. Albert wasn't moving. She rode up, jumping down from her mare. She ran up to the two boys, pounding her fists on each one of them. "Leave him alone. You're going to kill him!" Tommy and Tim backed off while Anna bent over Albert. "Albert, are you all right? Come on, Albert."

"What's the matter, squaw, can't you make your magic work on him?"

Anna looked up at Tommy Leland. She felt the murderous rage rise in her. She stood up. "Why do you two have to beat up on him like this? What has he ever done to you?"

"He's alive. That's enough."

"You're disgusting." Anna spat out the words. She saw the anger appear on Tommy Leland's face. He walked toward her.

"I never liked you much. You came in here and acted as if you owned the place. Hell, that squaw and the man she married aren't even your own parents."

Anna lashed out before she could stop herself. She punched Tommy in the face, hard, knocking him backward. "Don't you ever call her a squaw again."

Tommy Leland rubbed his jaw and looked over at Tim. "I'm tired of letting this little redskin push me around. I think it's time she got paid back."

"Yeah, I think she's overdue." The two boys approached Anna but she didn't back up. She stood her ground.

"Does it make you two feel big to beat up on girls and guys who are smaller than you? If Garrett were

157

here you wouldn't even have the guts to stay around."

"Yeah, where is your boyfriend? Thought he might be around to protect you."

"I don't need him to protect me. I can take care of myself."

"Well, if that's so, why don't you come here." Tommy reached out for Anna, yanking her roughly toward him. "You know, you are a pretty little thing for a squaw." Tommy tried to kiss Anna but she pulled away.

"Stop it, Tommy!"

"Or what? What are you going to do?"

"Don't come near me."

"Come on, Tim. I think it's time we taught this little girl a lesson. She still doesn't know how to respect her elders." The two boys walked toward Anna. "What's wrong, little girl, you afraid?"

"I'm not afraid of you two." Anna backed up as the two boys got closer to her. "Why are you doing this?" Anna tried to keep the fear from her voice but she could feel it come over her. She knew these two, and she knew what they were capable of. She didn't stand a chance against the two of them together. She stopped, refusing to back up any further. "What do you want?"

Tommy Leland moved forward. He touched Anna's long, dark hair, twirling it around his finger. "How come you never liked me, Anna? What did I ever do to you?"

"You hurt me when you hurt people like Albert, Tommy. You don't have to act like that. Albert doesn't hurt anybody. Why can't you just leave him alone?"

"Would you be nice to me if I left him alone?" Tommy stepped closer to Anna. "I never realized your eyes were so blue." He reached out and pulled her to him. "What're you afraid of? I thought you'd be used to this by now."

"Leave me alone!"

"Oh, come on, you can't fool me. I know you and Garrett have been making real sweet to each other for a long time."

"That's a lie!" Anna struggled to get free of Tommy's hold but she could not. "Garrett and I are only friends."

"That's not what he told us, is it Tim?" Tommy smiled.

"He's lying. He and I have never done anything together. Let me go, Tommy." Anna struggled but Tommy held her tightly. She felt Tim behind her. He put his hands on her shoulders.

"You've never been real nice to me either, Miss O'Leary. I think it's time you learned who your real friends are."

Anna continued to struggle but Tommy managed to pull her to the ground, kicking and screaming. He tried to hold her down but she punched him in the head. She got up to run but Tim grabbed her skirt, pulling her back down on the ground.

"She's a feisty little thing, isn't she, Tommy?"

"Yeah, I heard my pa say once that all Indian squaws are full of fire. He says they're the best because they'll do anything you want." Tommy grabbed Anna's arms and pinned them to the ground. "Is that true, squaw?"

Anna watched Tommy as he lowered his face to hers. Just as his face was about to touch hers she spit. "You make me sick."

"You little bitch!" Tommy slapped Anna. "Hold her down, Tim. She's gonna pay for that." Tommy got on top of Anna, laughing at her as she tried to fight. "She don't look too mean right now, does she?"

"Not at all. In fact, I'd say she looks real scared."

Anna felt Tommy's hands on the bodice of her dress, and she felt a stabbing pain in her stomach. She couldn't bear it if he touched her. She had to make him stop somehow. But he began to touch her, and then he unbuttoned her dress. When he became too impatient for the tiny buttons, he ripped the bodice apart. "Well, look here, Tim. Look at the pretty lace she's got under here. Shall we see what's under that?"

Anna struggled so hard her arms felt as though they were being pulled from their sockets. There was no way she could stop the two boys. "Tommy, please don't do this. Please."

"Why shouldn't I? I don't owe you anything."

"Please, it's not right."

"You hear that, Tim? She says it's not right." The two boys laughed, and then Tommy ran his hands over Anna's breasts. "You're not very big. Hell, I thought you'd have something there."

"Let's see." Tim knelt next to Tommy. He, too, ran his fingers over Anna's breasts. "I think she feels pretty good, Tommy."

"Ah." Tommy pushed Tim away. "What do you know. You don't know anything about how it's done anyway. Well, I'm gonna show you, Tim. I'm gonna show both of you." Tommy pulled the skirt of Anna's dress up around her thighs. "It's time you learned what it's like to have a real man, little girl."

"That's enough!" Albert's voice came out of nowhere. He stood battered and bruised, his thin body looking as if it would be blown over by a small gust of wind. He held a large piece of wood tightly in his hands. "Get off of her, Tommy."

Tommy laughed. "You've got to be kidding,

160

Perkins. Why don't you come over here and I'll teach you all about what it's like to be a man."

"I told you to get off of her."

Tommy looked over at Tim. Slowly they both stood up. "What do you think you're going to do with that piece of wood, Perkins? Christ, you can't even hold it. Look at yourself. You're hands are shaking." Tommy laughed loudly and Tim chimed in.

Anna pushed her skirt down and slowly stood up. She started to inch away but Tommy grabbed her arm.

"You're not going anywhere. We're not through yet."

"No!" Anna screamed and twisted away from Tommy. She ran away from him but he caught her, tackling her from behind and knocking her to the ground. "Let me go, Tommy."

"No, not till we're through." Tommy started to rip the lace material that consisted of Anna's slip but a thumping sound made Anna look up. Albert had hit Tommy across the back of the head and he had fallen forward on Anna. While Anna pushed Tommy off of her and stood up, Albert confronted Tim.

"Now, listen, Albert. I never meant you no harm. It was just a game, that's all."

"A game? A game?" Albert said, his voice quivering. He walked toward Tim, the piece of wood held high. "How would you like it if someone beat you up every day? How would you like it?"

"I, I wouldn't. I wouldn't like it."

"Then why do you do it?"

"I told you, it's just a game. It's fun."

"It's fun?" Albert screamed, throwing the piece of wood directly past Tim's head. "Well, I've had it, Tim. I won't be the butt of your jokes anymore."

Albert walked up to Tim, standing face-to-face with him. "And I don't ever want you touching Anna again. If I ever see either you or Tommy touch her again I swear I'll kill you."

"Okay, all right. We'll leave you both alone." Tim started to back up.

"No, that's not all, Tim." Albert walked up to Tim. He stared at him for a moment, then brought his fist back and hit Tim square in the face. Tim fell to his knees, holding his nose, but Albert grabbed his shirt and punched him another time. Tim was flat on the ground this time, knocked out cold. Albert stood over him, a disbelieving look on his face.

Anna walked over to Albert, putting her arm through his. "Albert, you were wonderful."

"I can't believe it. I can't believe I actually fought back, Anna." He turned to look at the girl.

"Sometimes you have to fight back, Albert. I know it's against your religion and all that but sometimes you just can't turn the other cheek. If you hadn't stepped in and helped me, there's no telling what they would've done to me."

"I know. I figured it was time for me to defend you for a change. You've always defended me, Anna. Always."

"Oh, Albert. Come on, let's go over by the stream. I want to wash some of that blood from your face." They walked to the stream. Anna tore a piece of her slip off and dipped it in the water. Gently she began wiping Albert's face. "You have nice eyes, Albert. I never noticed them before."

"Oh, my glasses. I lost my glasses. My father will kill me." He started to get up but Anna pulled him back down.

"We'll find your glasses later. Let me finish cleaning you up first." Anna wiped the blood from

162

Albert's face. "You're a mess, Albert. They really gave it to you this time."

"I asked for it, I guess."

"What do you mean you asked for it?"

"I shouldn't have laughed at Tommy in class." He smiled sheepishly at Anna. "But I just couldn't help it."

Anna laughed. "I know, I couldn't either. When Mrs. Ford showed him a picture of the *Last Supper* and asked him to identify it," Anna said, giggling uncontrollably, "I almost died when he called it *The Knights of the Round Table*." She and Albert laughed together. "I suppose we both asked for it today, Albert. We should never have laughed at Tommy."

"I suppose you're right, Anna," Albert replied seriously, "but *The Knights of the Round Table?*" They both laughed again. Suddenly, Albert stopped and looked behind them. "Do you suppose they're all right? Should I check on them?"

"They'll be fine but we should be getting out of here. If they wake up and find us still here, there's no telling what they'll do." They stood up and walked toward Anna's horse, which had moved further into the pasture. "Come on, Albert, I'll take you home. Climb on up behind me." Anna mounted her mare and leaned down, extending her arm to Albert.

"No, I can't do that. My father would never permit it." He looked around him. "Besides, I still haven't found my glasses."

Anna kneed her horse and quickly rode back to the place where the fight occurred. She found the glasses in seconds. "They're over here, Albert." Anna dismounted and picked up the round, wire-rimmed glasses. One of the lenses was cracked. "Here Albert. I'm afraid they're broken."

Albert shook his head dejectedly. "My father will never forgive me for this."

"But it wasn't your fault, Albert."

"It doesn't matter. He'll say I should have avoided it somehow."

Anna remounted and again extended her arm to Albert. "Please come up here behind me. It's silly of you to walk when you can ride with me. Your father will never know."

Albert slipped on his broken glasses and picked up his scattered books. "All right." He took Anna's arm and climbed up behind her on the mare, sitting awkwardly on the rump of the mare.

"You'll have to scoot close to me, Albert. Put your arms around my waist. Come on, don't be afraid."

Cautiously Albert slipped his arms around Anna's waist. "I've never ridden a horse before. Doesn't it scare you?"

"I love it better than anything in the world. I love the freedom of riding on a horse as fast as I can and feeling the wind against my face and the strength of the horse beneath me."

"I like you, Anna. You're so different."

"You mean because I'm Indian. Your father probably wouldn't approve of me either would he, Albert?"

"Probably not but I don't care. You're the only friend I've ever had in this town. You're the only person I've ever been able to talk to."

"What about Garrett? He sticks up for you sometimes."

"Sometimes but it wasn't always that way. Before you came, Garrett was just as mean to me as Tommy and Tim were."

Anna reined in. She turned around in the saddle. "I don't believe it. That doesn't sound like Garrett."

"I'm not lying, Anna. I know you like Garrett and he's your friend but I don't trust him."

"Albert, I can't believe you're talking about *my* Garrett. He just wouldn't do anything to hurt anybody."

"He pushed me out of a hayloft once. He talked me into climbing up and then pushed me out when we got up there." Albert shook his head, tears stinging his eyes. "I liked him, Anna, I really liked him. I thought he liked me, too. But he just wanted to make fun of me the way everybody else did. He's no different from those other two. I want you to be careful of him, Anna."

"Garrett would never do anything to hurt me, Albert. Never."

"Maybe."

"I don't want to hear anything more about Garrett. He's my very best friend. You should remember that he's helped you out quite a few times."

"He's helped me because you asked him to. He hates me as much as the others. Maybe more."

"What do you mean?"

"I never told on him when he pushed me out of the loft. I think it made him feel kind of guilty. I think he feels like he owed me something because of that."

"We're not talking about the same person, Albert. Garrett just isn't like that."

"Maybe not or maybe so. I do know one thing, though. He has changed for the better ever since you came here. Maybe he really is a different person now."

"Everyone can change, Albert."

"Even Tommy Leland?"

"I wouldn't go that far." Anna laughed, kneeing her horse. They galloped across the open land until they reached the white fence that led to Albert's farmhouse. "I'll drop you here, Albert. I wouldn't want your father to see me."

"I'm sorry, Anna. It doesn't have anything to do with you. It just has to do with his beliefs."

"It's all right. Take care of yourself, Albert. Make sure you do something for that eye."

Albert climbed down off the mare. He stood, staring at the ground. "I'm sorry I said those things about Garrett, Anna. I know how you feel about him."

"It's all right. You just don't know him the way I do."

"You're probably right. Thank you again, Anna. You always seem to be there for me."

"Well, you were there for me today, Albert. I'll never forget it. See you in school." Anna reined her mare in the opposite direction and rode toward home. She rode hard. They galloped across the open pastures. Anna pushed her mare harder and harder until she heard the animal breathing heavily. She pulled up and walked the mare the rest of the way. Anna was afraid that what Albert had told her about Garrett was true. She had seen signs of his temper in the past but had always chosen to ignore them because he had always been so good to her. And she knew for a fact that he had been close friends with Tommy Leland and Tim Stimson before she had come. She shook her head. "No, I don't believe it. I won't." Anna rode home, trying to push the nagging thoughts from her mind. Garrett was her friend and she wouldn't doubt him.

Anna glanced anxiously at Aeneva and Trenton as they rode in the wagon. "Are you sure I look all right? Does this color look good on me? What about my hair?"

"I've already told you a hundred times, Annie, you look wonderful. Every boy there will be falling all over himself to get at you."

"I don't think she cares about every boy there, Trenton."

"Oh, yes, I forgot. Garrett is back, isn't he?"

"Why do you two always tease me about Garrett? I've told you a hundred times we're just friends. Are you sure my hair looks all right?"

Aeneva and Trenton smiled while Anna fussed with her hair and dress.

"I hear this social is going to be a good one. People from all around are coming."

"Sally James said it's going to be the best social we've had around here in years."

"Sally James says that about every social."

"She does not. Oh, look, there's Garrett's house. Isn't it beautiful?"

"You'd probably say that if it were an old shack."

"Oh, Trenton," Anna replied dramatically but she had to admit that her father was right. She adored Garrett so much that it hardly seemed possible for her to go through a day without him. When he had gone to California to check on his land, she thought she would die without him but she had somehow survived. But when he returned, she was sure she had never seen a boy more handsome than Garrett. He had grown even taller and stronger, and his dark brown hair was cut and combed. He even wore city clothes. When she looked into his hazel eyes, she was sure she would never feel that way about anyone again.

Trenton drove the wagon into the courtyard. He got down and helped Aeneva and Anna down. They walked through the high adobe wall and into the large garden area. Musicians played and people danced and talked. Tables were set up all around the garden with food, plates, utensils, and beverages.

"Looks like a lot of people from Prescott came. I can't believe the crowd."

"Aren't those some of your friends from school, Annie?" Trenton pointed to Tommy Leland and Tim Stimson.

Anna frowned. "They aren't friends of mine." Over two years had gone by since Tommy and Tim had attacked her but she couldn't forget it. It seemed as if it had happened yesterday. "There's Sally. She's already dancing. I bet she has all the boys fighting over her tonight."

"I don't know why," Trenton replied absently. "She's a little too small for my tastes. She's not much bigger than you were when you were eight years old, Annie."

"That's not true and you know it. Sally's a nice girl. She just talks a little too much sometimes." Anna stopped talking. She looked across the garden and saw Garrett standing tall. He was talking to a group of men and shaking their hands. He seemed to be so much older all of a sudden.

"There's Garrett, Annie. Why don't you go over and say hello."

"No, I'll wait. He looks busy right now."

"All right. Aeneva, why don't we go over and say hello to Garrett's parents. We'll see you later, Annie."

"Okay." Anna watched as Aeneva and Trenton walked away, and the sight of them tugged at her heart. She loved them so much. She felt a tap on her shoulder and turned around.

"May I have this dance, miss?"

"Well, I don't really—" Anna never saw the boy

before, and she wasn't really in the mood to dance yet.

"Please, miss. I'm not from around these parts. I need to talk to someone."

"All right." Anna took the boy's arm and followed him to the dance area. "What's your name?"

"Adam, Adam Rivers. What's yours?"

"Anna O'Leary. I can tell you're not from around here. You have some kind of an accent."

"I'm from Boston. I'm out here visiting my cousin."

"Who's your cousin?"

"Garrett's my cousin."

"But he didn't tell me he had a cousin visiting."

"Well, I just recently arrived. So, Miss O'Leary, what do you do out here all day long?"

Anna's mouth twisted up at the corners. "Oh, nothing really. I mostly sit around and wait for rattlesnakes to crawl by so I can shoot their heads off. I keep a collection of rattlesnake heads right next to my scalp collection."

Adam looked at Anna a minute, then smiled. "I'm sorry. I guess I deserved that. I must have sounded rather pompous."

"You could say that."

"I really do want to know, though. What do you do for fun?"

"I ride and I help my parents on their ranch. I go to school and read. I read as many things as I can. Sometimes my parents and I will go into town and see a play or attend the opera. I'm sure it's not like Boston but good drama is the same anywhere, don't you agree?"

"Yes, I suppose you're right. You know, you're much different from most of the girls I've met out here. You seem to know a little bit more about life than marriage and children."

169

"There's nothing wrong with marriage and children, Mr. Rivers. If it weren't for marriage and children, neither you nor I would be dancing together right now."

Adam laughed, clapping loudly when the music stopped. "May I get you some punch?"

"Yes, you may."

"May I also have the next dance? I promise not to say anything too insulting."

Anna smiled. "Yes, I'll dance the next dance with you, Mr. Rivers."

Anna watched Adam as he walked away, thinking to herself how little she really knew of the world. The music began again, and she laughed as she saw five boys fight to ask Sally to dance. She saw Adam coming toward her when she felt a hand go around her waist, leading her to the dance area.

"You've been saving this dance for me, right?" Garrett took Anna's hand and put his other hand around her waist, guiding her around.

"I promised this dance to Adam, Garrett. I don't want to be rude." She started to pull away but Garrett pulled her to him.

"Adam can wait. I haven't seen you for three months. Do you know how much I've missed you?"

"If you missed me so much, why didn't you write?"

"I didn't have time. I was working on the land every day."

"Is it very beautiful out there, Garrett?"

"Yeah, it is. It's better than I thought it would be."

"Are you sorry you came back?"

Garrett stared into Anna's deep blue eyes and shook his head, a serious expression on his face. "Never. I couldn't have stayed out there without you."

Anna leaned her head against Garrett's chest.

"That's a sweet thing to say. Thank you."

"Come on." Garrett took Anna's hand and led her through the garden out by the back wall. There was an adobe bench under an oak tree. Garrett led Anna to the bench and they sat down. "I want to talk to you, Anna."

"About what?"

"I'm going to be going back to California to live at the end of the month. I want you to come with me."

"Garrett—" Anna was speechless. She couldn't believe what she was hearing. "Garrett, what about all of our plans?"

"Those were just childish dreams, Anna. This is reality. I want to marry you and take you back to California as my wife."

"Garrett, I'm only sixteen years old. I'm not ready to get married yet."

"Lots of girls your age are married."

"I'm not lots of girls, Garrett. I thought you knew that." Anna stood up and walked over to the tree, running her hand up and down the rough bark.

Garrett stood up and walked to Anna, putting his arms around her. "I love you, Anna. I always have. I don't want to go back to California without you."

"But I want to finish school first."

"You're already way ahead of the kids in this school. You're ready for something else now."

"Garrett, why are you doing this? We were going to wait until we were grown up, remember? We were going to travel and do everything we ever wanted to do before we settled down. What happened to those plans?"

"I told you, Anna, those were just childish dreams."

"I thought they were good dreams. Why don't you want to do that anymore, Garrett? What happened?"

"I can't just shirk my responsibilities, Anna. I have a thousand acres of land in California that belong to me. Lots of people are depending on me to make the land profitable. I can't just take you and travel around the world because it sounds like fun. I have a responsibility to those people. Do you understand?"

"Yes, I do understand."

"Then marry me and come back to California with me. We could start a whole new life. It's beautiful, Anna. You'll love it there."

"I can't, Garrett. I promised Trenton and Aeneva I wouldn't leave home until I was eighteen years old. I can't break that promise to them."

"They won't hold you to it if you decide to get married."

"I won't do that to them. They have done too much for me, given too much of themselves. I won't deprive them of two more years."

Garrett walked back over to the bench and sat down. "I knew that's what you'd say. You're always so practical."

Anna sat down next to him. "I'm not practical, Garrett. I'm the one who wants to run off and travel around the world. But this is different. These people took me in and raised me as if I were their blood child. I cannot leave them. Not now."

"Will you ever leave them?"

"What do you mean?"

"Just what I said. Will you ever leave them? Do you think you owe them the rest of your life?"

"That's not fair, Garrett."

"Maybe not but you've got to grow up sometime, Anna. There's a whole world outside of this place."

Anna reached for Garrett's hand. "Don't be angry with me. You know how I feel about you. I've never cared for anyone the way I care for you."

"I'm not really sure how you feel, Anna. If only you weren't so young."

"Damn you, Garrett McReynolds. One minute you ask me to marry you, and the next minute you tell me I'm too young to feel. You don't know anything that I feel." Anna stood up and started to walk away but Garrett pulled her back.

"Come here." He pulled her to him, seeking her lips in the darkness. He pressed his mouth against hers, holding her tightly. He moved his lips from her mouth to her cheek to the line of her neck. "God, you're so beautiful, Anna. You drive me crazy. You always have."

"I think we should stop, Garrett." Anna tried to pull away but Garrett held her tightly. "Garrett, please let me go."

"Why? So you can run back to your parents?" Garrett kissed her again, this time more passionately.

Anna struggled against Garrett's demanding kiss and tight hold, but she found that she enjoyed the kiss much more than she had ever thought possible. She loosened her arms from Garrett's grasp and put them around his neck, pulling herself even closer to his body. She felt Garrett move his body against hers, and she was weak with delight. When the kiss ended, Anna rested her head against Garrett's chest. "Why didn't you ever kiss me like that before?"

"You were never ready for it before."

"How will I live without you when you go back to California?"

"You don't have to."

"Please, Garrett, you know that I have to stay here for two more years. If you want me then, I'll come to you. I don't think I can be without you much longer than that."

Garrett looked at Anna in the moonlight. "Do you mean that? You will marry me in two years?"

"Yes, but you have to promise me something."

"What?"

"I don't want to have children right away. I want to help you on the ranch and I want to keep studying. I couldn't bear it if you made me stay in the house all the time and have your babies. I'd grow old and fat and you wouldn't love me anymore."

"I'll love you no matter what."

"Please, Garrett, it's important to me. I want to do something else for awhile. If we can't travel around the world together, then at least I can learn about the world and maybe even write about it."

"All right, I won't saddle you with children right away. But once we've got the ranch running smoothly, I want to have lots of children. I want at least three little girls, all of them to look like you."

Anna shook her head. "I can't believe we're talking like this. It seems like just yesterday when we were kids. Now we're talking about marriage and children. It doesn't seem possible."

"But it is possible. We've grown up, Anna."

"Garrett! Garrett, you out here?"

Garrett took Anna's hand. "There's Pa. We'd better be getting back inside. "Coming, Pa." He squeezed Anna's hand tightly. "I've got to talk business with Pa but I'll be back for a dance later." He kissed Anna on the cheek and walked toward the group of men who were standing together, her father among them. She saw Sally James and smiled. While she and Sally did not share many of the same beliefs or ideas, she liked Sally because she always had a good time no matter where she was.

"Anna, I do declare, you're getting prettier all the

time. I never realized you had so much up top before."

"Stop it, Sally. I see you're having fun. You've been completely surrounded by boys all evening."

"Yes, but there's no one here half as interesting as Garrett." Sally looked in Garrett's direction. "I tell you, Anna, you better hold onto him. He's getting more handsome all the time. One of these days, someone is going to come along and snatch him away from you."

"I don't own him, Sally. He's free to do as he pleases."

"You're always so logical, Anna. It drives me crazy." Sally looked around the garden. "There isn't anyone here even remotely interesting."

"Have you met Adam Rivers? He's Garrett's cousin from Boston."

"You don't say? Where is he?"

Anna looked around and pointed to Adam. "Over there, the tall, slim boy. He's very nice. A little snobby but nice."

Sally put her arm on Anna's and dragged her in Adam's direction. "Come on, Anna. You must introduce me. I need some new blood."

Anna approached Adam tentatively, touching him on the arm. "Excuse me, Adam. This is my friend Sally James. Sally, this is Adam Rivers."

Sally curtsied deeply. "Pleased to meet you, sir." She put her arm through his. "I'd just love to hear about Boston. I've always wanted to go there."

Anna smiled and shook her head as they walked off. She wished that she had Sally's confidence.

"Well, don't you look pretty this evening, little girl. Haven't seen you in a long time."

Anna froze at the sound of Tommy Leland's voice.

She had rarely seen him around anymore. Both he and Tim had quit school to work for their fathers. She turned around to face him. "I didn't know you were allowed to come to functions like this, Tommy. I'm surprised you even knew how to dress for the occasion."

"I see you dressed mighty fine for the evening. You're getting prettier and prettier, Anna. I bet you drive old Garrett crazy, don't you?"

"I don't have to listen to this." Anna started to walk away but Tommy grabbed her arm.

"What's wrong? The truth hurt? I bet you make his blood boil, and then you don't do anything about it." Tommy shook his head. "It's your own fault, you know. If you'd been giving him what he wanted all these years he wouldn't have to go to other girls for it."

"I don't know what you're talking about, and let go of my arm." Anna jerked her arm away.

"Do you actually think old Garrett's been faithful to you all this time? Why, hell, girl, he's had just about every girl in this county. Ask your friend, Sally. She'll tell you."

"I don't believe you."

"Ask her and then ask Garrett. And be sure to ask him about the little señoritas he had while he was in California. You see, Anna, Garrett is the kind of man who will never be satisfied with one woman. You better learn that right now."

Anna turned away from Tommy and walked through the garden to the food table. She went to the punch bowl and quickly got herself a cup of punch. Her hands were shaking as she brought the cup to her lips.

"Hi, Annie. You sure look pretty tonight."

Anna looked at the person standing beside her, and she smiled in relief. "Oh, Albert, it's so good to see you. I didn't think you were allowed to come to these socials."

"My father said it might be good for me to get to know some people around the county. But I really came because I knew you'd be here."

Anna put down the punch. "Albert, I need to talk to a real friend."

"Sure, Annie."

"Will you dance with me?"

"I don't know how to dance very well." Albert backed up a few steps.

Anna grabbed Albert's arm. "Come on, Albert, it's easy. Just take hold of my hand like this and put your other hand around my waist. That's right. Now we move in time to the music. That's good. You know how to dance, Albert."

Albert shook his head. "Why are you so nice, Annie? It's going to get you into trouble some day."

"That's what I want to talk to you about."

"What?"

"Remember a couple of years ago when Tommy and Tim beat you up so badly and they tried to hurt me? After it was over, you told me not to trust Garrett. You said he would hurt me. Do you still believe that?"

"Why are you asking me this now after all this time?"

"Garrett asked me to marry him tonight. He wants to take me back to California with him."

"No," Albert said quietly, shaking his head. "You're too young to get married, Annie. You're still just a girl."

"I know, Albert, that's what I told him."

177

"Oh, good."

"But I need to know something, Albert. I want you to be honest with me."

"I'll try."

"Has Garrett had other girlfriends besides me? Do you know, Albert?"

"He doesn't take me into his confidence, Annie. You know that. Garrett is the one you should be asking."

"But you must have heard things, Albert. Please, tell me the truth. I need to know."

Albert stopped moving suddenly. "Do you mind if we stop? I'm not very good at this." Albert walked to one of the benches and sat down. Anna sat down next to him. "Why are you asking me this, Annie? I don't want to hurt you."

"You do know something, don't you?"

"I've heard things."

"What've you heard?"

"I've heard that Garrett is still as wild as he used to be. He still hangs around with Tommy and Tim."

"What else?"

"They and some other guys had an old shack someplace. They took girls there and had wild parties. But even if Garrett did that, it doesn't mean he doesn't love you, Annie. It's normal behavior for a young man to act wild with other women." Albert shrugged his thin shoulders. "At least that's what I'm told."

"You don't do things like that, do you, Albert?"

"Let's face it, Annie, I'm not like all those other guys. I'm different."

"Yes, and that's what makes you so special." Anna leaned over and kissed Albert on the cheek. She stood up.

"Annie, where are you going?"

"I have something to do, Albert." Anna walked through the garden to where Sally was dancing cheek-to-cheek with Adam. She walked up behind Sally and took her arm. "I need to talk to you, Sally."

"Anna, what's the matter with you. Can't you see I'm dancing with Adam right now?" She started to turn back to Adam but Anna jerked Sally away.

"I need to talk to you *now*, Sally."

"Oh, all right. I'll be right back, Adam. Don't you go away." Sally pulled her arm away from Anna's rough grasp. "What in hell's the matter with you, girl? Can't you see I've got something good going with Adam?"

Anna stopped, confronting Sally. "Did you have something good going with Garrett, too, Sally? Is it still going on between you?"

"I don't know what you're talking about. Garrett and I are just friends."

"Cut the bull, Sally. I want the truth and I want it now, or so help me God, I'll beat it out of you."

Sally looked around her, acutely uncomfortable. "All right, all right. Keep your voice down." Sally walked over to one of the trees. "Yes, Garrett and I have been together."

"More than once?"

"Yes, more than once."

"Has he been with other girls, too?"

"I don't know. I don't keep a record book."

"Damn it, Sally, answer me!"

"I've never seen him, mind you, but I've heard he's pretty wild. Supposedly he and Tommy Leland and some of the boys had an old shack where they took girls. Your Garrett is not an angel, Anna."

Anna stepped closer to Sally, her face very close. "And what about you, Sally? I thought you were

179

my friend.''

"I am your friend. Garrett doesn't care for me. He loves you and he always has.''

"What's the matter with you? Doesn't it bother you that you went behind my back like that?''

Sally shrugged her shoulders. "A little, I guess. But I just figured that Garrett would have his fun, then marry you and settle down.'' Sally touched Anna gently. "Look, Anna, you're just not the kind of girl a boy does those things with. You're the kind of girl a man marries.''

"You mean I'm the kind of girl a man marries and continues to lie to.'' Anna looked across the garden to the circle of men where Garrett was standing. "Well, I won't be lied to anymore.''

"Anna, don't. He'll settle down after a while. These little flings don't mean anything. A man is supposed to sow some oats before he marries.''

"If you really believe that, Sally, you're a lot more stupid than I ever thought possible.'' Anna strode across the garden to the group of men. She smiled engagingly, walking up to Garrett. "Excuse me, gentlemen, can I borrow Garrett for this next dance?''

All of the men smiled and nodded assuringly. Garrett took Anna's arm and led her to the dance area but when he reached for her she pulled away.

"What's the matter, Anna?''

"How stupid do you think I am, Garrett?''

"What're you talking about?'' He tried to touch her but she pulled away.

"Did you think you could play this game forever and never get caught?''

"What the hell are you talking about, Anna?''

Anna threw him an angry look and stomped out of the walled garden to the tree where only a short time before they had made their declarations of love to

180

each other. "You know something, Garrett? I've loved you from the first time I saw you in school. When you smiled at me that day I felt as if my heart were being ripped from me. You were my friend, my very best friend. We talked about everything together. I let you know my innermost thoughts and feelings. And you betrayed me."

"What are you talking about, Anna? I've never betrayed you."

"What about Sally James? Or what about the shack that you and Tommy Leland take girls to? How many girls did you have in California, Garrett? My God, I thought I knew you."

"Anna, it's not what you think."

"What is it then? Tell me it's all a lie. Please, tell me it's a lie."

Garrett looked at Anna and shook his head. "I can't do that. I told you a long time ago that I didn't deserve to have a friend like you but you wouldn't believe me. You kept trying to make me into something that I wasn't."

"So that makes it right? It's all right that you've lied to me all of these years?"

"I lied because I didn't want to hurt you."

"And did you lie about loving me, too?"

"I've never lied about that, Anna. I've never loved anyone the way I love you. I meant it when I said I want to take you to California with me. I still want to marry you."

"Marry you? I wouldn't marry you now if my life depended on it." Anna started to pull away but Garrett held her to him. In spite of her effort not to, she began to cry. "Why did you lie to me, Garrett? I feel like such a fool. I thought we had something so special."

"We do have something special, Anna. We do." He

pulled her close to him, kissing the top of her head. "Give me another chance, Anna. I love you; I don't want to lose you."

"No, I can't." She tried to pull away but Garrett held her, and part of her didn't fight him. She buried her face in his chest.

"I'll go back to California and give you some time to think. I'm going to make something of myself out there, Anna. You'll be proud of me. I'll make you proud of me."

"How do I know if I can ever trust you again? I can't live a lie."

"I'll never lie to you again. I lied to you because I didn't want to lose what we had together. I know it was wrong. I'm sorry, Anna."

Anna pulled back, wiping the tears from her eyes. "We'll see what happens, Garrett. Maybe after two years, you will have found someone else. Someone who can please you the way I cannot."

"Don't say that. The very thought of you excites me, Anna."

"Then why didn't you come to me? Maybe I would have wanted to be with you."

"No, I didn't want that. You're too good. The only way I'll ever have you is after we're married."

"And if we do get married, how many more women will you have?" Anna took a deep breath. "Let's just see what happens in the next two years. Maybe by then you'll know your true feelings for me."

"I already know my true feelings for you, Anna."

"But when I marry, I want my husband to love me and only me. You better think about that, Garrett."

"Anna—"

"I don't think we should see each other before you go. I'll write to you in California when I've had time to think. Take care of yourself, Garrett." Anna looked at the boy she had always considered her best friend, the boy whom she had always loved. She was torn: Part of her despised him but part of her understood him. She walked to him and touched his chest lightly. "I will miss you, Garrett. It won't be the same without you." She kissed him on the cheek, feeling as if her childhood was gone forever.

Chapter VII

Nathan picked at the wall, his forearms burning from the long hours. Tong and he were sure the vein was here. They just had to find it. He wiped the sweat from his face and kept on working. Rocks and gravel rolled down the side of the mine as he picked. He looked around him and heard sand falling through some of the boards. Something was wrong.

"Tong!" he screamed, standing up and walking toward the other end of the mine. "Tong, are you all right?" Nathan picked up the lantern and headed toward the opposite end of the mine when he heard a rumbling sound. The boards overhead began to creak and shake, and dirt fell all around him. The very ground beneath his feet began to move. "Jesus," he muttered to himself, running through the twisted maze. "Tong, you have to get out. It's an earthquake! Get out, Tong!" Nathan ran toward the area where Tong was working but was forced to stop. Pieces of rock and board came flying down. He always knew there was a possibility of a cave-in but it had never seemed real to him. Even after his brush with death, he felt himself to be immortal. Now he knew how ridiculous he had been to think that. "Tong!"

Nathan kept running deeper into the mine shaft, knowing all the while that he might never get out. He saw the light from Tong's lantern. He saw the old man crumpled on the ground. "Tong, are you all right? Can you walk?"

Tong coughed. "You must go, Nathan. You must save yourself."

"Stand up, Tong. I'm going to get you out of here." Nathan pulled the old man to his feet just as the walls of the tunnel started collapsing. "What about the other way out, Tong? Can we still get out that way?"

"Is very dangerous. Could be closed off."

"Well, we can't get back the other way now. That's our only chance." Nathan hoisted Tong onto his shoulder, grabbing the lantern from the ground. He continued on through the tunnel. He had been to this end of it only once before. Normally, they stayed closer to the middle because that was where Tong was convinced there was a deep vein of gold. Nathan held the lantern up in front of his face as rocks and dust fell around him. He couldn't see so he laid Tong on the ground.

"We will never get out this way. Why did you not listen to me and save yourself?" Tong coughed on the dusty air.

"You're just a might impatient, aren't you, Tong? You're the one who told me to learn patience."

"This is different. You are being foolish. Do you think I will think you are a great hero because you sacrificed yourself for me?" Tong waved his hand in the air. "I will not forgive you for this if you die."

Nathan turned to look at Tong in the dim light of the tunnel. He shook his head angrily. "That's what I hate about you people. You think you have all the answers. Have you ever stopped to think that there are others of us who like to think for ourselves? I don't need you to tell me what to do all the time, Tong."

"Then why is it you have been with me for almost ten years? I think you are very used to being told what to do."

"You know why I've stayed so long."

"Then humor a foolish old man and tell me again."

"I want to help you realize your dream. I know there's gold here, and I want to help you find it. I want to help you help your people in China."

"And you want to help yourself."

"Of course I want to help myself. I want to be rich, too." Nathan turned back toward the tunnel. "I don't have time to sit here and talk with you, old man. I'm going to try and find a way out of here before we suffocate to death." Nathan picked up the lantern and inched his way through the tunnel. He took the pick from his belt and picked at the small piles of dirt that lay in front of him. He heard a rumbling sound again and knew that the quake hadn't quite settled. He braced himself for another shock, leaning against the wall, covering his head. It was over in seconds, and more dirt was pushed into the tunnel. He held the lantern up in front of him but he couldn't see anything. The tunnel was filled with dirt and rocks. "Damn!" he exclaimed loudly. He ran back to Tong, making sure the old man was all right. Tong was coughing. "Are you all right?"

"I'm fine. The tunnel is closed, yes?"

"Yeah. I'm going back the other way to see if we can get out."

"Do not waste your energy, boy. If it is our time we must not fight it."

"Damn you, don't you give me any of your philosophical crap. I won't give up that easily. If you want to lay here and die, you go ahead. I'm going to find us a way out of here." Nathan went back toward the tunnel entrance but his way was blocked immediately. Boards, rocks, and dirt had fallen into the tunnel blocking the way. He tried to climb through them but he couldn't. Dust filled the air. He started coughing and took off his bandana, tying it around his mouth and nose. He went back in the direction he had come. He didn't stop to check on Tong; he was determined to get them out of the tunnel, no matter what Tong thought. When Nathan reached the area that was filled with dirt, he set the lantern on the ground and began digging with his hands. The more he dug, the more dirt came from the sides of the tunnel and filled the space. He looked around him. "There has to be a way out of here." He went back to Tong. "How far from here to the end of the tunnel?"

"I do not know for sure."

"Think, damn it!"

Tong lifted his head, looking more frail than he ever had before. "Were you difficult as a child?"

Nathan squatted next to Tong. "I probably was but please answer my question."

"I bet you were a joy to your parents as well. Very bright." Tong nodded his head. "You must see your parents when you get out of here, Nathan."

"I will, Tong. I will."

Tong reached out and touched Nathan, grasping his hand firmly. "Promise me."

"I promise you, Tong."

"Good, good. It is not good to be separated from family for too long for whatever reasons. Family are the only people on this earth who will accept you unconditionally."

Nathan gently wiped some dirt from the old man's

188

face. "And some friends."

"Yes, and some friends." Tong closed his eyes. "From here to the end of the tunnel it is approximately two hundred feet. But it was not possible to get through it before. How do you propose to do it now?"

Nathan thought for a moment. "That means that from where I got to the end, it's probably only a hundred feet." He chewed on his lower lip. "I'm going to dig us out, Tong. It may take some time, but we're getting out of here."

"One hundred feet is a long way when you must crawl on your hands and knees and use your fingers as a shovel. It is too dangerous."

"We don't have any other choice, Tong. It can't be that hard to get to. That's where we're getting our air from. The other end is sealed up too tightly." Nathan took the extra bandana out of his back pocket and tied it around Tong's nose and mouth. "Keep that on. It'll help some." He started to turn away but Tong grabbed his hand.

"You are a good man, Nathan. Unlike many of your kind, the true meaning of honor has not eluded you."

Nathan nodded his thanks and headed off toward the end of the shaft. He looked back at Tong one more time, praying that he could get the old man out to see the light of day once more.

"Why in hell do you have to drive this damned thing so slow? I could've been there and back by now!" Joe exclaimed loudly.

Chin's expression never changed. "You most probably did not make a good slave, Joseph. It does not seem possible that you would pick cotton all day long while someone stood over you with a whip."

"You're right, I didn't make a good slave. That's why I bought my freedom and got the hell out of that godforsaken place."

"You like being a rich man better?"

"No, Chin, I like being a free man most of all."

"But money gives you power, does it not?"

"You should know about that."

Chin nodded, loosely holding the reins of the horses. "What time is it? Are we in time for lunch?"

Joe took out his pocket watch and snapped it open. "Yep, they should be coming out anytime soon. Why don't you stop this rickety old thing and let me out. I can't take it anymore." Joe jumped down off the wagon and walked toward the mine. He went to the entrance. It was completely covered with boards and rocks. "Chin, get over here. There's been a cave-in," Joe yelled. He started pulling boards and rocks away but the more debris he pulled away, the more fell into the opening.

"They are inside?"

Joe heard Chin's voice behind him. "You don't see them anyplace else, do you?" Joe looked around. "It'll take us forever to clear this out. They'll be dead by then. Is there another way into the tunnel?"

"Yes, it comes out on the other side of the hill. But it was closed many years ago. Tong never used it."

"Yeah, well he may have had to use it today. It may be their only way out. Show me where it is."

Joe followed Chin up the hill to the other side. They walked down to an old mine opening that was completely covered with dirt and rocks. Joe started picking up rocks and throwing them to the side. "Go back to the shack, Chin. Bring me a shovel and a pick. And water in case we find them." Joe moved away as many of the boards as he could, then sorted through the dirt for large rocks. When Chin returned, Joe took the shovel and began digging. He dug for over an hour and had made very little progress. He stopped, leaning on his shovel. "There's got to be a better way to do this."

"Perhaps if we wet the dirt?"

"What?"

"If we could wet the dirt, it would not fall back into the tunnel. It would take us a long time but it might help until we can actually get inside."

"It's gonna take a lot of water. How are we going to get all that water up here?"

"Tong has many buckets in his shack. We simply fill the buckets and put them in the wagon and bring them here. We wet the dirt and go back for more. It is worth a try."

"Sure, why not?" Joe agreed.

The two men worked for hours, filling buckets, emptying them, and refilling and bringing them back to the tunnel entrance. As soon as the ground surrounding the entrance had been well saturated with the water, Joe began to dig. This time the dirt stayed in place. When he got down deep enough and the dirt was dry again, they did the same thing with the water. By sunset, Joe had dug his way into the tunnel entrance.

"Perhaps you should rest, Joseph. You have worked hard all day."

"I'll rest as soon as I find Nate and Tong. Why don't you go get me some lanterns from the shack and set them up around here. I'm going to keep digging till I find 'em, Chin."

Nathan felt the cool dirt against his cheek. He was tired, and his fingers were bleeding and sore. He had no idea how long he had been digging. It seemed like days. The only thing he knew for sure was that there was air coming in from this side of the tunnel. He just had to get to it. He hadn't seen Tong in hours. He hoped that the old man was still alive. He thought for a moment what a strange way this was for it to end, here in a dark tunnel, trying to crawl his way out to the light. The light from the lantern was growing dim; the fuel was getting low. Nathan forced himself to get on his hands and knees and start digging again. He found a board that he used to push the dirt behind him as he dug but he still had to use his hands to move the dirt. He stopped suddenly as dust fell all around him. He tensed his body, ready for another quake, ready for the end. But the end didn't come. Instead, Nathan heard a noise. It sounded like someone digging. He sat up. "Hello!" Nathan screamed. "Is anybody there?" He began frantically digging with his hands, throwing dirt back through his legs. "Hello!" He yelled again and listened. The digging stopped.

"Nate? That you, boy?" Joe's voice traveled down the tunnel to Nathan.

Nathan laughed loudly, banging his fist in the dirt. "Yeah, Joe, it's me. It's Nathan."

"You hang on, boy. We'll get you out of there real soon. You just hang on."

Nathan breathed a sigh of relief and turned around, crawling back through the tunnel to Tong. He put his hand on the old man's shoulder and gently shook him. "Tong, we're going to be all right. We're getting out of here."

Tong slowly opened his eyes and looked at Nathan. "You were right it seems. It was not our time to die."

"Damned right." Nathan sat down next to Tong,

192

taking the old man's hand in his. "How do you feel, Tong? Are you all right?"

"I am well enough. I have been meditating. It keeps my mind from thinking about my stomach."

"Yeah, I know what you mean. I could eat a horse right now." Nathan wiped some of the dust from Tong's clothes, brushing his hands against his pants. Something caught his eyes, and he lifted the lantern up. The dust was very fine and shiny. "Tong, look at this." He pointed to the shiny gold particles.

Tong bent forward, examining the dust. "It is probably pyrite. We have found it before."

"But not here, not in this place." Nathan crawled over to the opposite wall, running his fingers along the dirt. He held the lantern up. "Jesus, Tong, I think you better take a look at this."

Tong slowly moved to the area where Nathan was looking. He got up very close to the wall, running his fingers over the shiny gold particles. "Hand me your pick," he said to Nathan. Nathan handed him the pick. Tong chipped at the wall until he had dislodged a piece of rock. He held it in his hand and examined it. He put it on the ground and chipped away at it. Gold chunks appeared throughout. He looked at Nathan. "It seems we have found our gold, boy."

"Really? This is it?" Nathan gave out a loud whooping sound, causing dirt to fall around their heads. He shrugged his shoulders. "Be just our luck to find the gold and have the whole damn place fall down around us."

"Have patience, Nathan. You have been willing to dig us out of here. We will find a way to get the gold out."

"I can't believe we really did it. We could be rich men, Tong."

193

"I do not wish to be rich. I only wish to help my family." Tong smiled. "I am glad for you, Nathan. This is what you wanted."

"Yes, I'm finally going to have the money I need to get Driscoll."

"You are still sure that is what you want to do?"

"There is nothing else I can do, Tong. He killed my brother. Should I turn my back and forget it ever happened?"

"Of course you cannot forget that it ever happened but you can go on with your life. You are a good man, Nathan. The most dangerous path of all is the one called revenge. Do not let it destroy you."

"It won't destroy me, Tong. But it sure as hell will destroy Driscoll. Don't worry about me, Tong. I'll be all right."

"And your parents, you will see them?"

"Yes, as soon as I've taken care of Driscoll, I'll go to my parents. It's been so long, Tong. Do you think they'll be glad to see me?"

"A parent is forever glad to see a child. Trust me, I know this."

"Do you have children, Tong?"

"I have no children but I had a father. He and I were separated for many years. We had a disagreement over something that lasted for over twenty years."

"But you saw him again?"

"I saw him on his deathbed. I went to him at my mother's request. When he saw me come into the room he held out his hand to me. It was as if we had never been apart." Tong blinked his eyes. "Your parents will welcome you back, Nathan. You will bring them as much joy now as you did when you were a boy."

"Thanks, Tong." Nathan clenched and unclenched

his fists. "It's been a long time, Tong. I've read everything I could. I've studied about places in the world I've never been to. I've taught myself to speak three different languages. Now I have to go to San Francisco and pretend that I'm a man of the world. I'm not sure if I can do it."

"You *are* a man of the world, Nathan. Even though you have not traveled you have learned about the world. You have learned about it through books, and you have learned about it through me, Chin, and Joseph. That will be the easiest part for you. The hard part will be willingly destroying another human being."

"Don't lecture me about it anymore, Tong. I'm doing what I have to do."

"Perhaps."

"Why do you always say that?"

"What will you gain by destroying this man? What good will it do? Will it make you a better person? Will it bring your brother back?" Tong shook his head. "It will only keep you separated from your parents that much longer. I think you are making a mistake."

"I know, you've told me enough times." Nathan picked up a handful of dirt and threw it across the tunnel. "You might be right, though. It's been almost ten years. I want to see my parents. I have a sister I've never even seen."

"Then take your gold and help your family with it. Repay your father's debt to Joseph and go home. Be the son to your parents that they have not had all of these years." Tong took Nathan's hand in his. He rubbed it gently. "Do this for me, Nathan. It would make me very happy."

Nathan looked at the frail hand that was holding his, and he nodded. "All right, Tong, I'll go home."

"You will give up this idea of revenge?"

"Yeah, I guess Driscoll's not worth it."

"Thank you, Nathan. You have made me very happy. I will die a contented man."

"Don't die on me yet, Tong. We've got to get out of here first."

"I will not die yet, Nathan. First, I want to see you reunited with your parents."

"Yeah—" Nathan stopped. "Do you hear that? I think they've broken through." Nathan crawled to the end of the tunnel. He was about halfway when he saw light shining through. "Joe!" Nathan crawled to the end and put his hand through the hole. He felt a firm grasp on the other side.

"Well, it's about time, boy. I thought we'd never get you out."

"It's good to hear your voice, Joe." Nathan held onto Joe's hand, not willing to give it up. He felt the warm sting of tears in his eyes. "I'm going home, Joe. I'm ready to go home."

"You just hang on a little while longer, and I'll take you home myself. Hang on, Nate. Hang on!"

Nathan looked out the window of his bedroom at the panoramic view of the city. He saw the blue water of the bay and the ships sailing in and out of the harbor. He looked down the neat tree-lined street at the lampposts that stood in front of every house. He took a deep breath, enjoying the fresh sea breeze that blew in. It felt good to be back to civilization, and it felt even better to know that he was going to see his parents soon. There was a knock on the door and Joe entered.

"Hey, you look real good in those clothes, boy. Just like a rich, successful businessman."

Nathan smiled broadly. "Thanks, Joe. You are going to invest that gold I gave you, aren't you? I want to make sure it's doing something instead of sitting around."

"Don't you worry about that none. I'll make sure you wind up with more money than you started with. Speaking of money, I don't want or need the money you gave me."

"Pa wanted you to have it. It was his last payment to you plus a little extra. That's part of the reason I worked all those years, Joe. I wanted to be able to pay you back for Pa."

"That's real good of you, Nate. Well, you ready to head on down to Chinatown? I'm sure old Chin and Tong are ready to see you."

"Yeah, I can't wait. They're like family to me, Joe. Just like you."

Joe pulled Nathan to him and hugged him fiercely. "You may be twenty-six years old and all grown up but I'm still gonna hug you when I feel like it. Let's go."

They left the house and walked down the street. The clang of a cable car caught Nathan's attention, and he couldn't help but think how much Berto would have enjoyed riding on one. Joe motioned Nathan after him, and they jumped up onto the car that took them through the busy city. Nathan noticed that there were many more buildings and many more multistoried buildings. Cable cars, carriages, omnibuses, and horse-drawn cars were everywhere. The city had grown immensely since Nathan had last seen it.

When the driver stopped, Joe paid him and nodded to Nathan. They jumped off. Nathan watched as the cable car continued on past him. He shook his head. Nothing stayed the same.

It had been almost ten years since Nathan had seen Chinatown. It had become even more crowded and busy. There were more stores and more buildings crammed into small spaces, and the number of people had seemed to triple. They were assaulted from all sides by vendors as they walked down the street, but Nathan and Joe just waved them away. They walked into Chin's butcher shop and through the back door. Joe followed Nathan up the back stairs to the room where Chin lived. Nathan knocked lightly on the door and waited for Chin to open it. Chin opened the door and bowed, waving Nathan and Joe into the room. Tong was seated cross-legged on the floor. There was tea waiting for them all. Nathan and Joe sat down.

"You look very prosperous," Chin said as he poured the tea.

"You have cut your hair," Tong observed aloud.

"What do you think?"Nathan smiled at Tong.

"You look like a boy. You will age well."

Nathan shrugged his shoulders. "How do you feel, Tong? Are you stronger?"

"Do not concern yourself with me, Nathan. When do you plan to leave for Arizona?"

"In about a week. I want to spend some time here with Joe and Larissa first, then Joe is going to go back with me." He smiled broadly. "It will be a great reunion."

"I am pleased for you, Nathan."

Chin handed the tea to each of the men. "I would like us to drink to friendship and the great love that we all have for this boy." Chin held his cup up and each of the others followed.

Nathan looked at each of the men and marveled how each one of them had helped and loved him. Each one of them had been more than a friend. "I want to thank each of you. I'm not sure I could have made it through the last ten years without any of you. Chin, you saved my life and gave me the will to go on where there was none. Tong, you have taught me so many things over the years but most of all you have taught me patience and caring. And Joe, you have loved me since the moment I was born, and you haven't stopped loving me since. Thank you all." The men all sipped at their tea and Nathan spoke again. "What will you do with your money, Tong? Will you go back to China?"

Tong held the cup in his thin, frail hands, as if letting the warmth seep into his body. "I thought I would never go back to China. There were so many problems when I left. But I think I would like to see my homeland once more before I die."

"You're not going to die for a long time," Nathan said confidently.

"Do you know something that I do not?"

Nathan shook his head. "You're just too stubborn to die, that's all. Take your trip to China then come back and visit me in Arizona."

"I would like that, Nathan. I would be most pleased to meet your parents." Tong reached into his pocket. "I want you to have something, Nathan. In case we do not meet again."

"Don't talk like that, Tong. We'll see each other again."

"Please, Nathan, it is important to me. You have become very special to me. You stayed with me for many years, and you helped me realize a dream. Without you, I would have never found the gold."

Nathan held up his hand. "No, I don't want anything from you, Tong. The gold was enough."

"This does not have great monetary worth but its worth to me is incalculable." Tong uncurled his

199

hand. "Take it, please."

Nathan took the gift from Tong's hand. It was a tiny dragon. It was of dark green jade, and it shone brightly, its onyx eyes staring out from its green body. "It's beautiful, Tong. I've never seen anything like it."

"Do you remember what I told you about the dragon and what it means to the Chinese people?"

"Yes, you said it brings good fortune."

"That is correct."

"But I've already found good fortune, Tong."

"It does not mean that kind of good fortune, Nathan. It means the emotional or spiritual kind." Tong was silent for a moment, his eyes staring into some unknown place. "Tai Shan is the mythical home of the benevolent Green Dragon. He is the lord of springs and streams. It is said that Confucious himself climbed Tai Shan and was inspired at the summit. I climbed Tai Shan to confront my own demons." Tong was silent. "It is a beautiful walk. There are wooded paths and stone steps all along the way, but it gets more and more difficult. One passes through three arches. The first is 'First Gate of Heaven.' Then comes 'Where Horses Turn Back.' Then 'Gate of Heaven' begins the steps that rise almost vertically up Tai Shan. When I reached the summit, I still had to walk another mile along the crest. It is impossible to describe its beauty. There are inscriptions on stones all along the way. The last one reads 'Enter With Awe This Region of Beauty.' I sat atop Tai Shan for a time, and I felt the dragon enter my body. I was able to confront my demons. I was able to go home again." Tong looked at Nathan, his old eyes as clear as a child's. "I want you to have this dragon, Nathan. My father gave it to me when I climbed Tai Shan, and now I want to give it to you.

200

Perhaps it will help you to confront your own demons."

"I can't take it, Tong." Nathan offered it to Tong but he refused.

"You are refusing my gift?"

"Yes."

"I do not know what to say. I feel deeply dishonored."

"Tong—"

Chin reached for Nathan's wrist. "You cannot refuse Tong's gift. He is giving you the thing that means the most to him in all the world. If you refuse it, it means this thing has no meaning anymore. You cannot do this to him."

"But his father gave it to him. I can't take it away from him."

"You are not taking it away from him. Tong is giving it to you. There is a difference."

Nathan looked down at the shiny green figure and realized the depth of feeling Tong must have for him to give up something so valuable. He closed his fist. "I am sorry, Tong. I didn't realize this was your custom. I am very honored that you would give me such a gift. I will treasure it always."

Tong looked at Chin and Joe and nodded approvingly, a slight smile appearing on his face. "Good. Chin, do you have any of that plum wine? I have a certain thirst."

"Yes, I have a bottle. Nathan, would you help me?" Chin walked to the cupboard and took out the glasses, setting them on a tray. "I, too, have a gift for you, Nathan."

"Chin, I don't want any more gifts. I have nothing for you and Tong."

"We do not want anything from you. Here." Chin handed Nathan a book.

201

Nathan looked at the brown leather cover and smiled, looking at Chin. "How did you remember? That was so long ago."

"I will never forget. You were just sixteen years old. You had just lost your brother. You were recovering from severe wounds, and you thought you had lost your parents. You kept talking about your mother and how much she liked to read. You said that someday you would like to get her an original of this book. You said it was special to her because of her French uncle. Now you can give this to her when you see her."

Nathan ran his hand over the smooth leather and shook his head. *A Tale of Two Cities.* It's beautiful, Chin." Nathan held the book to his chest. "I'll never forget you, Chin. Ever." He hugged the small man, knowing that Chin was uncomfortable at such open displays of affection but nevertheless showing him how he felt.

"Hey, Tong wants to know where the wine is."

"Yes, it is coming." Chin picked up the tray and brought it to the floor. He handed everyone a glass.

"This time it's my turn to make a toast." Joe held his glass up. He looked around him. "We have sitting here two Chinese, one black man and a half-breed. Here's hoping that people in the future can get along as well as we all do. Here's hoping that when people look at other people, they will look past the color of their skin to what's inside. Here's to freedom." The four men clinked glasses. "Well, what do you say I buy you all dinner in one of them fancy Chinese restaurants. I'm mighty hungry."

"I respectfully decline, Joseph. I promised Tong that I would let him see the fights tonight."

"Well, we could stay and go later," Nathan said.

"No." Chin's voice was hard. "You must never come in there again. Driscoll still comes in. You

202

cannot take the chance."

"I'm not going to do anything, Chin. I already promised Tong."

"That does not matter. You are going home. We cannot take that chance."

"He's right, Nate. Let's just say our good-byes and get on out of here. You can come back again before you leave."

"No, I'll just say my good-byes here." Nathan stood up, walking over to Tong. He carefully helped the old man to his feet, handing him the cane he had just recently acquired. "Thank you for the gift, Tong. I will treasure it always. Perhaps someday if I ever have a son, I can pass it on to him."

Tong nodded his head and smiled. "That is good. You are a good boy, Nathan."

Nathan reached out and hugged Tong. "Have a safe trip to China. I hope it's as you remember it."

"It will be."

Nathan walked to Chin and held out his hand. "I know you don't like to shake hands, Chin, but it is an American custom." Reluctantly Chin took Nathan's hand. Nathan put his other hand on top of Chin's. "Thank you for my life, Chin. I don't think I can ever repay you for that. But please, let me know if you ever need me for anything."

"I will, Nathan. Take care of yourself. I would like to see your children someday."

Nathan smiled and walked out of the small room, knowing that he was leaving a part of himself there. One part of his life was over, and now he was beginning another. It was up to him how he lived the rest of it. It was up to him to make it a life that both Chin and Tong would be proud of.

Joe and Nathan sat in the kitchen eating sandwiches and drinking milk. They had already had their share of whiskey that evening. They had gone out to dinner and then come home and spent the evening with Larissa. Now, after too much whiskey, Larissa made them sandwiches, poured them milk and went to bed.

"She's a nice woman, Joe. How did you ever get someone so pretty to marry you?"

"Don't rightly know. Surprises the hell out of me sometimes."

"It would be nice to know a good woman like Larissa. Aside from my mother and Larissa, I haven't known many women."

"Hey, boy, you mean to tell me you haven't—"

Nathan almost choked on the milk he had in his mouth. "What do you think I did up in the mountains all that time? Read?"

"Well, as far as I could see there weren't many women around. In fact, I didn't see any women."

"But they were there. Wagonloads of women would come up there and visit the miners."

"Ah, you mean prostitutes. Hell, boy, there's nothing wrong with that. That's a real good way to learn about women."

"Except it's real hard to fall in love with one."

"I did."

"I'm sorry, Joe. I didn't mean anything by it."

"I know you didn't. Well, it's time you got yourself introduced to some fancy young ladies."

"I won't be here long enough for that."

"You'll be here long enough." Joe stood up. "How about another sandwich. I'm still hungry."

"No thanks, I'm full. In fact, I think I'll head on up to bed."

"Okay. I'll see you in the morning. It's good to have you here, Nate."

"Thanks, Joe. It's good to be here." Nathan started out of the kitchen but stopped when he heard the kitchen door open. It was Charley, running into the room, obviously out of breath.

"Hey, Charley, what you doing home so soon? I thought this was your night out on the town."

"Mister Joe, there has been a terrible accident."

"What is it, Charley?"

"Chinese man has been killed. Old man in Chin's."

Nathan stepped forward. "Who was it, Charley? What was his name?"

Charley looked from Joe to Nathan. "His name was Tong."

"No," Nathan uttered. "Are you sure?"

"Yes. He friend of Chin's."

"What happened, Charley?"

"Can I have drink, Mister Joe? I run all of the way."

Joe poured Charley a glass of whiskey. "Sit down, Charley. Now, tell us what happened."

"We were at the fights in Chin's. Everything was going well. I win lots of money tonight. We all have good time. Then the rich white man and his body-guards come." Charley looked at Nathan. "The same white man that killed your brother."

Nathan looked at Joe. "Driscoll." He sat down at the table across from Charley. "Then what happened, Charley?"

"Tong had been betting well all night. When this white man comes Tong bet a lot of money that white man lose. He did lose and get very angry. He tell Tong to bet again, that this time his bird would win. But it did not. He start to push Tong around but Tong not try to fight back. White man hit him hard and knock him down. Chin and some others try to

205

help but the man's bodyguards step in with their guns. Driscoll beat Tong to death, then he leave with his bodyguards. It was terrible thing."

"Jesus," Nathan said softly, taking the jade dragon from his pocket. Tong had never gotten to go home after all, and it was because of Driscoll. Driscoll. He stood up. "I'm going down there, Joe. You want to come?"

"Yeah, let's go." Joe patted Charley on the back. "Thanks, Charley."

Joe and Nathan grabbed their coats and went around back to the carriage house. Quickly they hooked up the horses to the carriage. They went through the deserted late-night streets. When they reached Chinatown, Nathan jumped off the carriage and ran into the back of Chin's store. The room where the fights were held was empty. Nathan ran up the back stairs to Chin's room. He threw open the door. Chin was sitting on the floor, washing Tong's face. He didn't look up.

"I am glad you have come, Nathan." He continued washing Tong.

Nathan knelt next to Tong, taking one of his lifeless hands in his. "Damn it, Chin, why did you let it happen? Why did you let Tong bet against Driscoll?"

"I had men there to protect us but Driscoll's men had weapons. I was very foolish."

"Why the hell did you even let Driscoll in here? Damn it!" Nathan rubbed Tong's hand. "He didn't even get to see China again."

"I am sorry, Nathan. Now I have been the cause of two deaths in your family. First your brother, now Tong."

"It's not your fault, Chin. It's Driscoll's. He'll pay for this."

"No, you cannot. You promised Tong."

"That was before Driscoll murdered him. I can't let that man get away with this, Chin. It's not right. He has to pay. He has to answer to someone."

Joe came into the room taking off his hat and kneeling next to Nathan. "I'm real sorry, boy. I know how much he meant to you."

"Will you help me, Joe?"

"I'll help you with anything I can."

"Will you help me get Driscoll?"

Joe looked at Tong, nodding slowly. "Yes, I'll help you. I know you'll do it without my help anyway. Are you sure this is what you want? Old Tong wouldn't have wanted you to do this."

"I'm doing what I have to do, Joe. This time Driscoll will pay." Nathan turned to Chin. "Don't say anything to me, Chin. Nobody will talk me out of it this time."

"I will say nothing to you, Nathan. I agree that this man must pay for what he has done to your brother and to Tong. But you must be very careful. He is an extremely dangerous man, even more powerful than before."

"I still don't understand why you kept letting Driscoll in here, Chin. The guy is obviously crazy."

"I wanted to watch him. It was the only way I could keep an eye on him. But I was wrong. I should have killed him the night he hurt you and murdered your brother."

"Don't worry, Chin. He'll pay." Nathan stood up and walked to the little window that looked out on the bay. "I'm going to have to move out of your house, Joe. I'll move in somewhere else, rent a house maybe."

"Why can't you stay at our place? I can introduce you around."

"No. I don't want anyone to know we're friends. I

don't want you hurt, too."

"I'm not afraid of Driscoll, Nate."

"I know you're not but I couldn't take it if something happened to you or Larissa because of me. I'm going to have to change my name for awhile until this is over. I need something that sounds rich and impressive."

Joe thought a moment. "How about Steven Randall?"

"How did you come up with that?"

"When I was a boy on the plantation, my master's son had a friend who visited him from England. He came from a very wealthy family. I think there were even a couple of princes in his family somewhere."

"I can't use his name, Joe. What if he were to come to San Francisco?"

"He can't come to San Francisco, Nate. He's dead. Got killed in a hunting accident. So as far as anyone around here is concerned, you're Steven Randall from England, but you've been living in the States for a long time now. You have lots of money, and you're looking for good investments."

"That's good, Joe. I like it." He looked at his dark skin and laughed. "They might wonder what an Englishman is doing with such dark skin."

"Just tell people you've been traveling in the West, riding your horse. Getting a taste of the wild life. They'll love it."

Nathan looked over at Chin, who was still holding Tong in his lap. Nathan walked over and knelt next to Chin. "What can I do?"

"You can do nothing. I want you to leave and not come back until this thing is over. Is best for you not to be seen here. If you need me for anything, you send word with Charley. Go now. We will be together soon."

"What about Tong?"

"I will see that he gets a proper burial. Do not worry. I will be thinking about you. I will find out how you are from Charley."

"Take care, Chin. And if Driscoll comes in here again, stay away from him. You hear me?"

"I understand. I wish you good fortune, Nathan. Remember, those of us with twin roots sometimes become the strongest trees. Go now."

Nathan adjusted his tie, picked up his hat and walked out of the room. He walked down the hall, tipping his hat to a young woman and her mother who were quite obviously taken with the good-looking blond-haired young man. He stepped into the elevator that took him seven floors down. He went to the desk clerk and told him he would be out for the day, and he crossed the lobby. He smiled and nodded to people as he passed them, never knowing if they might somehow be helpful to him. When he was on the street, he looked back at the imposing facade of the Palace Hotel.

The desk clerk told him that every room had a fireplace, a clothes closet, and a private toilet. Every two rooms shared a bath. It had seven stories and five hydraulic elevators to supplement the seven staircases. The entire hotel centered around the Grand Court, one of three interior courts into which carriages drove. Gas-filled flares lit the columned enclosure, which was domed over in glass and surrounded by a tropical garden. It even had its own music pavilion. Nathan smiled to himself as he recalled the look on the clerk's face when he told him he had a castle in England that was bigger than the hotel.

It was costing him a lot of money to stay here but

that was good. Only people of great wealth could afford it and that's what he wanted people to believe. Already he had met a woman in the restaurant who had invited him to a luncheon at her home. Her family was from England, she said, and she wanted to make him feel at home. Nathan was surprised how really easy it had been to infiltrate San Francisco society but there had also been a great deal of luck. He had met a very important person at the luncheon, someone whom he was meeting today. He couldn't believe it had been that easy but perhaps fortune was smiling on him now. Whatever the reason, he had met Rebecca Driscoll, and it was easy to see that she was infatuated with him. Nathan took advantage of that and he preyed upon her innocence, as one might lead a lamb to the slaughter. Part of him hated that he was using Rebecca but the other part knew that it was the only way to get to Driscoll. And today was the day. He and Rebecca had been seeing each other every day for almost a month. Now it was time to meet her father.

Nathan flagged down a carriage. "Nob Hill," he said to the driver. "The Driscoll Mansion." Nathan took his hat off in the carriage, laying it on his knee. He had been obsessed with Driscoll; he thought of nothing else. He had almost been willing to forget what Driscoll had done to Berto and go on with his life, until Driscoll had senselessly murdered Tong. That had been too much for him to take. He thought about Tong many times when he was alone, remembering the bits of wisdom the old man had given him over their years together. He would never forget Tong. He would never forget what Driscoll had done to him.

"Here you are, mister. The Driscoll Mansion."

Nathan hopped out. He reached into his pocket

and handed the man a five dollar gold piece. "Thanks."

"Thank you, mister!"

Nathan walked up the long, flower-lined drive to the mansion. Every time he came to this place he reminded himself how Driscoll had built it. He pulled on the bell cord that hung on the ornate porch. The door opened and a tall, black man stood ready to receive visitors.

"Oh, hello Mr. Randall, sir. It is good to see you."

"It's good to see you, Henderson. Is Miss Driscoll at home?"

"Yes, she is, sir. She's waiting for you in the sitting room. Along with Mr. Driscoll."

"Thanks, Henderson." Nathan followed Henderson into a marble entryway. He looked up at the huge, circular staircase and the expensive oil paintings that were hung all the way up the wall to the second floor. He had never seen the upstairs but Rebecca had told him that there were ten bedrooms and five sitting rooms, as well as a small library for those who didn't want to go downstairs to find a book. The downstairs floor consisted of a large formal dining room and cook's kitchen to the right of the entryway, while to the left there was a large sitting room, a large library, an office, and a music room. Nathan wondered how many people had died so that Driscoll could live in such opulence.

"Coming, Mr. Randall?"

"Yes, Henderson." Nathan followed Henderson to the sitting room and waited while he opened the door. When he walked through he saw Rebecca sitting on a brocade-covered sofa. Driscoll was standing at the mantelpiece smoking a cigar. Nathan took off his hat. He smiled as he entered the room.

"Oh, Steven, I'm so glad you could come."

Rebecca took Nathan's hand, leading him to the mantelpiece. "Steven Randall, this is my father, Franklin Driscoll."

Nathan watched as Driscoll turned from the mantelpiece. He wondered if the man remembered that he had once tried to murder him but Driscoll didn't remember him. He noticed that Driscoll had grown even paunchier, and his skin was red and mottled. He's a drinker, Nathan thought to himself as he extended his hand to Driscoll. "I am pleased to meet you, Mr. Driscoll. I've heard very good things about you."

Driscoll shook Nathan's hand. "Mr. Randall."

"Daddy, Steven's family is from England. He's even related to the queen."

"What queen is that?" Driscoll asked absently.

"Queen Victoria, sir." Nathan tried to keep the contempt from his voice.

"She been your queen long?"

"Over forty-three years now, sir. Some say she'll last to the new century."

"I don't know much about kings and queens. They don't really concern me."

"I can understand that, sir." Nathan looked around the room, an approving look on his face. "You have a beautiful home, Mr. Driscoll. It's very much like our country home in Nottingham."

"Nottingham? Isn't that where Robin Hood was from?"

"So they say. We don't live too far from Sherwood Forest. It's really very beautiful there. Perhaps you and your family can visit my family sometime."

Driscoll suddenly perked up. "You don't say? Visit your family in England?"

"Of course. My family would be delighted to have some real Americans. Of course, I've been here so long now they consider me an American."

"My wife has always wanted to see England. Do you suppose we could see London as well?"

Nathan smiled inwardly. Driscoll was quickly taking the bait. "Yes, we have a large townhouse in the city. I have traveled all over the world, and I think London is my favorite city."

Driscoll suddenly straightened up, attempting to pull his brocade vest over his bulging stomach. "Well, how about some brandy, Mr. Randall? I've just recently acquired some fine old Napoleon brandy. It's as smooth as velvet."

"I'd like that, Mr. Driscoll." Nathan smiled at Rebecca, kissing her lightly on the cheek while Driscoll's back was turned. Rebecca blushed and giggled, leaning against Nathan. "I think you have a very special daughter, sir."

Driscoll went to the sideboard that contained various bottles. He brought out the brandy and poured two glasses, handing one to Nathan. "Yes, I think she's pretty special myself. She's my pride and joy."

"Oh, Daddy," Rebecca replied, leaning forward to kiss her father.

"It's true, honey." Driscoll looked at his daughter lovingly. "Why don't you go check on lunch, Rebecca. I'd like to talk to your young man alone for a few minutes."

"All right, Daddy." She gazed at Nathan with loving eyes. "Don't be long."

Driscoll sipped at the brandy, making contented sounds in his throat. "So, Mr. Randall, you're interested in my little girl?"

"I care for Rebecca a great deal, Mr. Driscoll."

"But you haven't known her a very long time. How do I know that you're not just some fortune seeker

213

coming here to marry my little girl for her money?''

"Sir, I haven't said anything about marriage. I care for your daughter, and I would like to get to know her better but I have no plans to marry her. As for your fortune, if you'll pardon me for being blunt; your fortune, Mr. Driscoll, doesn't come close to the fortune my family has. In fact, I should be careful that you're not pushing Rebecca to marry me for my money.''

Driscoll drank some more of his brandy and walked to the window that overlooked the gardens. "I'm considered a wealthy man in this city, Mr. Randall, and I have a lot of powerful friends in high places.'' He turned from the window. "What is it exactly you're doing in San Francisco?''

"My family is interested in investing some of their money over here. I want to buy some land but I'm also interested in banking.''

"Banking?''

"Yes, my family owns a bank in London and one in Paris. They are interested in investing over here if I can find them the right bank. Would you know of anything, Mr. Driscoll?''

"As a matter of fact, I sit on the board of directors of a bank right here in San Francisco. This would be a good place to invest, Mr. Randall. People are starting to come west in droves. The more people we have the more money we'll need. I could take you down there myself and introduce you to the director.''

"Yes, I would be interested in taking a look around. But do me a favor, Mr. Driscoll. Don't tell your director my name.''

"Why not?''

"If he finds out who my family is, he'll go to the owners and they'll raise the price of the stock. Just because we're wealthy doesn't mean we're stupid. You understand what I mean, Mr. Driscoll?''

Driscoll laughed and downed the rest of his brandy. He put his arm around Nathan's shoulders. "I like you, Steven. Can I call you Steven?"

"Yes, sir. Please do."

"Well, Steven, I think we might become good friends, you and I."

"I'd like that, sir. Oh, Mr. Driscoll, my family would be interested in any other investments you might know of. If we make a profit, we would pay you a percentage, a very healthy percentage."

Driscoll slapped Nathan on the back. "Well, well. This could be a very lucrative partnership for both of us, Steven."

"Yes, my father always said you get what you deserve. Do you agree with that, Mr. Driscoll?"

"Absolutely. I always get what I deserve, if you know what I mean." Driscoll laughed loudly, again slapping Nathan on the back.

"Yes, sir, I know just what you man. I hope you get just what you deserve." Nathan followed Driscoll out of the room, thinking of the day when he would let Driscoll know who he really was. And then Driscoll would truly get what he deserved.

Chapter VIII

Anna adjusted her hat, looking out of the carriage as it rolled through the city. She couldn't believe that Trenton and Aeneva had let her make the trip to California alone, especially after what had happened to Nathan and Roberto ten years earlier. But they had decided that she was old enough, and the railway system was much better, so they gave her their blessings and sent her off. She was to stay with Joe and Larissa but she would visit Garrett as well. She knew that they had many things to resolve before they decided on a future together, but still she was anxious to see him. She was totally enchanted with the city of San Francisco, and she smiled as the carriage wound its way through the downtown and up the hills to the larger homes. When the carriage stopped in front of a large white three-story home, Anna's breath caught in her throat. She couldn't believe that she would be staying in such a beautiful place.

"Here you are, miss." The driver got off the carriage and opened the door, helping Anna down to the street. "I'll get your trunk and bags if you want to go on up to the house."

"Yes, thank you." Anna adjusted her hat once

more and held herself straight. She remembered everything Trenton and Aeneva had told her about Joe and Larissa, and she was able to contain her fear. Although she had met Joe once, ten years before, it had been a long time. She was afraid they might not welcome her. She walked up the white stone steps and lifted the door knocker. A beautiful dark-skinned woman opened the door. She had a big smile on her face.

"Anna, I'm so glad you're here." Larissa grabbed Anna's arm. "Joe, she's here. Anna's here." Larissa hugged Anna, then looked her over from head to toe. "You are a beauty. Trenton and Aeneva must be so proud of you."

"Thank you, ma'am."

"Please, call me Larissa. Come on, we'll go into the kitchen. You must be starving."

"I'm not that hungry, thank you." Anna looked around her at the beautiful polished wood. "You have a beautiful home."

"Thank you. We like it." Larissa pushed open a swinging door that led to the kitchen. "Charley, do you have some of that good soup left? And how about one of your sandwiches for Miss Anna here. Anna, this is Charley. He has completely taken over my kitchen. He won't let me cook anymore. He doesn't trust me."

Anna curtsied slightly. "I'm very pleased to meet you, Charley."

"Pleased to meet you, too, missy. You sit down and I fix you right up."

"Thank you." Anna was about to sit down when the swinging door flew open and Joe walked through. Anna remembered that he was a big man, taller even than Trenton, but he seemed gigantic to her now. He had a big smile on his face, a face that

218

wore its love and kindness like a badge. She felt immediately at home.

"Well, I'll be. Is this that little girl I met ten years ago? Is it possible."

"Yes, sir." Anna smiled.

Joe stepped closer, a stern expression on his face. "You do know who you're talking to, don't you? I've known Trenton since he was younger than you are now, and I've known Aeneva since she was about your age. So I am part of your family. Please don't call me 'sir,' Anna. Call me Joe."

"All right, Joe."

"That's the way." Joe stepped forward and hugged Anna. He gave her a kiss on the cheek. "I swear you look like Aeneva. It's remarkable."

"Many people have told me that. It's probably the Cheyenne blood."

"Or maybe it's that you've lived with her for so long now that you've grown to look like her and be like her."

"I hope so. She's a wonderful person."

"That she is, girl. Hey, you sit down and eat or Charley will have my skin. He's very particular about his cooking."

Anna sat down, taking off her hat and handing it to Larissa. "Thank you. Are you sure I won't be an inconvenience to you?"

"We have this big house and no children to put in it so it would make us very happy to have you stay as long as you want, Anna."

"Thank you." Anna began eating the soup. "It's wonderful soup, Charley. You've used a different spice. What is it?"

Charley walked to the table, butcher knife in hand. He looked at Larissa and Joe. "You see, missy is only here a few minutes, and she notices that I put dif-

219

ferent spices in my soup. You two never say anything. I am never appreciated around here."

"Don't mind him, he's always that way." Joe nodded toward Charley. "So, Anna, tell us about this fiancée of yours. Where exactly is his ranch?"

"He's not really my fiancée. We're only talking about marriage. I don't think I'm ready for it yet."

"Smart girl." Larissa agreed. "You've got plenty of time for marriage."

"So, where's his ranch?"

"He says it's south of San Francisco, and it's very beautiful. He's been building a new ranch house."

"With lots of extra rooms for children, no doubt," Joe said playfully.

"We've only seen each other a few times in the last two years, and that's only been for a few days at a time when he's come back to Arizona. It's a little scary."

"What is, dear?"

"Thinking that you might want to spend the rest of your life with a person but realizing you haven't even known that person for the last two years. A lot could have changed between us."

"Well, that's what you're here for, isn't it?"

"And to have fun," Larissa added. "I hope you'll be rested up by tomorrow because tomorrow night there's a big ball being held. It'll be lavish and beautiful. I'm sure you'll enjoy it."

"But I don't have a ball gown."

"I took the liberty of ordering you one. When Joe described you to me, I decided we had to get you a gown in deep blue. I can take you there tomorrow for alterations."

"That's so nice of you, Larissa. Thank you. I've never been to a ball before. I'm not even sure what to do."

"You just walk in, honey, and you won't have to

worry about what to do. There'll be so many young men clamoring to meet you, I'm going to have to beat them off with sticks."

Anna laughed. "Speaking of young men, Garrett is going to come here in a week. I thought it would be best if we met here first. It didn't seem quite proper for me to go out to his ranch alone."

"Well, he can stay here as far as I'm concerned. That way I can keep an eye on him."

"He's a nice man, Joe, you'll like him. We were the best of friends as children but it changed as we grew older."

"You wanted to stay friends and he wanted something else?" Larissa asked in a gentle tone.

Anna nodded. "I'm still not sure when it happened but all of a sudden he told me he loved me and wanted to take me to California with him. I knew I had to wait. I needed time." She lowered her head. "It sounds silly, I'm sure."

Joe put his arm around Anna's shoulders. "It doesn't sound silly at all. It's important that you make the right decision when you marry someone. You can't just marry someone because you think it's the right thing to do. Ask your mother. She'll tell you the same thing."

"She told me about Ladro. She told me she loved him but not the way she loved Trenton."

"Well, Garrett might be the man for you but on the other hand, there might be some man waiting for you right now, somewhere in this city. So you eat up and then go get some rest because tomorrow night we're going to a party."

Anna felt giddy as a schoolgirl. She twirled around and around in her dress. She ran her hands down the

221

smooth deep blue satin. It was a beautiful dress. She bent over the vanity and looked again at the sapphire necklace and earrings Larissa had lent her. The stones sparkled on her neck and ears, and the blue of the stones and the dress only served to make her eyes stand out more clearly. Larissa had curled her hair and brushed it all back, holding it in place on either side with diamond combs. Anna wrapped her arms around herself. She felt like a princess. Now if only she would meet her prince. There was a light knock on the door. "Come in."

"Oh, you do look lovely. Here." Larissa handed Anna a long satin cloak that matched the dress.

"It's so beautiful, Larissa. Thank you. You've done so much for me."

"I like doing things for you, Anna. I've never had children of my own, and I never had a chance to really know Nathan and Roberto."

"What were they like, Larissa?"

Larissa got a faraway look in her eyes. "Roberto reminded me so much of Ladro, it broke my heart to look at him but it also gave me great joy. He had the same coloring as I but he was tall, like his father. I regret never having been able to know my brother's son better."

"And Nathan?"

Larissa smiled and nodded her head. "I felt as if I knew Nathan before I even met him. God, but he was beautiful. He had dark Indian skin from Trenton but his hair was very light and his eyes very blue, much lighter than yours. He was a very loving child. The first time he met me he threw his arms around my neck and told me how beautiful I was. I loved him instantly."

"I wish I had been able to know them. I look at Trenton and Aeneva sometimes, and I see the looks of

222

pain that they have. They still miss their sons."

Larissa lowered her eyes. "I'm sure they do but at least they have you to give them joy. Now, are you ready to go?"

"I think so. I'm so excited."

"You both ready?" Joe walked into the room whistling loudly. "Good God, girl, you're gonna drive every man in San Francisco crazy tonight."

"It's the dress and the jewels."

"No, it's the sweet thing that's inside 'em." He walked to Anna and took the cloak from her hands. He slipped it around her shoulders. "Are you ready for your first ball, Anna O'Leary?"

Anna took a deep breath. "I think so."

"Well, then, let's go."

Anna stood next to Larissa, clutching her purse. The ballroom was filled with hundreds of people, all laughing and dancing. Swirling across the dark polished floor, women in brightly colored silks flashed discreet smiles at the formally dressed gentlemen. The graceful sound of the music ebbed and swelled over the tinkling of crystal glasses and the deep, low voices of the men. Anna took in all the sights and sounds, sure that she would never see anything like it again.

"It's wonderful, isn't it?" Larissa leaned next to Anna. "It's so much fun to watch the people, especially some of the young men and women."

"I've never seen anything like this. We have socials and parties but nothing on this grand a scale."

"Believe me, Anna, this is fun but the people here are no better and sometimes far worse than the people you know." Larissa looked around. She pointed discreetly. "Take that man, for instance. Mr. Franklin

Driscoll. He's one of the richest and most powerful men in this state, and he's also one of the most corrupt."

Anna looked at the man Larissa was pointing to but her attention was caught by another man. "Larissa, who's—" Larissa was talking to some of the women next to her so Anna decided to venture out on her own. She was looking for the young man who had been standing next to Driscoll. She walked around the periphery of the dance floor, smiling as she passed people. Young men asked her to dance but she graciously declined. She suddenly felt lonely. She wished Garrett were here. With him, at least, she could feel at home. She started back toward Larissa but collided with someone, losing her balance. Strong hands caught her before she fell. When she looked up, she saw the same dazzlingly blue eyes she had just seen for the first time that day. His blond hair was combed away from a face that was strong, yet handsome.

"Are you all right, miss? I'm very sorry. I didn't see you."

"I'm all right." Anna could barely speak.

"Are you sure?"

"Yes, I'm fine. I'm afraid I wasn't watching where I was going. I'm not used to this many people in one place."

The handsome young man smiled. "I know what you mean. I know one place where there's a bit more room. Would you care to dance?"

"I don't know . . ." Anna hesitated, suddenly very unsure of herself.

"Please, then I can repay you for almost knocking you down."

Anna let the man lead her onto the dance floor. He took her into his arms as if they had always danced

224

together. She was embarrassed, yet she wasn't afraid.

"What's your name?" Nathan asked.

"Anna."

"My name is Steven, Steven Randall. Do you live here in San Francisco, Anna?"

"No, I'm just visiting but I love it here. I've never seen anyplace quite like it."

"Yes, it's a wonderful city." Nathan looked past Anna to the people surrounding the dance floor.

"Are you looking for someone?"

"No, I just thought I saw someone I knew. So, how long will you be here?"

"That depends."

"On what?"

"On whether I decide to get married or not."

"Oh, so you're engaged?"

"Not really." Anna laughed. "Never mind. I don't want to talk about that right now. I just want to enjoy this dance. I'll probably never have a chance to do this again." Anna felt Nathan's arms tighten around her waist. When the dance ended she started to pull away but he kept his arm around her.

"Would you care for the next dance?"

"Yes," Anna replied simply, completely caught up in the atmosphere and the attractive man with whom she was dancing. "Have you lived in San Francisco long, Mr. Randall?"

"No, I haven't. And please call me Steven."

"Do you plan to stay here?"

"That depends on my plans."

"And what are your plans?"

"I might get married also. So it seems we're both engaged to be engaged."

"Yes." Anna looked over Nathan's shoulder, trying to hide the irrational disappointment she felt at hearing he was engaged. "Where is your fiancée?"

"I don't think she's arrived yet. We were supposed to meet here. And what about your fiancé? Is he here?"

"No. He'll be here in a week."

"You don't seem too excited."

"I don't know how I feel right now, Mr. Randall," Anna responded honestly, unable to look at Nathan. She felt his hand as it lifted her chin.

"Are you all right?"

"Yes, why?"

"You seem sad for some reason. A woman as beautiful as you shouldn't be so sad."

"Thank you. Maybe I just don't want the night to end. It's almost like a dream."

Nathan looked around. "I still don't see my fiancée. Would you like to dance with me again?"

Anna studied the handsome face in front of her. It would have been easy to say yes to this man but she could not. He was engaged. He was only toying with her. "No, I don't think so. Your fiancée might not appreciate me taking all of your dances. Thank you, Mr. Randall." Anna started to walk off the dance floor but Nathan took her hand.

"The music has already started. You can't leave yet."

Nathan smiled and Anna found herself unable to resist his charm. She found herself thoroughly captivated as Nathan waltzed her around the large dance floor, smiling at her constantly.

"Do you mind if I ask you something personal, Anna?"

"That depends."

"Do you have Indian blood in you?"

Anna's stomach knotted up. Was he going to be like so many other people she had met in her life who discriminated against Indians? She looked him straight in the eyes. "Yes. My mother was Cheyenne Indian. Does that bother you, Mr. Randall?" Anna looked at the man, and she was almost sure that his face looked sad for a moment.

"No, it doesn't bother me in the least. I happen to find Indians fascinating myself." He looked at her a moment. "I would say your father was Irish. Would that be a correct guess?"

"Yes. O'Leary is my last name, and my father was as Irish as they come."

"Was? Is he dead?"

"I don't know. I haven't seen him for ten years. I hope that he's alive somewhere, possibly Ireland. He'd be happy there."

"So you've lived with your mother since he left?"

"No, I—" Anna stopped when she saw Nathan's eyes go past hers. She turned her head and saw a lovely young girl with blond hair and fair skin. She was waving to Nathan. "Is she your fiancée?"

"Yes."

"She's lovely."

"Yes, she is." Nathan smiled at Anna. "Now, you were telling me about your mother."

The music stopped and Anna removed her hand from Nathan's. "Thank you very much for the dance, Mr. Randall." She started to walk away but he took her arm.

"May I see you again, Anna?"

Anna looked at him and was surprised that his eyes seemed so sincere. She shook her head. "I don't think that would be a good idea. I don't think your fiancée would approve. Good-bye, Mr. Randall."

"Ne-sta-va-hose-voomatse. I will see you again," Nathan replied.

Anna stopped, startled by the familiar words. "You speak Cheyenne?"

"A little. I've traveled quite a bit. I was very impressed with the Cheyennes. They're a strong people with great honor and dignity. You should be proud to have Cheyenne blood in you."

"I am proud."

"Steven!" Rebecca Driscoll ran up to Nathan, taking his arm possessively in hers. "I'm sorry I was late. But I'm here now." She leaned closer to Nathan, eyeing Anna suspiciously.

"Rebecca Driscoll, this is Anna O'Leary."

"Hello, Miss O'Leary. Are you just visiting San Francisco?"

"Yes, I am."

"Will you be here long?"

"I don't know." Anna looked at Nathan and smiled. "Well, I must be going. It was nice meeting you, Miss Driscoll. Thank you for the dances, Mr. Randall."

Anna hurried from the dance floor, afraid to look back at Nathan. She had never in her life met anyone quite like him. He seemed so strong, yet gentle. She gently pushed through the people who were standing around the dance floor until she found a space to stand. She watched Nathan dance with Rebecca, and she noticed the way Rebecca looked at him. She was obviously very much in love with him. Anna turned away, embarrassed by her strange reaction to this man, yet unable to keep from thinking about him. She wondered what it would be like to love someone like Steven Randall.

"Isn't this wonderful, Steven? Daddy says there are a lot of important people here tonight that he can introduce you to."

"Good," Nathan replied absently, looking at

228

Anna as she milled through the crowd. He watched her as she stopped once and turned to look at him and Rebecca. She was stunning. She stood out from every woman there. The deep blue of her dress brought out the blue in her eyes, and they contrasted with her dark skin and hair. When she had said she was Cheyenne it was like a connection to his past. He wanted to talk to her some more. He needed to talk to her again. "Where is your father, Rebecca?"

"I think he's in the library with Mr. Jameson and some of the other men discussing business. Just like always."

"Well, after this dance I think I should try to find him. It's time for me to meet some of these friends of your father."

"Oh, Steven, don't go. I want to dance."

Nathan smiled, kissing Rebecca on the cheek. "Don't worry. When I leave, every man in this room will be fighting to dance with you."

"Oh, Steven," Rebecca sighed. "Who was that girl you were dancing with? She looked very young."

"I don't know. I just met her. Seems she's visiting someone in San Francisco. She said she plans to be married."

"Oh?" Rebecca suddenly seemed very interested. "To anyone I know?"

"She didn't tell me his name, Rebecca." The music stopped and Nathan led Rebecca from the dance floor. "You'll be fine until I get back. Just don't flirt too much." Rebecca giggled girlishly and immediately accepted a dance with another young man. Nathan breathed a sigh of relief. He walked through the people and looked around. Where was Anna? He had to see her one more time. He walked slowly around the room but he didn't see her. He walked to the terrace and went out, needing some fresh air. He despised the game he was playing. He didn't want to hurt Rebecca but it was the only way to get to her father. He leaned against the stone wall that overlooked the gardens. He shook his head in disgust. All of these people lived in such opulence. Their world consisted of parties and balls and money. They were not concerned with the more mundane things in life such as work and friendship. He wondered if one person here had a true friend. He heard a noise in the garden below him. He saw a figure move in the shadows, and he heard the rustle of satin. He couldn't see her face but he felt that it was Anna. He walked down the steps that led to the garden and went up behind Anna.

"Hello."

"Oh!" Anna jumped slightly.

"Are you all right?"

"I'm afraid I've cut myself on this rosebush. You caught me red-handed. I was trying to take one of these roses." She smiled broadly, bringing her finger to her lips.

Nathan reached into his pocket and pulled out a handkerchief. "Here, let me see your hand."

Anna tried to pull away. "No, it's fine."

"I insist." Nathan took her hand and looked at the cut. "I think you'll live but you don't want to get blood all over that pretty dress." He wrapped the handkerchief around the cut. "There. That should keep it from bleeding."

Anna pulled her hand away. "Thank you. I'm sorry about the handkerchief."

"I'd gladly sacrifice that and more if I could help you." He reached up and broke off the rose that Anna had tried to take. He carefully snapped the thorns from it and handed it to her. "There. I'm sure the rose will be much happier in your hands than it was on

230

the bush."

"Thank you." Anna brought the flower to her nose and breathed deeply, looking at Nathan as she did so. She knew she should go but she was afraid she might break the spell. She held the flower in front of her, touching its delicate petals. "Shouldn't you be dancing with your fiancée, Mr. Randall?"

"I suppose I should be, yes," Nathan answered. "But I wanted to see you again. I looked everywhere for you. Luck brought me out here."

Anna looked at him, then down again at the flower. "I think you should go."

Nathan stepped closer to Anna. "I don't want to go." He cupped her chin in his hand, lifting it slightly. "You don't even realize it, do you?"

"What?"

"How beautiful you are."

"Please—"

Nathan ran his fingers along her jaw and up to her lips, gently touching them. "I hope your fiancée appreciates you."

Anna was mesmerized. She stared at Nathan as he moved still closer, his body directly in front of hers. She felt as if this moment had already been planned for them both. She closed her eyes and felt his hand as it moved down her neck and pulled her close to him. She leaned against him, feeling the strength of his arms and his body as he held her. "Anna," Nathan said softly. Anna looked up at him, and he was completely captivated by her expression of innocence and beauty. He knew at that moment that he couldn't do to her what he was doing to Rebecca. Rebecca would survive it. Anna might not. He could already see how deeply her emotions ran. He dropped his arms and stepped back. "I suppose we should be getting back inside."

"Yes," Anna replied, a puzzled expression on her face. She unwrapped the handkerchief from her hand and handed it to Nathan. "Thank you for the handkerchief. I won't be needing it anymore." She walked out of the garden and up the steps to the ballroom.

Nathan watched Anna as she walked away, wanting to reach out to her but unable to. There was something in her eyes so trusting, so good, that he couldn't bring himself to use her, too. He looked at the handkerchief in his hand. Was it possible to fall in love with a woman he had only just met? He shook his head, forcing himself to remember what he was here for. He couldn't think of Anna. He had to think of Driscoll. He walked up the steps and through the ballroom to the library. There was a servant standing in front of the doors.

"May I help you, sir?"

"Yes, would you tell Mr. Driscoll that Mr. Randall would like to speak with him?"

"Yes, sir." The servant knocked on the door and went inside, returning moments later. "Mr. Driscoll says for you to go on in, sir."

"Thank you." Nathan walked through the doors and into the large library. There was a group of men sitting at a round table. They were playing cards. So much for the business, Nathan thought to himself. Smoke filled the room, and there was an unmistakable odor of whiskey.

Driscoll approached Nathan. "Steven, come over here. There are a few people I'd like you to meet." Driscoll put his arm around Nathan's shoulders as they stood in front of the table. "This is the young man I was telling you all about."

"Ah, Mr. Randall. Franklin has been telling us a lot of good things about you."

"Well, thank you, sir. I haven't had the pleasure yet."

The man stood up. "I'm William Jameson. I'm an attorney. Frank tells me you're interested in making some investments."

"Well, yes. My family would like to invest over here. I'm the first of my family to come to America, and they think it would be wise and profitable for me to invest in something over here if I'm going to stay."

"Yes. I agree. Have a seat, Mr. Randall. Can I get you something to drink? I can't stomach that awful punch my wife always serves at these functions."

Nathan sat down, taking the proffered glass of whiskey. "Well, Mr. Jameson, since you're an attorney, perhaps you could advise me on some of the ways I could invest my money."

"Exactly how much money are you talking about, Mr. Randall?"

"Millions," Nathan answered nonchalantly. He tried to keep a straight face when he saw Driscoll almost choke on his whiskey. "Will there be any problem with that, Mr. Jameson?"

Jameson shot a quick glance to Driscoll. "No, there shouldn't be any problem, Mr. Randall. No problem at all." He downed a shot of whiskey and poured another. "How about a game of cards? You a gambling man, Mr. Randall?"

"That depends on the odds, Mr. Jameson." Nathan stood up. "Sorry, but I have a lovely young lady waiting to dance with me. I'll see you gentlemen soon, I hope." Nathan walked to the door but was stopped by Driscoll.

"I'll be in touch, Steven. I'm sure we can work out something that will be lucrative to us all," Driscoll said.

Nathan nodded and left the room, barely able to conceal the contempt he had for Driscoll. He stopped. He didn't want to go back to the ballroom; already he was tiring of playing the doting lover to Rebecca. Almost without thought, his eyes searched the room for Anna. She was the one he wanted to be with. He walked around the room again. It seemed even more crowded than before. He saw Rebecca dancing with a young man, appearing to all the world as if she was having a wonderful time. Nathan made sure she didn't see him. He walked behind some people. He was about ready to give up looking for Anna when the blue of her dress caught his eyes. She whirled past on the dance floor, her dark hair swinging over her shoulders, her smile lighting up the room. Nathan went onto the dance floor. He tapped Anna's partner on the back.

"May I cut in?"

The man seemed reluctant to give Anna up. "It's up to the lady."

Nathan looked at Anna. When she nodded, he swept her into his arms and moved her around the dance floor as if he had never enjoyed dancing so much. When the music stopped he led Anna through the crowd, past the library to the entryway. "Where's your cloak?"

"I don't know. Someone took it."

"What color is it?"

"It matches my dress."

"Wait here." Nathan left and returned with Anna's cloak, placing it around her. "Come on."

Anna hesitated. "Where are we going?"

"I want to get out of here. I can't take these people anymore. Do you want to walk with me?"

"I have friends who will worry about me."

"I'll have you back before the ball is over." Nathan

held out his hand and Anna took it. They went out into the carriage-lined drive.

"Where are we going?"

Nathan laughed. "I don't know. I just wanted to have you all to myself." He took Anna's arm and tucked it into his. They walked down the long, lantern-lit drive until they found a place where they could see the ocean.

"Oh, look," Anna said. "Isn't it beautiful?" She walked further into the trees and looked out over the city. "I wonder what it's like to live in a house like this."

"The view is beautiful but I wouldn't take this kind of life for anything in the world."

"You sound angry when you say that. Why?"

"I have my reasons." He stood behind Anna. "I wish my parents could see this. Someday I'm going to bring them here."

"Why don't you?"

"I just can't right now."

"Are you in love with Rebecca Driscoll?" Anna asked suddenly. She felt Nathan behind her, and she was afraid of his answer. She turned around, searching his face in the eerie glow of the lantern light.

Nathan smiled at Anna and pulled her into his arms. "You know I'm not in love with her." He looked at her face in the dim light, and he was overcome with a sudden desire to love and protect Anna. He touched his lips to hers, seeking, hoping that her desire for him was as strong as his was for her. When she did not pull away, he held her closer, kissing her more passionately. He was filled with the kind of desire he had never felt before. He had had women but he had never desired a woman the way he desired Anna at this moment. He pulled away and held her head against his chest, stroking her soft hair. "I'm sorry. I can't seem to control myself around you."

Anna looked up at Nathan. "I'm not sorry. I'm glad you kissed me."

Nathan smiled broadly, hugging Anna to him. "God, I like you. You're so unlike any woman I've ever known."

"What about Rebecca, Steven?"

He took Anna's hands. "I can't tell you everything right now, Anna, but I need Rebecca Driscoll."

"I don't understand."

Nathan turned away and looked out toward the ocean. "Her father killed my brother, and I'm trying to get as much on Driscoll's dirty dealings as I can."

"So you're using Rebecca?"

Nathan turned back. "Yes, I'm using her. It's not a very honorable thing to do, I know, but I don't have a choice. Driscoll also murdered a very close friend of mine."

"Why can't you turn him in to the police?"

"Men like Driscoll are beyond the law. He has too many connections in this city. He's completely protected. The only way to get to him is to find out as much as I can about him."

"If he is that dangerous, shouldn't you be more careful? If he finds out about you and his daughter and he finds out that you are just using her, he could do something horrible to you, too."

"I'll be careful." He took Anna's hands, covering them with his own. "Anna, I don't quite understand what's happening with us. I just know that I have to see you. I have to be with you. But it could be dangerous. If Driscoll even suspects that I'm seeing another woman behind his daughter's back, there's no telling what he'll do. I don't want you placed in a position like that."

"I don't care. I'm not afraid."

"Well, I am. I don't trust Driscoll." He shook his head in anger. "Damn it, I just wish all this were over and I could go home. I wish I could take you home with me."

"We don't even know each other."

"Does that matter?" Nathan pulled Anna to him, wrapping his arms around her, covering her mouth with his. He heard her small sigh of pleasure and it excited him. He moved his mouth against hers as if he would never be able to kiss her again. "Oh, Anna," he murmured.

"Steven?"

"Yes."

"Maybe my friend can help you."

"No, I need to do this alone."

"But he's an influential man. He knows lots of people."

"No, no thank you. I don't want to involve anyone else in this."

"Well, at least talk to him."

"No!" Nathan snapped angrily. "Just forget I said anything, Anna."

"I'm sorry." Anna turned away, wrapping her cloak around her. "We should go back now. Rebecca will be wondering where you are."

"Anna." Nathan pulled her to him. "I don't love Rebecca Driscoll. I want you to know that. I'd like to see you and be with you but I don't want to endanger your life. Perhaps when this is all over—"

"I don't want to wait until it's all over, Steven." Anna surprised herself. She put her arms around Nathan's neck and drew his face to hers. She kissed him passionately, feeling his arms tighten around her. She wanted nothing more at that moment than to be loved by Steven Randall.

"You make me crazy, Anna."

"I'm glad."

"And what about your fiancé? What are you going to do when he comes to San Francisco?"

"I don't know. Until tonight I thought I loved him."

Nathan held her close. "And what happened tonight?"

"I think I fell in love with you."

Nathan was silent as he held Anna in his arms. Had he fallen in love with this woman or was he just attracted to her? Whatever he felt, it was stronger than anything he had ever felt in his entire life. He didn't want to let Anna go. Maybe that was love, he thought to himself. But he didn't even know her, yet it was as if he had known her all of his life. "Let's go back. Your friends will be worried about you."

"Will I see you again? Maybe you could come to my friend's to see me."

"No, I don't think that would be wise. I can't take any chances being seen with you."

"Oh, I see." Anna pulled her cloak around her. "Would you marry Rebecca Driscoll if you had to, Steven?"

"It'll never come to that."

"But if you had to?"

Nathan knew the answer. "Yes."

Anna looked out at the bay once again. "I've just decided I don't like the view from here after all." She started off toward the house.

"Anna." Nathan reached for Anna but she pulled away.

"It's best this way, Steven. This way I can just remember tonight as a fairy tale and you as my handsome prince. This way I can't be hurt."

They walked toward the mansion in silence and when they reached the entryway, Anna turned

238

to Nathan.

"Good luck, Steven. I hope this works out for you. Take care of yourself."

Nathan watched Anna as she walked away. He didn't try to stop her this time. He knew it was best this way. Until Driscoll was either put away for life or dead, no one that he cared about would be safe.

Chapter IX

It had been a week since the ball but Anna couldn't get Steven Randall off her mind. She had prayed that she would see him when she and Larissa went around the city but she didn't. She couldn't stop thinking about him or the way he had held her in his arms, or the way he had kissed her. And he had been as surprised by their attraction as she had been; that's what made it all the more exciting.

"Anna?"

Anna looked up from the book she was supposedly reading. "I'm sorry, Larissa. Did you say something?"

"Someone is here to see you. A young man."

Anna stood up, and the book fell to the floor. She immediately began smoothing her skirt and her hair. Was it possible? Had Steven decided to come see her? "Do I look all right?"

"You look lovely. Aren't you even going to ask me who it is?"

"Of course, who is it?" Anna held her breath.

"It's your friend Garrett. He decided to come early."

"Oh," Anna responded somewhat unenthusiastically.

"Are you all right, Anna? You do want to see Garrett, don't you?"

"Oh, yes. I do. It's just been so long, that's all."

"I'll go and bring him here. It'll give you a few seconds to compose yourself."

"Thank you, Larissa." Anna was surprised at her disappointment. But it didn't last long. When Garrett walked into the room, a smile lit her face. "Oh, Garrett." She ran to him and he put his arms around her, swinging her around.

"God, but you've gotten even prettier, Anna. I didn't think that was possible."

Anna looked at Garrett and decided immediately that hard work had been good for him. He was lean and hard, and his skin was dark and healthy looking. His dark brown hair was neck length and curling at the ends, and Anna thought he looked wonderful. If Sally James had thought he was gorgeous before, she would've died if she'd seen him now. "You look wonderful, Garrett. This life's been good to you."

"I love it, Anna. The work is hard but it feels so damned good to be doing something on my own."

"I'm so happy for you."

"I want you to come see the ranch."

"I'd like that."

Garrett took off his hat and held it in front of him, looking very much like a red-faced little boy. "Have you forgiven me yet, Anna?"

Anna reached up and ran her hand through Garrett's hair. "There's nothing to forgive, Garrett. We were both much younger then. I can't judge you for what you did. That's not my place."

"But what about us, Anna? Is there a chance for us?"

Anna turned around, walking across the room. "Let's just take it slow, Garrett. We haven't seen each

242

other in a long time. We need to get to know each other again. We're different people now. We might not even care for each other in the same way."

"Are you in love with someone else, Anna? Is that what you're telling me?"

"Why do you say that?" Anna asked in a shocked tone.

"You just sound so noncommittal, that's all."

"I just think we should take our time." She looked at him and smiled. "Sally James was right, you know."

"About what?"

"You are gorgeous. The first time you smiled at me in class I thought I would die. Remember, you even walked me home and picked me some wildflowers?"

"I'll never forget it. When you walked into the classroom you looked so small and frightened. You stood in the front of the class while Mrs. Ford introduced you, and all I could see were your big blue eyes. I fell in love with you right then."

Anna walked over to the sofa and sat down, motioning for Garrett to do the same. "Garrett, I need to ask you something. And I want you to be honest with me."

"Sure."

"You're the best friend I've ever had, Garrett. I've always shared everything with you."

"What's the matter, Anna? Are you sick or something?"

"No, no, it's not like that." Anna clasped her fingers together. "Have you ever met anyone and thought right away that you loved them? Is that possible?"

"Yes, it's possible."

"You're so sure."

"Of course I'm sure. It happened to me the first

243

time I saw you. I wasn't kidding about that, Anna. I've loved you ever since that first time I saw you." He took Anna's hand in his. "I'll never love anyone the way I love you."

Anna stood up, a look of anguish on her face. "But how do you know that for sure, Garrett? Have you met many other girls?"

"I've met a lot and you know it. None of them have come close to what I feel for you." Garrett stood up and walked to Anna. "What is it really, Annie? Tell me."

Anna turned and looked up at Garrett. He had always called her Anna except when he tried to pin her down about something. He knew her so well. "I met someone, Garrett." She was unable to look him in the eyes.

Garrett lifted her chin. "Tell me about him."

"There isn't much to tell. We met at a ball over a week ago. We danced a few times and we talked."

"And what else?"

"Nothing else."

"Annie—"

Anna looked at Garrett. "He held me in his arms, and he kissed me. That's all."

Garrett put his hands on Anna's shoulders. "That's not all, Annie."

"I swear, Garrett, nothing else happened."

"Are you in love with him?"

"I don't know. I don't know much about love."

"I always thought you were in love with me." Garrett shook his head. "Or maybe I always hoped you were in love with me. You never did feel the same way about me as I felt about you."

"That's not true, Garrett." Anna touched his arm. "You have always been so special to me. I used to wake up each day looking forward to school because

I knew I would see you, and afterward we would do something exciting. I even remember the first time you kissed me down by the stream."

Garrett smiled. "I remember, too. I practically had to fight you off, you were so anxious to see what it was like."

"Liar." Anna hit Garrett in the arm. "I was scared."

"But you liked it."

Anna nodded, a smile touching her lips. "Yes, I did like it. I think it was the sweetest kiss a girl could ever have."

Garrett stepped closer to Anna. "Should we see what it's like now?" Garrett kissed Anna, gently moving his lips against hers. When she didn't resist, he pulled her into his arms. "Do you still like it?"

Anna backed away from Garrett, walking over to the sofa. "I'm confused, Garrett. You've always confused me."

"That's good. It means you're still thinking about me."

"It scares me. How can I feel something for you and the man I met the other night? Is that possible?"

"I think it's possible, Anna, but you can't have us both. One of these days you'll have to decide." He sat down next to Anna. "Would you do me a favor? I have to meet some people tonight for dinner. Would you come with me? It would make it so much easier to have you to look at all evening."

Anna smiled. "I'd like that."

"All right. I'll be back at seven o'clock to pick you up."

"Do you have a place to stay, Garrett? There is plenty of room here."

"No, I have a room. I'll see you at seven."

"Garrett." Anna got up and walked to Garrett.

245

"Thank you for always being there for me. You are so special to me." She kissed him on the cheek and watched him as he walked out. Her stomach was twisted in knots. What was the matter with her? How could she be attracted to a complete stranger and yet have the same feelings she had always had for Garrett? She decided the best thing to do now was to relax and enjoy Garrett's company. After all, she might never see Steven Randall again, and she would never have to worry about her feelings for him. For the time being, she resolved to just have a good time, and perhaps her feelings for Garrett would sort themselves out.

Anna laughed uncontrollably as Garrett told her the story about his first try at bull fighting. She realized suddenly that being with Garrett was like being home. She felt safe and secure.

"How long was it before you were able to sit down?"

"At least a week. I never knew a bull's horns could be so long."

"Oh, Garrett." Anna leaned her head on Garrett's shoulder. "It feels so good to be with you. Are you sure we have to go to this dinner?"

"I have to, Anna. It's important. I need to discuss some business."

"All right, but let's leave as soon as we can. I'd love to take a walk in the moonlight, just like we used to do when we'd sneak out of our houses and meet by the stream. It was fun then, wasn't it?"

Garrett squeezed Anna's arm. "Yeah, it was. I'll never forget those times."

The carriage pulled into a lit courtyard. "Here you are, sir."

Garrett got out of the carriage and helped Anna down. He paid the driver and took Anna's arm. "You're going to like this place."

"You've been here before?" Anna looked around at the magnificent structure.

"Business."

"Of course."

They walked through large turning doors and into a lobby. Anna looked into the mirrored restaurant and smiled broadly. She wished her mother could see it. The maitre d' approached them immediately. "May I help you, sir?"

"Yes, Mr. Driscoll's table, please."

"Oh, yes sir. Right this way."

Anna felt herself stiffen at the mention of Driscoll's name. Not only had Larissa commented how corrupt Driscoll was, but Steven Randall had accused him of murdering two men. What, Anna wondered, was Garrett doing having dinner with a man like Driscoll?

They followed the maitre d' to a large table in a private section of the restaurant. The walls were mirrored and heavily draped. Everyone was elegantly dressed, and Anna noticed that all of the women had on expensive jewels. She silently thanked Larissa for the green silk dress and the emerald necklace she had lent her. At least she wouldn't look too out of place.

"Here you are, sir."

Anna brought her attention away from the other customers to the table where the maitre d' had led them. When she looked at the people seated at the table she wasn't quite prepared for Steven Randall, who, dressed in a dark gray suit, looked incredibly handsome as he stood up and smiled at her.

"Mr. Driscoll, sir. Hope we're not late. I'd like to introduce my friend, Anna O'Leary."

Anna smiled as beguiling a smile as she could possibly force. She held out her hand to Driscoll who also had stood. "I'm very pleased to meet you, Mr. Driscoll."

"And I, you, young lady. I can't remember when I've seen anyone as pretty as you."

"Franklin."

"Sorry, dear. Miss O'Leary, this is my wife Rachel and my daughter Rebecca. And this is Rebecca's fiancé, Steven Randall."

"How do you do." Anna smiled at all of the people.

"We met the other night, Miss O'Leary," Rebecca said. "You were dancing with Steven. Or have you forgotten?"

Anna shrugged her shoulders. "I danced with so many men that night I hope you'll forgive me, Mr. Randall, if I admit I don't remember you."

"That's all right, Miss O'Leary."

"Miss O'Leary, why don't you be seated by Mr. Randall. I'd like to talk to your friend for awhile, if you don't mind."

"Here." Garrett held the chair out for Anna. "It's good to see you again, Rebecca. You're looking lovely tonight."

"Why thank you, Garrett. You're looking rather well yourself this evening."

"Franklin, I don't want you to talk business right now. I want to dance."

"Rachel—"

"Don't argue with me, Franklin. I love to dance in this place."

"Very well, dear."

"Well, Garrett, would you like to dance with me? It seems Steven isn't in the mood to dance tonight. Perhaps he and your friend can entertain themselves while we're gone." Rebecca drank the rest of her champagne and stood up.

Garrett looked over at Anna. "Do you mind?"

"No, it's fine. Go ahead."

Anna sat with her hands in her lap, afraid to look at Nathan. She felt his eyes on her. Finally she looked up. His eyes seemed lighter than before, his face more handsome. "If I had known you would be here I wouldn't have come."

"You didn't know?"

"All Garrett told me was that he wanted me to go to dinner with him. He said he had to discuss business with someone. I didn't know it was Driscoll."

"What do you think Garrett has to do with Driscoll?"

"I don't know. I have no idea." She leaned forward, afraid her voice would carry. "Garrett is an honest person. He would never do anything corrupt. I'm sure he doesn't even know about Driscoll."

"That's possible."

"It's true."

"He's your fiancée?"

"He's my friend. We've known each other all of our lives. I feel safe with Garrett."

"And you don't feel safe with me?"

"I don't even know you. How can I feel safe with you?"

"You look beautiful tonight. When I saw you walk in, I wanted to take you in my arms and carry you out of here. I wanted to take you someplace where we could be alone forever."

"Don't." Anna reached for her glass of water but Nathan put his hand on hers.

"I haven't been able to stop thinking about you, Anna."

She jerked her hand away and took a sip of the

water. "You and I are from different worlds." She looked all around her. "I don't belong here. I can dress up in pretty clothes and jewels but I just don't belong."

"What makes you think that I do?"

"Because you're here, that's why."

"I told you why I'm here. I want to talk to you, Anna."

"I don't think that would be a very good idea."

Nathan drank his glass of wine. "I guess you're right." He looked back through the restaurant at the dance floor. "I suppose I should ask Rebecca to dance. I wouldn't want her to think I was neglecting her." He stood up.

"Don't be angry, Steven."

"I'm not angry. You're right. I can't involve other people in this until it's over. Its just that when I saw you walk in—" He shook his head. "Good-bye, Anna."

Anna had a sinking feeling in the pit of her stomach as she watched Steven walk away. She got up from her chair and went after him. "Steven." He turned, his eyes seeking hers. "Never mind."

Nathan took Anna's arm and escorted her toward the dance floor. "I'm sure your boyfriend would like to dance with you." They walked to the dance floor. Nathan tapped Garrett on the back. "Your fiancée is waiting for you. May I cut in?"

"Sure. Thank you, Rebecca. I enjoyed it."

"Thank you, Garrett." Rebecca watched Garrett as he went over and took Anna in his arms. "They certainly are friendly. Do you suppose they're lovers?"

Nathan tried to look nonchalant as he looked at Anna dancing with Garrett. "Who knows. Frankly, you're the only person I'm interested in this evening."

"Daddy says you're a bright young man. He says you'll make a real future for yourself here."

"I hope so." Nathan looked over at Anna and Garrett. Anna was laughing, and she laid her head against Garrett's chest. They seemed comfortable together; they seemed right for each other.

"Don't you think so?"

"What?" Nathan asked absently, still watching Anna. He admired her grace and beauty but he was really attracted to the person. She was kind and good, and it was easy to see she wasn't easily impressed with wealth.

The music ended and they all walked back to the table. Nathan seated Rebecca, all the while watching Anna and Garrett. He couldn't stand the sight of them together yet he could see that there was something very special between them.

"So, Miss O'Leary, where is your family from?"

"They're from Arizona." She looked over at Garrett and smiled. "Garrett and I grew up together."

"So, your folks are ranchers too, Anna?"

"Yes."

"Her father raises some of the primest beef in Arizona."

"So, your folks are Irish?" Driscoll asked.

Anna took a deep breath. She knew that by telling Driscoll the truth she might jeopardize a business deal for Garrett but she didn't care. "My real father was Irish and my mother was Cheyenne Indian." She waited for the words to sink in and for the Driscolls to exchange glances. She looked over at Nathan and found an approving look on his face. She continued. "My mother died when I was very young and my father went away. I have been raised by some wonderful people since I was nine years old."

"Well, that's quite a story, young lady." Driscoll

251

took a drink of his whiskey and looked at his wife. "Well, if you're all ready for dinner, I'll go ahead and order." Driscoll looked at the menu, tapping his pudgy fingers on the table. "Well, I think we'll have some of those sand dabs in that special French sauce, some fresh salad with that dressing your chef makes, some artichokes, and three grizzly bear steaks. And bring us two more bottles of this wine."

"Yes, sir."

Dinner was a long, drawn-out affair. Everyone was supposed to enthuse over the food as much as Driscoll did. Nathan noticed that the Driscolls were snubbing Anna, and he knew it was because of her Indian blood. He wanted to defend her but he couldn't. Not now. At one point, Driscoll stood up, asking Garrett to come with him. They had to talk business, he said. Nathan sat at the table with the three women.

"So, Miss O'Leary, what is it like to be an Indian?" Rebecca asked, twirling the stem of her wine glass.

"I'm sure it's no different from being a blonde, Miss Driscoll."

Rebecca's mouth tightened. "But do you go in for all that savagery? I mean, Indian men treat their women like dogs. I know, I've read about it in books."

Anna leaned forward, a conspiratorial look on her face. "You're absolutely right, Miss Driscoll. Why, I've even seen Indian men throw their wives to packs of wolves if they don't obey."

Rebecca's face went white. "Oh, my God." She looked at her mother. "Did you hear that, Mother? I knew they were savages."

Anna leaned back in her chair, winking at a bemused Nathan as she did so. "Yes, I was lucky to get out alive after my mother died. They wanted to keep me as a slave but I managed to escape and find my white father. I am so lucky to be in the civilized world."

"Yes, you are, dear." Mrs. Driscoll reached out and patted Anna's hand.

"Well, you don't have to worry about us, Miss O'Leary. We'll be sure to keep your secret. You're just lucky that you're skin isn't very dark."

"Yes, I am lucky. But I get frightened sometimes."

"Why is that?" Rebecca asked.

Anna picked up the steak knife alongside her plate and ran her fingers along the edge. "Sometimes I get these strange urges." She looked at Rebecca and Rachel Driscoll, a wild look in her eye. "Like I want to harm someone."

Rebecca looked at her mother and stood up. "I think it's time we were going, Steven. I have a bit of a headache."

"I am rather tired myself. Would you mind dropping me off, Steven?"

"Not at all, Mrs. Driscoll."

"Goodnight, Miss O'Leary. I hope you'll take care of those urges." He smiled broadly as he ushered the two women away.

Anna watched Nathan as he walked away and for the first time she realized there was something familiar about him. She couldn't quite figure out what it was. She shrugged her shoulders, drinking down the rest of her wine. Just when she was about to get up and leave, Garrett returned, an angry look on his face.

"Come on." He pulled her out of the chair.

Anna stood up. "What's the matter. Where's Mr. Driscoll?"

"Let's get the hell out of this place. It stinks in here."

Anna followed Garrett to the foyer, where they got her cloak. They went outside. The chill night air touched Anna immediately. She leaned against Garrett. He started walking down the street, taking great strides.

"Garrett, stop. I can't keep up with you in these shoes." Anna stopped. "Damn it, Garrett. Wait for me." Garrett slowed his pace and finally stopped. His hands were thrust into his pockets, and he was looking down at the ground. Anna went up to him. "Garrett, what's the matter? What happened between you and Driscoll?"

"Nothing. It's nothing."

"Garrett, I'm not a little girl anymore. Please, tell me. It might help."

Garrett was silent, unable to look at Anna. Finally he nodded his head. "I got into a business deal with Driscoll that I never should have gotten into in the first place. Now I owe him some money. A lot of money."

"Well, you have money. You can pay him."

"I don't have enough. If I don't find the money in one week, he's going to take my ranch from me." He shook his head. "I feel like such a fool, Anna. I thought I was doing the right thing. I should have known that Driscoll was too slick for me. He duped me. I'm finished."

"What do you mean you're finished? Go to your father. He'll help you out."

"I can't, damn it!"

"Why not? He'd be glad to help you. I know he would. Especially if he thought you were swindled."

Garrett began walking. "Just forget it, Anna."

"I want to help you, Garrett. What exactly did Driscoll do to you?"

"I said forget it!" Garrett yelled, walking faster.

254

Anna ran after him and pulled at his arm. "I'll help you, Garrett. I have some money that my father left for me."

Garrett stopped. "Oh, Anna," he said softly. "You are so incredible. You have always been there for me and I have always taken advantage of that friendship." He shook his head. "I won't do that now." He turned to face Anna. "Driscoll didn't swindle me, Anna. I gambled the ranch away in a poker game."

"You what?" Anna took Garrett's arm. "Let's walk. You tell me about it."

"There's nothing much to tell really. I came here and did some good work on the ranch. I heard Driscoll's name come up in lots of different conversations. I heard he owned all the land around me and wanted to buy me out. Well, Driscoll came to me himself, came on all nice and generous. Even when I said I didn't want to sell to him, he said that was fine. He invited me to his home in the city."

"So you have been there before. I thought you had."

"Why?"

"By the way Rebecca looked at you."

"Rebecca's a spoiled child. Daddy's little girl."

"So what happened when you went to Driscoll's home?"

"He said he liked me, that he thought I had good business sense. He told me if I stuck with him I could make a lot of money."

"And you believed him?"

"Why not? I looked around his great big mansion, and I saw the way people acted around him. I thought he could help me out."

"What happened next?"

"I stayed at his mansion for about a week. I went a lot of different places with him. Then one night he invited me to a card game at Jameson's."

"That was where I went to the ball."

"Well, you saw what kind of a place it was. I didn't have that kind of money so Driscoll staked me for the game."

"How much?"

"Two thousand dollars."

"Two thousand dollars!"

"Yeah, I figured that if he'd stake me that kind of money, he had to be honest."

"Didn't you learn anything in those poker games with the ranch hands? Usually the guy that was willing to stake you was the guy who'd beat the pants off of you."

"And that's what happened. I started off winning. At one point I even got up to around five thousand dollars. But then I started betting higher and higher until I was down to almost nothing."

"But how did Driscoll talk you into betting your ranch?"

"He just kept at me. He told me that if I won, I'd win a lot of money and if I lost, all I'd be out was a ranch. And he told me he'd help me out if I lost."

"But of course he won't do that. He's going to take your ranch and you'll be left with nothing."

"I'm afraid so and it's my own damned fault. Two years of work and it's going to wind up in Driscoll's hands."

"When does he want the money?"

"I have one week."

Anna thought for a moment. "Walk me back to the Palace, Garrett. Don't ask me any questions."

"What are you going to do? If this has something to do with me, I don't want you involved. Driscoll is a dangerous man."

"Just take me back to the hotel, Garrett. If you

don't take me, I'll go there myself.''

"Just tell me what this is all about."

"No. I'm a big girl now."

"They're not going to let you wait around the lobby of the hotel. They'll think you're a prostitute."

"Don't worry about it, Garrett."

Garrett gave in and walked Anna back to the Palace. He started to walk her inside but she stopped him. "I'll be fine from here. Come to see me tomorrow at Joe and Larissa's. We'll talk more then."

"Anna, I don't like leaving you here alone."

"Don't worry about me. I can take care of myself." Anna kissed Garrett on the cheek and walked into the lobby of the hotel. She rumpled her hair and pinched her cheeks, running up to the large desk. Two clerks were on duty. "Help me, please!" she said in a helpless voice.

"What is it, miss?"

Anna breathed heavily as if she'd been running. She could see that one of the clerks had already observed her clothing and jewels and decided that she wasn't a lady of the evening. She played on the man's sympathy. "Oh, please, sir, could you help me? I've just arrived from the East Coast to visit my brother. I got off the boat and the man who was supposed to meet me wasn't there. So I took it upon myself to take my things and come here. I attempted to get a carriage but some men came. They tried to assault me but I managed to get away. They took all of my things. I was lucky to get away with my life." Anna acted as if she were going to faint, and the flustered desk clerk came out from behind the desk and ushered her to one of the chairs.

"Wait here, miss. I'll get you a glass of water."

Anna waited patiently, trying to keep herself from

laughing until the clerk returned. She looked up at him with her big blue eyes when he returned with her glass of water. "Thank you so much, sir. I don't know what I would have done without your help." Anna drank some of the water and handed the glass to the man. "Please, sir, can you tell me if my brother is in? I just want to see my brother."

"What is your brother's name, miss?"

"Steven Randall. I am his sister, Anna. He is in, isn't he?"

"No, I'm afraid Mr. Randall hasn't come in yet."

"Is there someplace I can lie down, sir? I feel slightly dizzy."

"Well, I don't know."

"Why don't you just let me into Steven's room? I just don't want to be out here by myself right now. What if I were to see those men again?"

"I don't think their type would show up here, miss. Besides, we have good security here at the hotel."

"Oh, I'm so pleased to hear that." Anna waved her hand in front of her face. "I am so weak. I think I might faint if I don't lie down somewhere, sir."

The clerk looked around the lobby. "Well, it is highly irregular to let someone into one of our customer's rooms."

"I'm not just anyone, sir. I'm Steven's sister." She looked at him imploringly. "Please. I'll make sure my brother compensates you well for your help."

"Wait here," the clerk said abruptly, walking over to the desk and getting a key. He said something to the other clerk and came back. "All right, miss. Let's go. Easy now."

Anna let the man practically hold her as they took the elevator up to Steven's seventh floor room. They walked down the long hall to the end room, where the clerk unlocked the door. "Shall I turn a light on for you, Miss Randall?"

"That would be lovely, thank you." Anna sat down in one of the large armchairs, leaning her head back against the chair. "May I ask your name, sir?"

"My name is Ronald Lawrence, miss."

"Well, I want to thank you again, Mr. Lawrence, for all you've done for me this evening. I'll make sure my brother repays your kindness.

"Thank you, miss. If there's anything you need, just call downstairs. I'll be here until morning."

"Thank you, Mr. Lawrence. Goodnight." Anna waited until Ronald Lawrence closed the door. Then she got up and made sure the door was locked. She looked around the large suite and couldn't believe her eyes. It was one of the largest suites she had ever seen. The only hotel she had ever been to in her life was the hotel in Prescott, where she and her parents stayed once when they were too tired to drive home after they had seen a play. That room couldn't compare to this one. She walked around, looking at the opulent furniture. There was a large fireplace and beautiful gas-lit wall lamps. Woven rugs of deep reds and blues were on the floor, and marble surrounded the fireplace. Anna opened a door and peered into a large clothes closet. Steven's suits hung in a neat even row. She ran her hand along each suit, caressing it as if it were Steven's arm. She shut the door. The room was perfectly neat; it didn't appear that there was even anyone staying in the room. She opened the door that led to the bedroom and walked in. She turned up the wall lamp and looked around. A large four-poster mahogany bed dominated the room. She walked to the dresser and looked for little signs of him, anything that would give her insight into the man. There was a brush and comb, a watch chain, three pairs of cuff links, shirt studs, and collar buttons. She walked to the night table next to the bed. She pulled out the drawer and looked inside. There was a small box and a book. She started to touch them but stopped. She felt as if she were intruding on something extremely personal. She sat down on the bed and lifted the book out of the drawer. She smiled when she saw the title: *A Tale of Two Cities*. She had read it many times. It was one of Aeneva's favorites. How strange that Steven should have a copy of a book that was one of Aeneva's favorites. She put the book back and picked up the box. She opened the lid. Inside was a small jade dragon with black eyes. She took it out of the box and held it in her fingers a moment. It felt cool and smooth to her touch. She put it back in the box, shut the drawer, turned down the lamp and shut the door. She walked back out to the sitting room and went to the sofa. She decided to stretch out and relax. There was no telling when Steven would be back. She lay on her side, pulling her cloak around her. She closed her eyes, not knowing what she would say to Steven when he came into the room, but hoping that he would help her.

Steven walked across the lobby of the hotel to the elevator. The desk clerk had his back turned to him. He considered asking him if there were any messages but he was too tired. He took the elevator up to his floor. He walked to his room and opened the door, surprised to find the lamp on; he didn't remember leaving it on. He closed the door and went into the bedroom. After throwing his hat and coat on the bed, he went back into the other room. He needed a drink before he went to bed. He noticed that being with Rebecca Driscoll and her family made him drink more than he normally did. It was the only way to get through an evening with them. He poured the drink and sipped at it, letting the hot liquid course through his veins. He closed his eyes, remembering how Anna had looked that evening. She was so beautiful. He smiled when he recalled how she had toyed with Rebecca and her mother. He took another drink. Driscoll was getting sucked in. Nathan just had to make sure that Driscoll invested enough money to completely bankrupt himself. He started to turn down the lamp but decided instead to sit down and look out on the lights of the city. He walked across the large room and pulled open the heavy drapes. He stood at the window and stared out at the city lights and the dark ocean beyond. He felt alone, more alone than he ever had in his life. He couldn't talk to Chin or Joe, and he couldn't go to his family until he had gotten Driscoll. And being with the Driscolls almost every night made him even more lonely. They were not the kind of people who understood love or loyalty. He took another drink. He decided it was time to go to sleep. He was beginning to feel sorry for himself. He started back toward the bedroom but stopped, shocked by the sight of Anna asleep on the sofa. He walked toward her, standing over her. She looked like a child with her cloak pulled up to her chin, her dark hair falling all around her, her dark lashes curled against her cheeks. He squatted down next to her, touching her hair and running his hand gently across her cheek. She moved, taking a deep breath.

"Anna," he said softly. He watched as her eyes slowly opened and she looked at him. She seemed unafraid as she smiled.

"Hello. I wondered when you would be back."

"What exactly are you doing here and how did you get in?"

"I told the desk clerk that I was your sister from the

East and that I had been robbed, and he had to let me into your room. I told him that you would repay him for his kindness."

"That was nice of you."

"I couldn't think of any other way to get in. He was really very kind."

"I'm sure he was."

Anna sat up. "He was."

"Oh, Anna." Nathan smiled, sitting down next to her. "So, what *are* you doing here? I thought we weren't going to see each other again."

"I need a favor, Steven." Anna looked into his eyes. "A really huge favor."

Nathan reached over and wrapped a piece of Anna's hair around his finger. "Anything," he said softly. "I'll do anything for you."

"I need some money." Anna looked away from Nathan, suddenly feeling awkward.

"How much do you need?"

Anna took a deep breath. "Ten thousand dollars."

Nathan was silent a moment. "That's a lot of money. What do you need it for?"

"Well, I'm not really the one who needs it."

"Who does need it, Anna?"

Anna looked around the room, trying to find the courage to tell Nathan the truth. "Garrett needs it for his ranch. If he doesn't have the money by the end of the week, he'll lose the ranch."

"Oh, I see," Nathan replied quietly. He got up and walked over to the sideboard, pouring himself another drink. "He means that much to you?"

Anna got up and walked over to Nathan. "It means that much to him. He's my friend, Steven. I have to try to help him."

Nathan turned to Anna. "Why does he need ten thousand dollars?"

262

"He was in a gambling game with Driscoll. Driscoll staked him two thousand dollars, and Garrett was doing well. At one point he got up to five thousand dollars."

"Let me guess the rest." Nathan drank the rest of his whiskey and put the glass down. "Driscoll made an all-or-nothing bet with him. Told him the odds were that he'd win and come out a rich man. But Driscoll dealt the cards, and Garrett lost his five thousand dollars and his ranch."

"And Driscoll told him it would cost ten thousand dollars to get the ranch back."

Nathan shook his head. "The stupid boy. He should've known better in the first place."

"He didn't know. He had heard that Driscoll was a wealthy, respectable person. He thought he could trust him."

"You can't trust anyone in a poker game."

"I knew it was stupid to come here." Anna pulled her cloak tightly and walked toward the door. "I apologize for coming into your room."

"Anna, wait." Nathan walked to the door and closed it. "Come in here and sit down. I want to talk to you."

Anna went back into the room and sat down on the sofa. "I know it's a lot to ask, Steven. I wouldn't do it if I didn't think it were important. And Garrett will pay you back someday. I'll make sure he does."

"We can talk about that later. Right now, I want to talk about you."

Anna watched as Nathan sat down on the sofa next to her. He stretched his arm over the back of the sofa. She could hear his breathing, and she could feel his power. She looked at him and she was suddenly afraid. "What do you want to talk about?"

"Do you love Garrett?"

263

"I don't know how I feel about Garrett. I've known him since I was a girl, and I've cared for him ever since. He was my best friend, and we shared things that I've never shared with another person."

"Do you love him?"

Anna twisted the tie on her cloak, unable to meet Nathan's penetrating blue eyes. "I don't know."

"You must love him to do this for him."

"Why are you asking me this? If you can't give me the money, I understand. But please quit asking me about my personal life."

"I think I have a right to ask, don't you?"

"Why?"

"Because of what we shared that one night."

"It was a dream, that's all. You said so yourself."

"Maybe it was." Nathan leaned closer, cupping Anna's chin in his hand. "But maybe it wasn't." He kissed her softly, feeling the fullness of her lips and their gentle yearning. He looked at her, holding her face in his hands, forcing her to look at him. "Are you in love with me, Anna?"

Anna's large blue eyes searched Nathan's for something, anything that would tell her what he wanted from her. "I don't know," she answered honestly.

"But you like being with me."

"Yes."

"Yet you are willing to come here in the middle of the night and ask me for ten thousand dollars to lend to your friend. Just what does that mean, Anna?"

Anna pulled her face away from Nathan's hands. "It means that I care for him and I want to help him." Her anger was starting to build.

"I think it means you'll do anything to help him. Isn't that true?"

"Why are you doing this? If you don't have the money, that's all right. If you do have the money and you're willing to lend it to Garrett, why don't you just do it? Why must you make me feel like—'' Anna got up from the sofa and walked to the open window. She felt trapped.

"What do I make you feel like?" Nathan stood behind her.

"You make me feel cheap." She turned to face Nathan, her blue eyes ablaze with anger. "I will do anything I can to help Garrett but I will not sell myself for him. I value myself too highly."

Nathan looked at Anna and smiled. "Good. That's what I was hoping you would say."

"I don't understand. Was this a test?"

"No, I just wanted to know how you really felt about Garrett."

"And what do you think now?"

"I believe you really do care for him and you're a loyal friend, but that's as far as it goes."

Anna turned back to the window. "What does it matter to you, anyway? You're practically engaged to Rebecca Driscoll. Who knows, you might even have to marry her."

"I wouldn't do that."

"But if that's what it takes?"

"I'll find another way." He turned Anna around to face him. I'll play this game only so far, Anna. I'm going to see that Driscoll gets what he deserves but I'm not going to suffer in the process. I thought I could do it before but I can't now. Not since I've met you."

"Oh, Steven." Anna threw her arms around Nathan, burying her face in his chest. "I want to be with you. I don't want to lose you."

"That won't happen." Nathan kissed Anna deeply, holding her tightly. He felt her young body move against his, and his excitement grew. He wanted nothing more than to make love to Anna right now. "I want you to stay with me tonight." He kissed her mouth and cheeks and neck.

Anna held onto Nathan, afraid that she would lose him. "I'm afraid, Steven. I've never been with a man before."

"There's nothing to be afraid of."

She smiled slightly, staring into some far-off place. "My mother once told me that making love to my father was one of the most beautiful things she had ever experienced."

"Your mother sounds like a wonderful person."

"She is." She laughed. "She told me once that the first time she saw Trenton Hawkins she knew she would marry him."

Nathan froze at the sound of his father's name. Slowly, his hands came away from Anna and he backed up. "Is that your father's name?"

"Yes. He's not my real father, of course, but he's been like a real father to me. Just like Aeneva has. She *is* the only mother I've ever known."

Nathan looked at Anna and was astounded. No wonder he liked her so much. She embodied so many of the qualities that he respected and admired in his own parents. My God, he thought to himself, no wonder I felt so attracted to her. She is a product of the two people who loved and raised him. She was his sister.

"Are you all right, Steven? Steven?"

Nathan blinked his eyes and looked at Anna. She was so beautiful and he still wanted her. But that couldn't be now; now that he had found out the truth. His parents would never forgive him if he told them that he had fallen in love with the girl they had raised as their daughter. "What?"

Anna stepped closer, touching Nathan's cheek

266

with her hand. "Are you all right? You look strange."

Nathan knew that he had to push Anna away. As much as it would hurt her, he had to do it. It was for her own good. He put his arms around her. "Please stay with me tonight, Anna. I need you."

"I can't."

"Why?"

"My friends will be expecting me home. They'll worry."

"I can have a note sent to your friend's home."

"No, Joe would come looking for me."

Joe, Nathan thought to himself. Of course. Where else would Anna stay but with Joe and Larissa? "You're a big girl now, Anna. Can't you decide for yourself what you want to do?"

"Yes, but I don't want to upset Joe and Larissa. They have been so good to me."

"Perhaps if I had a talk with your friend. Maybe it's time you moved out of there."

"What do you mean?"

"I could get you a room here at the hotel. That way we could be together whenever we wanted." Nathan could see the shocked and confused expression on Anna's face, and it pained him that he put it there. He held her even tighter. "You could even move in here with me." He lowered his mouth to hers but she pulled away.

"No!" She walked across the room and turned to face him. "I thought you cared for me."

"I do care for you. That's why I want you to be close to me."

"You don't care for me. You only want what you can get from me. And then when you're through, you'll forget I ever existed. Oh, God." She started for the door but Nathan grabbed her arm.

"I'm sorry, Anna, I thought you understood. I'm

267

not ready for marriage. But I'm a very generous man. I could take good care of you." Nathan watched as Anna ran for the door but he stopped her before she opened it. "Wait, Anna."

"What for?"

Nathan touched her face, seeing the tears that welled in her eyes. "I thought you understood about these things, Anna. I didn't mean to insult you."

"It doesn't matter now." She put her hand over her face. "I feel like such a fool."

"There's nothing to feel foolish about." He took her arm. "Come on, I'll walk you out. I'll get you a carriage."

Anna yanked her arm away. "I can do it myself. Please do me a favor and forget that I ever came here."

"What about Garrett? How will he get his money?"

"Never mind about Garrett, I'll help him some other way."

"Anna, I'd like to be your friend. If you ever need anything—"

Anna confronted Nathan, her tear-streaked face beautiful in its anger. "I'll never ask you for another thing as long as I live. Never."

Nathan watched her hurry down the hall to the elevator. He crossed the room to the window and looked down on the street. He watched as the doorman hailed a carriage for Anna. She was on her way back to Joe's.

He had been successful—he had driven Anna away from him. She despised him now and that was how it should be. It was better for her to hate him than to love him. "But if only it would be that easy for me," he said to himself. "I am in love with Anna, and there is nothing I can do about it." He stood at the window and stared out at the city that had brought him nothing but pain. As soon as he was finished with Driscoll he was going to leave San Francisco and never return. Perhaps he'd go to China. He felt more of a kinship to the Chinese than he did to any other people right now, except his family. There was no place for him right now. After ten years, he was still alone. And he couldn't go home.

Chapter X

"I want to pay off what Garrett McReynolds owes you."

Driscoll dipped his piece of lobster in butter and sucked at the meat. He didn't bother to wipe his mouth before he spoke. "Now why in hell would you want to do that, Steven?"

"It's personal."

Driscoll continued eating the lobster, stopping only to sip at the champagne that filled his glass. "I didn't even think you knew McReynolds. So why do you want to help him out?"

"I never said I wanted to help him out."

"Then what is it?"

"I don't like him."

Now Driscoll stopped, wiping his hands and mouth. "And why is it exactly that you don't like a man you've only just met?"

"But I have met him before. About a year ago."

Driscoll leaned forward. "He never told me that."

"Why should he? He probably doesn't remember it."

"Do you mind explaining this to me?"

"I was traveling through Arizona, looking for

271

places to invest in. I stopped in a small town and went into the saloon to have a drink. I sat at a table and minded my own business when a group of young men came up to me. They started making fun of my clothes and they started knocking me around a bit."

"And?"

"I stood up and started fighting back. But there were five of them and only one of me. They dragged me out behind the saloon and beat the hell out of me. They also stole all of my money, a watch that belonged to my great-grandfather, and most of my clothes. Garrett McReynolds was one of them."

"Are you sure? He's been in California for the last two years."

"Not the entire time. I'm sure if you'll recall, he was in Arizona about a year ago at this time."

"Well, why didn't he recognize you?"

"He was so drunk that night he could barely walk. I don't even think he remembered doing what he did to me."

"But you want to pay him back just the same?"

"I've already paid back everyone else who was involved. He's the only one left."

"So you knew he was out here?" Driscoll smiled and sipped at his wine. "I like the way your mind works more and more, Steven. You planned to come here and invest your family's money but you also planned to make McReynolds pay for what he's done. I like that."

"So, you'll let me pay you what he owes?"

"No, I don't think so. I think we'll just consider this an even trade for the money I'll be getting from you for lining up investors. Deal?"

"Deal," Nathan said evenly.

"And what about that pretty little thing McReynolds brought to dinner the other night? I think he's planning on marrying her. Are you planning on ruining her, too?"

Nathan shrugged his shoulders. He decided now was the time to see how Driscoll really thought. "Who knows? She might prove to be useful to me, if you know what I mean."

Driscoll laughed. "I do like the way you think, Steven. In fact, if you weren't going to take her for yourself, I had plans for her for me. Umm, she is a lovely thing."

"So it wouldn't bother you if I kept a mistress? I know how much you love Rebecca."

"Hell, Steven, you're only a man. No matter how much you care for my daughter, you've got to have someplace to go to get away." Driscoll leaned forward and spoke in a conspiratorial tone. "Hell, I've had more than my share of women since I've been married. Couldn't have made it without them. In fact, I've got me a little gal now who's a real spitfire. She's Chinese and does she ever know how to treat a man." Driscoll whistled.

Nathan stared at the man across the table from him and felt nothing but disgust and hatred. The man was worse than he could have imagined. "Well, now that that's taken care of, how are our investors coming along? I received a cable from my father. He's very anxious to get into something over here. He may even come over himself sometime in the next few months."

"Well, I'd be real pleased to meet your father. The investors are falling right into line. I don't think we'll have much problem."

"Good. And what about you, Mr. Driscoll? Are you going to invest any of your own money in this little venture?"

Driscoll smiled, finishing his glass of champagne

and pouring more. "First of all, I think it's time you called me Franklin. Second, I don't venture into things like this much. I'm just the man who puts the deals together."

"I can understand that. That's why I'm going to check everything out very closely before I put any of my family's money into this." He looked around him and then at Driscoll. "I'll tell you something in confidence, though, Franklin. I'm going to put some of my own capital into this. There is no way a man can lose on this deal. I figure if I put in a million of my own I'll come out with at least two million in just a few years." Nathan saw Driscoll's interest peak for the first time.

"How is that?"

"Because the people we're dealing with aren't as smart as I am. I'm used to getting investors, taking their money, investing it, then paying them back with a tidy profit." Nathan lowered his voice. "The one thing I don't tell my investors is what I'm investing their money in."

"But I thought you said banking and land."

"Of course that's what I said. Do you think they'd put their money out if I told them I was investing in white slavery, prostitution, and drugs?"

Driscoll looked shocked for the first time. "You are kidding."

"Come on, Franklin, don't act so innocent with me. Did you actually think that I wouldn't have you checked out?"

Driscoll put down his wine glass. "What do you mean?"

"I mean I know how you've made most of your money, and it wasn't by being a good neighbor."

Driscoll finished his drink and poured the rest of the bottle into his glass. He took another gulp.

"What exactly do you know?"

"I know lots of things. I know that you've been dealing in white slavery for years, that you spend a lot of time in Chinatown, and that you're very familiar with the opium dens down there."

"How did you find all of this out?"

"I have my sources."

"Well, your sources are wrong." Driscoll finished his glass and slammed it on the table. He stood up. "I've had enough of this conversation."

"Sit down, Franklin." Nathan's voice had a hard edge to it. Driscoll complied. "Good. Now, here's what I want you to do."

"What the hell are you talking about? Nobody tells me what to do."

"Is that right? Well, how about your wife's father? He might be very interested in your activities of late. Especially concerning the Chinese boys." Nathan stared at Driscoll with hard eyes, thankful for the information Chin had sent him on Driscoll. "Are you ready to listen now?"

"Yes," Driscoll replied in an unsteady voice.

"I want you to secure those investors for me, and I want you to do it quickly. Tell them whatever you want, but get the money. And I want you to put up one million of your own dollars."

"Are you crazy?" Driscoll's voice was frenzied.

"Quiet down or you'll have the entire city knowing about your activities."

"I can't give you a million dollars. What if something happens and the deal goes sour? I'll lose everything."

"Nothing will go wrong, Franklin. I'm putting up one million of my own."

"But why me? I thought you just wanted me to put the investors together?"

"If you put in your own money, I'll be sure that you won't do anything behind my back. You'll take good care of me because you'll want to take care of your money, won't you Franklin?"

Driscoll lowered his head into his hands. "I thought you were an honest, upright citizen, Randall. You lied."

Nathan drank his champagne and stood up. "Well, that's what we all do, isn't it, Franklin. Contact me soon." Nathan walked out of the restaurant feeling better than he'd felt in a long time. Driscoll was more scared than he thought he'd be. He was deathly afraid of losing his fortune. Nathan smiled to himself. He couldn't wait to tell Driscoll that he'd lost all of his money and why. It was Driscoll's turn to suffer.

Nathan looked at the ranch as he rode toward it. It was beautiful. He could see why Garrett loved it so much. It was one thousand acres of fertile land that extended west to a cliff overlooking the ocean and east to the foothills. Cattle grazed lazily in the warm sun, and Nathan was reminded of his parents' ranch and the many times he had helped in the roundup. He rode across the rolling hills and into the flat country. He closed his eyes and remembered riding his Indian pony as fast as he could across the prairie. He remembered laughing with the Cheyenne children as they played at war. He remembered playing the same game with Berto. He pulled up, slowing the horse to a canter. He wondered what kind of man Berto would have grown to become. He knew that he would have been a good, fair man, the kind of man his parents would have been proud of. But Berto never had the chance.

Nathan rode into the yard. He saw Garrett in the large corral where they broke the horses. He was climbing onto a horse, while the ranch hands tried to hold the animal. When they let go, Garrett held on while the horse bucked and ran and tried everything he could to knock Garrett off his back. But Garrett tenaciously stayed on until the horse gave up. Garrett rode him around the corral for a while until the horse got used to the man on his back, then he dismounted and walked to the side of the corral. The ranch hands clapped and Garrett smiled. Nathan rode his horse to the corral.

"Garrett."

Garrett climbed up the side of the corral. "Mr. Randall, what're you doing out here? Get lost?"

"I need to talk to you."

"I'm pretty busy, Mr. Randall. I've got a lot of horses to break today."

Nathan looked toward the corral. "Could you use some help?"

"You? It's very dangerous trying to break a wild horse. I think you'd best stay out here."

"I'd like to try if you don't mind."

Garrett shrugged his shoulders. "Sure, why not? We've got one ready right now. He's a nasty one, too." Garrett turned to one of the men. "Jessee, take Mr. Randall's horse. Come on, Mr. Randall."

Nathan dismounted and walked to the corral. "Do me a favor, Garrett. Don't call me Mr. Randall anymore. Call me Steven."

"Sure, Steven."

Nathan climbed between the poles of the corral. He looked around. It felt good to be back in a familiar place. He took his gloves out of his pocket and pulled them on. He watched as the ranch hands fought the buckskin into the corral.

"You're sure you want to do this?" Garrett asked.

"Yeah, it's been some time but I'd like to give it a try."

"We haven't even been able to get a saddle on him yet." Garrett shouted over to the men. "Can't four of you even get a saddle on that animal?"

"He's crazy, Garrett. I don't think this one's breakable. I think you ought to let him go."

Garrett looked over at Nathan. "What do you think, Steven? You still want to give him a try?"

Nathan nodded and walked closer to the horse. He squinted. The buckskin was tall. His long legs were clean, and he moved with the kind of strength and grace that would make him an excellent saddle horse. *If* somebody could break him. "Do you have a pond around here? I won't need a saddle if you have a pond," Nathan said.

"Sure. Why?"

"Is it very deep?"

"I don't know. I guess so."

"Deep enough to make the horse swim?"

Garrett smiled slowly. He nodded his head. "I think so."

"Good. Let's get him down there."

Garrett mounted his horse. "Jesse, let's see if we can get him down to the pond." He looked over at Nathan. "Why are you doing this? This seems like a strange thing for a man like you to be doing."

"You don't even know what kind of man I am, Garrett. Let's go."

Garrett kneed his horse and waved for his men to follow. He rode next to Nathan. "You're here about Anna, aren't you?"

Nathan looked at Garrett in surprise but he remained silent.

"I saw the way you two looked at each other at the

restaurant. You're the man she met at the ball. You're the one she told me about."

"What did she say?"

"She wanted to know if it was possible to fall in love with someone after just meeting him."

"And what did you tell her?"

"I told her yes. I fell in love with her the first time I saw her. There's the pond."

Nathan glanced at the pond but he was thinking about what Garrett had just told him. Anna thought she was infatuated with him. He had to make sure it didn't go any further than that. As they started down the hill toward the pond, Nathan forced his thoughts back to the stallion.

"We need deep water close to the edge. I don't want to fight him in the shallows."

"Jesse, the far side," Garrett yelled.

Nathan took off his shirt.

"What're you doing?"

"I'm going swimming!"

"How do we get him in?"

"I said I'd ride him. It's up to you to get him to me." Nathan jumped in the water and swam to the middle. "Come on, Garrett," he hollered. "I'm waiting."

"Give me a minute to talk him into the idea," Garrett yelled back. "Form a half circle," he said to the men. "When I give the signal make as much noise as you know how to make. This horse is going swimming." He loosened the lariat from where it hung on his saddle and tossed the end to Jesse, who caught it neatly. "Drop his lead rope, Jesse, and back away from him slowly."

Jesse wrapped the end of the lariat around his saddle horn, nodding when he was ready. The buckskin shifted nervously. Garrett and Jesse rode forward slowly, the lariat stretched between them like an advancing barrier. "Now," Garrett shouted. The cowhands whooped, waving their hats and moving forward.

The buckskin trembled, whirling once to face the men, then back to the water. "Now," Garrett shouted again, spurring his horse forward. The rope slapped against the buckskin's hindquarters, startling him into a terrified leap that carried him thrashing and wild-eyed into the water.

"He's all yours, Steven." Garrett pushed his hat back, grinning.

Nathan swam close to the buckskin and caught the end of the floating lead rope. He swam closer, stroking smoothly, trying not to scare the already frantic horse. The buckskin snorted, clearing his nostrils of water, then swam, veering toward the opposite shore. Nathan waited until the horse was close enough and slid smoothly onto the buckskin's back.

A cheer went up from the shore but Nathan ignored it, concentrating on pulling the buckskin around in a circle that led him to deeper water. The horse was strong and fought the pressure of the rope but Nathan held firm, talking and stroking his neck. After nearly ten minutes the horse began to tire, and Nathan eased the pressure of the rope. He bent low over the horse's neck to tie the end of the lead rope to the halter, making a set of reins. He leaned forward, talking low. "Don't make an ass out of me, boy. This is supposed to work." Freed from the pressure of the rope, the buckskin headed for shore, his breath rasping. When Nathan felt the horse's hooves strike bottom, he readied himself for the worst. But it didn't happen. Nathan decided to press his luck. He dug his heels into the stallion's sides, and the buckskin broke cleanly into a gallop. Nathan balanced himself carefully, letting the buckskin get used to his weight. At the far end of the small valley, Nathan pulled up, then walked the horse slowly back to Garrett and the cowhands.

"How'd it feel?" Garrett asked with a smile, walking up to the stallion and rubbing his hand along the animal's smooth coat.

"It felt great. He's a strong animal. He'll make a good mount."

"Where'd you learn that about taking the horse into the water?" one of Garrett's men asked.

"I lived with the Cheyennes for awhile a long time ago. They did that with most of the horses they had trouble breaking. It saves the horse and the man."

"Come on, men. Let's get back. We've got some more horses to break." Garrett and the others mounted up, and they all rode back to the ranch. Nathan dismounted by the corral, handing the reins to one of Garrett's men.

"Thanks, Steven. You did a great job. I didn't think you could do it. You didn't seem the type."

"Like I said before, you don't know what type of person I am, Garrett."

"You said you wanted to talk to me."

"You have lots of work to do. I'll help you with it. We'll talk later."

Garrett agreed, and Nathan spent the day helping break horses. He talked and joked with the other men, and for the first time in years he felt relaxed and at home. Maybe because this was the first place to remind him of home. At the end of the day, Nathan cleaned up alongside the other men by the pump, and then he and Garrett had dinner in the ranch house. It was a small house, much like his parents' ranch had been until they had made it larger.

"You seem to like it here, Steven. I thought you'd

281

miss that fancy hotel of yours."

"I like it here because I come from a place like this, Garrett." Nathan looked out the window that faced the ocean. "I paid off your loan to Driscoll. The ranch is yours."

"Why would you do that? You don't even know me."

"But I know Anna."

Garrett shook his head. "She went to you that night at the hotel, didn't she? She asked you for money. Damn it, I told her not to do that."

"She did it because she cares for you. She was right to do it. A man like Driscoll shouldn't own a place like this."

"You paid Driscoll ten thousand dollars because you don't want Driscoll to own this land?" Garrett shook his head. "That's not why you did it, Steven. You did it for Anna. You're in love with her."

Nathan looked out the window again. "There's a condition attached to this, Garrett."

"What condition?"

"If I give you the deed to the land, I want you to marry Anna."

"What?"

"You heard what I said."

"I heard what you said but I don't believe it."

"Will you do it?"

"Why? Why would you want me to marry the woman you love?"

"Because I can't love her."

"I don't understand, Steven. I think you'd better explain it to me."

"I'm going to tell you something that you can't tell anyone else, Garrett. Especially not Anna."

"All right."

"I'm Nathan Hawkins. I'm Anna's brother."

Garrett stared at Nathan, nodding his head. "Why didn't I see it before. You look just like your father." He looked puzzled for a moment. "It was right after you and your brother disappeared that my folks moved closer to your folks' place. No wonder we don't know each other."

"Now you understand why I can't see Anna anymore."

Garrett shrugged his shoulders. "I don't see why it matters. You're not really her brother anyway. You're not related. Hell, you weren't even raised together. Anna never knew you."

"It's not right, Garrett. I could never do that to my parents."

"I don't understand this one bit. Why haven't you told your parents you're alive? And why in hell are you using the name Steven Randall?"

"It's a long story but believe me, I have a good reason."

"Does it have something to do with Driscoll? Is that why you're pretending to like his daughter?"

"Yeah, it has a lot to do with Driscoll."

"Can you tell me?"

"He's responsible for my brother's death and the death of someone else who was very special to me. Men like Driscoll always seem to get away with things but not this time. I've been waiting ten years so I could repay Driscoll for everything he's done to me."

"Can I help? I'd do anything to help you after what you've just done for me."

"I already told you how you can help. I want you to marry Anna and I want you to make her happy."

Garrett laughed. "Christ, Nathan, you don't ask for much, do you? Have you ever considered that Anna may not love me?"

"That doesn't matter. She cares for you a lot. She'll grow to love you."

"You're more naive than I am."

"I'm not naive. I just want what's best for her."

"Why don't you let her decide that for herself? Maybe she wants to be with you."

"Damn it, Garrett!" Nathan slammed his fist down on the table. "She doesn't even know me. How can she want to be with me?"

"She knows you, all right. She knew from the second she met you that you were the kind of man who was good and honest."

"She can't know that."

"Why are you fighting your feelings, Nathan? She loves you and you love her. You both should be together."

"I've already hurt my parents too much. I couldn't do this to them, too."

"God, you don't make any sense to me at all." Garrett stretched out and propped his feet on the edge of the table, leaning back in his chair. "You're not giving Anna or your parents much credit, Nathan. They'd all love you if you'd let them."

Nathan leaned forward, his expression intense. "And what about you, Garrett? Don't tell me that you don't love Anna. I saw you two that night at the restaurant. She seemed happy with you."

"Of course she's happy with me. I'm like a brother to her. Don't you see, Nathan? I *am* more of a brother to her than you ever were or will be." He put his hands behind his neck and looked past Nathan. "I'd be lying if I said I didn't love Annie. God, I've loved her from the first second I saw her standing in the front of our classroom. She singled me out right away, and I knew I had to be her friend. And I have been ever since."

"She loves you, too. You two are right for each other, Garrett."

"I won't force her to marry me, Nathan."

"Even if it's right for her?"

"Just because you think it's right for her doesn't make it right. I'd marry her in a minute if I thought she really wanted to be with me, but I won't marry her just to save you from your feelings for her."

Nathan sipped the glass of wine and put it down. "Do you have anything stronger than this? I'm so damned sick of wine. That's all the Driscoll's and their kind drink."

Garrett dropped his chair to the floor and walked to a desk that was against the wall in the small living room. He opened a door and reached in, producing a bottle of whiskey and two glasses. He came back to the table and sat down, pouring a drink for each of them. He held his glass up to Nathan's. "Here's to you, Nathan. You better face up to it, man. You're in love with Anna."

Nathan held his glass up and drank the contents, wincing at the feel of the whiskey going down. He poured himself another glass. "I'm not playing games, Garrett. I need you to do this for me. You're the only man I can trust to take care of her. You love her, and you've known her a hell of a lot longer than I have. You can make her happy. I can't. I don't know how to make anyone happy." Nathan downed his second glass of whiskey and poured another. "Least of all someone like Anna."

"You surprise me, Nathan. I thought you'd be the kind of man who would fight for the woman you love. But here you are practically throwing her into my arms. What's the real reason?"

"My life has been in turmoil ever since that day ten years ago when Driscoll murdered my brother and

285

almost murdered me. I swore then that I'd get even with him. I wrote my parents to let them know I was alive but I never heard from them. I assumed they didn't want to see me again. I didn't blame them. I held myself responsible for Roberto's death.''

"But your folks aren't like that, Nathan. They are some of the kindest folks I ever met. I can't believe they wouldn't welcome you back."

"I have a friend who says they never received the letters I mailed them."

"So why didn't you go back then?"

"Because I had decided that I was going to make Driscoll pay. I knew it would take time, and I knew it could be dangerous, so I decided just to let my folks keep believing I was dead, in case something happened to me. I mined for gold for nine long years."

"That's how you made your money."

Nathan nodded. "I knew in order to impress Driscoll I had to appear to be extremely wealthy. So I came up with a name and a reason to be in California."

"And what about Rebecca Driscoll? You don't really care for her, do you?"

Nathan shook his head. "I'm just using her. I feel badly about it but—"

"Don't feel too badly. Rebecca will be just fine. I happen to know she's not the faithful type. She's a lot like her father."

"And all this time I thought she was in love with me," Nathan replied in a hurt tone. He looked at Garrett and they both laughed loudly. "God, this is crazy, isn't it? The one woman I fall in love with is my own sister."

"But she's not your sister."

"Try telling my folks that." Nathan took another

drink of the whiskey. "I don't know what's going to happen with Driscoll and me. I want you to promise me right now that you'll take care of Anna."

"You know I'll do that, Nathan."

"And I want your promise that you'll marry her soon. Just as soon as you can."

"Jesus, Nathan—"

"If you don't promise me that, Garrett, I won't pay off your loan to Driscoll. That's the deal. Take it or leave it."

Garrett picked up his glass of whiskey and stared into the amber-colored liquid. "I'd be crazy not to take it, now, wouldn't I?"

"I think you would."

Garrett downed the whiskey. "But I won't. Go ahead and let Driscoll take the ranch away from me. I could live with that. I couldn't live with ruining Anna's life." He stood up and walked to the window that overlooked the Pacific. "We always talked about getting married when we were young. We were crazy for each other. We couldn't be separated. But young kids grow up, and feelings change. Anna's changed, mine didn't." He stared out at the ocean, then turned and walked back to the table. "But if I thought for one second that Anna wanted to be with me, I'd fight for her."

Nathan looked at the young man who stood in front of him, and he realized more than ever that Garrett was the one Anna should be with. He stood up. "I underestimated you, Garrett. I'm sorry. The ranch is yours, no matter what."

"I can't let you do that."

"Sure you can. Just promise me you won't get into any more poker games with men like Driscoll."

"I'm cured. I play with the hands around here, and the most I bet is a couple of dollars." Garrett looked at Nathan. "You still don't have to do this, Nathan. It's my problem, not yours."

"But I want to help and I can help. Besides, it's one less thing Driscoll will have his dirty hands on."

"And what about Anna?"

"I already told you, Garrett, I can't be a part of her life. Not now, not ever. I'm going to have to forget I ever met Anna O'Leary."

Garrett and Anna walked along the cliff, hand in hand. It had been weeks since Anna had seen Steven, and she tried to force him from her mind. She looked over at Garrett, the wind blowing his dark hair and she smiled. She felt so comfortable with him, and he always knew how to make her feel better.

"What's wrong, Annie?"

Anna looked up at Garrett. "Nothing's wrong. I was just thinking how much I like being with you."

Garrett squeezed her hand. "And you know how much I like being with you. I'm glad you came out here."

"It is beautiful, Garrett. I can see why you love it so." She stopped and looked out at the ocean. It was smooth and glassy, and the sun's reflection on it made it look like light blue glass.

"When are you going back to Arizona?"

"I don't know. I don't really want to go back. I like it here."

"Then don't go back."

"But I just can't stay at Joe and Larissa's forever."

"Why not? They love having you."

"I want to do something, Garrett. I want to make myself useful."

"Make yourself useful here."

"Garrett, I—"

"I don't mean as my wife, at least not yet. I mean, help me make this into a really productive ranch. You know as much about ranching as I do, maybe more. You know a lot of people through your father who'd be willing to take a chance on us."

"It does sound exciting. But it's an awfully long way to drive cattle, Garrett. They'd be so thin by the time we got them to Wyoming. They wouldn't be worth two cents a head."

"I'm not thinking about Wyoming. I'm thinking about Oregon."

"Oregon?"

"Sure, why not. It gets damned cold up there. They can't raise as much beef as we do down here. There'll probably be a lot of people up there who need beef."

"That's a wonderful idea, Garrett. It would be good to be doing something useful again."

"What about college? You always said you wanted to go."

"I know, but this is something I could do right now. And it's something I know. Maybe I can go to college later. Even if I don't, I can always learn. A person doesn't ever have to stop learning things."

"Are you sure, Anna?"

"Yes, I think it's a wonderful idea. I can move in with you, and we can be partners. I'll even use the money my father left to me to help rebuild the ranch. Oh, Garrett, I haven't been this excited about something in a long time." She threw her arms around Garrett's neck. She saw the intense look in his eyes as he pulled her close to him, but she didn't fight him. She loved Garrett, and she wanted to be with him. She closed her eyes, waiting for him to kiss her. But he did not. She opened her eyes. "This reminds me of when I was thirteen and wanted you to kiss me, and you wouldn't."

Garrett laughed. "This is a little different."

"How?"

"Because I love you, and I want to marry you. But I won't force you into anything you don't want to do. I want it to be your decision."

Anna reached up and touched Garrett's face. "You are so special, Garrett. You always have been. What would I do without you?"

"You'd be fine without me."

"No, I wouldn't." She pulled away from him, wrapping her arms around herself and staring out into the ocean. "You've always been there for me, Garrett." She turned to face him. "Now, I want to be here for you. I want to stay here with you. As your wife."

"Anna, I don't want you doing this out of a sense of loyalty. I want you to marry me because you think you can learn to love me."

"Garrett, I already love you." Anna leaned against him, feeling the security of his arms around her. Tears welled up in her eyes as she thought of Steven Randall but she forced them away, just as she would force his face from her memory forever.

"Are you all right? You seem sad."

"I was just thinking that I'll miss my parents but they can visit. They'll like it here. So will I." She looked up at Garrett. "Would you kiss me now?"

Garrett covered Anna's mouth with his, feeling the soft fullness of her lips. He pulled her to him. He had never needed anyone as much as he needed Anna. "I love you, Annie. I do love you."

"I love you, too, Garrett," Anna said softly, knowing that she could be happy with Garrett and praying that she wouldn't think of Steven every day.

"Come on, we should be getting back to the horses." Garrett put his arms around Anna. "You know, Annie, we can still be partners and not get married. You know that, don't you?"

"Of course I know that. But I like it better this way. It was meant to be anyway, Garrett. You and I always said we'd get married."

Garrett nodded. "I need to ask you something, Annie."

"Ask me."

"What about Steven Randall?"

The color left Anna's face. "What about him?"

"What if he were to come back into your life?"

"Why are you asking me about Steven Randall? I hardly even know the man."

"Come on, Annie. I'm not that stupid. He's the man you were telling me about. He's the man you said you thought you fell in love with."

Anna lowered her head, a look of guilt coming over her face. "I'm sorry, Garrett. It seems so silly and foolish. There's nothing worse than a girl falling in love with a man who doesn't love her."

"How do you know he doesn't love you?"

"I know he doesn't. He wanted to get me a room at his hotel. He wanted me to be his mistress."

"Well, you considered staying here with me and not marrying me. What's the difference?"

"You sound like you're defending him."

"I'm not defending him. I just want to know how you feel about him. Can you forget him, Anna?"

"Yes, of course I can forget him. I don't even know him, Garrett. He was just a fantasy. He wasn't real." She took the reins to her horse. "Can we go back now?"

"Sure," Garrett replied, swinging up on his horse, wondering what Anna really felt about Nathan. He liked Nathan, and he felt sorry for him. He really belonged with Anna but he wouldn't permit himself to love her. It was as if he were punishing himself for his brother's death. He hoped, at least, that Nathan's luck with Driscoll was better than it had been with Anna.

Nathan sat at the table, surrounded by some of San Francisco's wealthiest men. He looked at them all, confident that they would believe what he said. He looked at Driscoll and his anger was renewed. This man had cost him so much: his family, his brother, Anna, his life. He stood up, holding the stack of papers in his hands as he did so.

"Gentlemen, as you probably already know, I am Steven Randall. I've come here as a representative for my family to make some investments in America. I've looked all around this great country of yours, and I'm most impressed with the West, particularly California." Nathan waited a moment, watching as the men nodded in agreement. "When I first came to San Francisco, I heard that Mr. Franklin Driscoll was a very influential man. So I contacted Franklin and told him what I was interested in doing. He was kind enough to bring you all together so I could speak with you. Now I and my family are prepared to put up enough money to buy a bank here in California, or open our own. But as you all know, it takes a lot of capital to open a bank. I will need investors, and that's where you come in." He passed the papers around the table. "You will notice on this paper that I've had drawn up for you that the figures are right there, and they aren't formidable. We are anxious to get started on this. My family is prepared to spend as much as five million dollars in this investment. If you gentlemen are likewise interested, I would like to hear from you right now."

"What exactly would our profit be, Mr. Randall?"

"You should all see a profit within a year, Mr. Jameson. We have dealings with a bank in New York that will reciprocate with any of their notes, as well as a bank in Washington which I've already contacted."

"Why banking, Mr. Randall?"

"Your name, sir?"

"Howard Findley."

"Well, Mr. Findley, California is a young and growing state. People are coming here in large quantities, and the number will only grow in time. As people come here, they will need places to live and land to live on. All of them won't have money so they will have to borrow the money from us in order to buy land and supplies to build homes. And then there is the matter of gold."

"Most of those mines are panned out, Randall," Driscoll said in a hostile tone.

"I can assure you they are not, Franklin. I know of a man who hit a vein a few months ago and has already made himself two million dollars. Where do you suppose that gold goes to, gentlemen? It goes to the banks, and it's worth much more to us than money is. Once those miners hit gold, they want to get rid of it, spend it. And where else will people cash it in?"

"When would your family be interested in either building or taking over a bank, Mr. Randall?"

"As soon as possible, Mr. Jameson. I'm sure you gentlemen wouldn't mind being on the board of directors of your own bank, would you?" Nathan put his papers together and pushed his chair back. "Well, if you gentlemen don't have any more questions, I have another appointment." Nathan started for the door and stopped. "Oh, Mr. Findley, I never did answer your question. Franklin here has drawn up a proposal in which he guarantees that each one of you will double your investment in one year. Good afternoon, gentlemen." Nathan walked out the door, smiling to himself as he recalled the look on Driscoll's face. Finally, the end was near. As soon as he had the money from the investors he'd deposit it in an account, all in Driscoll's name. And then Driscoll would finally pay. He went back to his hotel and sent a letter by messenger to Joe, saying that he wanted him to send Chin some important information. Chin would know just what to do. Nathan sat by himself, waiting for the time when his revenge would be complete.

Anna and Garrett were eating dinner, absorbed in their stories of the past, when a knock on the door interrupted them. Garrett went to the door.

"Joe, what are you doing here? I thought you weren't supposed to be here for another day."

"I have to talk to Anna, Garrett. I've got some bad news."

Garrett held open the door. "Come in."

Joe walked to the table and smiled when he saw Anna. "Hi, girl. You look real good." Joe took off his hat and held it in front of him, twisting the edges of it.

"What's wrong, Joe?"

"It's Trenton, girl. He's real sick."

Anna stood up. "What's the matter with him?"

"I just got a cable today from Aeneva. She says he's real sick, and they don't know if he'll get well. She wants you to come home, Anna."

"Oh, God." Anna covered her mouth with her hands. "I'll go right now."

"Wait a minute. I can't go yet. I have some business to take care of. But Larissa has already planned to go with you."

"I'll go with her." Garrett walked over to Anna, putting his arms around her. "We can leave as soon as we're packed."

"That's good enough for me, boy." Joe put his hands on Anna's shoulders. "I'll be there just as soon as I can. I love Trenton like a brother. There isn't anything that can keep me away. Do you understand that?"

Anna hugged Joe. "Of course, Joe. Thank you."

"Well, I've got to be getting back to the city. You all be careful. I'll see you as soon as I can."

"You have to get me back to town, Garrett. I need to get packed and get home. I don't know what I'd do if I couldn't see Trenton again. The first time I met him he was so kind to me. He made me laugh, and not long after that he gave me a pony. My own pony." She breathed deeply. "He has been the father I've never had. I want to be there for him."

"I'll throw together some things, and we'll go into the city and get Larissa. Then we'll get the first train out of here."

"I just hope we can get there in time. I don't know what I'd do if I was too late, Garrett. I don't know what I'd do if I lost him."

"You won't lose him, Anna. Just hold onto that thought. I'll go pack."

Anna nodded, folding her hands in front of her. "Let him be all right, God. I've already lost one father. Please don't let me lose another. Please."

"Mr. Randall, this is certainly a surprise."

"Sorry to bother you tonight, Mr. Jameson. But this is extremely urgent."

"Well, come in then. Close the door."

Nathan walked into the library of Jameson's mansion. He sat down in one of the chairs that was by the fireplace. "I've found out some rather disturbing news."

"What is that?" Jameson asked absently, lighting his cigar.

"How well do you know Franklin Driscoll, Mr. Jameson?"

Jameson looked at Nathan, dropping the match into the ashtray on the table. "I know him very well, sir. Why do you ask?"

"I have reason to believe that Mr. Driscoll is planning to embezzle the money that we invest in our company."

"That's preposterous!" Jameson laughed but stopped abruptly. "Do you have any proof of this?"

Nathan reached into his pocket, pulled out a sheet of paper and handed it to Jameson. "You'll find facts and figures on here much different from the proposal I gave to you at the meeting. This shows a tremendous profit for Driscoll and not much of one for us."

"Are you sure Driscoll wrote this?"

"It's his handwriting, isn't it?"

Jameson nodded. "Well, nothing's lost yet. He doesn't have our money."

"But he does."

Jameson sat up straight. "What are you talking about? I gave that money to you."

"No, you didn't, Mr. Jameson. You gave it to Driscoll to give to me. I never received it."

"Well, where the hell is it, anyway?"

"It's in an account in the bank under Driscoll's name."

"What!"

"Yes. I found out through a friend of mine who

works there. He said Driscoll came in and opened a new account. He said it was for a special business investment."

"Well, what do we have to worry about then? He's just keeping it safe for us."

"Do you want to know what the special business investment is, Mr. Jameson?" Nathan waited until Jameson could hardly stand it. "Your friend is dealing in white slavery, drugs, and prostitution. Is that what you men plan on making your profits from, Mr. Jameson?"

"See here!" Jameson stood up to confront Nathan but Nathan was much angrier.

"Sit down! I'm going to tell you a few things about your friend, Franklin Driscoll." Nathan began walking around the room. "About ten years ago he went to a place in Chinatown where they have cockfights. He was enjoying himself, having a good time, until a young boy accidently fell into the ring, and the bird that Driscoll had bet on lost. Driscoll got angry and started pushing the boy around. So the boy's brother tried to help him but Driscoll decided to push him around, too. Driscoll wound up killing one brother and severely wounding the other."

"How do you know this?"

"I was the brother who made it." Nathan could see the look of shock on Jameson's face. "I'm surprised, Mr. Jameson. I thought you'd have something to say."

"I don't know what to say. I'm sorry about your brother but it has nothing to do with me."

"It has a lot to do with you, Mr. Jameson. You were there that night, too, weren't you?"

Jameson remained still, staring off into space. "I've often thought about that night. I couldn't believe that Franklin would kill a boy."

"But you stood by and let him do it. Why?"

"I don't know. Maybe it was that whole atmosphere. It was strange. I've never been back since."

"Do you recognize me yet, Mr. Jameson? Has it come back to you?" Nathan waited as Jameson stared at his face. "Can you remember what my little brother looked like? Well, I can. I see his face every second of every day. I'll never forget what Driscoll did to him. Never."

"You didn't come here for an investment at all, did you? You came here to get revenge."

"You catch on quickly."

"Then why the story? Why didn't you just tell me?"

"Do you actually think you would have listened to me? No. You're in too tight with Driscoll and his friends. This way, you've all implicated yourselves in Driscoll's dirty dealings."

"Now wait a minute." Jameson stood up. "I admit I've always known that Franklin has fooled around down there in Chinatown, but I never went along with it."

"You went along with it once, didn't you, Jameson?"

Jameson sat down. "What do you want, Randall?"

"My name isn't Randall. It's Nathan Hawkins. Remember it, Mr. Jameson."

"What do you want from me, Mr. Hawkins?"

"I want you to tell Driscoll that you found out I've set him up. I want you to tell him to get the money out of the bank because I plan to leave with all of it."

"What good will that do?"

"I'll have police waiting for him when he goes to get the money out."

"It won't work. Driscoll owns the police department."

"It'll work. Especially when I show the chief of police what Driscoll has on him and his family. Driscoll has an entire log that he's kept of people over the years. I'll just simply tell the chief to help me out or my friends at the newspaper will start printing some of the things they've found out about some of the prominent citizens in this city. And I'll testify that Driscoll murdered my brother and attempted to murder me."

"It won't matter. That was ten years ago. It'll never hold water."

"It'll hold all right. Driscoll murdered another man less than three months ago. I have more than ten witnesses who can testify."

"What about his family? If the police seize that money of Driscoll's they'll be bankrupt."

"They'll only be bankrupt in your terms, Jameson. I'm sure you'll see fit to help them out."

Jameson nodded. "When do you want me to go to Driscoll?"

"Right now. I've waited long enough. Make sure he gets to the bank within one hour. I'll have the police waiting." Nathan walked to the door. "And don't try anything, Mr. Jameson. That little book I was talking about has quite a few interesting things about you and your wife in there. I'm sure you wouldn't want those things to be public knowledge."

"I'm Franklin Driscoll, I tell you. Where is the manager?" Driscoll looked around him. "I demand to see the manager or I'll have your job right now, young man."

"Wait just a moment, sir." The young man went into an office and came out with an older man. "Yes, Mr. Driscoll. Can I help you?"

"Yes, I'd like to make a withdrawal."

The manager looked at the withdrawl slip and compared it with the signature on the other slip that the young man handed him. "I'm sorry, Mr. Driscoll, but your signature doesn't match."

"What do you mean my signature doesn't match?" Driscoll grabbed the piece of paper out of the man's hand and looked at it. "Of course it doesn't match. It's not my signature."

"You're saying this isn't your signature, Mr. Driscoll?"

"No, this is my signature. Now that we cleared that up, can I have my money?"

"I'm afraid not, sir."

"Look here, man. I am Franklin Driscoll. I am a very powerful man in this city. If you don't give me my money right now, I'll have the police here and have you arrested."

"Don't bother, sir. The police are already here."

Driscoll looked over at the uniformed men who walked in the door. "Ah, good. Now, if you don't give me my money I'll have you arrested."

"This man says he's Franklin Driscoll. He's trying to take out an enormous sum of money but his signature doesn't match the signature on our slip. I can't let him have the money."

"Can you write your name for us, sir?"

"What?" Driscoll was angry but he gave in and signed his name once again. He thrust it into the policeman's face. "There. That will prove it to you once and for all."

The policeman glanced from the paper to the slip that the bank manager had given him. "I'm sorry, sir. I'm going to have to take you in."

"What? Are you crazy? I'll have your jobs. Wait until Chief Larimer hears about this."

"Chief Larimer is the one who sent us, sir."

"What? I can't believe it."

"Come on, sir. Don't make it hard on yourself."

"I won't go to jail. I won't."

"You don't have a choice, sir." The officers began dragging Driscoll out of the bank but Driscoll kicked and fought.

"You let me go, damn it! You don't know who you're dealing with. I'm Franklin Driscoll.

"Sure, sure, Mr. Driscoll. Now come on with us."

Driscoll was dragged, kicking and screaming, to the police wagon. When the wagon pulled away, Nathan stepped out from behind the crowd that had quickly gathered. It had finally begun but it wasn't over yet.

Nathan walked into the dark corridor and stood in front of Driscoll's cell. He looked inside. Driscoll was lying on his back, snoring loudly. Nathan walked up to the bars and wrapped his fingers around them. He couldn't imagine what it would be like to be locked up in a place like this forever. He hoped he never had to find out.

"Wake up, Driscoll!" He shouted. Driscoll turned over onto his side but he didn't wake up. "Come on, Driscoll. Wake up. I don't have all day." He watched as Driscoll opened his eyes and looked around him as if he couldn't believe where he was. Driscoll sat up and ran his fingers through his hair. "Over here, Driscoll." Driscoll finally looked in Nathan's direction, squinting his eyes in the dim light.

"Who is it?"

"It's Steven Randall."

"Randall? That really you?" Driscoll hurried from the bed to the bars. "It is you. Did you come to get

301

me out?"

"That depends."

"On what?"

"On you."

"I don't understand."

"Look closely at my face, Driscoll. Are you sure you don't recognize me?"

"Of course I recognize you. You're Steven Randall."

"I'm Steven Randall to you now but how about ten years ago? What was I to you then, Driscoll?"

"I don't know what you're talking about."

"Well, see if you can remember this. You went to a cockfight with some of your friends one night in Chinatown. You bet a lot of money on one of the cocks, and it was doing well. In fact, it was winning. But some kid fell into the ring, and your bird wound up losing. You started pushing the boy around, and his brother stepped in to help him. Ring any bells yet, Driscoll?"

"Wait a minute." Driscoll got closer to the bars, staring at Nathan through the slits. "You can't be. I thought—"

"You thought you killed me that night, didn't you?" Nathan shook his head in mock disappointment. "Too bad, Mr. Driscoll, but somehow I managed to survive, even with a gunshot and a knife in the back."

"Listen, I didn't mean to do it. Honestly, Steven."

"My name's not Steven. It's Nathan. Nathan Hawkins."

"All right, Mr. Hawkins, I didn't mean to hurt you or your brother that night. It's just that I had been drinking, and you know what it's like when you've had too much to drink. The kid got in the way, and he made me lose a lot of money. I lost my temper."

"You didn't just lose your temper, Driscoll. You

302

murdered an innocent boy."

The expression on Driscoll's face changed as soon as he recalled something. "Even if you can prove that I killed your brother, no one in this town is going to go against me. Besides, who cares what happened to some stupid kid over ten years ago?"

"I care," Nathan replied coldly, grabbing Driscoll through the bars. "I have been waiting a long time for this, Driscoll. You robbed me of ten years of my life, and I'm going to make sure that the same thing happens to you."

"What do you mean?"

"How do you think it will feel to lose all of your money?"

"I'm not going to lose all of my money. I've got money in places you'd never even think of."

"Where? The ranch in Los Angeles? The ships in Monterey?"

"How did you know about them?"

"I know, Driscoll, because I bought you out."

"You can't do that. I never heard of that. My people didn't tell me one word about it."

"Your people didn't tell you because they're as scared as you are right now. They gave me all the information I needed on you. They were more than willing to let me buy you out. I think if you'll do some checking, Driscoll, you'll find that you don't have very many assets left."

"You can't do that to me. I'll have you torn apart for this, kid."

"You're not going to do anything of the kind. I'm calling all of the shots now." Nathan backed away from the bars and leaned against the wall. "Do you care what happens to your wife and daughter, Driscoll?"

"Of course I care what happens to them. If you've

303

done anything to hurt them—"

"I'll make sure they're taken care of as long as you leave them alone."

"You can't be serious."

"I'm very serious. I'll even see to it that the charges are dropped if you don't go back to your family."

"Where am I supposed to go?"

"You're going on a trip, Driscoll. A long, long trip."

"Where?" Driscoll's voice was tremulous.

"China. You're going to China, Driscoll."

"No! I'll never go there. Never!"

"It's either China or you can rot in prison here for the rest of your life. It's up to you."

Driscoll backed up until he sat down on the bed in his cell. He lowered his head into his hands. "I'll do what you want me to do, Hawkins. Just make sure my family is taken care of."

"They'll be taken care of."

Driscoll looked up, a look of anguish on his face. "How long do I have to stay in China?"

"For as long as you live, Driscoll," Nathan replied coldly. "For a man of your many talents you shouldn't have any trouble finding a way to live. Who knows. You might even wind up being wealthy and powerful again. But I doubt it."

"Why China, for God's sake?"

Nathan walked up to the bars, his blue eyes appearing as cold as ice. "Because of the way you have treated the Chinese all of your life, Driscoll. You treat them like dirt. You killed a Chinese girl years ago. Hell, you even killed an old man a few months ago, didn't you? Probably thought no one would even notice. Well, I noticed. He was a friend of mine, and he was the kind of person you could never hope to be. I figure if you live in China, you might be smart enough to learn something from them. You might even turn out to be a decent human being if you're lucky." Nathan walked toward the door but Driscoll's voice stopped him.

"How long have you been planning this, Hawkins?"

Nathan turned around, his young face cold and impassive. "Since the day you murdered my brother." He turned and walked out, hoping that he'd never have to see Franklin Driscoll again.

Chapter XI

Nathan turned over, disturbed by the loud sound. He tried to go back to sleep but the sound kept intruding. He opened his eyes. Someone was knocking on the door and wouldn't stop. He got up from the sofa where he had fallen asleep fully clothed and went to the door.

"Joe, what in hell are you doing here so early?"

Joe walked in, slamming the door behind him. "Where in hell you been, boy? I've been looking all over this city for you."

"Why are you so mad? In fact, what are you doing here? I told you not to come here until I was all through with Driscoll."

"Well, I don't give a damn what you told me. You got something more important to worry about now."

"What is it?"

"Your pa is real ill, boy. I got a cable from your mother yesterday. She's not sure if he's going to make it."

"Pa," Nathan said softly, walking across the room to the window. The sun was just coming up, and the entire city was about to be illuminated by its glow. "What happened?"

"She didn't say. She just told me to send Anna home right away. You didn't even know your sister was staying here, did you, boy?"

"I knew," Nathan said absently, walking over to the sofa and sitting down. "God, Joe, I feel as though my life is falling apart."

"What is it, Nate? What's the matter?" Joe sat down next to Nathan, putting his arm around his shoulders. "You met her, didn't you?"

Nathan nodded, running his fingers through his thick blond hair. "We met a number of times. I fell in love with her, Joe. I fell in love with my own sister."

"She's not your sister. Your parents raised her but she's not related to you."

"They might not see it that way."

"They will in time. If you love her, Nate, tell her so. She was miserable when she left here."

"She's gone?"

"She and Garrett and Larissa left last night. Took the first train out."

"How did she seem with Garrett?"

"Happy enough. She likes him. He's her friend. She'll probably even marry him if you drive her to it."

"He's good for her, and he loves her a lot."

Joe stood up. "Fine, you do what you want to do but I'm on my way to Arizona. You coming?"

"I haven't finished completely with Driscoll."

"Who cares? He's in jail. He's not going to go anywhere until you come back."

"I'm scared, Joe. I haven't seen my parents in over ten years."

"Has your love for them changed in that time, Nate?"

"No."

"Then you don't have anything to worry about.

Pack your things and let's get going."

Anna hurried into the house, ahead of Larissa and Garrett. She embraced Aeneva, holding onto her as if she would never let her go. "How is he, Aeneva?"

Aeneva kissed Anna on the cheek, pushing the hair from her face. "He's resting now, dear. You can go in and see him if you like."

"No, I don't want to wake him. What happened?" Anna put down her bag and untied the ribbons of her bonnet. She sat down in the rocking chair her father had made for her on her ninth birthday.

Aeneva stopped as she saw Larissa and Garrett come in the door. "Larissa," she said with great affection, taking the woman in her arms. "I am so glad you are here. I need the company."

"Joe is on his way."

"I'm glad." Aeneva looked at Garrett. "Hello, Garrett. Thank you for making sure Anna got here safely."

Garrett removed his hat. "My pleasure, ma'am. How is Mr. Hawkins?"

"He's a strong man, Garrett. We'll just have to pray that he makes it."

"What did happen, Aeneva?" Anna walked to Aeneva.

"He and some of the hands went up into the hills after that cat that's been going after our cattle. Someone wounded it but it ran off. Trenton and a few of the men kept tracking it. The rest of them gave up and went home, thinking that the cat would die from the wound. On the third day out, Trenton got jumped by the cat. She'd been protecting some cubs. He stumbled on them accidently. The cat thought he was trying to hurt them. He tried to get away but she

309

attacked him."

"Oh, God." Anna put her arm through her mother's. "How badly was he hurt?"

"She ripped open his neck and part of his cheek. He tried to protect his face so his arms and chest were badly cut. She played with him like he was a mouse."

"Did anyone kill her?" Garrett asked.

"No. She stopped attacking Trenton when he played dead. She apparently got to her cubs and moved them. Trenton managed to drag himself away from the area. He fired his rifle three times. The other men found him and brought him home."

"Will he be all right? Is he healing?"

"He was badly torn in places, Anna. I did the best I could for him. I put every medicine I could think of on the wounds. Infection has already set in. He has a fever and he's very weak. We'll just have to see."

"I want to go in and see him. I won't wake him up."

Aeneva hugged Anna. "You stay with him as long as you want. He would love to wake up and find you there."

Anna hugged Aeneva. "I love you, Aeneva. I'm sorry I wasn't here."

"Don't be sorry. There was nothing you could have done. Go on now."

Anna went to Garrett, taking his hands in hers. "Thank you, Garrett. I don't know what I would have done without you."

"It'll be all right, Annie. I'll be at my folks if you need me. I'll probably ride over tomorrow to see you."

"'Bye, Garrett." Anna walkd up the stairs to Trenton's room. She quietly opened the door and went inside. The lamp on the table next to Trenton was turned down so she could barely see his face.

There was a chair next to the side of the bed. It was, she assumed, where Aeneva had been sitting since it had happened. Anna walked across the room and stood at Trenton's side. Half of his face was covered with a bandage, and his neck, right arm, and chest were wrapped as well. He was pale and his breathing was labored. "Trenton," Anna said softly, reaching over to touch his forehead. He felt hot. She saw the bowl on the table, and she put the cloth into it, rinsing it out and putting it on his head. She wiped his face, then folded the cloth and left it on his forehead. She sat down in the chair, watching him as he slept. She held her stomach, feeling almost sick inside. She never realized until now how much she loved this man who had taken her in and loved her as his own. She felt the tears run down her face. "I love you, Daddy. I love you." She laid her head on his chest and closed her eyes, silently praying that he would live.

Larissa handed Aeneva the cup of tea and sat down opposite her. "Are you sure you're all right?"

"I am fine. I just don't like to think about the possibility of losing him."

"I know, Aeneva. I don't know what I'd do if I lost Joe."

"I can't wait until he gets here. Maybe he will be what helps Trenton to recover."

Larissa nodded as she sipped her tea. She wanted to find a way to tell Aeneva that Nathan was alive. Joe thought she should be prepared when he came through the door. "What would you do if you found out that Nathan was alive, Aeneva?"

Aeneva stared at Larissa with her dark eyes. "What are you talking about?"

"How would you feel?"

311

"I would feel overjoyed. And it would make all the difference in the world to Trenton."

Larissa reached across the table and took Aeneva's hand. She squeezed it tightly. "Nathan is alive, Aeneva. He's alive."

Aeneva stared at Larissa, her large eyes filling with tears. "You are sure? You are not lying?"

"No, I'm not lying. He's on his way here with Joe. They'll be here very soon."

"Oh, my God." Aeneva's voice broke, and suddenly she began to cry. "I can't believe it. Nathan."

Larissa got up and put her arms around Aeneva. "It's all right, Aeneva. Cry. You deserve to cry."

"I just can't believe it. Just this last week Trenton was talking about the boys. He said he wondered what Nathan would have grown up to be like. I haven't seen him that sad in a long time."

"Well, maybe Nathan can help him recover. It would be the best thing for Trenton."

"What happened, Larissa? How long have you known?"

"It's a long story and one I think Nathan should tell you himself."

"Oh, it doesn't matter. The only thing that matters is that he's alive." She wiped the tears from her eyes. "I'll make sure his old room is fixed up for him. He'll like that."

"There will be time enough for that tomorrow." They both looked up when they saw Anna coming down the stairs.

"Have you told Anna yet?" Aeneva asked.

"No, I thought you should do that."

Aeneva smiled as Anna walked toward her. "It's wonderful having you here. Sit down. I want to tell you something."

"I'll get you some tea." Larissa got up and went to

the kitchen.

"What is it?"

"I just found out that Nathan is alive."

"Nathan? Oh, how wonderful. What happened? How did you find out?"

"Larissa told me. She said he'll be here tomorrow with Joe."

"But they didn't tell me they had found him."

"They probably only just found out. It doesn't matter anyway. Your father will be ready to get up out of that bed when he sees Nathan."

"I've heard so much about him. I can't wait to actually meet him."

"He was a wonderful boy. I'm sure he's a fine man." Aeneva shook her head in disbelief. "I can't believe he left here a boy and he'll be returning a man."

"Tell me again what he was like, Aeneva."

"He was a beautiful child. When he was small he was always happy and very, very curious. We couldn't keep him out of anything. My people loved him because he was so different from them. He would play with the Cheyenne boys, and you could always see him with his golden hair next to the dark-haired boys. He loved everyone in the camp, and they all loved him. He was very sad when we left there."

"Did he and Roberto get along?"

"They fought as any two brothers would, but they loved each other very much. In fact, Nathan was always getting in fights with boys who made fun of his brother's dark skin and hair. Trenton tried to tell him that he couldn't win every battle with his fists but he didn't seem to understand that. All he knew was that some boys were trying to hurt Berto, and he couldn't let them get away with it."

"He was like your real son, wasn't he?"

"Yes, he was. When I found out he was dead or I thought he was dead, I felt his loss as much as I did Berto's."

"I'm sorry." Anna took Aeneva's hand. "I'm sorry that Berto isn't alive, too."

"We must be thankful for what is, Anna. Tomorrow Nathan will come back into our lives, and we will be a family again."

Everyone was on edge. Joe and Nathan's train had been delayed, and they weren't to arrive for another day. So the three women kept busy tending Trenton and visiting with each other. The day had passed quickly, and now it was the day when Joe and Nathan were to arrive. Aeneva tried to keep busy but her mind was constantly thinking of Nathan and what it would be like to see him again. Larissa was wondering how Aeneva would react when she found out she and Joe had known all these years that Nathan was alive. And Anna was wondering how the brother she had never seen would react when he found out he had a sister.

"Anna, why don't you go for a ride? We don't know when Joe and Nathan will be here."

"I might go over and see Garrett. I need to take my mind off of this. The waiting is terrible."

"I know." Aeneva gave Anna a hug. "Go on. Tell Garrett I said hello."

"I will. 'Bye." Anna went to the stables and saddled her mare. She led her outside and swung up on her, immediately feeling at home in the saddle. She rode quickly, jumping the small stream that ran along their property to Garrett's property. She felt her mare running hard, as if she had missed the exercise, too. Anna had just reached the grove of oaks when she pulled up. Garrett was standing by the stream throwing rocks into the water, skimming them along the surface. She slid off her horse. Garrett smiled as she walked over to him. "Hello."

"Hello." Garrett held out his arms, and Anna went into them. "Are you all right?"

"Yes. I'm just worried about Trenton. You should see him, Garrett. He looks terrible. I'm afraid he won't get well."

"He'll get well. Trenton Hawkins is one of the strongest men I know. He's not going to let a mountain lion get the best of him."

Anna smiled, looking up into Garrett's hazel eyes. "You really do love me, don't you, Garrett?"

"You know that I do."

"I meant what I said in California. As soon as Trenton gets well, I'm going to go back to California with you as your wife. And I'll help you make that ranch into one of the best ranches in the whole state!"

"Just take it easy. Let's take it a step at a time. Wait until Trenton gets well first, then we'll talk about marriage."

"You're not afraid, are you? Do you think I'll be too much to handle?"

"I *know* you'll be too much to handle but I'd like to give it a try. But let's just take our time now. You need to spend time with your folks. I'll stay here a while and then I'll head back to Frisco. When you're ready to come back, you let me know. Then we'll talk about marriage."

"What is it, Garrett? You act like you don't want me to marry you."

"I want to marry you more than anything in this world," Garrett said warmly, pulling Anna into his arms again. "But I want to make sure it's what you want. I don't want you to have any regrets."

"But—"

"Shhh." Garrett put his finger over Anna's lips. "I don't want to talk anymore. Let's just enjoy this beautiful day at this place where we have so many good memories." He kissed Anna, holding her tightly against him, hoping that she would always be his but feeling that she would not.

Nathan reined in the horse at the entrance to the ranch. He stopped and looked all around him, shaking his head. "I can't believe I'm really here."

"How does it look to you, Nate? Does it feel good to be home?"

"It feels great, Joe. I never realized how much I missed it here."

"Well, let's get going. I'm sure your mother is real anxious to see you."

They rode into the yard, hitching their horses at the corral. They walked up to the house, and Nathan stopped when he got on the porch. He looked out at the view of the mountains, trees, and rolling grass. He recalled all of the times that he and Berto had raced along those fields, and all of the times he had cheated Berto. I'd give anything if I could race him just one more time, Nathan thought to himself. He heard the door open behind him and turned. His mother was standing at the door, her dark hair pulled back, her large eyes quickly filling with tears. Even after ten years she looked beautiful to him. She held out her arms to him.

"Mother," he said softly, wrapping his arms around her. He held her tightly, tears stinging his eyes as he felt anew the warmth and security he had always felt as a child with Aeneva.

"Let me look at you," she said lovingly, running

her hands over his face. "Oh, Nathan, you look so much like your father. You are so much like him."

"It's all right. It'll be all right." He held her to him, wondering if she would ever forgive him for staying away for all of these years.

Aeneva wiped the tears from her face. She kissed Nathan on the cheek. "Now, how about you, Joe? Do I get a hug from you?"

Joe took off his hat and slapped it against his thigh. "I was wondering when you was going to notice me, woman. You should've married me, you know. I always was the more handsome of the two."

"Just don't tell Trenton that." Aeneva kissed Joe on the cheek and threw her arms around him. "Oh, it's so good to have you here. Trenton will be so glad to see you."

"How is he, Mother?"

"He's still very weak."

"What happened, Aeneva?"

"Let's go inside. I'll tell you about it later. You have a wife who is anxious to see you."

They went into the house. Joe went to Larissa, while Nathan and Aeneva went up the stairs to Trenton's room. Aeneva opened the door and walked in, followed by Nathan. They walked to Trenton's side. Aeneva reached into the bowl of water and rinsed the cloth that was on Trenton's head. She wiped his face and replaced the cloth on his forehead. She kissed him on the cheek and stepped back by Nathan.

"What happened to him, Mother? He's been torn apart."

"A mountain lion attacked him. He's lucky to be alive."

"He looks bad. Is he healing?"

"I'm worried about the gash on his neck. It doesn't

317

seem to be healing well at all. I've even had the doctor from town look at it."

"You had a doctor look at Pa?"

"Yes. I was afraid that I wasn't doing enough for him. I wanted to see if the doctor knew something I did not. But he wasn't healing well so I removed the medicine the doctor told me to put on it, and I mixed my own. I just hope it does some good."

Nathan walked closer to the bed, sitting down in the chair. He reached out and touched Trenton's arm. "Pa, Pa, can you hear me?" Trenton didn't move. Nathan looked back at Aeneva, and she nodded her encouragement. "Pa, it's Nathan. I'm home, Pa." Trenton still didn't move. "Why don't you go and visit with Joe, Mother. I'm going to stay here for awhile."

Aeneva leaned down and kissed Nathan on the cheek. "It's so good to have you home." She walked to the door. "Nathan, you have a sister. Her name is Anna. We've had her for the last ten years, since right after we lost you and Berto. You will love her. She is the light of your father's life."

Nathan nodded and looked back at his father. Anna was the light of his father's life. How could he ever tell him that he was in love with her? He rubbed his father's arm. "I love you Pa," he said sadly, wondering if his father would ever hear those words from him again. Trenton made a moaning sound and turned suddenly. "Pa!" Nathan called to Trenton but Trenton didn't wake up. Nathan sat next to his father, prepared to stay with him until he woke up.

Anna came riding into the yard, feeling much better than she had when she left. She was growing more and more dependent on Garrett and she knew it. But she liked the feeling. She knew that Garrett

318

would never let her down. She started to unsaddle her horse but one of the men came to take the mare from her.

She patted her mare's nose. "You've taken good care of her, Jake."

"She missed you, Miss Anna. She hasn't been ridden that hard since you left."

"Well, I'll be riding her like that every day. Thanks, Jake." She walked across the yard, stopping to pick one of the roses for her mother. She smelled the sweet flower and smiled. The sunshine felt warm on her shoulders, and she looked up at the clear blue sky. She couldn't believe in her heart that her father was going to die. It just wasn't possible.

"What you doing there, girl? We wondered when you were going to get back."

"Joe!" Anna ran up the stairs to meet her friend. She hugged and kissed him. "Have you seen Trenton? Is he any better?"

"No, he's not stirring. But he's a strong man. I think he'll make it."

"So do I."

"So, where you been? With Garrett?"

"Yes. We went riding. We have this place where we go. It's a grove of oaks by a stream. It's beautiful there, Joe. Wildflowers grow and it's always cool there. We used to go there in summer when we were kids. We'd take picnics and spend whole days just swimming and riding and eating."

"Sounds like you and Garrett have been close for a long time. You've never been in love with anybody else, have you Anna?"

"Of course not, Joe. Why would you ask?" Anna answered too quickly.

"Oh, I was just hoping that you wouldn't use Garrett."

"What do you mean? I would never do that to

Garrett. I really do love him, Joe."

"I think you mean that, girl, but what kind of love is it? Is it the kind of love I have for your mother, or is it the kind of love I have for Larissa?"

Anna turned away, crossing her arms defiantly across her body. "Why are you asking me all of these questions?"

"Because I know about Steven Randall."

Anna looked at Joe. "How do you know about Steven Randall?" But before Joe could answer Anna, Aeneva came out onto the porch. "How was your ride?"

"It was wonderful. Garrett and I had a good time. How is Trenton?"

"No change." Aeneva put her arm around Anna's shoulders. "Nathan is here, Anna. He's up with Trenton now. Do you want to meet him?"

"Oh, yes."

"Anna, wait." Joe tried to stop Anna.

"We'll talk later, Joe. I want to meet my brother first."

Joe followed Anna into the house, shaking his head. He went up to Larissa. "I didn't have a chance to tell her."

"If only I'd known. I could have prepared her."

"I don't know that it would have done much good. Either way, it's going to come as a real shock to her."

"I just hope this family isn't torn apart." Larissa leaned against Joe. "I feel for them all but I especially feel for Nathan. He's been alone for so long. He's done what he thought was the right thing to do. I hope they will understand that."

"Trenton and Aeneva will. I'm not so sure about Anna."

*   *   *

Anna held onto Aeneva's arm. "What if he doesn't like me? What if he resents me?"

"Nathan isn't like that, Anna. He'll welcome you into this home just as we have."

"I'm afraid. I've heard so much about him, I feel as if I know him. I want him to accept me."

"Trust me, Anna. He will accept you." Aeneva opened the door. "Do you want me to go in with you?"

"Yes," Anna replied uncertainly. She walked ahead of Aeneva, staring at the blond-haired man who sat in the chair next to her father's bed. It was hard to see what he looked like but she could tell he had Trenton's coloring. She was excited yet scared. She was finally going to meet her brother. She walked up behind him and tentatively touched his shoulder. "Nathan," she said softly. The man stood up, turning slowly around. Suddenly Anna had a sinking feeling in the pit of her stomach. Her legs felt weak as she leaned on the chair for support.

"Hello, Anna."

Steven Randall's face shone in the place of her brother's. Why hadn't she seen it before? Why hadn't she listened to that part of her that told her he wasn't right for her?

"Anna, this is your brother, Nathan."

Anna heard Aeneva's words but she couldn't speak. She felt herself begin to shake all over. How long had he known? How long had he let her make a fool of herself? She turned and walked out of the room, listening to Aeneva's voice calling her but ignoring it. She ran down the stairs and out of the house, ignoring Joe as he tried to reason with her. She had to get away from here. She had to be alone. She started for the stables but she heard footsteps behind her. She started to run but a firm hand on her arm stopped her. Nathan turned her around.

"I want to talk to you, Anna."

Anna stared into the face of the man she had once loved, the man who was her brother. She began to shake all over. "How could you do this to me? How could you?"

"I didn't know, Anna. I didn't know."

"You liar!" Anna ran away but Nathan caught up with her.

"Let me try to explain it to you. As soon as I found out I pushed you away from me. I never wanted to hurt you. Never."

Anna stared at Nathan, her eyes filled with anger. "I hate you for this. Our family will never be the same because of you. I wish you had never come back." She ran to the stables, and this time Nathan didn't follow her.

He watched her as she rode out of the yard. He considered going after her but he knew it wouldn't do any good. He turned back toward the house and saw his mother and Joe standing on the porch. He knew it was time to tell his mother the truth about everything. He had put her through too much already. He walked back to the porch.

"Nathan, I'm sorry. I don't know what got into Anna. That's not like her."

"I do." Nathan took his mother's arm and went into the house. "Joe, I'd like you to be here for this."

"For what?" Aeneva looked from Nathan to Joe.

"Just sit down, Mother. Please." When Aeneva was seated at the table next to Joe, Nathan proceeded to tell his story. He could see the anguish on his mother's face when he told her about Roberto, and he reached out and held her hand. She didn't try to take it away. As Nathan proceeded with the past ten years of his life, Joe filled in portions of the story that he knew. When Nathan finally came to the last few months he stopped, unable to tell his mother about Anna.

"So, you haven't told me yet how you managed not to meet Anna if she was staying with Joe and Larissa all of this time."

"I did meet her, Mother. Several times." Nathan looked at Joe for support. Joe nodded his head confidently. "But I didn't know she was my sister." He said the words measured and slow, hoping that he could convey to his mother the meaning without actually having to tell her.

Aeneva was silent for a time, thinking, considering. When she looked at Nathan, her expression was neither stern nor approving. "She is in love with you," she said simply.

Nathan nodded his head. "When I found out she was my sister I knew we had to end it. So I pushed her away. I made her think I didn't love her."

"But you do love her, don't you? It was written all over your face when you stood up and looked at her."

Nathan reached for his mother's hand. "I'm sorry, Mother. I never meant for this to happen. I'd give anything if we'd never met."

"You cannot change what has happened." Aeneva pulled her hand away. "There is something I still don't understand, Nathan. Why didn't you let us know you were alive? Do you know how much pain and anguish we went through when we thought you were both dead? If it hadn't been for Anna I'm not sure your father and I would have survived the loss."

"I did the only thing I could at the time. I knew it would take a long time to get the money I needed to fight Driscoll, and I was afraid if something happened to me, you would have to go through it all again. I didn't want that for either of you."

Aeneva looked at Joe for the first time. "I cannot believe you did not let us know our boy was alive. Why, Joe?"

"Because I couldn't betray a trust. Nathan begged me not to tell you two he was alive until this thing with Driscoll was all over and he could come home safe and sound."

"You know how much we suffered, Joe."

"Yes, I do know, Aeneva. It wasn't an easy thing for me to do but I figured it's what you and Trenton would've done. I kept an eye on him and made sure he was all right until he could come home to you."

Aeneva stood up. "I am going up to sit with your father."

Nathan stood up and went to his mother. "Please try to understand, Mother. I did what I thought was right. I never meant to hurt you or Pa or Anna."

Aeneva reached up and gently touched Nathan on the cheek, then went up the stairs.

Nathan sat back down at the table. "I should've never come back here. I don't have a family anymore, Joe. I just don't fit."

"Bullcrap! Give them both some time. It's quite a lot for them to digest right now, especially your mother. She feels betrayed and so does Anna. They need time to get to know you again."

"If Mother reacted that way, Pa will never forgive me."

"Don't you believe it. Your Pa is one of the fairest men I've ever known. Once he hears the facts, he'll understand."

"I don't know." Nathan ran his hands through his hair. "I've got to get out of here. I've got to think."

"There's a real nice grove of oaks near a stream. Real pretty place to think."

"Yeah, I know the place. I used to go there all the

time when I was a kid."

Joe walked to Nathan, patting him on the back. "Don't worry, boy. Everything will work out in time. You just have to hang on."

"I'll try, Joe. I'll try." Nathan went upstairs and quickly changed out of the constricting city clothes to the clothes he was used to wearing. He put on a pair of jeans and a blue working shirt, rolling up the sleeves to his elbows. He pulled on an old pair of boots and hat and went to the stables, looking for a horse to ride. He saw several horses in the stalls and went up to a large Appaloosa stallion, patting him on the neck and rubbing his nose. The animal threw his head but Nathan continued to talk to him. Nathan backed him out of the stall and put on the tack. After leading him out of the stable and into the yard, he mounted the large stallion and headed off in the direction of the oak grove. He kneed the horse into a gallop, feeling the need to get away from the house as quickly as he could. He knew he wasn't wanted there, and the further away he got the better he felt. He rode hard, feeling the strength of the animal beneath him as it took its great strides. Nathan jumped a wide part of the creek and rode along it for a time until he came to the grove. He reined the stallion in, slowing him down to a canter as they neared the grove. Nathan dismounted, letting the horse graze freely on the lush grass that surrounded the creek. He smiled as he looked up at the large, old trees. They had grown even larger in the last ten years, and their branches leaned toward the earth as they weakened with age. He walked over to the creek and knelt down, cupping some of the fresh water into his hands. It tasted good, fresh and cool. He walked over to his favorite tree and sat down against it. He turned to look at the trunk of the old tree, running his hand along the rough bark, feeling the years it had been on this earth. He crossed his legs and leaned back, closing his eyes. How many times had he come here as a boy to get away from everything? He smiled when he thought of the times he had hidden in the tree from Berto, who always wound up crying because he couldn't find him. He missed Berto now more than ever. He knew that his brother would understand what had happened. He was probably the only one of his family who would. He closed his eyes, feeling the weariness come over him. He hadn't slept in two days, not since he'd found out about his father. He felt his body relax and felt the cool breeze against his face. His head felt heavy, and he leaned it back against the trunk of the old tree. Perhaps this old tree was the only thing that could give him solace now, he thought. Thoughts went through his head; thoughts of how he had missed his family, thoughts of Berto, thoughts of Anna. Images and colors flashed in his brain, and he felt his body jerk. He wanted to wake up but he couldn't. He thought he heard other sounds but his body was too intent on sleeping.

"What are you doing here?"

Nathan jerked when he heard the sound of Anna's voice. He forced himself to open his eyes. She was standing in front of him, her long hair in tangled disarray, her cheeks flushed, her eyes blazing. "What?" He couldn't remember what she'd just asked him.

"What are you doing here?"

"I needed to go for a ride. I used to come here when I was a kid. This was my favorite place."

"You have to ruin everything for everyone, don't you?" Anna said angrily. "Why did you come back? Why didn't you stay in San Francisco with the Driscolls?"

"That's all over now. I'm finished with Driscoll."

"Are you finished with Rebecca now, too?"

"Yes." Nathan stood up. "I didn't know who you were, Anna. I didn't find out until that night in my hotel room. When you said who your parents were I couldn't believe it. I knew then that I had to push you away from me. That's why I did what I did."

"Why didn't you tell me who you were? Why, Nathan?"

Nathan shook his head and walked out of the grove of trees toward the stream. "I didn't know how long I was going to be involved with Driscoll. I didn't want you getting involved. You know what he did to Garrett. That's the least of some of the things the man has done."

"You should have told me the truth. I deserved to know the truth. I feel like such a fool."

Nathan went up to Anna, touching her arm. "It's not your fault."

"Don't touch me. Don't you ever touch me!" She ran to her horse. She started to mount the mare but stopped. "Why did you even come back here? You didn't care about your family for ten years. I wish I'd never met you, Steven Randall!" Anna swung up and rode away.

Nathan walked to his horse and mounted. He rode slowly back to the ranch. He took the Appaloosa to the stable. Jake walked up to him.

"I'll take him, Mr. Nathan. It's real good to have you back. Your folks missed you mightily."

"Thanks, Jake. Looks like you've taken real good care of the place."

"I try. What do you think of Miss Anna? Isn't she something?"

"Yes, she is. My parents really love her, don't they?"

"Yes, sir. She kept them going when they thought you and Roberto were dead. She's a good girl. She loves your folks."

Nathan patted Jake on the back. "Thanks a lot, Jake." He walked up to the porch, hesitating before he went inside. He knew Anna wasn't back because her mare wasn't in the stable but he was still bothered by his mother's reaction. Joe wasn't around when he walked inside but he heard his mother and Larissa working in the kitchen. He went through the living room and up the stairs to his parents' room. He sat down next to his father. "Hello, Pa," he said sadly, leaning forward onto the bed. "I wish you could hear me, Pa. I need you. I need to talk to you." Nathan closed his eyes, wishing that he could escape forever from his past. He felt relaxed being next to his father, even though his father didn't know he was there. Right now, here was the only place he felt wanted. He felt his father's legs move under his head, and he looked up. "Pa? Pa, can you hear me?" He watched as his father started to move his head. Nathan moved closer to his father. "Can you hear me, Pa? It's Nate. It's Nate, Pa." Nathan's voice was pleading. But Trenton didn't move again, and Nathan lay his head back down on the bed. For the first time in his life he felt as if he had nowhere to go.

"Nate?"

Nathan looked up. Trenton's eyes were open, and he was lifting his good hand. "Is that you, Nate? Is it really you?"

"Yeah, Pa, it's me. I'm here. God, I'm here." He lay his head on his father's chest, not ashamed of the tears that fell. "You're going to be okay, Pa." He felt Trenton's hand on his head, and he breathed a sigh of relief. This man had always loved him, understood him and been there for him. "Do you want me to get

Mother?" Nathan started to stand but Trenton held his hand.

"No, wait. I just want to look at you a minute." Trenton's eyes filled with tears. "I thought I was dreaming when I opened my eyes and saw you sitting there. But you're really here." He ran his hand through Nathan's hair.

"I'll tell you all about it later, Pa. Right now you should rest. I'll go get Mother. She's been worried sick about you."

"Is she all right?"

"She's fine. Joe and Larissa are here, too."

"I guess everyone was expecting me to die. Could you get me a drink of water, son?" Trenton stopped. "I never thought I'd say that word again. Come here." Trenton put his arm around Nathan, pulling his head to his chest.

"I've got a lot to tell you, Pa. You might not be so happy to see me when you hear everything."

"I don't care what you've done. Right now I'm just glad to have you right here."

"And I'll be here as long as you need me, Pa. As long as you need me."

Aeneva and Anna went to the door. Anna quietly opened it for her mother, who was carrying a tray of fresh bandages and medicines. She was astounded to hear her father and Nathan talking. She started forward but Aeneva stopped her. They both stood still, watching Trenton and Nathan together. Aeneva was totally overwhelmed at seeing her husband and her son together again, and Anna was touched at seeing the love Trenton and Nathan had for each other. Aeneva started forward.

"I see you've found our good news."

329

Trenton smiled, his blue eyes twinkling as he looked at his wife. "I thought I was dreaming when I woke up and heard him talking to me. I still can't believe it."

Aeneva threw Nathan a stern look but kissed him on the top of the head anyway. "I can't get used to seeing him all grown up. He looks so much like you I can't believe it."

"Hello, Trenton."

"Anna," Trenton said enthusiastically. "Come here." Nathan moved out of the way as Anna leaned down next to Trenton. "I swear, you've gotten prettier than the last time I saw you."

"You always say that."

"It's true." Trenton looked at Nathan. "I take it you've met your little sister." Trenton kissed Anna on the cheek. "Isn't she the prettiest thing you ever saw?"

Nathan looked at Anna, trying to avoid her cold eyes. "Yes, she is. I can see why you love her so much." He didn't look away from her.

"I want you two to become real close. It's time we were a family again."

"I'm sure Nathan has other things he'd much rather do. He doesn't want to spend his time getting to know a young, unsophisticated girl," she said coldly. "Besides, I'll be spending most of my time with Garrett."

"Well." Aeneva pushed her way between Anna and Nathan. "It's time for me to clean those wounds. And I would like to have some time alone with my husband." She turned and looked at Anna and Nathan, her dark eyes narrowing. "You two go downstairs and find something to talk about."

"I'll see you later, Pa."

"You bet you will, Nate."

Anna kissed Trenton on the cheek. "'Bye."

"'Bye, Annie." Trenton watched Anna and Nathan as they walked out of the room. He looked at Aeneva. "What the hell is going on with those two? There's so much tension between them you can practically see it."

Aeneva sat down next to Trenton on the bed, pushing his hair back from his face. She kissed him softly. "It's a long story. I'll tell you later."

"No. I want to hear about it now."

"No. Right now I am going to hold you and make sure you are still here with me. I want you all to myself." She leaned back against the bed and gently lifted Trenton's head onto her chest. "I have missed you, husband."

"I had strange dreams, Aeneva. Almost like the kind you and your grandmother used to have."

"What do you mean?"

"I kept dreaming about Nate. It's like I knew he was going to come home. I felt it."

"You talked about him last week. Do you remember?"

"Yes. I remember feeling that I missed him more than I had in a long time. Do you suppose I felt he was alive? Is that possible?"

"I think many things are possible. Right now, I want you to rest while I clean your wounds. Then I will bring you some soup."

"I want to see Joe and Larissa."

"You will see them soon enough. Please, Trenton, rest for now. I want to have you for many years to come."

"All right. I'm pretty tired anyway. Did any of the men go back and look for that cat?"

"Some of them went back up the day after you were found but they didn't see her."

"I feel badly about her. She's only trying to feed and protect her cubs. Maybe if we were to take some beef and leave it up in the mountains for her she wouldn't keep coming down here."

"None of the men would agree to that."

"Why not? I'm the one who got attacked!"

"Yes, but many of them keep losing cattle. I think it is more than the one cat."

"Why do you say that?"

"Once in my camp when I was a little girl, we found a bear who had killed one of our horses. He kept coming back, and the warriors kept going out after him but they couldn't find him. When they finally got the bear and killed him, the next morning another horse was killed."

"You're probably right. They've wounded that poor female until she's going to go crazy, and they'll wear her down and kill her and her cubs. And she's probably not the one responsible. I wish I could talk to some of the men."

"No. You are going to stay right here until you are completely rested. They will take care of it themselves, no matter what you say."

Trenton ran his hand along Aeneva's jawbone, tracing its line. "You always were a stubborn woman."

"And I haven't changed since you've been sick. I am still very stubborn, especially when it comes to you. I love you, Trenton."

"I love you, too." Trenton kissed his wife, moaning as he tried to maneuver himself in another position. "I'm afraid that's going to have to wait for awhile."

"I don't care if it has to wait forever as long as I have you back with me again."

"Let's not get carried away. I'm not so old that I can't make love to my wife."

"And I'm not so old that I can't enjoy it." She kissed him again and stood up. "But right now I think it's time to check those wounds."

"What about Nathan? Where's he been all this time?"

"It's up to Nathan to tell you that."

"Well, I don't care what he tells me. All that matters is he's back and he's going to stay. I'll have you, my son, and my daughter. What more can a man ask for?"

Nathan came downstairs, smiling when he saw the lovely woman who was waiting for him. "Clare," he said, genuinely glad to see her face. Although it had been over ten years since he'd seen her, she didn't look much older than the last time they had been together. "You look wonderful."

"So do you." Clare stepped closer, examining Nathan's face. "I can't believe you're really alive. Oh, Nathan!" She threw her arms around him.

"It's really me, Clare." Nathan kissed her on the cheek. "What about you? Mother told me that you got married. She also told me your husband is dead."

"Yes. I married a man much older than I. His name was Elliot Richardson. He came from a wealthy shipping family in Boston. We met when I was going to school in Boston."

"Were you in love with him?"

Clare looked shocked. "Of course not, and he knew it. He married me for my beauty, and I married him for his money."

"So now you're a rich young widow. What are your plans?"

"I'm going to marry for love the next time," Clare said softly, her hand touching Nathan's cheek. "I thought I was carrying your baby, Nathan.''

"What?"

"Don't you remember the last time we were together?" Clare smiled sheepishly.

"How could I forget!"

"I was two months late. I didn't know what to do. I wanted to see you. Then I heard you'd been killed, and I prayed that I was carrying your child."

"But you weren't, were you?"

"No, it was just nerves, I think."

"I'm sorry I put you through that, Clare."

"I'm not. I've never forgotten it." She reached up and put her arms around Nathan's neck. "I've missed you, Nathan." She kissed him in a way that meant only one thing.

"Clare," Nathan said gently, trying to pry her hands from his neck. But Clare refused to be denied. She pressed her body against Nathan's until he felt himself respond. He pulled her to him, returning her passionate kiss.

"Will you come to my house tonight for dinner? I'll have the cook make whatever you want."

"I don't care about the food," he answered in a daze.

Nathan watched Clare as she walked away. She was beautiful and desirable, and she wanted him. He'd be crazy to ignore a woman like her. He forced Anna from his mind and tried to think about the night ahead with Clare. It would do no good to think about Anna.

Chapter XII

Nathan sat next to his father on the porch. He was trying to find the right words to tell him about Anna.

"I still don't understand why you didn't let us know you were alive. I would have stayed away if that's what you wanted."

"I couldn't take that chance, Pa. Driscoll was a dangerous man. I didn't want anyone close to me involved."

"You were alive and in San Francisco all this time. I can't believe it."

"I didn't do it to hurt you, Pa. I did what I thought was right. Maybe you or Mother will never be able to understand that but I wanted to make sure I'd make it back here alive. And don't blame Joe either. I made him promise. He had no choice." Nathan watched his father, unable to judge his reaction. "I can't blame you if you don't forgive me, Pa. I'd probably be mad if I was you."

Trenton tried to sit up but winced at the pain in his neck and arm. "Listen, Nate, I've done lots of things in my life that I'm not proud of. I still feel badly about your real mother. I could have been better to her. And there was a time when I thought I had to get revenge for my father's death and no one, not even Aeneva, could stop me from going. So I can understand why you did what you did. You thought in some small way you were atoning for Berto's death by getting revenge on Driscoll."

"Yeah, I guess so. And I felt responsible for what happened to Berto. He was my little brother, Pa, and I couldn't even take care of him. I let him down."

"You didn't let him down, Nate. If anybody let him down it was me. I should never have allowed you two to go on by yourselves. I'll never forgive myself for that."

"We were there, Pa. We were safe. If I hadn't let Berto talk me into going to Chinatown—"

"Don't, Nate. We can't keep going over 'what if.' We have to deal with what is."

"I have something else to tell you, Pa." Nathan looked at his father, meeting the clear blue eyes that were a reflection of his own. "I met Anna when I was in San Francisco, but I didn't know she was my sister. You've got to believe me, Pa. I didn't know."

Trenton touched Nathan's arm. "What happened? It's obvious that something went on between you. She doesn't like you much, Nate."

"She has good reason not to like me. We met a few times, and we were attracted to each other. The first time I saw her I knew I could love her. I knew I could spend the rest of my life with her." Nathan was afraid to look at his father.

"So what happened?"

"I found out who she was one night when she was telling me about you and Mother. I couldn't believe it. I couldn't believe that the one woman I would fall in love with would be my sister." He shook his head, a look of despair on his face. "I feel like all I've done for the last ten years is mess things up."

"Nate, I want you to look at me. Come on." Nathan looked at his father. "We have had Anna since she was eight years old. We have loved her, nurtured her and looked upon her as our own daughter. But the fact of the matter, Nate, is that she *isn't* our daughter, not by blood, anyway. And that's what matters. She's not really your sister, either. You two were never even raised together. Hell, you never even met until a few months ago. You have no reason to feel guilty about Anna."

"I suppose I should've told her who I was right when I found out but I thought it would be best for her if she thought of me as Steven Randall. At that point I wasn't sure what was going to happen to me."

"So she's pretty upset with you, huh?"

"Why are you laughing? She hates my guts right now. I think she'd sooner see me dead than walking around this place."

"She's got a stubborn streak in her a mile long, just like your mother. That's probably where she got it from. Although as I recall, her real father was as stubborn as they come."

"I knew you'd understand, Pa. I just knew it."

"I want to tell you something, Nate. And I want you to listen real good. I don't know if I'll ever understand why you didn't at least let us know you were alive. I felt as if a part of me had been ripped out, and your mother went through hell. You are her son, Nate, just as much as Berto was."

"I'm sorry, Pa. I don't know what to say. When I woke up in Chin's place and found out Berto was dead, I wanted to be dead, too. Then I wanted to live because then I could get the man who did this to me and to Berto. I made good friends—Chin and Tong—and Joe was always there, but it was never the same. I hated being away from you and mother and I missed

Berto. I kept thinking what it would be like to have him all grown up as a brother."

"I don't want you blaming yourself anymore. It's over and done with. No matter what we do, we can't bring Berto back. But we can always remember how much we loved him. No amount of time will ever dull that love." Trenton rubbed Nathan's head as if he were a boy again. "So, what are you going to do about Anna?"

"There's nothing to do. She's going to marry Garrett, and that's how it should be. He's good for her. They're good for each other."

"You're going to give up just like that? You're practically pushing her into the arms of another man."

"That's what Joe said."

"Well, he's right. If you love her, why don't you fight for her?"

"That's just it, Pa. I don't know if what we felt for each other was love or just attraction."

"Well, how will you ever know if you don't get to know her better? She's special, Nate. Like your mother."

Nathan shook his head and smiled. "I can't believe you're saying this to me."

"It wasn't that long ago that I was your age. I came pretty damn close to making the same mistake you are."

"What's that?"

"I almost pushed Aeneva into the arms of another man."

"You're talking about Ladro?"

"I hated him but I liked him. He was a good man. Hell, he gave his life to save mine. There was a time I was ready to ride away and leave her with him because I thought that's what she wanted."

"But you didn't. You fought for her and you won."

"In a way. I sometimes wonder if Ladro had lived—" Trenton stared ahead for a moment. "He might have been your father, not me."

"You almost seem sad when you say that, Pa. Why?"

"Because he was a good man. It was a waste for him to die. He should have known Berto. He should have known his son." Trenton shook his head. "Joe and Anna should be back soon. Why don't you talk to her then."

"I guess it'll be sooner than I wanted it to be. Look." Nathan pointed to the dust beyond and squinted his eyes to see the riders in the distance. He stood up. "There's something wrong."

"What is it?"

"It's Joe but he's alone. He's leading Anna's mare." Trenton attempted to stand up. "Damn it!"

"Stay there, Pa. I'll find out what's wrong." Nathan ran out into the yard and met Joe as he came riding in. "What's wrong?"

"I was riding up by the hills, and I found Anna's mare grazing in the valley."

"Damn her. Do you have any idea where she is?"

Joe turned and pointed toward the hills he had just ridden from. "She went riding up in there. I tried to follow her tracks but she knew exactly where she was going. I rode all over the place looking for her. I decided I'd better come back here for more help."

"Go tell Jake to saddle me up Pa's Appaloosa. We'll need water and a lantern." Nathan ran up to the porch, skipping the stairs to the top. "Anna's missing. She went riding in the foothills by Bear Hill. Joe looked all over for her but couldn't find her. He found her mare. I'm going after her."

"Nate, wait." Trenton's face had drained of all

339

color. "That's where I got attacked by the cat. I want you to take my gun and holster and a rifle for both you and Joe. And get yourself some food and water."

"I'll be right back, Pa."

"All right."

Nathan ran into the house and went to the gun case. He fastened his father's holster, got the two ivory-handled Colts, and made sure they were loaded. Then he got out two of his father's best rifles, the Winchesters, grabbing enough ammunition for both him and Joe. He then walked into the kitchen and packed up some food, wrapping it in a cloth. He walked back outside with the guns and food. "I'll find her, Pa. Don't worry. Tell Mother I'll bring her back."

"Good luck, Nate."

Nathan ran down to the corral, meeting Joe as he led the two horses out. "We'll need water."

"I've already got water. Just give me that rifle and pack the food away and let's get going."

Nathan put his rifle in its holder and packed the food in one of the saddlebags that Jake had thrown on, and he climbed up. "Let's go, Joe." He reined his horse in the direction of the mountains. The Appaloosa galloped hard, as if sensing Nathan's urgency. Nathan didn't let up until he reached the foothills, then he reined in, walking the stallion so he could lean down and check the ground for signs of tracks. Joe slowed up behind him.

"Anything?"

"Just the prints from your horse and Anna's. Show me which way she rode."

Joe went in the lead, riding slowly on the narrow path that wound through the trees and rocks. "Look, Nate. Over here." Joe pointed to footprints on the ground.

Nathan dismounted and checked the prints. "No, they aren't Anna's. These are too big and they're not fresh enough. See, the edges of the print have already started to wear down." Nathan stood and looked around him. "I'm going to ride in a little further." Nathan mounted and rode slowly on the trail, occasionally patting his horse to calm him down. He couldn't figure out why Anna would even want to ride in a place like this. In a matter of minutes the terrain had changed drastically. The trail was almost nonexistent, and it was getting too steep for the horses. Nathan stopped and dismounted, tying the stallion to a small tree. Joe did the same. Nathan got the food and water and threw them over his shoulder and then removed the rifle. He looked back at Joe. "Are you ready?"

"Yep, ready as you are."

The two men climbed up the narrow trail looking for signs of Anna. They climbed for over an hour before Nathan saw a print from Anna's boot. "It's hers." He looked around him. "What the hell is she doing climbing up here?"

"That's what I wondered. It's a strange place for a girl to go all alone."

"Berto and I used to come up here all the time when we were kids. There were all kinds of caves and things. We used to pretend like we were holding off entire armies, just the two of us."

"Well, maybe she just wanted to get away like you two used to do. It is real pretty up here."

"Yeah, it is. But I'd still like to find her before it gets dark. I don't think she knows that her mare is gone." They kept climbing, following Anna's tracks. Her tracks led farther and farther up the side of the mountain, and Nathan couldn't find any sign of them coming down. By the middle of the afternoon they sat down and had something to eat and drink. "If we don't find her in the next hour, I want you to go back to the house, Joe."

"I'm not leaving you out here alone."

"I want you to go back and tell Pa. He'll be able to tell you what men to organize. I know this place a lot better than you, Joe, even after all these years. I know most of the caves and most of the hiding places."

"It's not real safe spending the night up here by yourself, you know."

"I know that. I'll be careful. But I want to be here in case we can't find Anna. She'll be scared. I don't want her being alone up here."

"All right, boy. Whatever you say. You're the boss in this." Joe finished off his sandwich and drank down some water, wiping his hand across his mouth. "What're you going to do when you find her?"

"I'm going to take her home. What do you think I'm going to do?"

"That's not what I meant and you know it."

"I don't know, and I'm not even going to think about that right now. Come on. Let's get going."

Nathan and Joe climbed to the top of one of the hills and looked out over the valley below. Nathan looked out over the other side. He cupped his hands to his mouth. "Anna! Anna!" He yelled as loudly as he could but there was no response. He took off his hat and looked up at the sky. "You should start heading back down now, Joe. It'll take you awhile, and I want you to get back to the ranch before dark. Tell Pa I want Garrett to be in the search party. He probably knows this area as well as anyone."

"All right, boy. You take care now. I don't want to lose you again."

Nathan slapped Joe on the arm and smiled. "I'll be all right. I'll leave signs wherever I'm going. I'll be easy to track."

"See you later, boy."

"'Bye, Joe." Nathan watched for a moment as Joe started back down the mountain. Then he went down the other side. He called Anna's name over and over but there was no response. He tried not to think that something might be wrong with her. He wouldn't let that thought enter his mind. He just kept walking, looking for signs that Anna was all right.

Anna opened her eyes and tried to move. She groaned, feeling a sharp, throbbing pain in her left foot. She sat up and examined herself. Her legs were cut and bruised, and her left foot felt broken. Both of her arms were badly banged up, and her head had a lump on it the size of a small rock. She looked above her and twisted her mouth into a silly grin. No wonder she was so sore. She had fallen a long way. She looked around, suddenly remembering why she had fallen. She was jumping from rock to rock, trying to balance on one foot, a game she and Garrett had played as kids, when suddenly she had frozen. On the next rock, out of nowhere, crouched a mountain lion. She had tried to remain calm but the animal snarled and started toward her. She tried to back up but slipped, falling to the ground below. She was lucky she wasn't badly hurt. She looked around again for signs of the cat but decided it hadn't meant to hurt her. If he had, he would've eaten her while she was unconscious.

Anna tried to stand up but stumbled when her foot wouldn't support her. She tried to stand on it but she wound up hopping. She looked up. There was no way she would get back up the rocks unless she had something to lean on. She half limped, half hopped around, looking for a stick until she found one that was strong enough. She leaned on it as she tried to climb back up the rocks, forcing herself to put weight on her sore foot. She looked up at the sky. It was already late in the afternoon. A chill went through her. She had never spent the night alone in the mountains. The very thought of it scared her to death. She wasn't sure if she could do it.

She willed herself to climb the rocks until finally she was at the top. She looked down at the hill she had to go down and still worse, the hill on the other side she had to climb up. She decided not to waste time. She sat down, pulling her skirt down around and between her legs and began to slide, stopping herself with her stick when she went too fast. When she neared the bottom she stood up, leaning on the stick. Then she started up the next hill. It had never seemed like such a large hill before but now it seemed insurmountable. She had gone only a short distance when she saw a movement out of the corner of her eye. She looked toward the trees but saw nothing. She continued up the hill but saw the movement again. This time she saw what it was. The cat was following her. It didn't make sense for him to be stalking her. If he had wanted to kill her he could've done that when she had fallen. Why was he following her? Uneasiness drove her faster but she stumbled repeatedly. Halfway up she sat, scanning the rocks. She didn't see the big cat but she knew he was there. She could feel him looking at her. She felt cold suddenly and rubbed her arms. The sun was beginning to go down behind the trees. It would be dark soon. She had to get to the top of the hill and find some shelter. She couldn't be out in the open all night long. There was no telling what the cat would do. She stood back up, and this time she stepped on her bad foot. The pain was almost unbearable but Anna reminded herself that she could easily be a mountain lion's dinner if she didn't find a place to hide for the night. Finally, after what seemed like hours, she reached the top of the hill. She hobbled as quickly as she could toward a mound of rocks. She knew there was a cave nearby but she refused to go inside. Garrett had always told her that caves were the worst places to go. You never knew what was inside.

She climbed up on the boulders by sheer will. At the top, she looked frantically at the trees surrounding her. Limping to the tree closest to her, she reached futilely for the lowest limb. It was too high. She jumped, trying to catch it, but fell, landing on her bad foot. She sprawled across the rocks. "Damn it!" Her voice sounded small and weak in her own ears, and she fought back tears. She forced away her fear and stood slowly. This far from the trunk, the limb curved closer to the ground. She grasped it tightly, ignoring the sharp stab of the pine needles. Anna pulled herself along until the height of the limb forced her to hang, gripping the rough bark. With what felt like the last of her strength, she pulled herself upward, bracing her good foot on the trunk. She managed to pull herself up onto the limb and sat trembling. After a moment she climbed higher and found a spot wide enough for her to sit more comfortably. She rested her bad foot on the branch in front of her and leaned back, dangling her good foot over the other side of the branch. She looked back through the tree and could just barely see the valley where she lived. It had never looked so good to her. "It was stupid of me to have come up here today," she said aloud. But she knew why she had come. She had to get away from Nathan. She couldn't stand being in the same house with him. It drove her crazy. She turned away from the valley and looked out at the darkening rocks in front of her. Fear instantly seized her. Thirty feet from the base of the tree sat the big cat, looking at her, watching. Instinctively she lifted up her good leg and rested it on the limb next to her other leg. She didn't want to give him anything to think about. She mentally measured the distance from the rock to the limb where she sat and prayed that it was too far for the cat to jump.

Darkness soon fell and Anna felt all alone, but she knew the cat was still watching her. She had seen his lean silhouette a number of times as he walked back and forth on the rocks, but he never left.

She leaned her head back against the tree trunk, trying to calm herself. She was cold and scared. She wished that someone would find her, but she knew that was impossible. No one would come for her this late. She would have to spend the night in the hills alone. A movement above her made her cry out. An owl flew into the tree, and her whole body jerked in response to the beating of its wings. She imagined the cat watching from below. She had never known such fear in her life. Closing her eyes, she forced herself to think of other things, but all she could think of was the dark and the animal who sat watching her. She thought she heard another sound and she turned, straining to hear from which direction it was coming. The cat stood up, instantly alert. It sounded like footsteps, but she couldn't believe that someone would be in the hills this late. She saw a light but was afraid to call out, suddenly afraid that it might be someone who would hurt her. She huddled in the limb of the tree as the person came closer. She could hear the heavy footsteps.

"Anna." She could hear a voice call out to her in

the darkness. But it wasn't just any voice.

"Nathan! Nathan, I'm here."

"Anna, where are you?"

"I'm over here in a tree by the rocks. Be careful, Nathan, the mountain lion is below me."

"I'm going to fire some shots, Anna. Then I want you to keep talking so I can find you." Nathan fired off three shots.

Out of the darkness Anna could see the silhouette of the large cat jump off the rocks. She could hear him run into the woods. "It's all right, Nathan. He's gone. I'm over here. Be careful. It's so dark. Oh, I see your light. Did you bring a lantern? I can't believe you found me. Nathan, are you there?" Anna kept talking, working her way down to the lowest limb. "Nathan?"

"Right here, Anna. Right below you."

Anna looked down and saw the light. Nathan climbed the rocks and set the lantern down. He walked over to the end of the branch. "Can you hang on the branch and scoot your way over here until I can grab you?"

"I think so. I hurt my foot, Nathan. I can't walk very well."

"That's all right. Just hang onto the branch and move toward me. As soon as you're close enough, I'll steady you."

"All right." Anna eased her sore leg off the branch. She held on tightly and let her body drop, moving her hands one over the other until she got close to the edge of the rocks and Nathan. She felt his arms go around her, and she let go of the branch, feeling his strength. She held onto him, lost in the warmth and safety she felt at that moment.

"It's all right now. You're okay."

Anna didn't move. She was afraid to. Just the

347

sound of his voice and the feel of his arms around her made her strangely uneasy in a way she had never known before. She had never felt this way with anyone, not even with Garrett. "How did you find me?"

"I tracked you. Your footprints were everywhere, but the problem was there were old ones and new ones. Why in hell did you pick this place to explore?"

"It's one of my favorite places. I always come here." She leaned heavily against Nathan. "I'm sorry. I hurt my foot when I fell."

"You can tell me about that later. Right now, we have to find a place to stay for the night. Isn't there a cave around here somewhere?"

"Yes, there's one in those rocks but I'm not going in. The cat might be in there."

"The cat is nowhere around now. He's too smart. He heard the rifle. He's not going to stay around where he can get shot at."

"I'd rather stay out here."

"Come on, Anna. You've got to get off of that foot, and it's too cold out here. We have to get in somewhere. I'll go inside first and make sure there are no mountain lions lurking anywhere."

"Don't make fun of me. He was watching me for hours. It was scary. I didn't know if he wanted to eat me or just scare me away."

"Probably just scare you away. Come on, lean on me."

Anna leaned on Nathan but she couldn't walk. Her foot had swelled up, and her leg was stiff. "I'm sorry, Nathan. Why don't I just wait here."

"Oh, no you don't." Nathan reached down and put his arms under Anna, lifting her in his arms. "I'll carry you into that cave if I have to."

"I guess you'll have to because I'm not going to walk into it willingly."

"Just put your arms around my neck and hold on. I'll give you the rifle and lantern so I can see where I'm going." Nathan carefully climbed down the rocks and walked in the direction of the cave. At the entrance he stopped, listening for any sounds. He pulled out his pistol and cocked it, slowly entering the cave. "Hold the lantern up higher, Anna." Nathan stopped, setting Anna down on the ground.

"What are you doing? You're not leaving me, are you?"

"Just stay here while I look at the rest of the cave. Have the rifle ready."

"Nathan, I want to go with you."

"Just relax, Anna." Nathan walked through the cave, holding the lantern out in front of him. He walked to the end. There were no mountain lions, nor was there any evidence of any. He walked back to Anna, who sat holding the rifle in front of her. "Don't look so scared. We're safe."

"I can't help but be scared. That cat followed me for a long time. Why was he watching me, Nathan?"

"I don't know. What happened earlier? You said you fell."

"I was on top of some rocks, and I saw the cat. I thought he was coming toward me, and I got scared. I started to back up and slipped. I fell off the rocks and down a hill."

"You're lucky you didn't break your neck." Nathan moved forward. "Let me take a look at your foot." He ran his hand from Anna's knee to the top of her boot. He tried to pull off her boot but it wouldn't move. "Your foot is real swollen. I'm going to try to cut that boot off."

"No. I won't be able to walk if you do that."

"You won't be able to walk anyway. By tomorrow that foot's going to be twice the size it is now."

Nathan took out his knife and started at the top of Anna's boot, making an incision and cutting downward to the ankle. The sharp blade of his hunting knife moved easily through the leather of the boot. "Now, let's try." Nathan moved the boot around and finally pulled it from Anna's foot. He started to roll down her stocking but she stopped him.

"I'll do it." She rolled the stocking down and off of her foot. "Oh, God, I'll never be able to walk again," she said, looking at her bruised, swollen foot.

"Have you always been so melodramatic?"

She laughed, unable to stop herself. "I suppose it's that Irish blood in me. I've heard that all Irish are actors."

"Well, there's nothing we can do for it now but rest it. How about the rest of you? Are you all right? You look like you got pretty cut up."

"I'm all right. Just a little sore in places." She looked at Nathan's saddlebags. "Do you have any food in there? I'm starving."

Nathan tossed her the bags and the water. "Help yourself. I'm going to try to make a fire. We don't have a blanket. We're going to need something to keep us warm." After he said it, Nathan clenched his teeth. He was trying to go easy with Anna. This was the first time she had even spoken to him in a week.

"Why did you come out here after me, Nathan?"

Nathan didn't turn around. He continued building a fire ring with small rocks. "Pa was worried sick about you."

"Is that the only reason?"

Nathan turned to look at Anna this time. "No, it wasn't the only reason. I was worried about you, too. I would have never forgiven myself if something had happened to you, too."

350

"What do you mean to me, too?"

"Roberto was killed because of me. If you had gone off because you were mad at me and something bad had happened to you, it would have been my fault."

"I went off riding because that's what I like to do. You didn't chase me away. I like to come up here and be alone. It's beautiful up here."

Nathan sat back on his haunches. "Yeah, I know. Berto and I used to come up here and pretend we were defending the entire world against the bad guys. I was always the general, of course. Poor Berto was always content to be just an officer."

"I'm sure he loved it, Nathan. I bet you two had fun together."

"We did. Even though he was younger than I was, we got along real well." Nathan shook his head in remembrance. "He was such a good kid. He was so full of adventure, and he never blamed anyone for anything. He was really Mother's real son. He was the most like her."

"I think you're like her."

"Why?"

"You're good like she is, and you do what you think is right."

"That's not what you said before. That last time we talked you said you wished I'd never come back here."

"Well, I'm glad you did. I think you're the main reason Trenton has recovered so quickly as he has."

Nathan reached into the bag and took out a hunk of bread and an orange. "How is Garrett?"

Anna was silent. "Garrett is wonderful, just like he always is."

Nathan considered her answer for a moment, then put down his food. "I'm going to get some firewood."

"You're not going to leave me here alone, are you?"

"Is this the girl who was sitting up in the tree all alone facing a mountain lion?"

"I didn't say I liked it." She looked at Nathan and then smiled. "All right, go on. I'll be fine." Anna sat eating an orange, trying to figure out why she was being so nice to Nathan. Part of the reason was because he had come up here to find her; the rest of the reason she didn't want to admit to herself.

"You'd better be careful. Mountain lions can sneak up on you up here."

Anna jumped. "That's not funny, Nathan. I can't believe you aren't more frightened. One of them almost killed Trenton."

Nathan knelt down, placing the armful of wood on the ground. Carefully he began building a fire. "Even Pa said the female was just trying to protect her cubs. He doesn't even think she's the one who's been killing the cattle."

"Do you think it's the one that was watching me? It was a male."

"It could be but for the most part they aren't dangerous. Berto and I used to see them all the time up here."

"And they didn't do anything to you?"

"That male didn't do anything to you, did he? You even said he could've killed you if he'd wanted to."

"They still scare me. I didn't like him looking at me."

"They should scare you. They're wild animals. But they're usually just as scared of us as we are of them."

"What about bears?"

"Pa said that bears are a lot different. They're much more aggressive than most animals. Mother told me that when her grandmother was a little girl, a grizzly came into their camp and started tearing down teepees and attacking people. Some warriors finally killed him. They never could figure out why he had come into the camp and attacked for no reason. Usually, wild animals will only attack humans if they are wounded or if they are protecting their young." Nathan got out his flint and struck it against a rock. The sparks flew into the small pile of twigs and leaves. He blew on the pile, and the smoke turned into small flames. Slowly he began adding wood until the flames grew higher. "Come on over here. It's nice and warm."

Anna moved herself closer to the fire, holding her hands close to it. "Were you old enough to remember the fires that the Cheyennes had in their camps and the stories they told around them?"

Nathan nodded, a thoughtful expression coming over his face. "It's amazing but I can remember everything about that time. I loved it there. I used to love to run and swim and ride with the other boys. They accepted me as one of them, even though I looked so different. I remember when Pa went away and left me with his mother's people. He went to look for Mother in Mexico, and they came back a year later with Berto. God, I missed them. I remember being afraid that I would never see them again." Nathan was silent, thinking that he had thought much the same thing for the last ten years.

"I'm sorry, Nathan."

He looked up from the fire. "For what?"

"I'm sorry for saying you didn't care about your parents. I had no idea what you've been through. But there's still something I don't understand."

"What's that?"

"Why didn't you tell me that you were my brother

353

that night in your hotel room? Why did you make me find out here?"

"I didn't know what would happen between me and Driscoll. I was afraid I might never come back here again. I didn't want any of you knowing I was alive."

"But you also did it because you were shocked that you had kissed your own sister."

"Yes, I felt terrible."

"So did I at first."

"And now?"

"Now I realize that there's nothing to feel terrible about. You and I are no more brother and sister than Garrett and I are. Your parents were good enough to raise me and love me, but that's the only bond you and I have in common."

"That's not the only bond." Nathan looked at Anna in the flickering firelight, and he thought she had never looked more lovely. He wanted to take her in his arms, but his instincts told him this was not the right time. He picked up a stick and stoked the fire.

"Did you ever know Sun Dancer?"

Nathan looked at Anna, surprised by her question. "What makes you ask that?"

"Aeneva has always talked so much of her grandmother. I wondered if you knew her."

"I knew Sun Dancer all right. If it had been up to her, she would have let me run the entire Cheyenne nation!" He looked at Anna, and they broke out into laughter. "She was wonderful to me. She treated me as if I were her real grandson." He turned to Anna, his eyes sparkling in the firelight. "Did you know that Sun Dancer met my Grandfather Hawkins?"

"How?"

"She had been married just a short time to Stalking Horse. Some French traders had come into the

354

camp. One of them thought she was beautiful and stole her away. He stopped at the farm one night and tied her in the barn. A little boy with blond hair and blue eyes came to look at her. She begged him to let her loose, and he did. She thanked him by giving him a turquoise and silver necklace that had been given to her by a friend's mother. My grandfather kept it until he grew up and then he gave it to Pa. When Pa met Sun Dancer, he gave it back to her."

"It's a wonderful story."

"That's not the end. When Sun Dancer was going for her walk to Seyan to meet Stalking Horse, she gave the necklace back to Pa to give to me. She wanted me to have it when I grew up. I'll never forget her face when she said good-bye to me." Nathan stared at the flames in front of him, as if in a trance. "I will miss you, Grandmother. *Ne-mehotatse.*"

"What does it mean, Nathan?"

"It means 'I love you.'" He looked at Anna for a moment, then back at the fire.

Anna rubbed Nathan's arm. "It's a beautiful story. You are lucky to have had someone like that in your life."

"What about you, Anna? What was your life like with your real father?"

"We moved from town to town mostly. He gambled and drank a lot. We made our money from gambling. If Papa had a good night at the tables, we celebrated. If he had a bad night, we starved. But he wasn't a bad man. He loved me in his own way. He always kept me with him, no matter where he went. He always called me his little lady. He said I was the respectable one in the family." She looked at Nathan. "Your mother and father saved us both."

"Anna, just because I'm back here doesn't mean you can't call them your parents anymore. They've spent a lot of years taking care of you and loving you. You are their daughter.''

"Thank you," Anna replied sincerely.

"What about your mother?"

"I don't remember much about my mother except that she was kind and very quiet. She died when I was very young." She looked at Nathan, her eyes soft. "Your mother is the only mother I have ever known."

"Do you think you'll ever see your real father again?"

"I don't know but I don't hate him for what he did. He did what he thought was right for me." She leaned closer to the fire. "If he hadn't left me with your parents, I never would have met you."

Nathan looked at Anna in the firelight and wanted to take her into his arms, but he knew he had no right. Although she was being kind to him, there was still the fact that they were raised in the same family. That was something that couldn't easily be forgotten. He stoked the fire and added more wood. "Why don't you lie against the saddlebags. We should try to get some sleep now."

"All right." Anna lay down on her side, resting her head on the saddlebags. "Nathan." Her voice was low but gentle.

"What?"

"Thank you. You didn't have to come up here after me."

"Yes, I did."

Anna didn't say anything; she didn't know what to say. She had never felt so confused about anyone in her life. She had always known how she felt about Garrett, and she had always been secure in those feelings. But it was different with Nathan. Nathan made her feel things she had never felt with anyone else before. She closed her eyes. The ground felt hard and bumpy but she was too tired to care. She was sore and her foot throbbed, but she felt safe with Nathan lying close by. She was afraid to think how it would have felt to have spent the night in the hills alone. Quickly Anna drifted into a deep sleep, her body and mind totally relaxed. Images of different people raced through her mind. She saw Rebecca Driscoll laughing at her and she saw Nathan next to her, holding her in his arms. He kissed Rebecca passionately and then suddenly Anna turned into Rebecca. She could feel the touch of his lips on hers and the warmth of his body as he pressed against her. She wanted him, and she wanted to know what it was like to have him make love to her. But he turned and walked away, taking Rebecca with him. She called out for him but he was gone. She heard someone calling her in the distance. It was a shrill cry, and it touched her to the very bone. It was almost inhuman. It called again and suddenly she was scared. She started to run but stopped. There was an enormous mountain lion standing in front of her, waiting to pounce on her. She backed up but there was another one behind her. She turned to run but they were everywhere. Their shrill cries echoed in her ears as they closed in on her. She screamed.

"Anna." Nathan moved to Anna, taking her in his arms. "Anna, it's all right."

Anna huddled against Nathan, listening as the shrill cry of the cat echoed in the hills around them. "It scares me. I know it's silly but it does. It doesn't sound earthly."

"It won't hurt us. It's probably just calling to its mate. Are you all right?"

Anna held onto Nathan's shirt, leaning her head against his chest. "Stay here for awhile, Nathan. Please."

"I'll stay here." Nathan put his arms around Anna, running his hands up and down her back for reassurance. "Just relax and go to sleep. I won't leave you." Nathan leaned his chin on Anna's head, feeling how natural it was to hold her this way. He could feel the tension begin to leave her body as she relaxed against him. He stroked her long hair. "It's all right, Anna." He held her until she fell asleep, and he lay down on the ground with Anna next to him. He kept his arm around her, and she lay with her head on his chest. He liked the feeling of having her lie next to him. He closed his eyes and wished she would lie next to him forever.

Anna woke up in the middle of the night. It was completely dark with only embers from the fire giving a slight glow in the dark cave. She moved her arm and touched Nathan's chest. She felt as if she should pull away but she didn't want to. She moved closer to him, and his arm automatically tightened around her. She ran her hand up and down his chest, feeling the hard muscles underneath the shirt. She closed her eyes and imagined what it would be like to lie next to him completely naked, and she felt strange, as if it were forbidden to even think such things. She ran her hand up to his face, running her fingers along his jaw and cheek. She loved his face. She had loved it the first moment she had seen him. Her body jumped as she heard the cry of the cat again, and she moved still closer to Nathan. She felt his hold tighten around her, and she felt his body stiffen. He was awake. She started to move her hand away from his chest but he took it, bringing it to his mouth. He brought her palm to his lips, kissing it softly, lovingly. She closed her eyes again, still not sure of the feeling that was threatening to overcome her. Suddenly his arms were around her, pulling her up to him, his mouth covering hers with an urgency she never before knew existed. She responded with equal urgency and heard herself moan, embarrassed but delighted that she could feel such unbridled passion. "Anna." She heard him say her name, and it excited her more than she thought possible. His mouth sought hers in the darkness, and she felt his arms go around her, moving down the length of her body, feeling, exploring. He stopped suddenly, his hands cupping her face.

"Are you sure you want to do this?"

"Yes," she said without hesitation, her body seeking his in the chill night air. She felt his hands as they unbuttoned her blouse and caressed her breasts. He lowered his head to her mouth and then gently, slowly, moved his mouth down the line of her neck to her breasts. Anna was afraid but she wanted Nathan more than anything in the world. Her arms went around him, and she arched her back. His hands moved slowly down her waist to her hips and thighs. He pulled her skirt up high, pushing the pantalets down. Anna closed her eyes and enjoyed the feel of Nathan's hands on her bare flesh. He moved and she felt him between her legs. She opened her eyes and watched as he took off his shirt and lowered his pants. She wasn't afraid any longer. She reached out to him and Nathan entered her, filling her with his love and passion. Anna ran her hands up and down Nathan's bare back, reveling in the feel of his skin against her fingers and the feel of him inside of her. She felt his hands pull her up to him and she arched her back, giving herself to him fully. His mouth sought hers and she felt the passion grow between them, threatening to explode. Anna cried out suddenly, unable to control herself. She held onto Nathan as he continued to move inside of her until he, too, was unable to fight his passion. He held onto her as his body gave itself to hers. They lay entwined, exhausted yet exhilarated.

Anna held onto Nathan, afraid to let him go. She was afraid to think about what might happen in the light of day. She didn't know what kind of future they had together, but at least they had had tonight. She knew she would never be loved by any man the way she had been loved by Nathan that night.

Chapter XIII

Nathan held Anna in his arms, his supplies slung over his shoulders. The cat had been following them all morning. He stopped, turning to look back at the animal. He was beautiful. He was long and tawny colored, his small head seeming almost incongruous with his large muscular body. His eyes watched their every move.

"Why is he following us?"

"I don't know. I think he just wants to make sure we're on our way out of here. I bet he's the female's mate."

"You think he's just protecting her and the cubs?"

"Probably." Nathan started walking again but stopped when the cat's shrill cry echoed around them. He looked back but the cat was gone. He heard sounds in the trees around them. He started running toward some rocks, putting Anna down and taking out the rifle.

"What's wrong?"

"I think we might be near the female and the cubs. He's either warning us or he's going to come after us. Get up higher on those rocks." Nathan climbed up after Anna, squatting down, looking all around him.

"I can't see anything. He ran into those trees down there. I wonder if that's where his mate is."

"Nathan, look." Anna pointed to the hill behind him. There was another mountain lion, smaller but just as frightening.

"It's the female," Nathan said quietly, lifting his rifle. "Look, she's wounded by her shoulder." Nathan looked down by the trees, and he could see the male through them. "The male's guarding the cubs, and she's trying to scare us away." Nathan took Anna's hand. "Come on. I want you to move slowly down the rock." When they got to the bottom, Nathan handed Anna the rifle. He picked her up and began walking slowly away from the trees where the male and the cubs were. The female stood on the hill above them, watching, but she didn't move. As Nathan started climbing the hill the female started moving slowly down toward the trees. When Nathan and Anna were at the top, Nathan looked down at the female, who, still watching them, disappeared into the trees. He walked over the other side of the hill and started down.

"How did you know she wouldn't hurt us?"

"All she wanted was for us to get away from her cubs. That's the only reason she attacked Pa. Look." Nathan stopped. "There's our valley."

"It's beautiful. I don't think I ever realized how beautiful it is before."

"We should be home by midday if my horse is still there. If he's gone, we'll make it by nightfall."

They continued walking for awhile until they heard voices. "Listen." Anna pulled Nathan's arm. "I hear someone."

"It's Joe." He waited for another minute until they heard another voice. "And Garrett." He looked at Anna a minute and started toward the sound of the voices.

"Nathan," Anna said in a quiet voice, her mouth next to Nathan's ear. She wanted to say something to him about the previous night but she didn't know what to say. "Nathan, I—"

"Anna!" Garrett's voice came out of nowhere. He burst onto the trail, running toward Anna and Nathan. He stopped in front of them, out of breath but with a smile on his face. "You're all right?"

"I'm fine, Garrett. I just fell and hurt my foot."

Joe came running up behind Garrett. "I sure am glad to see you two. When your horse came back in the middle of the night we got a little concerned."

"The cat must've scared it away."

"Why don't you put me down now, Nathan. I'm sure I can walk all right."

"There's no way you're walking," Garrett said, taking Anna from Nathan's arms. "We'll start back toward the horses. Thanks, Nathan."

"Sure," Nathan replied, watching as Garrett and Anna walked away.

"Everything all right?"

"Yeah, fine." Nathan continued to stare after the two.

"You and Anna seem to be getting along better."

Nathan looked at Joe. "When I found her she was real scared, and she was being followed by one of the cats. She would've talked to anyone at that point."

"Right," Joe replied in a sarcastic voice. "Your lady friend came over to see you last night. She got real worried when we told her where you were. I don't know if it was because of the cats or because of Anna."

"Stop it, Joe." Nathan walked ahead of Joe on the trail. By the time they reached the horses, Garrett was helping Anna onto hers. Nathan watched as Garrett

363

kissed her cheek. He felt a sudden uncontrollable anger. He walked to his horse.

"Hey, Nathan. I've just asked Anna to marry me. I think that's the only way I can keep her from running around places like this. What do you think?"

Nathan stared at Anna a minute, his mind unable to forget what had happened between them the night before and how passionate she had been with him. He didn't want to think of her being that way with Garrett. "I think it's none of my business," Nathan replied coldly, mounting his horse and quickly galloping off.

"What got into him?"

"He's just probably tired." Joe tried to placate Garrett, all the while knowing why Nathan was so upset. He looked up at Anna and saw how she watched Nathan, and it wasn't hard for him to guess what had happened between them. "I think I'll leave you two alone. I'm going to ride on ahead with Nathan." Joe galloped off in Nathan's direction, riding hard to catch up with him.

Nathan turned around and saw Joe following him and he pulled up on his horse, walking him until Joe caught up. "I'm not in the mood for any lectures, Joe."

"I wasn't about to give you any, boy. Did you run into that cat up there?"

"Yeah, a couple of times. The male followed us almost all of the time, and the female came out once. I think we got a little too close to her cubs. But they didn't bother us."

"That's good to hear. How'd Anna get hurt?"

"She was climbing on some rocks and saw the male walking toward her. She got scared and slipped. She fell quite a ways down and hurt her foot, and she got some bumps and bruises. But the cat never went near her.''

"Clare was at the house last night. In fact, she stayed over. She's real worried about you.''

"She should've gone home.''

"What's the matter with you, Nate?'' Joe reined in his horse, leaning over and tugging at Nathan's reins. "I want to talk to you.''

"I thought you said no lectures.''

"I lied,'' Joe replied loudly. "You're twenty-six years old, Nate. You've been through a lot in your lifetime, and you have a lot to be angry about but it's time you figured out what you want to do with the rest of your life. Do you want to marry a prosperous young widow like Clare and live the rest of your life comfortably and passionless? Or do you want to fight for Anna and have an exciting life like your parents have had? I know you love her, Nate. It's written all over your face. What I don't understand is why you fight it and why she fights it. Why don't you two just be together?''

"It's not that simple, Joe. There are others involved.''

"Garrett? Yeah, he loves Anna, but she doesn't love him the way she loves you.''

"How do you know? Damn it, Joe. Why don't you just stay out of it.''

"I won't stay out of it because I love you both.''

"I know you love us, Joe, but you have to let us decide for ourselves what to do.'' Nathan looked over his shoulder. "Here they come. I want to get home before they do.''

"Nate!'' Joe yelled after Nathan but Nathan had already ridden off toward the ranch.

Nathan rode hard, trying to drive the image of Anna from his mind. If he couldn't have her, he'd have to try and forget her. He rode into the yard, practically jumping from his horse. "Will you take care of everything for me, Jake?"

"Everything all right, Mr. Nathan?"

"Everything's fine. Anna is safe. She'll be here soon." He walked up to the ranch house and went inside. Aeneva ran to him immediately.

"Is Anna all right?"

"She's fine, Mother. She's riding back with Garrett." He looked at his father. "She took a nasty fall and hurt her foot, but she'll be all right." He looked around him. "Where's Clare?"

"She's upstairs putting fresh flowers in Anna's room." Aeneva ran her hand over Nathan's cheek. "Are you all right? You look tired."

"I'm all right. I'm going up to see Clare." Nathan took the stairs two at a time. He walked into Anna's room and saw Clare arranging flowers in a vase. She looked lovely with her brown hair pulled back, and she was wearing a simple white dress. "Clare."

She turned, smiling, her face lighting up. She ran across the room and threw herself in his arms. "Oh, Nathan. I was so worried about you. I was afraid something had happened to you."

"I'm fine now." He pulled her close, kissing her passionately. "I missed you, Clare. I want to be with you."

"I want to be with you, too. Why don't you come to my place for dinner tonight?"

"Do you think that's wise? You know people will talk."

"I don't care. Besides, all of the help will be gone tonight."

Nathan smiled. "Then that makes it even better." He kissed her again, trying unsuccessfully to put the memory of Anna's full lips from his mind.

"My, you really did miss me, didn't you?"

"Yes, I did. I think we should talk tonight, Clare."

"Talk about what?"

"I think we should talk about our future together."

"Oh, Nathan." She threw her arms around his neck and held onto him tightly. "I knew you would finally give in. I knew that you would see that we were made for each other."

"I'm just not sure I'm ready to settle down."

"I don't think any man is ready to settle down. But I'll make sure you want to come home to me." She unbuttoned the top two buttons of his shirt and ran her fingers over his chest. "Do you know how long I've waited for you to come back? I'll never forget the first time we made love. It will always be like that for us, Nathan." She kissed his chest, reaching for the third button.

Nathan took her hands. "Not here, Clare. They'll be back at any second." He kissed her hand. "There will be enough time for that tonight."

Garrett carried Anna into the house amid greetings from her parents and Larissa.

"I'm fine, Aeneva. There's nothing to worry about." She smiled over at Trenton, who attempted to get up. "Don't get up, Trenton. I'm fine, really."

"Are you sure?"

"Yes. I'm just hungry and I need to take a bath. I'm covered with dirt."

"What happened to your foot?" Aeneva was already looking at the swollen foot.

"I fell down some rocks. Can I tell you about it later? I'm pretty tired right now."

"Would you mind carrying her up to her room, Garrett?" Aeneva asked.

"I wouldn't mind at all, Mrs. Hawkins." Garrett

said and smiled in reply.

"I can get up the stairs by myself, Garrett."

"I'll carry you up."

Anna looked at Aeneva and Trenton. "Just give me some time to clean up and rest. I'll tell you all about it later." She held onto Garrett as he carried her up the stairs. She was tired, physically as well as emotionally. She tried not to think about Nathan and what had happened between them the night before, but she couldn't put it out of her mind. She closed her eyes, remembering how it felt to have his hands on her, remembering how it felt to have him love her.

"Here we are," Garrett said happily. "Oh, sorry. Didn't know you two were in here."

Anna opened her eyes. Nathan was holding Clare in his arms. Her cheeks were flushed and it was obvious that they had been in a passionate embrace. "Hello, Clare," Anna said brusquely.

"Hello, Anna. I'm so glad you're all right."

Anna noticed that Clare didn't seem to be the least bit perturbed that she and Garrett had walked in on them. "Thank you." Anna forced her eyes away from Nathan's.

"Well, I'll see you tonight, darling." Clare kissed Nathan on the cheek.

"I'll walk you out."

"No, don't bother. Why don't you stay here and make sure your little sister is all right."

Anna bristled at Clare's tone and her choice of words. "Put me down, Garrett. I can walk now." Anna leaned against Garrett, limping to the bed and sitting down. She looked up at Nathan, an angry look on her face. "Your little sister is just fine, so why don't you go after Clare. You two look like you can hardly stand to be apart anyway."

Nathan looked at Garrett and then at Anna. "I'll

see you later, Garrett."

"Thanks again, Nathan." Garrett turned to Anna. "What is it between you two? I thought you were getting along better?"

"I don't want to talk about Nathan." Anna fell back onto the bed, her arms thrown up over her head. "I never knew a bed could feel so good." She felt the bed sink down as Garrett sat down next to her. "I'd like to show you someday how good a bed can feel." He leaned down and kissed Anna. "I want you to marry me, Anna, and I want your answer soon. I'm going back to California next week. I'd like you to come back with me."

"Oh, Garrett, I'm so tired. Please let me think about it."

"I will, but make sure it's what you want. I want you to marry me because you want to be with me, not because you're afraid to be with someone else."

Anna sat up, her eyes large. "What do you mean?"

"You know what I mean." He kissed her on the cheek. "I'll be back tomorrow to check on you. 'Bye, Annie."

"'Bye." Anna sat on the bed for a moment, then she pulled off her boot. She unbuttoned her blouse and took it off, standing up to drop her skirt. She was dressed only in her camisole and pantalets. She stood there, wondering what she looked like to Nathan. She knew she wasn't the woman that Clare was, and she wondered to herself whether she could hold onto a man like Nathan. Could she love him in the ways that Clare obviously could? She lay down on her bed, pulling the comforter over her. She closed her eyes. She was so confused. Had last night been just a dream, just like the night of the ball when she had danced with Nathan? Had it all been a fairy tale meant to show her that Nathan wasn't the man for her? She didn't know. She knew that Garrett loved her and wanted her just the way she was, but she didn't know if after having been loved by Nathan she could be content to be loved by Garrett. She fell asleep, hoping that when she awoke there would be some clear answers.

Nathan brushed his hair and finished buttoning his shirt. He pulled out a jacket from his closet and walked out of the room. He stopped by Anna's door and knocked lightly, but when there was no answer, he opened it. It was dark in the room, and he could see from the light in the hall that Anna was still asleep. He walked in and turned the lamp up just enough to illuminate the room. He walked over to the bed and looked at her. She was rolled up in her quilt, but her arms were thrown out and her long hair was like a dark spray over the white pillow. He watched her chest rise and fall with every breath, and he looked at her mouth, the mouth which he had so eagerly kissed, the mouth which had so eagerly sought his the night before. He sat on the edge of the bed. Anna turned toward him, throwing an arm across his lap. He lifted her arm and kissed it lightly, then lowered his head to kiss her mouth.

Anna moved. "Nathan?"

"Yes." He sat up. "I wanted to see if you're all right."

Anna squinted at the light and looked around her. "Yes, I'm all right." She shook her head. "I guess I was dreaming." She looked at Nathan. "You look handsome. I'm sure Clare will think so, too."

Nathan lowered his head. "I think you were right. It would've been better if I'd never come back here." He stood up. "Do yourself a favor, Anna. Marry

370

Garrett. He'll make you happy.'' Nathan walked to the door.

"Nathan?'' Anna's voice stopped him.

"What?''

"I'll never forget last night. Never.''

Nathan hesitated at the door a moment, then walked out, trying to forget that he had ever loved Anna.

Weeks had passed since Anna had gotten lost in the mountains, and she had seen very little of Nathan. He spent all of his time at Clare's, and Anna couldn't stand it. She wanted to see him and talk to him but he never gave her a chance. It was as if he had decided that they never should have loved each other, and he was forcing it from his mind. He was determined to fall in love with Clare, and Anna was afraid that it had already happened. Clare was having a party that night, and Anna didn't want to go. She was afraid that Clare was going to tell everyone that she and Nathan were going to get married. Anna sat in the garden behind the house, attempting to read a book but finding it impossible. She sat on the bench and looked at the colorful flowers, wondering why her life had turned out the way it had.

"What's so interesting about those flowers?'' Trenton walked up to Anna and sat down next to her.

Anna smiled. "Hi. I'm just looking at the flowers because they're so pretty. I tried to read but I just can't concentrate.''

"Why's that?''

Anna shrugged her shoulders. "I don't know.''

"It wouldn't have anything to do with Nathan, would it?''

"Why would it?''

Trenton took Anna's hand, rubbing it gently. "Do you know that the very first time I saw your mother I fell in love with her? And I was only a boy. But I knew that I loved her, and I knew that I would never love anyone else."

"How did you know that so young?"

"I just did. I felt it inside. Even when I married Lydia, Nathan's mother, I couldn't forget Aeneva. She was always on my mind, every minute of the day."

"Why did you marry Nathan's mother? Did you love her?"

"No, I didn't love her. I married her because she was pregnant with Nathan. I thought it was the right thing to do." He shook his head. "But I was wrong. I cheated myself and I cheated Lydia. She should have had a man who really loved her, not just a man who was trying to do the right thing by her."

"If she hadn't died, would you have stayed with her?"

"I don't know, Anna. I've asked myself that question lots of times. If I had left her I probably would have lost Nathan, and I don't know if I could've stood that. But if I had stayed with her, I would've lost Aeneva and that was just as unbearable to me."

"Is it possible to get over a love like that, Trenton?"

"I don't know. I suppose it is. I suppose you learn to get on with your life. But I don't know if you ever forget that kind of love." Trenton cupped Anna's face in his hand. "You are in love with Nathan, aren't you, Anna?"

Anna looked up into Trenton's eyes, eyes that were exactly like Nathan's, and she couldn't lie. Tears filled her eyes. "Yes, but he doesn't love me. He's in love with Clare."

"Are you sure?"

"Yes. And that's the way it should be. Nathan and Clare are good together, just like Garrett and I are good together."

"Are you trying to convince me or yourself of that, Annie?"

"That's just the way it is. Besides, it wouldn't be proper for us to be in love."

"Why? Because you were raised by the same people? That's hogwash." He took Anna's hand and walked over to a large oak tree. "Let's sit under here. I can't stand those damned benches." They sat down. "Did Aeneva ever tell you about her parents?"

"Not much. Why?"

"Well, Little Flower and Young Eagle were her parents. Little Flower was Cheyenne and Young Eagle was Crow, taken captive when he was very young. He and Little Flower were raised as brother and sister by Little Flower's parents."

"Stalking Horse and Sun Dancer?"

"Yes. But from the time they were very young, Little Flower and Young Eagle cared for each other in a way that was unlike what a brother and sister should feel for each other. They both tried to fight it but eventually they fell in love. Stalking Horse would not forgive them, and they left the tribe disgraced. But it didn't matter because they were together."

"Did Stalking Horse ever forgive them?"

"Yes, but it was too late. By the time he went to them, they had been murdered by Crow warriors bent on revenge."

"It's a sad story. Everyone would have been spared the sadness if Little Flower and Young Eagle had never run away together."

"No, everyone would've been spared the sadness if

they had been allowed to love each other freely without being made to feel like they were doing something wrong. They were raised by the same people but they were not brother and sister, just as you and Nathan aren't brother and sister."

"I don't know, Trenton. I'm so confused. When I'm with Garrett I feel good but when I'm with Nathan, I feel wonderful, special."

"And how do you feel when Nathan is with Clare?"

"It makes me angry. I don't like to think of the two of them being together."

"Then why don't you do something about it if you don't like it?"

"I don't know what to do. I don't really know Nathan. All I know for sure is that we're very attracted to each other. That doesn't mean we're in love."

"But you could try to get to know each other. That's the best way of finding out whether or not you're in love with someone."

"I don't know." She looked up, hearing Nathan's voice.

"I wondered where you two were."

"Why?" Trenton asked.

"I have something to tell you. Clare and I are going to be married."

"Oh." Trenton stood up, walking to Nathan. "You're sure this is what you want, son?"

"Yeah, I've thought it over, Pa. Clare and I have known each other a long time."

"Yes, but you haven't seen each other in ten years, Nate. Don't you think you better give it some time?"

"I don't need to give it some time. It's the right thing to do. I thought you'd be happy for me, Pa."

"I am happy for you, Nate, if you're sure that it's

what you want.''

"It is.'' Nathan walked to Anna. "What do you think?''

Anna stood up, forcing the tears from her eyes. "I'm sure Clare will make you a very good wife, Nathan. I hope you're both very happy together.'' She walked past him and out of the garden. Nathan watched her as she walked away, knowing the hurt he had caused her.

"Why are you doing this, Nate?''

Nathan looked at his father, his eyes locking with those of Trenton's. "I'm doing it because it's the best thing for Anna, Pa.'' He shoved his hands into his pockets and walked past Trenton.

Trenton shook his head, wondering if he had been so stubborn when he was that age and then instantly knowing the answer. He knew there was nothing he could do. He just had to hope that Nathan and Anna learned before it was too late how much they really loved each other.

Anna held Garrett's arm, dreading the party. "Are you sure you want to go to this party, Garrett? Why don't we just take a ride. It's such a beautiful night.''

"It'll be a great party, Annie. Besides, Nathan will be disappointed if you're not there when he announces his engagement.''

"Why should he be disappointed. I'm not his sister.''

"Come on, Annie. Don't ruin this night for him.''

"All right. I'll try to have a good time.''

Anna and Garrett walked up to the large doors of the house. Garrett pulled the bell, and they were immediately admitted into a wide entrance that led to a ballroom. "I hate this house,'' Anna muttered to herself.

"What did you say?"

"I said I hate this house. It doesn't fit. It's too out of place for this country. She only made her husband build it because she wanted to be like the people in the city. Look at it—all those columns and arches. It looks like a palace."

Garrett stopped, taking Anna by the shoulders. "Stop it, Anna. This isn't like you. You're not like those gossipy old women who have nothing better to do than to tell lies about other people. I thought you liked Clare."

"I do like Clare."

"Is it so hard for you, Annie?"

"Is what so hard for me?"

"Is it so hard for you to accept that Nathan is in love with another woman?"

"No, I can accept that. That's not what bothers me."

"What does bother you then?"

"I think he's rushing into this relationship, that's all. He hardly even knows her."

"He's known her most of his life."

"But he hasn't even been here for the last ten years of his life!" Anna pulled herself away from Garrett's grasp. "I don't want to go in there. I'm sick of women like Clare Richardson. She married a rich old man when she was just a girl, and when he died she got all of his money. Now she's ready to have Nathan all to herself."

"Why does that bother you so much?"

"I told you why it bothers me. It's not fair."

"Why isn't it?"

"Would you stop it? Just leave me alone. I didn't want to come to this party anyway."

"Just take it easy." Garrett put his arms around

Anna. "We'll stay for awhile, and then we'll go for a ride. I'll take you out to the oaks. But you'd better be careful. I've been known to go crazy on nights like this."

Anna finally smiled. "Why Garrett McReynolds, I never knew you were the type."

"I am around you." He kissed Anna. "Should we go in now?"

"All right." She took Garrett's arm, and they walked into the ballroom. Anna looked around her at the huge marble floor, the crystal chandeliers, and the heavy drapes. She hated this room, not because of its richness but because it belonged to Clare Richardson. Anna saw most of the people she had grown up with, many of them married and with children. She looked around the room and felt acutely uncomfortable. She felt suddenly as if she didn't fit, and she couldn't figure out why. She saw Nathan and Clare dancing. They made a beautiful couple. Nathan was tall and fair-haired, and Clare was delicate and fine-boned. She was dressed in a deep green silk dress that made her skin look like ivory.

"Do you want to dance?"

"Not now, Garrett. Would you mind getting me some punch?"

"Sure."

Anna watched Garrett walk away, and she felt good inside. He was a handsome man, and she saw more than a few heads turn to watch him as he walked by. The music stopped, and she saw Nathan and Clare walking toward her. She steeled herself for what was to come.

"Hello, Anna. You look lovely this evening. You're looking more grown up all the time."

Anna smiled graciously. "Thank you, Clare. Perhaps in ten years I'll look just like you." I can play the game too, Anna thought.

"Why don't you ask your sister to dance, Nathan? I see her escort is gone."

"He's just getting me something to drink. I'll wait for him."

"Oh, nonsense." Clare pulled Anna toward Nathan. "You might as well dance with him now, Anna, because after I marry him, I'm not going to let any woman touch him."

Anna smiled half-heartedly and walked with Nathan onto the dance floor. She took his hand and put her other hand on his shoulder, but she didn't look at him. She refused to be taken in by him again. She could feel his hand tighten around her waist as they moved around the dance floor, but she didn't say anything.

"You do look lovely tonight, Anna."

Anna looked up at Nathan for the first time, refusing to be drawn in by his eyes. "Thank you," she replied abruptly.

"I'm surprised you came. You didn't seem too enthused about my announcement."

"I don't really care what you do, Nathan. In fact, the more I think about it, you and Clare Richardson deserve each other."

"Clare is a nice person."

"Yes, I'm sure she is. I wouldn't know."

"Then why are you judging her? You don't even know her."

Anna stopped dancing. Her eyes were filled with fury when she looked at Nathan. "If you don't know that, then you're more cold-hearted than I thought you were." She started to walk off the dance floor but Nathan caught her arm and swept her back into the dance. "Let me go!"

"Why? So you can run off and pout? Don't you think it's about time you grew up, Anna?"

"Me? What about you? Chasing after a rich widow."

"I'm not chasing after her. We happen to be getting married. There is a difference."

"Yes, I'm sure there is." Anna looked past Nathan. "What's it like when you make love to her, Nathan? Do you tell her all of the things that you told me that night? Do you kiss her the way you kissed me?" Her eyes filled with tears in spite of her efforts to stop them. "Damn!"

"Come on." Nathan led Anna out of the ballroom to the garden. He took her down the steps to the gazebo. Taking out his handkerchief, he wiped the tears from her face. "Anna, I want to tell you something, and I hope you hear me."

"I don't want to hear anything you have to say, Nathan. It will all be lies anyway."

"No, what I'm about to tell you is the truth." He placed his hands on her shoulders. "I will never forget the night we made love. We shared something very special. I'm not sure I will ever be able to love another woman the way I loved you that night." He dropped his hands from her shoulders. "But we are different people, and you don't belong with me. Clare and I are alike. She understands me and she understands my needs. You are too good, too innocent to be with me, Anna. You should be with Garrett. He will make you happy."

Anna covered her mouth with the handkerchief, afraid that she would start sobbing. "Did you love me that night, Nathan?"

Nathan tilted Anna's chin up and kissed her lightly on the lips. "Yes, I did love you that night,

379

Anna." He looked at her a moment longer, then he walked away. And I will always love you, he said to himself.

Anna held Garrett's hand tightly. She looked up at the star-filled sky. "It's beautiful out here, isn't it? Sometimes I wish we could be children again."

"What's wrong, Annie?"

"I don't know. I'm just feeling a little sad tonight."

"Does it have anything to do with Nathan? I saw you two talking earlier."

"He just made me realize that it's time to grow up."

Garrett slipped his arms around Anna's waist. "You feel grown up to me."

Anna turned around in Garrett's arms. "Do you want me as a woman, Garrett? You still don't think of me as a little girl, do you?"

"No, I haven't thought of you as a little girl for a long time." He kissed her passionately. "I want you, Anna. The way a man wants a woman."

"Then show me, Garrett. Show me how much you want me." She put her arms around his neck and kissed him deeply.

"Not here, Anna."

"Why not?"

"Because this isn't the place I want to make love to you. You deserve more than a dirt bed."

Anna felt a stabbing pain in her heart. Nathan hadn't thought she deserved more than that. She felt like such a fool. She felt Garrett's arms tighten around her.

"I love you, Anna, and I want to take care of you if you'll let me. I want to build a home with you and have children with you, just like we dreamed of doing." He kissed the top of her head. "You're worth more to me than one night out here under the oaks."

Anna knew then that Nathan was right. Garrett was the person for her. He loved her and he wanted to care for her forever. To Nathan, she had been nothing more than a conquest. And now that he had conquered her, he wanted nothing more to do with her. "Do you still want to marry me, Garrett?"

"More than anything in the world."

"Then let's do it right now. If we ride into town, we could be there when the judge gets back from the party. He could marry us tonight."

"No, Anna. When I marry you I want the whole world to see it. I want a big wedding with all the fancy trimmings."

"Are you sure?"

"I'm real sure. And I want a honeymoon in someplace special, like Europe."

"Europe? Garrett, are you kidding?"

"No, my father said that if I settled down and married you he'd send us to Europe as a wedding gift. It would be just like we always planned, Annie."

"Oh, Garrett, it sounds so wonderful."

"Then let's set a date and we'll do it. It'll be the biggest wedding this territory has ever seen."

"What about Nathan and Clare?"

"What about them?"

"They'll be getting married soon. I don't want to ruin things for them."

"The hell with them. You and I have been talking about getting married since we were kids. I think it's about time we did it, don't you?"

"Garrett, are you sure? It scares me. I'm afraid I won't make you happy."

"You make me happy no matter what you do, Annie. Don't you know that?" Garrett hugged Anna.

"I just want you to make sure you're making the right decision. I want you to be happy."

"I will be happy, Garrett. I will be." Anna hugged Garrett and closed her eyes. This was what she had always dreamed of and hoped for. She and Garrett were getting married. They would spend the rest of their lives together. But as much as she tried, Anna couldn't find the joy she thought she would feel on that day. She hoped that it would come soon.

Anna walked around the garden, smelling the roses and smiling to herself. She remembered the story that Aeneva had told her. When they first moved to this property, Trenton had told her she couldn't raise flowers in this heat, but Aeneva had protested and made Trenton buy seeds when he went to town. The first year there were no flowers, but the second spring flowers bloomed all over her garden until every year Aeneva planted new varieties of flowers. Finally Trenton had to admit that he liked the garden. It had become a favorite place for everyone to escape to.

Anna sat down under the old oak and looked around her. She loved this place. It was filled with such love. She was partly afraid to leave and go off to California with Garrett, but the other part was yearning for adventure. She looked up at the sky. Clouds moved briskly along, and the air was beginning to cool. She wondered if they were going to have a storm. She hoped that her parents and Joe and Larissa had a good time in Prescott. They had gone in to see a play and to stay the night at the hotel. They had all looked so happy going off together. She wondered if that's what it would be like when she and Garrett were married. She shivered and rubbed her arms. The sky was beginning to darken. She decided to go for a ride before it rained.

She went to the stable and saddled her mare. After riding for a long time, she felt her mind clear. Aeneva had asked her if she would be all right staying alone and she had said yes, that she needed the time alone. Nathan was now spending almost all of his time at Clare's, and Anna was glad she didn't have to deal with him. Soon they would both be married, leading lives of their own.

Anna brought the mare back into the yard and unsaddled him, brushing him down and taking him into the stall. She went back to the house and stopped on the porch, looking out at the horizon. It was clouding up quickly. A storm was coming. Anna walked into the kitchen and cut off a piece of bread. She chewed on it absently and headed back into the living room, walking over to the bookshelf to pick out a book. She sat down and opened it up but she closed it immediately. She couldn't concentrate long enough to read. She went over to her father's desk and poured herself a glass of whiskey, staring at the amber-colored liquid in the lamplight. After taking a small sip, she twisted her face in a grimace. She hated the taste of whiskey but she was in the mood to get drunk, and if she had to drink whiskey to do it, that's what she would drink. She sipped at the whiskey again, still hating its taste but forcing it down. She felt warm inside. Now she understood why all the hands drank it when they were cold. She took another sip and got up, walking over to the windows that looked out on the mountains. It was dark. Although the sun had not yet set, the clouds had all but obliterated the sun. She could see the hands getting horses in the corral and closing the doors to the stable and barn. She decided she was hungry and went back into the kitchen to make herself a sandwich. She came back out to the living room and stood at the window where she could see lightning in the distance. Seeing Jake walking toward the house, she went out on the porch.

"What is it, Jake?"

"Looks like it's going to be a rough one, Miss Anna. Make sure your shutters are closed and all the windows are shut tight. Wouldn't want anything to get ruined."

"Thanks, Jake. Are you all going to be warm enough out there? Do you have plenty of blankets and food?"

Jake smiled his lopsided smile. "We have plenty of everything that counts."

"You mean whiskey?"

"Yes, ma'am."

"Jake, are you and the hands going to play poker tonight?"

"Well, yes, ma'am. We play poker every night."

"Do you mind if I play?"

"Now, Miss, I don't think that would be a very good idea."

"Why not?"

"Your father would kill me if he knew you were gambling."

"Of course he wouldn't, Jake. He's the one who taught me how to gamble. Oh, please, just for a while."

"Oh, all right. But not for long. Those guys can get pretty rowdy."

"Thanks, Jake."

"I'll come up and get you when it's time, miss. But please mind me when I say it's time for you to go back to the big house. I don't want any trouble."

"Whatever you say, Jake."

*   *   *

Nathan rode into the yard, taking his horse straight into the stable. The doors to the stable banged open behind him as he led his horse inside. The wind blew furiously as he unsaddled his horse and gave him a grain bag. He patted his horse on the neck and walked outside into the blinding rain. Thunder crashed around him, and he ran across the yard and onto the porch. He went inside, wiping the rain from his boots and clothes. "Anna?" he called as he walked inside, dreading the moment when he would have to see her. He knew his parents and Joe and Larissa would be in town, and Aeneva had asked him if he could stay home just this one night and watch after Anna. He said he would. "Anna." Nathan walked into the kitchen and saw the bread and meat out on the counter. He walked back through the living room and ran up the stairs, checking each room—no Anna. He went back downstairs. The house was completely lit but Anna was nowhere in sight. Thunder crashed overhead and he jumped slightly. Where was she? He walked over to the window and looked out into the yard. Seeing the light from the bunkhouse, he thought that if she were frightened, she would go to Jake. He went out on the porch, pulling the collar of the jacket up around him and running across the yard. He knocked on the door of the bunkhouse and walked in, not waiting for an answer. Upon entering, he was surprised to see a table full of men and Anna playing poker. Anna was drinking whiskey out of a shot glass and intensely scrutinizing her hand of cards.

"I'll see your twenty dollars and raise you ten," she said confidently. Her face betrayed nothing.

"I think you're bluffing, girl," said Pete, one of the younger hands. "Let's see the cards."

Anna spread out her cards. "A full house, kings

high." She smiled devilishly as she pulled in the money from the middle of the table.

"I thought you said this would be a nice friendly game," Pete said to Jake. "Hell, she's come down here and took all our money."

"She's done it fair and square," Jake replied adamantly. "Oh, hello Mr. Nathan. Your sister here just wanted to play a few hands of cards."

Anna looked up at Nathan, swigging at her glass of whiskey. "Well, if it isn't my big brother. What brings you home, brother dear?" She looked at him, downing the rest of her glass.

"I wanted to make sure you were all right in this storm."

"How sweet but I'm fine as you can see." She reached for the bottle and poured herself some more whiskey.

"Don't you think you've had enough of that, Anna?"

"I don't need you to tell me when I've had enough, Nathan." Anna took another drink. "Would you like to play? I'd like nothing better than to take your money."

"I think it's time you went up to the house, Anna."

"I don't care what you think. I'm staying here. Whose deal is it?"

Nathan walked over to the table. "Will you gentlemen excuse me?" He reached down and pulled Anna from her chair, throwing her across his shoulder kicking and screaming.

"I hate you, Nathan Hawkins. Put me down!"

"You split her winnings between you, Jake," Nathan said as they reached the door. Nathan walked out into the rain, this time in no hurry to get to the house.

"Damn you, Nathan. You have no right. Put me down."

Nathan ignored Anna as he walked through the heavy rain to the house. He put Anna down on the porch, holding onto her arm while he opened the door. He dragged her into the house after him and closed the door. Anna took a swing at him but Nathan caught her arms and held them at her sides. "I bet you were a mean little girl."

"Only to boys who beat me up." Anna struggled out of Nathan's hold.

"I'll let you go if you promise me you'll go upstairs and get out of those wet clothes. And no more whiskey and poker tonight."

"You're not my father, Nathan. You can't tell me what to do."

"Well I am telling you what to do, and you can't argue with me. You either do as I say or I'll do it for you."

Anna stopped struggling. "All right, I'll do as you say as long as you leave me alone the rest of the night. What are you doing back here anyway? I didn't think you and Clare could live without each other."

"Mother didn't want you to be alone. I told her I'd stay with you tonight."

"You're such a thoughtful brother," Anna replied coldly. She walked up the stairs.

Nathan shook his head, wondering how he had ever thought he could be in love with such a child as Anna. He poured himself a glass of whiskey and sat down in his father's leather chair. He liked the sound of the storm raging outside but he didn't like the one that was raging inside. He sipped at the whiskey, letting it warm his insides. He shivered, realizing that he had forgotten to remove his wet clothing.

Standing up, he removed his wet jacket and shirt and threw his hat on top of the wet pile. He quickly built a fire in the fireplace and struck a match. Standing in front of it, he felt its warmth go through his body. He downed the rest of his whiskey and poured another, walking back to the fire. Closing his eyes, he let the warmth from the fire sink into his body and thought of Clare, wondering what she was doing right now. He enjoyed being with her and enjoyed their love-making. She was very experienced and was well-schooled in the many ways there were to please a man. She knew exactly how to please him. But still there was something missing, and he knew what it was. Anna. It had been so different when he had made love to her. She wasn't at all experienced but her love-making had been more passionate than Clare's could ever hope to be. Anna possessed the kind of natural qualities that he so admired and desired in a woman. If only she wasn't so young. If only she wasn't part of his family.

"Nathan."

Nathan opened his eyes. Anna stood before him in an ice-blue satin nightgown with a thin robe tied over it. He looked at her with her dark hair brushed out over her shoulders and her large blue eyes confronting him with honesty, and he was hard put to ignore her. He looked at her long, graceful neck and the swell of her breasts. He remembered how it had been to touch her breasts, how it had felt to run his hands over the length of her slim, young body.

"I'm sorry."

"What?" Nathan forced himself out of his reverie.

"I'm sorry for the way I acted earlier. I was trying to make you angry."

"It's all right. How do you feel?"

"I have a headache and I'm tired. I think I'll go to

bed now."

"All right. Goodnight."

"Goodnight. Thank you for keeping me from making a complete fool out of myself."

Nathan smiled. "You're a good card player. Pa must've taught you."

"He started teaching me when my real father was still here. The three of us used to play together. It used to drive Aeneva crazy."

"I bet it did. She hates gambling, but don't ever get into a card game with her. She'll win every time."

"I've never seen her play."

"She plays now and then, and when she does she always wins."

Anna laughed. "She's full of surprises." She looked at Nathan. The firelight danced along his bronze skin, and she couldn't take her eyes away from his lean body. She remembered how it had been the night they had made love. She wasn't sure if she could ever forget it. She flinched as thunder cracked all around them and covered her ears. "I hate it when it's so loud."

"It's all right. It won't hurt you."

Anna stood next to Nathan, wrapping her arms around herself as she stood next to the fire. "I remember crossing the prairie in our wagon. I was eight years old. We were caught in a big storm. My father was drunk and had passed out. All I can remember was lightning and thunder. I thought it was going to rip our wagon apart. I kept trying to wake my father but he wouldn't move. I don't think I've ever been that scared." Lightning lit up the room, and Anna looked anxiously around her. Several seconds went by, and the distant rumble of thunder turned into a loud cracking sound around them. Instinctively Anna moved closer to Nathan, closing her eyes. She felt his arms go around her and she didn't fight him.

"It's all right, Anna. It won't hurt you."

"I hate it. I wish it would stop." She buried her face in his chest, reveling in the smell of his bare skin. She wanted to give herself to him again right there and then, but she knew she could not. He had refused her once before; he could do it again. She pulled away. "I think I should go up to bed now." She pushed the hair back from her face. "Goodnight."

"Goodnight, Anna."

Anna climbed the stairs to her bedroom and went to bed, pulling the quilt high over her head. She still hated the sound of the thunder but she refused to turn to Nathan for comfort. She knew it would be a mistake. She closed her eyes and tried to push the sound of the thunder from her mind, but she had a more difficult time trying to push the feel of Nathan's skin from her thoughts. She hoped that sleep would bring her solace.

Anna turned, throwing her arms over her head. They were all against her now. She had no one to turn to. Tommy and Tim were holding her while Garrett hit her, over and over again. She screamed for him to stop but he only laughed. Then he turned to someone who came out of the darkness. It was Nathan. He walked out of the darkness holding Clare's hand. He stood in front of Anna, kissing Clare and telling her how much he loved her. He turned to Anna, telling her that she was nothing to him. He laughed as Garrett and the others dragged her away, tying her to a tree. When she screamed for Nathan to help her he turned and walked away, holding onto Clare. Anna begged Garrett not to hurt her but he slapped her, telling her it was what she deserved. He told her she wasn't good enough for any man. Thunder shook the room and Anna screamed louder than before, feeling as if her entire body had been ripped apart. She was suddenly alone on the prairie with no one, in the middle of the storm. She yelled for help but no one would help her. No one. She saw the lightning as it lit up the darkness and she ran to get away from the thunder, but it caught up with her and shook her entire body. She screamed again. She reached out for someone to help her, and this time someone did. She felt arms around her and suddenly felt safe.

"It's all right, Anna. There's nothing to be afraid of. It's all right."

Anna slowly opened her eyes to the dim lamplight of her bedroom. She had been dreaming. Nathan was sitting on her bed, his arms around her. "I'm sorry."

"Don't be sorry. You had a nightmare. You were scared to death."

"It was a strange dream," she said in a soft voice. "I was all alone. There was no one to help me."

"You'll never be alone, Anna." Nathan held her closer, stroking her hair.

"I feel so silly."

"Why? Because you're afraid of thunder and lightning? That's a lot more real than what I used to be afraid of."

"What was that?"

"I used to be afraid of horny toads."

Anna laughed. "You? I can't believe it."

"It's true. When I was a kid one of my friends caught one and put it down my pants. I've been scared of them ever since."

"You're lying." Anna laughed again. "But thank you anyway." Anna huddled against Nathan as the thunder cracked again and the wind banged a loose shutter against the window. The rain battered the outside of the house, and Anna felt unnerved.

"It's all right." Nathan wrapped his arms tighter around her.

"Don't leave me, Nathan. I don't want to be alone tonight."

"I won't leave you alone." Nathan put his legs up on the bed, crawling under the comforter with Anna. He pulled her close. He stroked her hair. He could feel her body begin to relax against his. "It's all right, Anna. Just relax." He ran his hand up and down her back, trying to ignore the feel of her soft skin. Soon he felt her even breathing as she fell asleep, her head on his chest, her arm thrown across his waist. He ran his hand along her arm up to her shoulder, bending over to kiss the top of her head. He wondered what it would be like to hold her like this for the rest of their lives, and he knew that it would always feel this good, this exciting. She made him feel something no other woman had made him feel, and he still wasn't sure how to deal with it.

Nathan closed his eyes, finally relaxing. He moved down into the bed, stretching out into the length of it. Anna didn't let go of him so he held onto her, unable to let her go. It felt good to hold her like this. It felt much better than when he held Clare. He had thought Clare had made him feel like a man, but he knew more about manhood now. The warmth he felt from Anna came from more than just her body; it was the flame of her spirit and the goodness of her soul that held him.

The storm started up again and the shutter again slammed against the outside of the house. Carefully, Nathan got out of bed, walked to the window and opened it, trying to fasten the loose shutter. A clap of thunder sounded so loud, even he was surprised by it. He slammed the window down and turned to find Anna sitting bolt upright in the bed, a look of absolute terror on her face. He ran to the bed, climbing back in and taking Anna in his arms. "Don't worry, Anna. It's all right now. It's all right." He could see the tears running down her cheeks and carefully, very carefully, he kissed each one away. Her mouth quivered slightly as he kissed her but she responded immediately, surprising him with her passion. Their bodies moved against each other as each one sought the other out. Nathan stood up, removing his pants in the dim lamplight as Anna watched. He sat down on the bed, pulling her gown over her head. He looked at her body in the light and ran his hands lovingly over it. Anna closed her eyes, enjoying Nathan's touch. He pulled her over to him, and she leaned against him, her breasts against his bare chest. She wrapped her arms tightly around his neck, pressing herself against him.

"Nathan," Anna whispered against his mouth. "Do you love me, Nathan? Do you want me?"

"Yes," Nathan replied eagerly, pulling Anna on top of him as he lay back on the bed. Her hair fell over them as Nathan ran his hands down the length of Anna's body. He kissed her deeply, feeling his desire grow. Lightning illuminated the room, and soon thunder filled the room with its deafening roar, but for the first time Anna was oblivious to it. She moved her body against Nathan's, feeling as she had never felt before in her life. Nathan rolled over, his body covering hers. She held onto him, wanting him to love her again. She opened herself to him, and their love was like the storm that raged outside—fierce and unrelenting. Their bodies were covered with sweat, and they moved in perfect unison, as if they had been

393

made for each other. When Nathan moved against Anna she moved with him, her body ready and willing to take him.

When she felt as if she would scream, Nathan held her, filling her again and again with his love. Anna cried, seeking Nathan's mouth in the darkness, feeling the fulfillment she had never known existed. She kissed Nathan gently, unable to stop the words that came to her lips.

"I love you. I love you, Nathan."

"I love you, too, Anna. My dear Anna." Nathan's voice came to Anna out of the darkness like a light that was leading her homeward. She knew then that there was no other man for her but Nathan. He was her love. He was her life.

Chapter XIV

Anna stretched, feeling warm and fulfilled. She reached out her hand in the darkness but she couldn't feel Nathan. "Nathan?" She sat up, looking around the room. "Nathan?" She got up, quickly putting on a heavy robe. She ran down the hall to Nathan's room and went inside. "Nathan, are you here?" She looked around the room. His bed was unmade and his cupboard doors were open. He had taken some clothes out to wear, and his clothes from the night before were thrown in the corner. She went downstairs but he was nowhere around. Anna ran upstairs and quickly dressed in some old pants, a shirt, her boots, a jacket, and a hat under which she tucked her hair. She went out to the barn.

"How you feeling this morning, Miss Anna?"

Anna turned around, smiling when she saw Pete. "Not too bad considering, Pete. I hope I didn't make too much of a fool of myself."

"No, we were all just angry that you were winning, that's all. We'd be glad to give you your winnings back."

"No, you keep them. Have you seen Nathan around this morning?"

"Yeah, he lit out of here at the crack of dawn. Said he had some business to take care of at the Richardson place."

Anna felt an ache in her stomach. So he had gone to Clare. "You're sure, Pete?"

"Yes, ma'am. Said he had to get back there."

"Thank you, Pete." Anna wandered back to the house, realizing too late that she had done just what she had promised herself she wouldn't do. She had gone right back into Nathan's arms, only to have him turn to Clare. She ran back to the stable, going to her father's big Appaloosa. She quickly got the tack and saddled him, leading him out of the stable.

Jake followed Anna. "You don't want to ride him, Miss Anna. Your father can barely handle him."

Anna held tightly onto the reins. "I want to ride him, Jake. I'll be fine."

"Please be careful, Miss Anna. Remember how spirited he is."

"I will, Jake." Anna stepped into the stirrup as the Appaloosa pranced around, throwing his head up and down. "Whoa, boy. It's all right." She held onto the horn and pulled herself up onto the saddle, holding onto the reins. "All right, boy. Let's go." Anna kneed the large horse, and he took off into a gallop. They rode through the yard and out into the open countryside, riding up the hills and jumping the stream that bordered the land. Anna rode until her anger had subsided into sadness, then she rode back to the grove of oaks. She dismounted, tethering the stallion to a nearby tree. She walked over to the stream and stared into the clear water. She looked up into the cloudless sky and couldn't believe that only last night there had been such a terrible storm, and she had again made such a fool of herself. She heard a horse and she started for her horse, afraid that it

396

might be Nathan, but she could see that it wasn't Nathan. She waited, watching as the lone rider on the horse reined in by her. It was Pete.

"Is something wrong, Pete?" She walked over to his horse.

Pete looked around him, slowly climbing off his horse. "Well, yes, ma'am, there is something wrong."

"What? Is it my family or Nathan?"

"No." Pete stepped forward, drawing his gun and aiming it at Anna. "I'm sorry, miss, but you're going to have to come with me."

"What are you talking about?" Anna stepped backward.

Pete grabbed her arm. "You just have to come with me, ma'am. That's all I can tell you for now."

"Well, I won't go with you." Anna yanked her arm away but Pete cocked his pistol. "I have orders to shoot you if I have to, miss. I think you just better come along with me."

Anna walked toward Pete, who shoved her toward his horse. "Now, you just stand there while I get me some rope. There we go." Pete took Anna's hands and tied them in back of her. "There you go. I don't think you'll be able to do anything. Come on now, step up here." He tried to boost Anna into the saddle but she fought him. Quickly Pete's demeanor changed. He shoved Anna against the side of his horse, putting his hand firmly around her neck. "Look, missy, I was paid a lot of money to get you someplace and that's just what I'm going to do. If you fight me, I'll just have to knock you out and drag you there. It's up to you."

Anna looked at Pete's cold eyes. There was no feeling in them. "All right. I'll do what you want. Just tell me one thing. Who are you working for?"

"Sorry, ma'am, I can't tell you that. Up you go

now." Pete boosted Anna up into the saddle and climbed up behind her, putting his arms around her to grab the reins. "Haven't had my arms around a girl as pretty as you in my whole life. Feels kinda nice."

"You'll never get away with this, Pete. My father and brother are the best trackers around here. They'll find you before you even leave the territory."

"That so?" Pete clamped his arms more tightly around Anna. "You and that brother of yours seem to be awfully close. Seems kinda strange to me."

"He's not really my brother. We're not related."

"I figured it musta been something like that."

"Pete, if it's money you want, I'm sure my father will be glad to pay you whatever you want."

"Sorry, ma'am, but I'm going to be getting more money out of this than I'm gonna know what to do with."

"What about my horse? As soon as my brother sees my horse he'll be after us. That was careless, Pete."

"No, that was on purpose, miss. It's your brother he wants."

"Who?"

"You'll find out soon enough."

Anna struggled to keep the fear from consuming her. Who would want to kidnap her in order to get Nathan? They were riding west, and Pete wouldn't tell her anything else. They rode until midday when Pete stopped and dismounted.

"I'll untie your arms for awhile miss, but if you try to escape, I'll have to hurt you. Do you understand?"

"Yes." Anna let Pete help her off of his horse, cringing as his hands slipped up the sides of her breasts. She waited patiently as he untied her hands. Rubbing her arms, she tried to get the circulation back into them. She looked around her. There was nothing. Nothing but hills, cactus, and sagebrush.

That meant they were headed west. She looked at Pete. "Please tell me something, Pete. I've never done anything to hurt you."

Pete shrugged his shoulders and handed the water bag to Anna. "All I know is there's some man who's hell-bent on getting your brother. I guess he thought he could best get to him through you."

"Why didn't he just have you kidnap Nathan? I don't understand."

"I don't either. He just told me to kidnap you and that your brother would follow soon enough. That's all I know. That's all I was paid to do."

"And if I tried to escape? Were you paid to kill me?" She noticed that Pete avoided her eyes.

"I'm not going to kill you, miss, but I will get you there. Come on. We better get going."

Anna climbed back up in the saddle and thought for a moment about trying to ride off, then thought better of it. She waited until Pete climbed up behind her. "I promise I won't try to do anything, Pete, if you'll just leave my arms free."

"I don't know if I can trust you, miss."

"You have the gun. You're behind me. What can I do?"

Pete thought a moment. "I guess that'll be all right. But don't try anything."

"All right."

They rode the rest of the day until after twilight. They stopped on a slight rise. "See down there, miss? That's where we're going."

"Where? I can't see anything."

"Can't you see that railroad track down there?"

"We're going on a train?"

"That's right." Pete urged the horse down the hill to the railroad tracks. He rode up to the water station, reaching up to pull down the arm with the red flag.

"There we go. The train should be along in no time at all."

Anna squirmed in the saddle, trying to turn around, but Pete wouldn't let her. "Pete, please let me go. I'll give you anything you want. You can have all the money I have in the world. I bet it's more than what this man gave you."

"I doubt it, missy. 'Sides, ain't no way I could trust you to give it to me once I let you go. No. This way I get myself some money and I get out of Arizona."

Anna's mind raced with thoughts as she sat on the horse with Pete. She tried to think of any number of ways to get away but none of them seemed possible. "What are we going to do when we're on the train? You don't actually think I'm going to keep my mouth shut once I'm on that train, do you?"

"That's not going to matter much, miss. Oh, look, here it comes." Off in the distance the light from the train shone into the darkness. "Just in case you decide to do something stupid, I'll have this gun right in the small of your back. And I ain't afraid to shoot."

Anna watched as the train approached, praying that it was too dark for the engineer to see the flag at night. But she could hear the squeak of the brakes as they grated against the rails, causing sparks to fly up all around. Pete dismounted and pulled Anna after him. He watched as the cars went by and he waited. He approached the caboose, meeting the porter as he stepped outside.

"Howdy, sir."

"Howdy, there. I do believe Mr. Rogers is expecting us in his private car."

"Yes, sir. Right this way." The porter led them through the caboose to the next car. He knocked on the door. "Mr. Rogers, sir. Your guests are here."

Anna felt the end of Pete's gun in the middle of her back as she smiled at the porter. He tipped his hat as he opened the door for her and Pete. "Thank you," she said politely, hoping that he would notice that she was scared. He noticed nothing.

"Mighty obliged, sir," Pete said in a friendly tone as he firmly pushed Anna into the car. He shut the door behind them.

Anna looked into the plushly decorated car and to the man whose back was to them. All she could see was his dark hair. She looked over at Pete.

"Go on in, missy. I think Mr. Rogers would like to see you."

Anna moved tentatively forward, not sure what to expect. But Pete shoved her, and she walked toward the man. "Mr. Rogers," she said softly, unsure whether the man was even awake. She walked to the side of his chair, and he turned around. She froze in her steps. It was Franklin Driscoll.

"Well, Miss O'Leary, how nice of you to come."

Anna stood, unable to move. "I thought—" Anna was unable to speak.

"You thought I was in jail. Yes, lots of people thought I was in jail, including your brother. But he's not really your brother, is he?" He patted the seat across from him. "Come, sit down, Miss O'Leary. I think we have a lot to talk about."

"We don't have anything to talk about. I don't even know why I'm here."

"Oh, I think you do. You're here because Steven Randall, or should I say Nathan Hawkins, is in love with you. He is, isn't he?"

"I'm sorry, Mr. Driscoll, but you have the wrong information. Nathan is not in love with me. He is engaged to marry another woman."

"He was engaged to marry my daughter just a few

months ago!" Driscoll said angrily. "But I have sources who tell me that he really loves you."

Anna looked disdainfully at Pete. "Who? Pete? He doesn't know anything. He can barely speak English." She saw Pete shoot her an angry glance but she didn't back down.

Driscoll laughed. "Yes, I do agree that Pete has his limitations but he does seem to like money. So, I expect he'll do what I tell him."

"Just how did you get out of jail, Mr. Driscoll?"

"I'm not without a few connections. What your brother seemed to forget is that my wife is from an extremely wealthy family. They would no more see me rot in jail than they would let a Chinaman run for mayor." He laughed, finding his little joke funny. "The police department owed my wife's family a few favors and I got out. It was that simple."

"So you're free, just like that?"

"Not quite, my dear. You see, you're brother ruined my reputation in that town for good. My wife gave me my freedom and enough money to live on comfortably for the rest of my life, but on the stipulation that I leave San Francisco and California for good. It's a shame, too. I liked that place. Gullible people all over."

"What about your family, Mr. Driscoll? Won't you miss them?"

Driscoll shrugged his shoulders. "Not much. You see, your brother went under the mistaken impression that I cared for my family, which I did not. Hell, my daughter was exactly like my wife. They both drove me crazy. All they cared about was money and clothes and which ball to go to next. I was glad to get away from them both. To tell you the truth, your brother did me a favor." Driscoll laughed.

"He's not my brother, Mr. Driscoll." Anna glanced

402

at the corpulent man in the brocade dressing jacket, reminding herself that he had murdered Roberto and had almost murdered Nathan. She didn't want to forget that he could do the same to her at any time. "I think you're wasting your time. He knows I'm in love with Garrett. If anyone comes after me, it will be Garrett."

"Oh, that young McReynolds. Not too bright. I could've owned his ranch if it weren't for your—" Driscoll hesitated a moment, eyeing Anna up and down. "What should I call him? Your lover?"

"Nathan Hawkins is not my lover."

"I think you're lying, Miss O'Leary. I've had you two watched ever since you left San Francisco. Pete here tells me that you two seem mightily attracted to each other. I saw it that night I met you in the restaurant. He couldn't take his eyes off of you. Poor Rebecca."

"Why do you say that?"

"I think she actually thought she was in love with Hawkins. Oh, well, she'll get over it. I'm sure she'll find herself some rich young man who'll spoil her just like I did."

Anna stared at Driscoll, not believing that he could be so callous about his own daughter. "What do you intend to do with me?"

"Do?" Driscoll looked at Pete and shrugged his shoulders. "What do you think I should do with the lovely Miss O'Leary, Pete?"

"I could think of a few things, Mr. Rogers, sir." Pete smiled as he looked at Anna.

"Would you like that, Miss O'Leary? Would you like me to give you to Pete?"

Anna met Driscoll's eyes, refusing to back down in spite of the cold fear that gripped her insides. "I'm sure you'll do with me whatever you want anyway,

Mr. Driscoll. I don't imagine you give a damn what I like or you wouldn't have brought me here."

Driscoll pounded his fist on the arm of the chair and laughed. "Did you hear that, Pete? I like this girl. She's got spunk. I knew it the first time I saw her."

"Yes sir, you shoulda seen her last night. She come into the bunkhouse and drank whiskey and played poker."

"Did she win, Pete?"

"Yes sir, she was real good."

Driscoll eyed Anna, nodding his head. "You can go now, Pete. Why don't you go up into the other car and get something to eat."

"You be all right alone with her, Mr. Rogers?"

"Do you think this little girl is going to do anything to hurt me? Besides," Driscoll said, reaching into the side of the chair, "I have this handy in case she tries anything."

Anna watched Pete as he left the car, then she looked back at Driscoll. "You still haven't told me what you want with me. I told you, Nathan won't come after me."

"And I think you're wrong. Even if he doesn't come after you because he loves you, he'll come after you because that's what your loving parents would want. He *will* be here, Miss O'Leary."

"What are you going to do with Nathan?"

"I have lots of plans for Mr. Hawkins."

"Why are you doing this, Mr. Driscoll? You are the one who tried to murder him all those years ago. Why don't you just take your money and leave?"

"I don't like people who deceive me, my dear, and that is just what Nathan Hawkins did. Mark my words. He will be sorry that he ever tried to ruin me."

*   *   *

404

Nathan paced across the room trying to keep patient. "Stop it, Clare. You knew this was coming. Hell, we hadn't even seen each other in ten years. You can't expect to fall in love all over again in a month."

Clare stood up, holding the handkerchief to her nose. "But that's what happened to me, Nathan. It was like we were never apart. It was just like when we were kids."

Nathan grabbed Clare by the shoulders. "But we didn't have anything when we were kids except a physical relationship. All we did was sneak around and kiss and find places to make love. We didn't really know each other, Clare. We still don't."

"It's her, isn't it? It's your sister. You're in love with her."

Nathan clenched his jaw, trying to keep his temper. "She's not really my sister and you know it."

"You haven't answered my question, Nathan. Are you in love with Anna?"

Nathan thought of the way he had left Anna earlier that morning and a warmth spread throughout his body. He had never felt quite that loved in his life. "Yes, I am in love with Anna. I'm sorry, Clare. I wasn't trying to use you. I honestly thought I could fight the feelings I had for Anna but I can't any longer."

"How long have you known, Nathan?"

Nathan couldn't lie to Clare. "I think I've known since the first time I saw her."

Clare walked back to her chair and sat down. "I knew I didn't quite have the hold over you that I did when we were younger. You couldn't bear to be away from me in those days. It was different this time. You weren't really with me, you were with her."

"I am sorry, Clare. I enjoyed our time together."

"So did I." She stood up, looking at Nathan, and

kissed him on the cheek. "It's probably for the best. I would've ruined you anyway. I have an insatiable appetite, and I probably would have had numerous affairs, and you would have never forgiven me and—"

Nathan pulled Clare to him, hugging her tightly. "You're a good friend, Clare. Thanks." He kissed her on the cheek and walked out of the room, anticipating Anna's reaction when he told her that he wanted to marry her.

Nathan saw the Appaloosa tethered to the tree from a distance. He smiled as he thought of Anna lying under the trees somewhere. He rode into the small grove and dismounted but Anna wasn't there. He looked all around but he couldn't find her. He untied the Appaloosa and rode back to the ranch, leading the stallion behind him. Jake met him when he rode into the yard.

"I was wondering when you'd return, Mr. Nathan. I've been looking for Miss Anna. She went tearing out of here early this morning on that stallion of your pa's, and I was afraid something would happen to her. I sent Pete to check on her."

"I didn't see Pete or Anna. How long ago did you send Pete out?"

"A couple hours ago. Do you suppose they went for a ride together? Pete being a young fella and all."

"I don't think so, Jake. That's not like Anna. Was it your idea or Pete's to go after her?"

Jake lifted his hat and scratched his head. "Now that you mention it, it *was* his idea. Said he'd be glad to go out and look for her. Then he went into the bunkhouse and came back out with a saddlebag. I didn't think nothin' of it at the time. I just thought he was taking some things in case he had to stay out looking for her." He shook his head. "I'm sorry, Mr. Nathan. Do you think he's done something to Miss Anna?"

"I don't know, Jake, but I'm going to find out." He dismounted and went into the house. He quickly climbed the stairs and went into his room, pulling out one of his drawers. He took out the knife his father had given him and stuck it down his boot. He got down a rifle and extra shells and a gunbelt, fastening it around his waist and went back outside. Jake had filled his saddlebags with supplies. Nathan mounted his horse. "Thanks, Jake. Tell my parents that I'll bring her back. No matter what it takes, I'll bring her back."

Nathan rode back to the oaks and followed the trail from there. It was fresh and easy to follow, almost too easy. They were traveling west, and Nathan kept up a hurried, almost frantic pace. When night fell, he kept riding. He had ridden for a couple of hours when he heard the sound of the train whistle in the distance. Then he knew: Pete was taking Anna to meet the train. For some reason he wanted her on it. Nathan knew that the next train didn't leave until midday of the following day, so he stopped and made camp. He tried to figure why Pete would want to kidnap Anna, and he couldn't come up with an answer. Pete had seemed to be a harmless fellow who cared a good deal about his work. That's what bothered Nathan the most. If Pete was working for someone else, which he probably was because he wasn't smart enough to do this on his own, then he would probably have blind loyalty to that person. But to whom? Nathan couldn't figure out who would want to get to him through Anna. There was only one person who would want to see him dead and that was Franklin

Driscoll, and he was in jail. A cold feeling gripped the pit of Nathan's stomach as he thought of the unthinkable: Somehow Driscoll had gotten out of jail. Was it possible? He thought he had covered all avenues of escape. He was sure he had fixed it so Driscoll would either rot in jail or be sent on a boat to China. But he didn't know for sure. He was gone, and for all he knew Driscoll could've gotten out. Although he'd taken much of Driscoll's money, Driscoll's wife was still an extremely wealthy woman in her own right, and her family was one of the most powerful in the city. If they had been able to arrange for Driscoll to get out and discreetly leave the city—Nathan was suddenly very afraid for Anna. Driscoll would do anything to get back at him, and somehow he had figured out that Anna was the best way. The man had found out his true identity and had even bribed one of the ranch hands to spy on Nathan and Anna. It probably hadn't been too difficult to figure out that they were in love with each other. Nathan tried to calm himself so that he could think clearly. Driscoll was probably going to lead him back to California, back to where he still had some influence and power. Somehow Nathan had to follow Driscoll's trail but when he got there, he had to let Chin know that he was back and that he might need his help. He had to get Anna back safely, no matter what.

"Are you sure you wouldn't like to change into something else, my dear? You look awfully uncomfortable in those clothes."

Anna wrapped her arms around herself, feeling secure in the pants and shirt, feeling much less vulnerable. "No, thank you. I'm quite comfortable."

"Well, I'll let you stay in them for now but when we get to where we're going, I'm afraid I'm going to have to ask you to change. You'll have to take a bath and fix your hair, and I'll make sure you have a suitable gown."

"Where is it I'm going, Mr. Driscoll?"

"You'll find out soon enough, my dear. Go ahead and finish your tea."

Anna sipped at the bitter-tasting tea. It quickly warmed her insides. She finished the cup and set it down.

"All done? Why don't you go lie down on that couch over there? Go on. I'm not going to hurt you. It's your lover I want."

Anna stood up and walked over to the couch, lying down on her side. She stared at Driscoll from across the room, afraid to close her eyes, afraid that Driscoll would do something horrible, but her body and mind were tired and she could feel herself relax immediately. The bumping motion of the train rocked her to sleep. She wrapped her arms around herself, trying to block the vision of Driscoll from her mind. Instead she thought of Nathan. She prayed that he cared enough about her to come after her. She felt herself panic. What if Nathan didn't even know she was missing? What if he had gone off to Clare's to marry her? He might not even care that she was gone. She felt tears sting her eyes but she refused to let them come. Nathan had loved her passionately the night before, and he had told her that he would never leave her. She had to hold onto those words and to the belief that he loved her enough to come after her.

"We'll be stopping here for awhile, Miss O'Leary. I've taken the liberty of ordering you some clothes and I'll have a bath sent in. While I'm out, I'd like you to bathe and dress suitably for an evening out. Please don't try anything foolish. There are guards at both doors and the windows are locked. I have all of the weapons so, please, use that pretty head of yours and don't try anything.''

Anna watched as Driscoll walked out. She waited for the tub to be carried in and the buckets of hot and cold water to be poured. Then she went to the frosted windows and looked out, but she couldn't see a thing. They had stopped but they weren't in any town that she knew. She thought of breaking one of the windows and trying to jump out but she knew that the guards would hear her. She resigned herself to the fact that she would have to play Driscoll's game until she could find a way to escape.

She took off her clothes and eased herself into the warm, soothing water of the tub. She took the soap that had been left with the towels and lathered her arms and legs. She had visions of Nathan's naked body and felt herself quiver; she had never wanted anyone as much as she wanted him. She only hoped that he felt the same about her.

She soaked in the tub for a time, sipping at the tea Driscoll had left for her. She suddenly felt thoroughly relaxed and almost drowsy and forced herself to stand up and get out of the tub. She started dressing in the undergarments Driscoll had left for her, pulling on the silk camisole and pantalets. She sat down to put on her stockings when the rear door opened and Pete walked in, slamming the door behind him. Anna picked up one of the towels and covered herself. ''What do you want, Pete?''

''Oh, don't let me bother you none, miss. I'll just watch.''

''Shouldn't you be outside? Mr. Driscoll said I was

to be left alone."

Pete took a step forward. "Well, what Mr. Driscoll don't know won't hurt him." Pete threw his rifle onto the couch and walked toward Anna. "You sure are a pretty thing standing there all clean. I bet you smell good, too." He went up to her and touched her hair. "You have real pretty hair, miss."

"Thank you, Pete." Anna moved slowly backward. "If Mr. Driscoll finds you in here he'll be very angry."

"Like I said before, what Mr. Driscoll don't know won't hurt him." He grabbed Anna's hair and pulled her forward. "That's right, come to old Pete. I've been looking at you for a long time now, you know. I was real sad when you went away but when you came back you looked even prettier than when you left. Bet you never even noticed me, did you?"

"I noticed you, Pete. I did. You were always nice to me."

"And you were always nice to me. I'd sure like it if you'd be nice to me right now, missy." Pete yanked Anna forward by her hair. She fell against him, and he pinned her with his arms. "Umm, you do smell real pretty." Pete buried his face in Anna's hair.

"Pete, please don't." She tried to pull away but Pete held onto her.

"What's the matter, missy? I'm not good enough for you? You'll let your own brother do things to you but you won't let me touch you. Now I think that's real sick." Pete nodded his head, squeezing Anna so tightly she had to gasp for breath. "I heard you two that night. I heard what you was doing. It's not right that a brother and sister should be doing such things."

"Please, Pete, let me go. Nathan's not my brother. Do you understand? He's not my brother."

"You're ashamed of what you done. I can under-

411

stand that. It's not your fault. I saw the way he carried you out of the card game."

"Pete, what do you want?"

"I want you just the way you gave yourself to him. I want you to say all of the things you said to him."

Anna stared at Pete in horror. "My God, were you listening? Were you in the house?"

"I was right outside your bedroom door. I heard it all." Pete licked his lips and smiled. "I coulda killed you both right then but I didn't. Now aren't you grateful to me for that?"

Anna stared at Pete's cold, blank eyes. "You make me sick. I'd rather die than have you touch me."

Pete's hand went around Anna's throat. "Yeah, well, that's just what might happen if you don't change your mind real quick. I'll give you one last chance."

"Never," Anna answered firmly, gasping for air as Pete tightened his hold on her throat. Anna pounded on Pete with her fists but it seemed to have no effect on him. He just stared at her with a crazed look in his eyes and tightened his hold on her. Anna felt dizzy, and she felt her body weaken. Was this how it was to end for her?

The door burst open and Driscoll and two of his men ran in. "Let her go, Pete."

Pete loosened his hold slightly, but still held Anna against hinm. "She's mine, Driscoll. You said I could have her."

"And you can, Pete, right after the deal is set."

"No, I can't wait until then. You all just get out of here. You can have her back when I'm through with her."

"Pete, it looks like you were trying to hurt her. She won't be any use to me if she's dead."

"She's not being nice to me, Mr. Driscoll. She

412

needs to be taught a lesson."

"And she will be, Pete. You just have to be patient." Driscoll walked slowly forward.

"You wait there. I don't trust you. I been promised things all my life."

"I'm not lying to you, Pete. I paid you the money, didn't I?"

Pete seemed confused. "Yeah, you done that."

"Well, do you think I'd lie to you about her? As soon as I make the deal, you can do anything you want with her. But I need her alive, Pete. She isn't worth anything to me if she's dead. Do you understand?"

"I think so." Pete loosened his hold on Anna. "She just looked so pretty all cleaned up like this. I just wanted to be with her. You can understand that, can't you, Mr. Driscoll?"

"Sure I can, Pete." Driscoll walked forward, taking one of Anna's hands. "But she has to get dressed now, Pete. Will you let go of her now?"

Pete ran his fingers through Anna's hair one more time, then released her. "I'll be waiting for you, missy." Pete walked toward the rear door.

"Pete?" Driscoll called in a kind voice.

"Yeah, Mr. Driscoll?" Pete turned around.

Driscoll quickly pulled the gun from his belt and shot Pete in the chest twice. The force of the shots knocked him back toward the door. Driscoll motioned toward the guard. "Get him out of here." He put the gun back in his belt and looked at Anna. "You look pale, my dear. I hope that ordeal didn't frighten you."

Anna looked at the blood that was on the floor where Pete had fallen. She had never seen anyone get shot before. She had seen people die but she had never seen anyone killed so violently. She realized how

413

easily Driscoll had pulled the trigger. She looked at him. "Can I get dressed now, Mr. Driscoll?"

"By all means, dear. Get dressed. Don't let what happened with Pete spoil the evening."

Anna walked to the pile of clothing and self-consciously began getting dressed. When it came to the bright red dress that Driscoll had selected for her, she stopped. There were buttons all along the back which she couldn't reach. She knew he would have to button them for her. She took a deep breath and steeled herself against his touch. "Could you please help me button this dress, Mr. Driscoll?"

Driscoll finished pouring two glasses of wine and walked to Anna, a wide smile on his face. "I'd be delighted, my dear. I used to help my wife and daughter with these things all the time. I'm pretty good at it, if I do say so myself."

Anna closed her eyes as Driscoll's chubby, cold hands rubbed against her back. She was astounded at the cheerful way he talked about his wife and daughter, as if they were still a part of his life. She was even more astounded that he had murdered someone in cold blood only minutes before. When he had finished she turned around, smiling. "Thank you very much. Now I have to fix my hair."

"No, don't do that. Leave it down. I like it that way. It shows the Indian in you."

"All right." Anna accepted the proffered glass of wine that Driscoll gave her. She sipped at it, enjoying its flavor. "It's very good. Thank you."

"Good. Sit down, sit down. Dinner will be brought in in a short while." He looked back at the blood-stained floor. "I do hope they clean that up before we eat, don't you?"

Anna nodded, realizing that the man was as sick as Pete. She was sure that he had actually convinced himself that he was right in everything he did, even if it was murder. "What do you plan to do with me, Mr. Driscoll?"

"That, my dear, depends on you."

"In what way?"

"It depends on whether you want to be sold as a white slave or whether you want to become my mistress. It's up to you but I suggest you decide soon. We'll be in San Francisco in a few hours."

Driscoll hadn't touched her yet, but Anna felt his hold on her tighten. She looked at the man, trying to imagine what it would be like to have him make love to her. She felt sick at the thought. "Why me?" she asked boldly.

"Because you're his, that's why." Driscoll sipped at his wine. "I would like nothing better than to see his face when I tell him I've made love to you." He laughed loudly. "Drink your wine."

Anna drank. "So it's entirely up to me. You won't force me?"

"No, I won't force you, although I must admit I would like to know what it's like to make love to an Indian." His eyes devoured Anna.

"What happens to me if you sell me to the slavers?"

"Oh, you'll get sent to China on a ship with other white women. There are many Chinese who will pay highly for the services of a white woman. But I understand that you must be good at what you do. They can be very cruel people. But who knows, you might find it enjoyable. I hear that Chinese men have very diverse tastes."

Anna lifted the glass of wine to her lips. She couldn't believe this man would honestly expect her to choose between him and white slavery. But she knew that he meant what he said. He was a cruel man, a man who thought nothing of human pain or suffering. "What if Nathan doesn't come, Mr. Driscoll? What will you do then?"

"But he will come."

"What if he doesn't?" Anna persisted.

Driscoll looked at Anna. "Then I suppose I will keep you for myself and sell you to someone else when I'm through with you."

"What about Nathan?"

"I'll think of another way to get to him. Through his parents, perhaps."

Anna felt the fear rise in her but she forced it down. "You don't scare him, Mr. Driscoll. He got you once. He can do it again."

"Don't count on it, my dear." There was a knock on the door and Driscoll turned. "Come in. Ah, it's dinner. Good, I'm starving. Why don't you have a seat over there, Miss O'Leary?" He pointed to the table that was set up for dinner. "And would you please get some people in here to take this tub out?"

Anna and Driscoll waited until the food had been brought in and the tub had been emptied and taken out. Then they sat down. "It's duck. One of my favorites. I hope you like it."

Anna looked at the food in front of her, trying to force herself to eat. She took a bite of the duck, feeling as if it were her last meal. "I'm not sure what you want from me."

Driscoll chewed on the greasy meat, obviously enjoying the meal and Anna's discomfiture. "I want you to come to me willingly, and then I want you to tell your lover that you are my mistress. I can't imagine anything I'd like more than the look on his face."

"Why don't you believe me, Mr. Driscoll? I'm not Nathan's lover. He is engaged to marry another woman, and he loves her. If he cares for me, it is only because of our parents."

"We'll see. Would you like to play some cards after dinner?"

Anna looked disinterested. "I don't really want to play cards. All I want is to go home. I don't want to play your game anymore."

"But I'm afraid you don't have much choice, my dear. You'll play the game as long as I want you to. Dessert?"

Anna shook her head. "I don't want anything from you."

"You may change your mind when you see the inside of that cargo ship filled with white women who are to be taken to China. I think then you'll be begging me for forgiveness."

"Never," Anna responded coldly.

"We'll see."

"Nathan won't come after me. He'll never come." Anna watched Driscoll's smiling face, and she knew even as she said it that she was wrong. Nathan would come after her, and she was frightened for him. Driscoll was capable of anything.

Anna held onto Driscoll as he led her blindfolded down a street. She knew they were by the bay because she could hear the water. Driscoll grabbed her arm more tightly.

"Step up, my dear. You're walking across a ramp."

Anna stepped tentatively on the wooden ramp but Driscoll pushed her forward, and she fell unseeing into the arms of a man.

"There you are, Captain. Take her down below and examine her. I think you'll find her to be the prize of

417

the lot."

"Thank you, Mr. Driscoll. She looks to be a pretty one."

"She is, and I won't go a penny lower than what I asked for her."

"We'll see after I take a closer look at her. For all I know you stole her out of some whorehouse along the wharf."

"One look will tell you for sure that she's quality merchandise, Captain. Do you mind if I have some of that brandy of yours? It's a touch cold this evening."

"Come down," the captain replied, pulling Anna down the narrow stairs that led to the hold of the ship. He opened a door and shoved Anna inside, locking the door behind her.

Anna quickly pushed off the blindfold and looked around her. It was a small cabin. She ran to the door and jiggled the handle. It was locked. She searched the cabin for any kind of weapon but she could find none. She felt panicked. If this man liked her, he would keep her on board this ship until they reached China. She realized for the first time that she might never see her parents, her home, or Nathan again. She ran to the small bunk and turned over the mattress, looking underneath for anything she might use as a weapon. Then she looked at the lamp on the table and picked it up, standing to one side of the door. She heard footsteps in the hall and a key in the door. The door opened slowly and someone peered in. Anna stayed behind the door. Suddenly the door came crashing against her, pushing her against the wall. She tried to throw the lantern at the man but he grabbed it from her hands and pushed her down on the floor.

"Well, you need a little lesson, I see." He walked

over to her, standing above her, slowly taking out his belt.

"What do you think, Captain?" Driscoll walked into the room and closed the door. He was drinking from a bottle.

"I think she's a might too spirited for her own good. She needs to be taught who's boss right now." The captain wrapped the belt around his hand and slapped it against his thigh. "I've lots of ways of taming women. By the time I get them to China, they'll do anything for any amount of money." He lifted his arm and whipped the belt against Anna's back. Instinctively she covered her face and head, but the captain kept hitting her.

"Don't you think that's enough, man?" Driscoll took hold of the captain's arm. The captain looked at Driscoll with cold, hard eyes.

"Don't you be telling me what to do on my own ship. I paid you good money for this bitch. I'll do whatever I damn well please with her."

"But if you scar her, you'll never get good money for her."

"I won't scar her. I'll just teach her a little lesson." The captain lashed Anna a few more times and then stopped. "Don't ever try to hurt me again, girl, or you'll regret it. As long as you're on this ship you'll do as I say. If you don't, I can make this a living hell for you. Do you understand me?"

Anna nodded her head, rubbing her arms. She watched as the captain and Driscoll left the room, locking the door behind them. She didn't know what to do. There was no way for her to escape, and she couldn't imagine living the life of a whore in China. She knew she would rather die than face a life like that. She decided then that if there was no way to

419

escape, she would find a way to kill herself. She would never let a man like the captain use her the way he intended.

Anna struggled against the men but they held her firmly as the captain held the pipe to her lips. "Breathe in, girl. You won't believe how good it'll make you feel."

"No." Anna tried to pull away from the men but they held her tightly. The captain's tight hold on her jaw caused her unbelievable pain. She still tried to jerk her head away but he held it firm. "You either do as I say or you'll be sorry." The captain reached into his boot and brought out a knife. "Hold her hand flat on the table." He held the knife to her little finger. "I'd hate for you to lose this finger, but I'll cut it off right now unless you smoke that pipe. I'm not like that pig, Driscoll. I don't play games."

Anna saw the madness in the man's eyes and she nodded, opening her mouth to take the stem of the pipe. She inhaled deeply, feeling the smoke burn her lungs. The captain told her to do it again and she complied, suddenly feeling dizzy. Her entire body felt as if it didn't belong to her. She looked at the man in front of her, and she suddenly didn't know who he was and what he wanted. She felt as if she were in a dream world of some kind. When the captain put the pipe to her lips again, she didn't struggle. She gladly inhaled the smoke that made her feel so good. She heard a noise and looked to see the door open. She thought she saw Driscoll but she didn't care. She didn't care about anything but how she felt at that moment.

"Are you crazy letting her smoke that stuff? Why she'll be hooked by the time she gets to China."

420

"Exactly. Then she'll do anything I ask her to do and gladly, just so I'll give her some of this lovely opium to smoke."

"Is that what you do with all of them?"

"It's the easiest way. That way I don't have to beat and scar them. I just get them hooked on this stuff, and they'll do anything I ask. It's real simple."

"How long do they last on this?" Driscoll saw the glazed, lifeless look in Anna's eyes.

"A year, sometimes two."

"And what happens after that?"

"They get thrown out into the streets. Who cares after that? They aren't my concern any longer. Once I get them to that godforsaken place, I get the hell out of there. All those foreigners make me nervous." The captain looked at Driscoll. "You did put it in her food and drink, didn't you?"

"Yes. But this is different."

"It's no different. Same drug."

Driscoll walked over to Anna, who was now sitting back on the bunk. "Hello, Anna. How are you doing?"

Anna stared at Driscoll from glazed eyes. "Hello." She looked past him to the captain. "Can I have some more of that?"

The captain winked at Driscoll, smiling. "Sure you can, girl. Here you are." He held the pipe to Anna's lips while she inhaled the smoke. "That's a girl. It feels good, don't it?" He ran his hand over Anna's cheek and down to her shoulder. "You're right about one thing, Driscoll. This one is lovely. She might be worth keeping for myself."

"What if I were to buy her back from you for double what I got?"

The captain looked thoughtful for a moment, then shook his head. "I don't think so. I think I'm going to keep her for me until I get there and then sell her for a big profit once I get there."

"Well, I envy you, Captain. I wish I had kept her for myself. Oh well, I made myself a nice profit, and it'll be worth seeing the look on my friend's face when he finds out I've sold his woman to a white slaver." Driscoll walked to the door. "When will you be setting sail, Captain?"

"I'll be here three more days and then I'll be off. I'd like it if you brought me some more women like this, Driscoll."

"There are no more women like that, Captain. I'll be back, hopefully before you set sail. I want this man to see what he's losing, and I want him to suffer just as he made me suffer."

Chapter XV

Nathan paced nervously in Chin's small room, occasionally walking over to the window and looking out at the bay. He had followed Driscoll to San Francisco and then lost him. He couldn't figure out where he would be taking Anna. Nathan had checked with the police and found out that Driscoll was released because of family connections but he was forced to leave the city. So Nathan surmised if Driscoll was in the city he was someplace where he didn't want to be found. Nathan went straight to Chin, hoping that with his connections he could find out something about Driscoll.

Nathan went back to the mat and sat down, crossing his legs in front of him and closing his eyes. He tried to push the horrifying images of Anna and Driscoll from his brain but he found it impossible. He knew that Driscoll would do anything to get at him, and he hated to think what the man might do to Anna.

Nathan heard footsteps on the stairs and looked up as the door opened. Chin walked in, ignoring Nathan as if everything were just fine. Nathan jumped to his feet. "Did you find out anything?"

"I must have tea first. You know I cannot talk without tea."

Nathan paced nervously as Chin prepared the tea and brought the tray to the middle of the room. They both sat down on the mat. Chin poured tea for Nathan and handed it to him. "Driscoll has been seen in the city."

"He has? Where?"

"Down by the wharf and here in Chinatown. He has a woman here that he has seen for many years."

"Where is she?"

"Listen to me. No one has seen the girl."

"What do you mean no one has seen the girl? I followed them both here. I know she was with him."

"How do you know it? Did you actually see them together?"

"Damn it, Chin, do you think I'm stupid? The man who kidnapped her was found dead, shot in the chest twice beside the rail where Driscoll had his private car. What do you want me to do?" Nathan stood up. "She's with him, Chin. I can feel it."

"All right. I believe you."

"So where do I go from here? I need to find out where the hell she is before it's too late."

"It may already be too late, Nathan."

Nathan came back to the mat and squatted down. "What are you talking about?"

"I have heard that there is a ship in the harbor."

"So? There are lots of ships in the harbor."

"Not ships like this. This is a white slaver ship. It is rumored to have many white women aboard who are to be taken to China."

Nathan felt as if someone had ripped his guts from his stomach. He had heard the rumors about those ships for years but he had never really thought much about it. Part of him believed that those ships really

424

did exist and the other part, unfortunately, didn't care enough to find out. He had heard of the things that were done to the women on those ships, and the thought of any of those things happening to Anna made his blood run cold. "Is it possible Anna is on that ship, Chin?"

"I don't know. The only way we find out for sure is to see for ourselves. But that very difficult. Ships cannot be searched because they pay police much money, and they have armed guards on board. If she is there, it will be difficult to find a way to get on ship."

Nathan shook his head. "Jesus, Chin, if Anna is on board that ship, she couldn't survive in a place like that."

"Do not torment yourself with those thoughts. You must use your anger and fear wisely. Let them guide you. We will find a way to get on the ship." Chin thought for a moment. "First thing we must do is find a disguise for you. Driscoll will be looking for you, and he will have given your description to the men on the ship. You need to change your clothes, and we must do something about your hair."

"It's going to be hard to change the color of my hair."

"Well, we can hide it if we cannot change the color of it. We can cover it with stocking cap and dirty your face. We can make you look like you work on docks."

"They're not going to let me on the ship just because I work on the docks."

"I will go on ship. You will wait on shore. You walk around and make a lot of noise and then you disappear. You walk farther down the wharf and get into water and swim up to ship. You must be careful; there will be many guards. But if I can create disturbance, you can climb on board."

"What are you going to do?"

"If it is a slave ship, they will want slaves. I must find some women who would be willing to come with me for the evening. Women who are nice looking but unafraid."

"Whores," Nathan said.

"Yes, but they must be white. They will not want Chinese. Can we do this?"

"Sure, for enough money I can get some to go along with us. All we have to tell them is there's someone on board we're trying to get off. We'll tell them to act like they're frightened. It could work."

"I will also have other plan."

"What's that?"

"I have many friends who owe me favors. I will have them waiting on shore with guns. If we do not come out in a few minutes, I will have them come in after us."

"Well, it's the best we've got right now. We don't have any time to waste."

Nathan appraised the women standing before him. They were all Caucasians, all attractive and all whores. He had taken them out and gotten them expensive dresses. He made them remove their make-up and brush their hair down. They all looked demure and lovely. He smiled and shook his head. "You ladies would fool me."

"I think this is going to be kinda fun," one of the girls named Rita said. "It's sort of an adventure."

"It's also very dangerous. You're aware of that, aren't you?"

"What we do is dangerous, sonny," another named Gina replied. "And hell, you've paid us well enough. This beats lying on our backs all night."

They all laughed. The third one spoke in a quiet, concerned voice. Her name was Lila. "Tell us again what your girlfriend looks like. We don't want to make any mistakes if we have a chance to get her out of there."

"She's tall, a little taller than you, Lila. She's got dark skin and black hair. And her eyes are blue, the kind of blue you see in sapphires."

"I've never seen me no sapphires, mister."

"Sorry. They're a deep blue color, the way the ocean looks before a storm."

"She sounds real pretty."

"She is and she's young, too young to have this happen to her."

"We were all too young for that, mister," Gina said caustically.

Nathan looked at them all. "Listen, if any of you want to back out, now's the time. You don't have to do this. The men we're fooling with are rough. It's possible you could get hurt."

"I'm not worried," Lila replied nonchalantly. "I get hurt all the time at this job, and I never even get to leave the bedroom." She looked at the others and laughed. "We're ready to help you and your friend."

"Good. I'll be back for you right at dark, and we'll go on down to the wharf. My Chinese friend, Chin, will be the one who takes you on board. He'll have some friends helping him."

"Where will you be?"

"I'll be in the bay swimming toward the ship. I'm hoping I can get on without being seen and help you get her out." Nathan walked to the door of the hotel room. "I'll see you ladies at dark."

"We'll be waiting."

*　　*　　*

Nathan pulled the dark stocking cap way down over his hair. He put the heavy blue wool coat over his shirt and pants and buttoned it all the way, pulling the collar up. He stuck his two pistols in his belt and his knife in his boot. He turned to Chin. "What do you think?"

"It not too bad but it not too good either. Good thing it will be dark when we go there. You make sure you not get too close to ship."

"I'll walk up with you and the girls, and then I'll disappear."

"Do not get your hopes up, Nathan. She might not even be on that ship."

"But I have to know for sure, and that captain will probably know where Driscoll is if Driscoll's been on board."

"All right. We go now."

Nathan and Chin left Chin's butcher shop, walking up the street to a shop that sold jewelry. Chin stopped for a minute to talk to the owner, and within a few minutes two large Chinese men appeared. Chin started walking.

"Who are they?"

"They are very grateful cousins that Huang Li brought over from China. They will do anything for him, and he, in turn, owes me many favors. Tonight they will do anything for me."

Nathan glanced at the two burly men behind him. "I didn't think Chinese grew to be very tall."

"You always assume, boy. You will never learn anything that way."

They kept walking until they came to a restaurant. Chin went inside and returned moments later with four more young men who walked silently behind them down the street.

"More favors?" Nathan asked, looking back at the

six men.

"Of course."

Chin and his men went to the wharf and waited while Nathan picked up the three women and brought them to Chin. While each of the women waited patiently, Nathan tied their hands behind their backs and tied handkerchiefs around their mouths.

"Good luck, girls," he said as he blended into the group that followed Chin to the boat ramp. Armed guards stopped them when they reached the ship Chin had heard about. He stepped forward, bowing his head. "My name Chin. I would like to speak to captain of ship."

The guard stepped forward, pressing the barrel of the rifle into Chin's chest. "Who the hell cares who you are, chink? I ain't disturbing the captain for no-body."

"I have three beautiful women here that I think your captain will be interested in." Chin looked at the man in front of him, thinking how best to get to him. "You do not appear to be a stupid man. If you let me speak to your captain, I will pay you money. If your captain likes the women I have brought him and he makes much money from selling them, he will also give you money for being smart enough to let me speak with him. Only a stupid man would say no to that."

The guard seemed confused. "I don't know. The captain said he wasn't to be disturbed."

"This is important, don't you think?" Chin looked back at the women. "They are beautiful, don't you think? I hear that your captain likes only beautiful women. If you let me talk to him for two minutes, I am sure he will buy the women." Chin reached slowly into the pocket of his jacket and brought out some gold coins. "I will also make sure to tell the captain what a smart guard he has out here. What is your name, sir?"

The guard took the money. "My name's Willie." He looked at Chin and then at the group of people behind him. "I guess it'll be all right. Follow me. The rest of them stay there until I say it's all right for them to come aboard."

"I understand." Chin followed Willie on board and down into the bowels of the ship. Willie knocked on what appeared to be the captain's cabin.

"Sir, I got someone here who wants to talk to you."

"I told you I didn't want to be disturbed, idiot!"

"But it's real important, sir. It's about some more women. I seen them. They're real pretty like you like, Captain."

There was a long silence and then a crashing sound inside the cabin. They could hear footsteps as the captain came toward the door and opened it. He looked outside. He squinted at Chin and shook his head. "I ain't dealin' with no chink. Get him out of here, Willie."

"Wait, sir. The women are right outside. All you have to do is take a look at them. I think you'll like them."

The captain considered what Willie said. "All right, but they better be worth it. Go get them." He looked at Chin for a minute, then opened the door. "Come on in. I suppose it doesn't matter who I deal with as long as I get good merchandise."

Chin bowed his head politely and walked into the dimly lit room. The sweet odor of opium was heavy in the air. He felt as if he would choke on it. He didn't realize there was anyone else in the room until he saw a figure lying on the bunk. "Could you turn up the lamp, Captain? It will be easier to see the girls."

"Might as well." The captain walked over to the table and turned up the lamp. "There." He lifted the pipe from the table and lit the match to it, inhaling deeply. He looked at Chin. "What's the matter? You must be used to seeing this all the time."

Chin had not even heard the captain. His eyes had traveled to the bunk and to the prone figure of the young girl who was lying there, dressed only in a slip. Her dark hair was tangled and spread all over, and her expression was impassive. Her deep blue eyes seemed lifeless. It was Anna. "Is this one of your girls?" Chin forced the emotion from his voice.

"Who, her? I just got her about ten days ago. Pretty little thing, ain't she? Yeah, I figure she'll keep me busy until we get to China, and then I'll sell her for a nice little profit." He lifted the pipe toward Chin. "You want some?"

"No thank you." Chin turned as the door opened, and Willie brought in the three women. Chin smiled inwardly, admitting that Nathan had done a good job in selecting whores who looked like everyday young women. They appeared to be lovely, innocent and, best of all, scared. Chin walked over to stand in front of them. "So, are you interested in any of them, Captain?"

The captain walked over to the three women and circled around them, looking at them as if they were prize beef. He lifted Lila's blond locks and ran his hand along her neck. "This one sure is pretty. Those Chinamen will go crazy over her. They love those light-haired ones." He looked at Rita and Gina, nodding his head as he did so. "You did good bringing them here, Chinaman. What's your price?"

"Six hundred dollars."

"Six hundred dollars! Are you crazy? I wouldn't pay that much if they were all virgins, which they probably aren't."

"Then I will take them and go. I do not have much time to waste. I heard you were a good businessman, Captain, not a thief. You know that you can sell each of these women for at least five hundred dollars once you get to China." Chin started pushing the women toward the door when the captain walked toward him.

"Hold on a minute. Maybe I underestimated you, Chinaman. I always like to see what kind of man I'm dealing with before I strike a deal."

"Now you know. I will take no less than six hundred dollars."

The captain walked over to Lila again, shaking his head. "I bet I could get at least a thousand for this one alone." He turned to Chin. "You got yourself a deal, Chinaman. Willie, take them and put them in with the other women, all except the blonde. I'd like to take a closer look at her." Willie ushered the other two women out while Lila stood by the door. "Go on over to the bed, honey. Have a seat. There's nothing to be scared of."

Lila walked over and sat down on the bunk, looking at Anna and then up at Chin. Chin nodded slightly while the captain puffed on his pipe. He walked over to the captain.

"Perhaps I could have some of that now, Captain. I never like to partake when I am doing business."

"Wise decision." The captain offered Chin the pipe.

Chin inhaled, quickly blowing the smoke out. He looked at Anna. "I wonder, Captain. Would it be possible for me to borrow this woman for the evening."

"Who? Her? Why would you want to do that?"

"I like the look of her. She is almost childlike."

The captain smiled broadly. "It'll cost you, Chinaman."

"How much?"

"One hundred dollars," the captain said coldly, anticipating Chin's reaction.

"How long will I have with her?"

The captain stared at Chin, a dumbfounded look on his face. "What do you mean?"

"I will not pay one hundred dollars to have a woman for only one hour. It will take me longer than that to wake her up. I like my women to know what they are doing when they are with me."

"Yes, I've heard some strange stories about you Chinese. You do some funny things to women. No wonder they're so afraid to go over there." The captain looked at Anna and shrugged his shoulders. "Hell, why not. She's not worth much that way anyway. I'll give you till the morning with her. But remember, I only have to pay you five hundred dollars for the other three."

"Which you will give me now, of course."

"Yeah, sure." The captain walked to a trunk and took out a small box. He counted out some bills and handed them to Chin. "Good doing business with you, Chinaman. Next time I'm in port, why don't you look me up."

Chin flipped through the bills, then put them into his pocket. "Yes, perhaps I will do that." He walked over to the bunk and pulled Anna to a sitting position. "Where do I take her?"

The captain walked over to Lila and yanked her to her feet. "Don't worry about it. You take my cabin. I'll take this one some place else. Have fun, Chinaman." He laughed as he slammed the door shut.

Chin pulled Anna to a sitting position. She was like a rag doll. Her eyes were glazed and unfocused. Chin held her against him and gently slapped her cheeks. "Anna, can you hear me? My name is Chin. I am a friend of Nathan's. I have come to help you."

433

Anna did not respond. Her body went completely limp, and she lay back down. Chin shook his head. Short of carrying her off the ship, there was no way he could get her off of it. It would take her days before she could fully concentrate again. He had seen the work of opium too many times. His gut twisted when he thought of what the captain had done to her. He didn't want to think what Nathan would do when he found out. He could do nothing but wait for Nathan and the others.

Nathan swam through the cold water toward the ship. He heard noises behind him and he stopped, treading water as he watched the silhouettes of the men who swam toward him.

"What are you doing here? You're supposed to be back on shore."

"Chin say we are to help you. He say we not to let you alone."

Nathan shook his head, knowing that Chin was right. "Okay, I want you to follow me. When we get to the ship, we'll go on one by one. We have to try to take out the guards so that I can get down below."

"We follow you."

Nathan took the lead and swam toward the big ship in the darkness. He heard the water slapping against its heavy wooden sides and could see one of the guards, sitting near the rail overlooking the bay, drinking what appeared to be a bottle of whiskey. Nathan silently swam around the ship to the starboard side. There was no guard on that side. He looked for a rope, for anything that might facilitate his climb, but he couldn't find anything. He couldn't get up on the ship without a rope.

"We can get on ship. Drop you a rope," one of the

Chinese said to Nathan.

Nathan turned to him in the darkness. "How can you climb the side of a ship without a rope? It's impossible."

"Nothing impossible." The man spoke to the others in Chinese. "You wait for us."

"All right." Nathan watched as the man in the water swam to the edge of the ship and held on, digging his fingers into the rough planking. The next man climbed on his shoulders, taking a moment to find his balance and set his grip. The smallest man spoke a single word in Chinese, then scrambled up the living ladder until he was able to reach the railing. Nathan watched in awed silence, ignoring the chill of the water as it numbed his hands and feet. The Chinese looked through the railing and then climbed over. Seconds later a body came over the side of the ship, then another. A rope snaked down the side. The other two Chinese climbed the rope, and Nathan pulled himself up after them. "Thank you," he said to the men.

"Two of us will go to front of ship to eliminate guards. I will go with you."

"I'm going down below. That's where I think she is."

"Please, I will go before you. I am more experienced at this than you."

Nathan nodded, realizing that these were the men of whom Chin had so often spoken, men who had been trained since childhood to defend themselves with their bodies. They moved silently down the stairs to the hold of the ship. The young Chinese stopped as they passed the bunks where the crew slept. There were a few noises, and he crept silently past the door. Nathan followed. They came to the end of a hall and a large door. Nathan looked inside

435

but he couldn't see anything. He tried the door but it was locked. "You wouldn't happen to know how to pick a lock, would you?"

The man went to the door. He took an instrument out of his pocket and worked it in the door a moment and then it was open.

Nathan looked at the man, silently thanking Chin for sending him after him. They went inside the dark room. Nathan knew immediately that it was filled with bodies. The odor of human suffering was everywhere. "Anna," he whispered her name in the darkness.

"That you, mister?"

Nathan recognized Gina's voice. "Gina? Where are you?"

"Over here."

Nathan started toward the voice but tripped on someone's legs. "Gina, can you come toward the door?"

"Sure. Come on, Rita."

Nathan waited as the two women talked toward the partially opened door. "Did you see her?"

"Yeah, we saw her all right. She didn't look none too good either."

"Where was she?"

"She was in the captain's cabin. She was on his bunk, and she was drugged or something because she hardly even moved."

"Drugged?"

"It was opium." Rita's voice came out of the darkness. "I've done it before. I could tell by the look in her eyes. There was nothing there."

"Where's Chin?"

"He stayed with her. He made a deal with the captain. Said he wanted to have her for the night, and the captain took Lila to another place. He was quite taken with her. Poor Lila."

"Don't worry about Lila. We'll get her out."

"Should we try to get out of here now?"

"No, you stay here until we're sure the guards upstairs are taken care of. We'll come back for you."

"Be careful, mister. That captain's a crazy one. No telling what he'll do."

"Sit tight, girls. We'll be back for you." Nathan left the room and followed the young Chinese. They walked to the end of the hall and stopped when they heard a noise. It was from the room closest to them. Immediately the Chinese stepped in front of Nathan and walked to the door, putting his ear against it.

"There is a man and woman in there. The man is beating her up."

Nathan started forward but the Chinese man stopped him. "I will enter first." Nathan started to object but the man moved quickly, opening the door. The lamplight was on and they could see the captain and Lila. The captain was telling Lila to do something, and she was fighting him. The Chinese man moved quickly, opening the door and moving across the room like a cat. Nathan joined him and they had the captain pinned to the floor before he could do anything. Nathan stared at the man, pulling Lila behind him.

"Where is the Chinaman and the other girl, the girl with the dark hair and blue eyes?"

"I don't know what the hell you're talking about."

The Chinese man looked up at Nathan and he nodded. The man applied pressure to the captain's throat until the man started kicking and flailing his arms about. The Chinese man released his arm. "All right. They're down the hall in my cabin."

"One more question. Where's Driscoll?"

The captain looked from Nathan to the Chinese

man. "This isn't very smart, you know. I have guards all over this ship."

"Not now you don't." Nathan put his foot against the man's nose. "Do you know how easily I could shove your nose through your brain? It would only take seconds but it would be extremely painful." Nathan pressed the heel of his foot into the captain's face.

"All right. Driscoll's staying at a place in Chinatown with a Chinese girl he's known for years. All I know is he's going to stay there until he finds a man—" The captain hesitated. "You're him, ain't you? You're the one he's looking for!"

"You haven't finished answering my question."

"After he finishes up with you and the girl, he said he was going East. Said there were lots of opportunities for men like him there."

"What is the girl's name?"

"What girl?"

"The Chinese girl."

"Hell, I don't know."

Nathan pressed his foot into the man's face. "Try to remember."

"All right. I think it's Kim. He said she was from a good family but she had lost face. Now she makes a living as a prostitute. That's all I know."

"That's not enough."

"I told you that's all I know."

"Well, then, I guess your worthless life is over a lot sooner than you ever expected." Nathan stood up tall and lifted his foot, taking aim at the captain's nose."

"Wait! I do remember something. He said she lived on top of a bakery. He said she even worked in the bakery every morning because the people who owned it had taken her in and been kind to her when her family threw her out. That's all I know, mister."

438

Nathan turned and went to the door, hearing a thud as the Chinese man knocked the captain unconscious. "Lila, I want you to go in with the other women until we're done. One of us will be back for you."

"Listen, Nathan, your woman's in bad shape. He was awfully bad to her. Don't let her suffer any more than she already has."

"Thanks, Lila. Now go, down the hall." Nathan went out the door and down the other way to the captain's cabin. He knocked on the door. "Chin, it's me."

The door opened and Chin stood, an exasperated look on his face. "She is over there, Nathan."

Nathan walked into the room and over to the bunk. Anna was lying on her side, still dressed in the slip, her arm flung up over her head, her hair a tangled, matted mess. Her face was very pale, and her lips were dry and cracked. He sat down, touching her face. "Anna, wake up. It's me. Nathan. Wake up, Anna." He slapped her face lightly. Anna opened her eyes to look at Nathan but there was no sign of recognition. Nathan was shocked by the lifeless look in her eyes. He pulled her limp body to him, holding her tightly. "Come on, Anna. I'm taking you home." He wrapped a blanket around her and lifted her into his arms. "Come on, Chin. Let's get the hell out of this hole." Nathan carried Anna out of the room. The Chinese man was waiting for them in the hallway. "Would you get the women out of that room? If they can't walk, carry them out. I want them all out of there."

"Let us make sure that all of his men are disposed of first," Chin said as he nodded to the young man. He ran off and returned within a few minutes, nodding his head. "All right, Nathan. We can go."

Nathan carried Anna up the stairs and onto the deck. He heard the women follow. Chin's men were standing all around the deck, rifles in hand. They watched as Nathan and Chin walked across the ramp. Nathan turned to the three women who helped him. "I want to thank you all. You took a great risk."

"I just hope she'll be all right, mister. Good luck."

"Good luck to you."

Chin walked up to Nathan. "I sent word to Charley. He will have a bedroom prepared for Anna at Joe's house. She will need you for the next few days. When she wakes up, she will want the drug. You must stay with her and help her. It will be very difficult for her."

"Is there anything I can do to help her?"

"Charley will know what to do. She won't want anything for a few days. She will be very sick. When she starts to feel better, Charley will have soup and tea for her. Make her drink them. It is important." Chin put his hand on Nathan's shoulder. "If you need me, send Charley for me. I will be there."

"Thanks, Chin. I don't know what I would've done without your help. You are a friend."

"No more thanks. Go. There is a carriage waiting for you. Bring her to me when she is well."

"I will." Nathan held onto Anna as he lifted her into the carriage. As the carriage bumped and jostled along the road, Nathan felt a fear grip him like no other. He was afraid he would lose Anna now that he had found her. He knew that she was strong but he was afraid that she wouldn't be able to face whatever the captain had done to hurt her. He held her to him, praying that she would be well.

Anna reached out but there was no one there.

There were flashing colors and then a white light that hurt her eyes. She turned away from it and closed her eyes. Her body hurt, and she felt hands touching her everywhere, but when she opened her eyes all she could see was emptiness. She saw a tunnel and she walked toward it. It was dark in the tunnel, and she was afraid to go inside but she heard someone calling her name. She hesitated at the entrance but she couldn't resist the sound of her name. She went inside the tunnel. It was black. She couldn't see anything, not even the dim outline of shapes. She reached out but she could feel no sides to the tunnel. She looked down and was able to see a swirling fog. She looked back but the entrance to the tunnel had disappeared. She was all alone in the darkness. She heard her name again, and she ran toward the sound, to the only familiar thing she had heard in what seemed like ages. She ran and she ran but still she couldn't find an end to the tunnel. Then, suddenly, there was a smell, a sweet, flowery smell of smoke. It comforted her and she breathed in, inhaling the smoke deep into her lungs. She felt the loneliness begin to disappear as the smoke took over her body. She walked farther into it and kept breathing, delighting in the way the magic smoke made her feel. She was happy and nothing mattered but the smoke. She twirled around and breathed deeply but the smoke was gone. She opened her eyes and looked around her, and the tunnel had disappeared. She felt frightened. She needed the smoke. It was the only thing that made her feel human. She heard voices and could see people in the distance but she couldn't see their faces. They were running toward her. She saw them as they got closer. She saw her parents, and she saw Nathan and Garrett, and she was afraid to face them all without the smoke, afraid that they would

441

see the awful things that she had done. She ran but the harder she ran the faster the smoke disappeared until finally she was left alone to face the people she most wanted to avoid. She felt the tears as they filled her eyes and ran down her cheeks. She felt naked and dirty. Nathan stepped forward and held out his arms to her but she shook her head.

"No, no, I can't. Go away."

"Anna, it's all right. I want to help you."

"No, you can't help me." Anna shook her head and pulled away from his arms but his grasp was too tight. "Let me go, Nathan."

"No, I won't let you go. Ever."

Anna opened her eyes. She wasn't dreaming. She looked around her and recognized the room in Larissa and Joe's house. She was sitting up, and Nathan had his arms around her. She looked down at herself, and she was still in the dirty slip that she wore on the ship. She suddenly felt sick to her stomach as she thought of the ship and the man on it. She covered her mouth with her hands until Nathan held a bowl in front of her. Her entire body was wracked with spasms as she vomited. She felt weak and her head ached. "May I have some water?" She ran her hands through her hair, shoving it out of her face. Nathan brought her the water and she took it, her hands shaking.

"Take it easy." Nathan put his arm around her, helping her hold the glass. "Why don't you lie back down?"

"I can't. I don't feel well. I need help."

"It'll be all right."

"I'm sick, Nathan. You've got to get me some of the stuff from the ship. It'll make me feel good as soon as I smoke some."

Nathan looked into Anna's eyes. They were not

442

bright and clear like he knew them to be. "Do you know what that stuff was, Anna?"

"No, I just know that it made me feel better. I need it, Nathan," she pleaded.

"It was opium, Anna. You were smoking opium and probably eating it, too."

"No," Anna replied. She had heard the stories about the opium dens in Chinatown. She had heard how the people went in there in the morning and didn't come out again for two days. She had also heard how many of the people had died trying to find enough money to keep getting the drug. "You're lying, Nathan. That wasn't opium. You just don't want me to have it." She pushed the covers aside and stood up. "I'll go back to the ship myself. I don't need you."

"Why bother going to the ship, Anna? Why don't you just go down to Chinatown. There are lots of places down there where you could lie all day and never come out."

Anna stood by the window. Something was wrong. She didn't feel like herself. She thought she needed the stuff to smoke but she knew that it wasn't good for her. She also knew that what Nathan had told her was the truth. She turned to face him. "I need your help, Nathan. I don't know what to do."

Nathan walked to her, putting his arms around her. "I'll be here for you. You're going to be sick for a couple of days, and you're going to want that stuff more than anything in the world. But if you can get through the next couple of days without it, you'll be okay."

"I'm afraid."

"Don't be afraid. I won't leave you."

Anna felt tears come. "You came for me."

"Of course I came for you. I love you, Anna. I told

443

you that that night."

"But when I woke up you were gone. You had gone to Clare's."

"I went to Clare's to tell her I was in love with you. I didn't want to be away from you any longer."

"Oh, Nathan." Anna put her arms around Nathan, holding onto him. She began to shiver uncontrollably, and Nathan led her back to the bed.

"I'm going to have Charley fill a tub for you. It'll help you warm up."

Anna pulled the quilt up to her chin. "I'd like that. I need to get clean."

"You just relax. I'll be back to get you when the tub is ready."

Anna watched as Nathan went out the door. He looked so strong and healthy. He looked so good. Tears filled her eyes again, and she began to shake but not from the cold. Visions of the captain flitted through her brain, and she recalled what he had done to her. She felt an anguish rise in her, and she began to scream, a scream that wouldn't stop. Nathan ran into the room but she didn't see him. All she could see was the captain's ugly face. All she could feel were his rough hands. All she could smell was his fetid breath.

"Anna, don't fight me. I want to help you."

"You can't help me. You can't help me."

"I can help you. I love you. I love you, Anna." Nathan held her to him, running his hands gently up and down her back. "Just relax. Everything will be all right. I promise you."

"I'm afraid, Nathan. I'm afraid I'll never be able to forget that man. You don't know some of the things he did to me. You don't know."

"It doesn't matter, Anna. You'll never have to worry about that man again." He pulled the covers

444

from her. "Come on. You'll feel much better when you've had a bath." Nathan led Anna down the hall to the bathroom, an exclusive room that Anna normally loved but now didn't have time to notice. Charley was filling up the tub with buckets of hot water.

"Thank you Charley. I think when she's done, Anna could use some of that soup."

"I bring you soup, missy. You like."

"Thank you, Charley." Anna stood looking at the bathtub.

"What's wrong, Anna?"

"I don't know. I feel so strange. Everything feels so unreal to me."

"Do you want me to help you?"

"No. I'll be all right."

"Just call me if you need help."

Anna nodded and stood, staring at the water. She had flashes of the sound of the water in the bay as she slept on the bunk. She could hear the captain laughing as he made her smoke from the pipe, then as she begged him for more. She shook her head, trying to clear the unpleasant memories from her brain. She undressed and stepped into the steaming water. It felt hot against her skin but it felt good. She lowered herself into the clean water and completely dunked her head, getting her hair wet. She took the bottle of Larissa's shampoo and washed her hair, scrubbing it until her head hurt. When she was through rinsing her hair, she started on her body, scrubbing until she had covered every inch of her body. She laid her head back against the edge of the tub, feeling clean for the first time in weeks. As she lay there, bright visions popped into her brain, colors and images, things that made absolutely no sense to her but things that made her feel good. She longed suddenly for the smoke that made her feel good, the smoke that helped her to see more clearly. She needed it. She stood up and got out of the tub, drying herself off. She opened the door and ran down the hall to her room. Quickly she dressed in one of the many outfits Larissa had given her. She pulled out a cloak and covered her wet hair. She went to the drawer and pulled out a box which she had put there that was filled with money. She was afraid it wouldn't be enough so she took the sapphire earrings that Larissa had lent her, and she shoved the money and the jewels into a purse. She went to the stairs and listened. She couldn't hear anything and assumed Nathan and Charley were in the kitchen. She hurried down the stairs and into the entryway. The heavy front door was locked, and she turned the lock and opened it, quietly shutting it behind her. She ran onto the sidewalk, looked down the street, and started running. All she knew was that she had to have more of that smoke. She was afraid to go back to the ship so the only place she could go to was Chinatown. The thought of it frightened her, but the thought of not having the smoke frightened her more. She ran until she was able to flag down a carriage to take her the rest of the way. When she got out she didn't know where to go. She felt panicked suddenly, afraid something would happen to her, afraid she wouldn't ever have that feeling that the smoke gave her. She continued on down the street until she came to a man on the corner. He babbled at her in Chinese but she couldn't understand him. She looked at him, her eyes frantic.

"Smoke. Do you know where I can smoke?" The man looked at her as if not understanding until she made a gesture of smoking with a pipe. "Please." She took out her money and handed it to the man. "Smoke." The man nodded and took Anna's arm, taking her down the street to a shop that was closed. He went around the back and knocked on the door. A guard stood at the door. The Chinese man spoke to the guard and handed him Anna's money, after taking some for himself. Anna let herself be led into the dark room. The smell of the sweet smoke calmed her immediately. A small, thin Chinaman led Anna to a cot where she lay down on her side, watching as he prepared the pipe. When it was ready, he held it to her mouth and she inhaled deeply, feeling the sweet smoke go through her body instantly. She lay back on the cot, reveling in the way the smoke made her feel. The Chinaman tapped her shoulder and held the pipe to her lips. Again Anna inhaled deeply, pushing all the bad things from her mind. Nothing mattered now. Nothing mattered but the way the smoke made her feel.

"Charley!" Nathan ran down the stairs. "Is Anna down here?"

"No, Mister Nathan, I no see her."

"She's gone, damn it!" Nathan paced the kitchen nervously. "She probably went back to the ship for more opium."

"Or she could go to Chinatown. Very easy to get the poppy there."

"Do you know the places, Charley? Can you take me there?"

"I can take you." Charley threw off his apron, shaking his head. "It is bad stuff. It make you feel as if nothing wrong. It take your body and mind away from you. Come, we hurry. We find her before she do very much."

They ran to the carriage house and hooked up the horses to the carriage. Nathan drove, and Charley held on for dear life as Nathan tried to avoid people, horses, and trolleys. When they reached Chinatown, Charley told Nathan to pull the carriage into an alley behind some of the shops. Charley led the way, first to a shop where he conversed in Chinese with a man who shook his head. Charley motioned to Nathan to follow him.

"What did he say?"

"He say he see no women go into his place tonight. There are others we will try." Charley stopped at the back of a shop, knocking on the door and waiting before he entered. Another man appeared, looking skeptically at Nathan. But Charley spoke to the man in Chinese, and the man shook his head. Charley motioned Nathan to follow him. "He no see women tonight. We check other place I know." They walked up a hill and down another row of shops. They walked behind the shops and stopped at another door. Charley knocked, again speaking in Chinese to a big man. The man looked at Nathan and shut the door.

"What's the matter?"

"He talk to owner. I think she in there."

"I'm going in."

Charley put his hand on Nathan's arm. "Do not, Mister Nathan. They will shoot you before we step in the door. Let me talk. I have told him that she stole jewels from you, and you want them back. I have told him you do not wish to cause him trouble. Please, be patient. Do as I say." The door opened and a small, frail-looking Chinese man appeared. He looked at Nathan and then at Charley. He said something to Charley, and Charley spoke to him, gesturing with his hands and pointing to Nathan. The small Chinese man was silent a moment and then nodded, saying something else to Charley.

Charley turned to Nathan. "He say there are two women in here. He say we can come in and look but he want no trouble."

"Tell him I understand." Nathan nodded toward the man.

They followed the man into a room that led to another door. The man opened it, and Nathan was immediately assaulted by the sweet smell of smoke. The room was dimly lit, and there were cots all over the room. People were lying on the cots, smoking the poppy, totally oblivious to anything around them. Nathan forced himself to get past the hatred he felt for Driscoll and the captain of the ship for doing this to Anna. Right now he had to find Anna and get her out of here. They went from cot to cot but Nathan didn't see Anna. He was quickly losing hope of finding her when he saw a cloak. He walked to the cot, and his stomach tightened at the sight before him. Anna was lying on her side, her arm hanging limply off the cot. Her eyes were open but she stared straight ahead of her, unable to see anything but what the drug made her see. Nathan nodded toward the Chinaman, and he left Nathan alone. Nathan squatted down next to the cot, moving the pipe and the tray that was there. He reached out and touched Anna's face. She was warm and sweaty, and she was mumbling something incoherent.

"Anna," he said softly but he knew as he said it that she couldn't recognize him. He put his arm underneath her and pulled her to him. She didn't fight him. She didn't even seem to notice that someone was touching her. Nathan picked her up in his arms and walked through the room, ignoring the blank stares of the people who lay all around the room. He got to the back door and kicked it open, inhaling the fresh air that literally burned his lungs. He hurriedly carried Anna to the carriage, waiting for Charley to catch up. Charley climbed into the carriage and drove as Nathan held Anna. When they reached Joe's house, Nathan carried Anna upstairs and stripped her, dressing her in a nightgown. She looked at him, trying to say something, but still nothing coherent would come out. When Nathan had put her in bed he went downstairs to the kitchen.

"Charley, I don't want her out of this house again. I want all of the doors locked, and I want her room locked when we're not in it. And I want you to make some of that tea for her that Chin told me about."

"It strong stuff. It make her very sick."

"Will it help her?"

"Yes, it will help her. It will help to get the drug out of her quicker. It will not be easy, Mister Nathan. She will fight you. I have seen this before. The people on the poppy get crazy. They hate anyone who takes their drug away from them."

"I don't give a damn. I just want her well. I'm going back up to sit with her until she wakes up. Just get some of that tea ready."

Nathan walked back upstairs and went into the room. He stood by the bed watching Anna. He would do anything it took to help her, even if he risked losing her. The only thing that mattered to him now was making her well.

Chapter XVI

Chin stood in the darkness on the wharf, watching the crew of the ship get ready to sail. He had thought about leaving the captain alone, but when he thought about what the man did to Anna and to countless other women, he knew he couldn't forget it. It reminded him too much of what had happened to his own sister. He would never forget the look on Nathan's face when he had seen Anna; he, himself was shocked when he first saw her. He nodded, satisfied that he was doing the right thing. He held up his hand to the men who were standing with him in the darkness. They moved quickly, climbing on board the ship and knocking out the crew that was up front. The rest of the crew was forced to jump overboard. Chin was waved on board, and he silently crossed the plank and went below. He walked to the captain's cabin, turning the handle of the door. He looked inside. The captain was sitting at his table, a glass in one hand. He was mumbling something but Chin couldn't understand what he was saying. Chin walked in behind the captain, two of his friends following close behind him.

"Hello, Captain."

The captain jumped. "What the hell?" He squinted his eyes in the dim cabin light. "Who's that? That you, Chinaman?"

"Yes, it is I, Captain."

"What do you want? If you got some more women for me I can't take them. I'm leaving without any women this time. Too dangerous."

"I'm not here about any women, Captain. I'm here about one certain woman."

"Which one's that?"

"The one that you bought from Driscoll."

"You mean the one that you had last night. I can't sell her to you, Chinaman. Some crazy man came in here last night and took her and all of the women away."

"Yes, I know." Chin stepped closer so the captain could see his face. "That crazy man is my friend and that woman you bought from Driscoll is the woman he loves. You have defiled an innocent girl and dishonored yourself before all men. You do not deserve to live, Captain." Chin's voice was quiet but filled with anger.

"Now wait a minute. Driscoll came to me. I didn't have no idea he was bringing that girl here."

"But still you bought her, and you and Driscoll hooked her on the poppy, didn't you? Isn't that what you do to all of the girls to make them do what you want?"

"Hell, there's nothing wrong with that. It's better than beating them, isn't it?"

"You do not understand, do you Captain." Chin stepped still closer. "When a man in my country has dishonored himself he does not deserve to live."

The captain started to stand up but looked at the men who stood behind him. "Now wait a minute. I don't know what you're talking about."

452

"Of course you do." Chin stared at the man with cold, dark eyes. "You have lived an honorless life. You have made your money by selling women for money, and you have used many of them for your own pleasure. Surely, Captain, it must have occurred to you at least once that this was not an honorable thing to do."

"Listen, I want you and those other chinks the hell out of here right now. Louie! Louie!"

"Yell all you like, Captain, but no one will hear you. It is just us. Now, I will give you a choice. You can die honorably or dishonorably. You decide."

The captain's eyes were frantic as they darted from Chin to his men. "Listen, I didn't mean the girl any harm. It just seemed like fun."

"Fun?" Chin stepped even closer, his dark eyes scrutinizing the man in the chair. "It seemed like fun to take an innocent girl and give her a drug like the poppy?"

"She didn't seem to mind. She kept asking for more."

"She asked for more because she was addicted to it." Chin shook his head. "I thought you might have some remorse for what you have done, Captain, but I can see that I was wrong." Chin reached into the wide sleeve of his tunic and pulled out a long, thin knife. He held it up, and the shiny blade reflected the lamplight. "I want you to take this knife and for the first time in your life do something honorable."

"You can't be serious." The captain tried to get up from the chair but Chin's men pushed him back down.

"I am very serious, Captain. You have a chance to redeem yourself right now."

"You're crazy. You're out of your mind."

"Quite the contrary, Captain. In many places this is

453

considered a very honorable deed."

"Well I think it stinks." The captain stood up, grabbing the bottle and hitting it against the edge of the table. He shoved the jagged pieces at Chin's men until they backed up. Slowly he stood up. He waved the bottle in front of him. "If I have to go, you're coming with me, chink."

Chin stood rooted to the floor, staring at the captain. "I am afraid, Captain, that you never had it in your soul to be honorable." Chin held the knife by the blade, then with a sudden flick of his wrist he sent the knife sailing across the room. It landed in the captain's chest, over his heart. The captain grabbed at the knife but he fell to the floor, a look of surprise and horror on his face. Chin walked over to him, removing the knife and wiping it on the man's clothes. He nodded to his friends and walked out. He didn't look back. The man was not worth the effort. Now there was one more matter he had to take care of for Nathan.

Nathan jumped as Anna screamed. He sat up in the chair and reached over to the bed, trying to take Anna in his arms but she fought him, hitting and scratching him. "Anna, stop it."

"I hate you."

"Stop it, Anna, or I'll tie you down."

Anna stopped struggling and looked at Nathan with pleading eyes. "Nathan, please, I need the drug. I need it. I can't live without it."

"Of course you can live without it. You have to tell yourself that you will be stronger than this drug, Anna. It's the only way you'll win."

Anna pushed Nathan away and turned onto her side. "You're doing this to me on purpose. You want to make me suffer.''

Nathan forced himself not to react. Charley had told him what to expect. "If you have to suffer to get this drug out of your body, then you'll just have to suffer. If you want to hate me, Anna, go ahead.''

Anna turned over and looked at him. "What about Clare? You really love her, don't you? You're only here because Trenton and Aeneva sent you. Well, I don't want you here. I want Garrett. Garrett is the only person who loves me.''

"If you feel that way when you're well, then I'll take you to Garrett. But you're not setting foot out of this room until you're over this.''

"Why don't you just give me a little in some tea? I could drink it in the tea. Please, Nathan.''

"Tea?''

"Yes, Driscoll gave it to me in my tea. It always made me feel so good. Please.''

Nathan considered Anna's request, then nodded his head. "All right, I'll get you some tea. But stay here, Anna. I'm locking the door.''

"I'll wait here, Nathan. I promise.''

Nathan left the room and locked the door, anguished at the sight of the woman he loved willing to do anything for a drug. He went down to the kitchen. "I'm ready for the tea, Charley.''

"She will drink it?''

"She said one of the men gave her the drug in tea. I'm just not telling her what I'm giving her in this tea.''

Charley shook his head, pouring the tea into a cup. "Tea very strong, make her very sick. She will be very weak afterward, but she will sleep." Charley handed the tea to Nathan. "Do you want my help?''

"No, I have to do this myself. I'll call you if I need you.'' Nathan went back upstairs and unlocked the door. Anna was sitting up in bed, a look of great anticipation on her face. He handed her the tea.

"Charley says it will taste a little bitter."

"Oh, I don't care." Anna blew at the steaming liquid and sipped at it, closing her eyes as she thought the opium was going into her body. She sipped at the tea again and smiled at Nathan. "I'm sorry about what I said before. I just needed something to help me."

"It's all right. Finish it up." Nathan watched Anna as she gratefully finished the cup of tea. She handed the cup to Nathan. "Feel better?" he asked, wondering how long it would take for the tea to take effect. Charley told him she would begin to get warm and start to sweat, then she would begin to get sick.

"Yes, it's just what I needed. You see, I don't need much, Nathan. There's nothing to worry about."

Nathan watched Anna closely. She leaned back against the pillows, mistaken in the belief that she had just taken something that would make her feel good. He could see the beads of sweat begin to form on her upper lip and her cheeks begin to flush. She moved her head from side to side, wiping her hand across her brow.

"It's hot in here, don't you think?"

"It feels just fine to me."

Anna kicked off the covers and pushed the hair back from her face. "Nathan, please open a window. I can't stand it."

Nathan didn't move. Anna was becoming more and more restless. Soon her body would begin to reject the tea that had just been put inside of her and soon, hopefully, she would begin to purge her body of the drug that had taken her will from her.

Anna bent forward suddenly. "My stomach. Something is wrong with my stomach." She moaned, rocking back and forth. Nathan brought the bowl to the bedside, along with towels and a wet cloth. He wiped Anna's face. "Oh, God, Nathan, I feel like I'm dying." She grasped her stomach even tighter until she couldn't control herself. She vomited into the bowl that Nathan held for her, spasm after spasm until she felt as if she couldn't stand it any longer. But soon she was sick again, and Nathan sat with her, holding the bowl, wiping her mouth and face, rubbing her back. Her body heaved convulsively for hours until finally Anna was worn out, her body completely spent. Nathan took the bowl out of the room to the bathroom and came back with fresh water. He undressed Anna and washed her, noticing how thin she had become. He dressed her in a clean nightgown and covered her up. He went down to the kitchen.

"Do you have any of that strong coffee, Charley?"

"It all over now?"

"Yeah. God it was horrible. I've never seen anyone get so sick. What do you put in that stuff?"

"Many strong herbs. In China we use it when people get poisoned. It help to get the poison out of the body. It do the same for the poppy."

"Will she still want it when she wakes up?" Nathan took the cup of hot coffee from Charley, sipping it gratefully.

"Don't know. Could be she still want the drug tomorrow but she will still be sick." He pointed to his head. "She thinks she needs it even after her body does not."

"But why?"

"Could be many reasons but probably because man hurt her. Maybe she cannot face what he did to her. Maybe she cannot face telling you."

"I love her, Charley. I would do anything for her."

"Just make sure she knows that when she wakes up. That will help her."

"I don't understand men like that. What makes them do the things they do?"

"Don't know but there will always be men like that in the world. But there will also be men like you and Mr. Joe and Chin. There is a balance."

"It's awfully damned hard to find the balance sometimes."

"Yes, but it is there. You must believe that."

Nathan stood up. "Thanks, Charley. You're one of those who helps create that balance. I don't think I would be the person I am if it weren't for you, Chin, Tong, and Joe. You've all helped me a lot in the last ten years. Thank you."

"No thanks needed, Mister Nathan. You get woman well and take her home. Give her love and many babies."

Nathan smiled. "Goodnight, Charley." He walked up the stairs, finally feeling how tired he really was. He walked into the room and lay down on the bed next to Anna. He looked over at her, brushing his hand lightly over her cheek. He had never even thought about having children with Anna but the thought excited him. He closed his eyes, feeling the weariness creep over him. He could think of nothing better than lying beside Anna every night when he went to bed and waking up next to her every morning.

Anna was in the tunnel again but this time it frightened her. The smoke around her made her sick; it was no longer something she looked to for release. She ran through the tunnel, hoping to get out of it but it went on forever. The smoke continued to swirl around her and engulf her. She wanted out and screamed for help. It was so dark, and she hated the smell of the smoke. She screamed for the only name that came to her. She said his name over and over, hoping he would hear her as he had heard her so many times before. She looked again at the end of the tunnel and saw a light coming toward her. She ran to it, unafraid of what was outside there now. She finally reached the end, and there in the bright sunlight stood Nathan, his arms opened to her. She ran to him, unafraid, unashamed. He said her name over and over. It was a sound she would never grow tired of.

Anna opened her eyes. She heard her name. She looked next to her and saw Nathan, asleep in his clothes, murmuring her name over and over. She reached over and touched his hair, running her fingers through its golden softness. She looked at his face and at the strength of his body, and she knew that she could love no other man but him. She leaned over to him, kissing him on the cheek. "Nathan." She said his name softly. Nathan stirred but didn't wake up. Anna held her stomach. She thought she was going to be sick again. She vaguely recalled the night before, and she remembered that Nathan had been with her through the entire night. She moved farther down in the bed so that she was lying next to him. She moved her head next to his and kissed him softly on the mouth. Nathan's body twitched, and he sat up, suddenly wide awake.

Anna sat up, looking at him. "Are you all right?"

"I was dreaming about you." He shook his head. "I thought you were still on that ship."

"I'm right here, thanks to you." She reached out and took his hand. "Nathan, there are some things I want to tell you. Some things that happened on that ship."

"Anna, you don't have to tell me anything."

"I want to tell you. I can't remember everything. All I know is by the time Driscoll got me to that ship I was hooked on the opium. He had been giving it to me in my food and drink, and I didn't even know it. Then the captain started giving it to me in a pipe. I was scared the first time but he forced me. After that I did it without argument. It didn't seem to matter at that point. I wasn't sure if you would ever find me. All I wanted to do was numb myself to him and everything else." She hesitated, looking down at Nathan's hand. "He would make me take my clothes off and stand in front of him. He would touch me all over. God, I can remember his hands. They were awful." She brought Nathan's hand to her lips, kissing it gently. "Not like your hands."

Nathan pulled Anna's head to his, holding her next to him. "It's all right. It doesn't matter what he did to you. He'll never touch you again."

"But it does matter. I'm not sure if I can ever forget it. He made me do things, Nathan—"

"Anna, listen to me." He cupped her face in his hand. "I don't care and you shouldn't either. Don't let him do that to you. Don't give him that much control over your life."

"I don't know if I can ever forget. I keep remembering things, and I feel so dirty."

"I will help you forget, Anna." Nathan kissed her softly, gently caressing her neck and shoulders.

"Oh, Nathan, I do love you." She opened her eyes and looked at him. "I love you more than I thought it was possible to love anyone."

Nathan pulled her next to him. "I want you to marry me as soon as you're well. Will you?"

"Yes." She threw her arms around him. "Yes, I

460

will marry you.''

"And will you have my children?''

Anna was stunned. "Are you sure, Nathan? Are you sure I'm what you want? Clare is so much more—''

Nathan touched his fingers to Anna's lips. "I don't love Clare. I love you. We have forgotten one other thing, though.''

"What?''

"Garrett. What about Garrett?''

Anna looked down, her eyes suddenly sad. "I do love Garrett but not in the way I love you. He deserves more than a woman who only loves him as a friend. But I don't want to hurt him. I want to tell him before we get married.''

"All right.'' Nathan hugged Anna, kissing the top of her head. "Will you be all right if I go out for a few hours today?''

"Yes. Where are you going?''

"I have a few things to do.'' He sat up, putting his feet on the floor. "I want you to eat some of Charley's soup. It'll fix you right up.''

"What was it he put in that tea last night? It wasn't opium, was it?''

"No. It was some ancient mixture that he says purges the body of all poisons. I'm sorry you suffered so much but I'm glad you're better. I couldn't stand seeing you on that stuff.''

"I'm sorry. I feel like such a fool. It was so strange feeling like I needed to have it. I actually felt like I would die without it. What a horrible feeling.'' She wrapped her arms around herself.

Nathan hugged her. "It's all right now. I want you to get some rest, and I'll see you this afternoon.'' He got up and walked to the door.

"Nathan.'' Nathan stopped and looked at Anna.

461

"I'll never be able to thank you for what you did for me."

Nathan smiled and left the room, confident for the first time since he was sixteen years old that his life was now his own.

Chin led Nathan into the dark warehouse. "Over here." They walked behind some boxes, and Chin opened a door. They went inside, and Nathan stopped when he saw Driscoll sitting naked on the floor, his hands and feet tied together. He was blindfolded and gagged.

"So this was your present to me?"

"What better present?" Chin asked. "I will leave you alone. You do what you must. No one will ever know."

"Chin." Nathan put his hand on Chin's shoulder. "I can't kill a man in cold blood."

"As I said, you do what you must. Then I will do what I must." Chin walked out, leaving Nathan alone in the room with Driscoll.

Nathan looked at the paunchy, overweight, lily-skinned man cowering in the corner before him, and he couldn't believe that he was once one of the most powerful men in San Francisco. Nathan walked over to him and lifted up the blindfold. Driscoll's eyes widened in horror. "What's the matter, Franklin? Did you actually think I'd forget about you?" Nathan yanked down the gag. "I'd like to hear what you have to say for yourself."

"Listen, I never meant your sister no harm. I just wanted you, that's all."

"That's all? You drugged her and then sold her to that pig who degraded her even more, and you say that's all?" Nathan kicked Driscoll in the thigh.

"You're a disgusting excuse for a human being. You don't even deserve to live, Driscoll."

"Listen, Hawkins, I still have money left. You can have it all if you'll just let me go."

"I don't need your money. I have enough money of my own."

"Land, then. I still own land all over this state. I can give it all to you."

"I don't want your damned land either." Nathan squatted down in front of Driscoll, looking into his eyes. "Do you even remember my little brother, Driscoll? Do you? Do you know that he was only eleven years old when we came here? He was just a kid and you murdered him. You never even gave him a chance."

"Listen, I'm sorry about your brother but—"

"You're sorry about a lot of things, aren't you, but that doesn't do anybody any good. You're just going to have to learn how to pay for what you've done."

"What do you mean?"

"I mean you have to be punished."

"Come on now, Hawkins. You can't start taking the law into your own hands."

"That's what you've done all your life, Driscoll. Why should I be any different?"

"Please, I'll do anything you ask if you'll just let me go."

"Sorry, Franklin. I can't do that. I gave you a chance once before, and you came after me. But your big mistake was taking Anna and not me. You never should have involved her in this."

"I'm sorry. I didn't know how much she meant to you."

"You knew exactly how much she meant to me." Nathan took out his knife, holding it in front of Driscoll's face.

Driscoll closed his eyes. "Don't cut me, Hawkins. Please don't."

Nathan brought the knife close to Driscoll's skin and cut the ropes that held him. He threw his clothes at him. "Get dressed. Now!" Nathan watched as the man hurriedly put on his clothes and his boots. "I've thought a lot about this, Driscoll. I thought that I could march you into the police station and have you confess to the murder of my brother and my friend, but knowing how corrupt the police are here, they wouldn't do anything to you. Then I thought of killing you outright, but I thought that would be too good for you. I wanted you to be able to think about what you've done in your lifetime." Nathan took Driscoll's arm but Driscoll pulled away.

"Where are you taking me?"

"You'll find out when we get there. Oh, and Driscoll, don't try anything. I'll have a gun on you, and Chin will have his men all around you. Understand?" Nathan took Driscoll's arm and led him out of the warehouse and into the midday sunshine. Driscoll shaded his eyes from the brightness. Nathan pulled Driscoll along.

"Where are we going? Why are we down by the bay?"

"Just keep walking." Nathan continued to pull Driscoll along until they reached a ship that was getting ready to sail. "Here we are."

"What do you mean?"

"This is your destination, Driscoll. Not your ultimate destination but this will be your new home for a few months."

"No, I won't go on that ship."

"You don't have any choice, Franklin. It's either that or I turn you over to Chin's men." Nathan stepped closer to Driscoll. "Have you heard of some

464

of the ways that the Chinese torture people? Especially people who have dishonored them or their friends?"

Driscoll looked at the cold, emotionless faces of the men around him and then looked back at Nathan. "What are you going to do with me?"

"Just what I wanted to do in the first place, only this time I'm going to make sure you'll get to China."

"China? No. I won't go. You can't make me go."

Nathan took out his gun and placed it in Driscoll's ribs. "It's up to you, Driscoll. If I have to, I'll kill you right now."

"But they'll kill me in China. I won't have a chance."

"Oh, you never know. If you work hard you might be able to buy your freedom in ten years."

"Freedom? What do you mean?"

"I've sold you, Franklin, just like you were going to do with Anna. You're a slave."

"You can't do that. It's against the law."

"I know but men like you manage to do it all the time, don't you?" Nathan shoved Driscoll forward. "See that man standing on the bow? He's the captain. He's been looking for a slave for his family. He wants one who is strong and will work hard. Naturally I thought of you."

Driscoll looked at the big Chinese man who stood on board. "You sold me to him? No. I can't believe this. You can't do this, Hawkins."

"I did it, Driscoll," Nathan replied coldly. "And this time you won't get away. The captain will make sure that you're chained for the entire trip. Then once you get to China, he'll take you to his province, and you'll be his personal slave. You'll have to do whatever he and his family want. Look at it this way, Driscoll. This will be a good opportunity for you to see how all those girls you've sold into slavery have

465

lived." He pushed Driscoll forward. "Now it's your turn."

"You can't do this, Hawkins. You can't." Driscoll looked around frantically. "Help, someone help me!"

"Do you actually think that anyone down here will help you, Driscoll?" Nathan dragged Driscoll to the ship and nodded to the captain. "Have a good trip, Franklin. Maybe if you're real lucky, you'll learn something about the Chinese people. Maybe you'll even turn into a human being." Nathan walked away, listening to the sound of Driscoll's screams in the background. But he didn't turn around. Like Chin, he believed that there was no reason to look back. He had only the future to look forward to now.

Anna tried to calm Trenton and Aeneva and Joe and Larissa. "I'll tell you all about it later but first I want to talk to Garrett. It's very important that I talk to him."

"What about?" Trenton asked.

"Well, you all may as well know. Nathan and I are going to be married." She smiled as everyone kissed her and congratulated her.

"I knew that boy had more sense than I gave him credit for," Joe replied. "This calls for a celebration. We'll have one tonight."

Aeneva hugged Anna. "I am so happy for you, dear. You know how much I love you both."

"It's all right with you and Trenton?"

Aeneva took Trenton's hand. "We couldn't be happier."

Trenton kissed Anna. "Now I don't have to worry about getting to know my daughter-in-law."

"You never did tell me how you all managed to

come here at the same time."

"We got a wire from a friend of Nathan's. He told us that you were safe and that we should all come here."

"And I told Garrett to come along because I know how close you two are," Trenton said.

"Who was it?"

"It was signed Chin."

Anna smiled, remembering the kind face of the man who had come to help her on the ship. "Chin is a wonderful man. I'm glad he told you all to come." She sat up in the bed, looking around at all of the people she loved so dearly. "I have so much to tell you, things that will upset you, things that will be hard for you to hear. But just know that I'm all right now. And I will be all right." She smiled. "Could someone tell Garrett to come up now. I'd really like to speak to him. But please don't tell him anything."

Aeneva kissed Anna once more. "I'll be in to see you later. I love you."

"I love you, too." Anna watched them all leave, and she was filled with love but she was sad, too. She loved Garrett and she didn't want to hurt him. This would be one of the hardest things she ever had to do. There was a knock on the door. "Come in." She smiled as Garrett took off his hat and walked across the room. He looked even younger and more handsome than she remembered. When he bent down to kiss her cheek, Anna held onto his neck, hugging him tightly. He sat down on the edge of the bed.

"Are you all right, Annie? I was worried sick about you. I didn't know what had happened to you."

Anna took Garrett's hand. "I'm all right now, Garrett. I'll tell you about it sometime but not now." She reached up and touched his face, the beloved face she had known and trusted for so long. Her stomach wrenched at the thought of having to hurt him. "How are you?"

"Better now that I see you're all right." He kissed her again, holding her tightly. "I was afraid I'd lose you, Annie. I couldn't imagine life without you."

"Garrett, don't. Please."

Garrett looked at Anna. "What's wrong?"

Anna looked away, unable to meet Garrett's eyes. "I can't marry you, Garrett. I'm not in love with you."

"But you said you loved me. You said you wanted to get married and build a life together."

"I know what I said and I'm sorry. I didn't really know what I wanted."

"But now you know?" Garrett responded angrily. "It's Nathan, isn't it? It's been Nathan all along. Why the hell couldn't you have been honest with me? Didn't I deserve that at least?"

"You deserved that and more, Garrett. I want to try to explain something to you." She looked at his hazel eyes, and she smiled, tears filling her eyes. "You are someone who will be with me the rest of my life, no matter where I go. You and I have the kind of friendship that will last forever. I have shared things with you that I'll never share with anyone else, not even Nathan. I've laughed and cried with you, and I've loved you with all my heart. But it's not the kind of love a wife gives to a husband, Garrett. It's the kind of love a woman gives to a man who has been and hopefully always will be her friend." She wiped the tears from her cheeks. "I'm not lying when I say I love you. I do love you. And I hope that someday you'll forgive me for hurting you."

Garrett was silent, staring down at the bed. When he looked up at Anna, his eyes were sad. "There's nothing to forgive, Annie. I think I've known all along how you really felt about me, and I was always afraid that someone else would come along and ruin it for us. But it's good that it did. I would've never made you happy. Not the way Nathan will." Garrett reached out and pulled Anna into his arms. "I'll always love you, Annie, and I'll always be there if you need me." He tilted her chin upward and kissed her softly on the lips. "You'll always be a part of me." He stood up and put on his hat, walking to the door.

"Garrett. I want you to be at my wedding."

"I don't know if I can do that, Annie. I'll have to think about it."

"I understand. Garrett?"

Garrett hesitated again. "What, Annie?"

"Can I name my first-born son after you?"

Garrett looked down at the floor, then back up at Anna. "You sure you want to do that?"

"Yes. Garrett Hawkins. It has a nice sound to it."

Garrett smiled. "I have to admit, it does." Garrett walked back across the room. "Stand up here. I want to give you a proper good-bye."

Anna pushed down the covers and stood on the floor. She looked up at Garrett, and again the tears filled her eyes. Why was it so hard to give this man up when she had found the man she loved? She felt his arms go around her and she began to cry, long deep sobs.

"It's all right. Hush, now."

"I don't want to give you up, Garrett," she said without even realizing it.

"But you can't have it both ways, Annie."

"I know." She buried her head in his chest, just as she had done so many times before, just as she had done the first time she had been laughed at and Garrett was there to protect her. It felt so good in his arms. It felt so right. She could have held onto Garrett forever but he finally pushed her away.

"You always did look pretty when you cried." He wiped the tears away with a finger. "It's all right, Annie. It is. Like you said, you and I will carry each other in here forever." Garrett took her hand and put it over his heart. "No one can ever take that away from us. No one." He covered her mouth with his, kissing her deeply, then he let her go. Anna watched him as he walked out the door, and she felt as if a part of her had been taken away. She felt somehow incomplete, and she wasn't sure if she could ever get that part of her back. Even with Nathan.

A month had gone by since the morning Nathan and Anna had confessed their love for each other, but Anna had become withdrawn since then. No one was able to get her to talk, not even Aeneva. She wasn't sure what was wrong. She knew that she missed Garrett, and she knew that quite suddenly she was unsure of her love for Nathan. But more than that, she couldn't stop thinking about what had happened to her on that ship as bits and pieces of it kept coming back to her.

For his part, Nathan was distraught. Just when he thought he had gotten Anna back again, he had lost her. When he returned from dealing with Driscoll, Anna wouldn't talk to him, and it had continued like that for the next several weeks. Finally, Nathan couldn't stand it any longer. He tried to talk to Anna one last time, but she wouldn't speak to him. So he packed up and went back up to the gold fields and to the shack where he and Tong had spent so much time together.

Anna continued her daily routine of washing,

dressing, and sleeping until Aeneva couldn't stand it any longer. "What is the matter with you, Anna? I thought you were in love with Nathan and you were going to marry him."

"I don't know what I want now. Nothing seems to matter anymore."

"Why not?"

"I don't know."

"That's not good enough, Kathleen Anna O'Leary." Aeneva took Anna by the shoulders and made the girl face her. "Tell me what is wrong."

"I'm afraid."

"Of what?"

"I'm afraid that what I feel for Nathan isn't real."

"Is what you feel for Garrett more real? Is that what you're worried about?"

"I don't know, Aeneva. I don't know."

"Only you can make that decision, Anna. I had to do it once myself."

"And you chose Trenton. But you always loved him. It was easy for you."

"It wasn't easy for me at first. I had a son by Ladro, and I felt I should stay with him. He was good to me and he loved me. But the thought of never seeing Trenton again made me realize that I couldn't be without him. That's what you must think about, Anna. Can you live with Garrett, knowing you'll never see Nathan again? Can you?"

Anna looked at Aeneva. "I don't know."

"Then why don't you find out?"

"What do you mean?"

"Go to Nathan. Talk to him. Find out if you really do love him. Don't torture him because you're unsure of yourself, Anna. Confront your feelings, whatever they may be."

Anna nodded, knowing that Aeneva was right.

471

One way or another, she had to find out her true feelings for Nathan.

Anna sat next to Chin in the wagon, bumping against him as they traveled on the rutted road.

"You are quiet, girl."

"I don't know what to say, Chin."

"Are you happy to be seeing Nathan?"

"I think so."

"You are not sure?"

"I'm not sure of much these days."

"What has happened to make you change your mind about Nathan?"

"I haven't changed my mind about Nathan. I still love him. But I love someone else also. Someone I've known all my life."

"I see."

"No, you don't. Garrett is my friend, and he knows me better than anyone else in the world. I feel safe with him."

"And you do not feel safe with Nathan? Did he not risk his life to get you from that ship?"

Anna looked down at her clenched hands. "I feel safe with Nathan but I am afraid also. When I look at Nathan I think of the ocean. The ocean can be calm but it can also be angry and rough. But when I look at Garrett, I think of a lake. A lake is always placid and calm and safe."

"Is that what you want? Safe?"

"I don't know, Chin. I can't stop thinking about Nathan. He touches me like no one has ever touched me before. But he has also seen me as no one else has ever seen me."

"And that frightens you?"

"Yes, it frightens me. He saw me at my very worst,

and I can't believe he still loves me."

"Whereas your other friend loves you for the way you have always been?"

"Yes."

"Is it not better that a man knows a woman for what she truly is and not for what he thinks she should be? You and your friend have a love based on childhood memories, but you and Nathan have a love based on what you have been through together. It is up to you to decide what kind of love you want."

Anna was quiet the rest of the trip, reflecting on Chin's words. She didn't know how she would feel when she saw Nathan, but she knew she had to make a decision about her life and get on with it. After a couple of hours Chin stopped the wagon. He pointed up a hill.

"The shack is up there. If Nathan is not there he will be in mine. You can wait for him."

"Where will you be?"

"I will go back to city. Come back for you tomorrow."

"What if I want to go?"

Chin shrugged his shoulders. "You will have to stay. Is best to confront your demons, girl. Do not let them torment you forever."

Anna took her bag and jumped down from the wagon, waving good-bye to Chin as he turned the wagon around and drove away. She walked slowly up the hill, looking around her. She could smell the pungent odor of the pines as she walked through them, and she noticed with mild interest the mines that were all around. She saw the shack and approached it slowly. She went to the door and called Nathan's name, but when he didn't respond, she went inside. Nathan was not around. She put down her bag. There was a small cot in the corner, a table

473

and two chairs, and a cupboard for supplies. She went over to the cot and lay down. She was tired. She didn't want to go out to look for Nathan because she knew he would come back when he was ready. She threw her arm over her eyes and forced herself to rest, but her mind couldn't forget what had happened to her. She felt as if she were a prisoner in her own body. Why couldn't she forgive herself when everyone else could? She felt herself relax and fell asleep. When she awoke it was almost sunset. She got up and went to the door. Nathan wasn't anywhere. She went over to the lamp on the table and lit it, turning it up. She brought out the bread, cheese, meat, and fruit that Charley had sent and put it on the table. She sat down to wait for Nathan, putting her elbows on the table and resting her head in her hands. She was tired of feeling tired. When, she wondered, would it be over?

"Hello."

Anna flinched at the sound of Nathan's voice. She looked up at the door. He was leaning against the side of the door, his hat pushed back on his head, his blond hair shining in the lamplight. His sleeves were rolled up to reveal strong, muscular forearms, and she noticed how healthy he looked. He was as exciting to look at as he was to be with.

"What's wrong?" Nathan asked as he walked into the shack and threw his hat on the cot.

"Nothing's wrong. You just startled me, that's all."

He sat down on the cot, pulling out his shirt. "I could say the same for you."

"I'm sorry," Anna said absently, watching him as he unbuttoned his shirt and took it off. His brown skin literally shone in the light, and he seemed even leaner than she remembered.

Nathan reached down to pull off a boot. "Why are

you here, Anna?"

She watched fascinated as he pulled off the other boot and set them next to the cot. Next came his socks. He unbuckled his pants and walked to the cupboard grabbing a towel.

"Where are you going?"

"Going to take a bath in the stream."

Anna watched him as he walked out, and she got up and followed him. She watched as he took off his pants and stepped into the stream. She could see his lean, tight body silhouetted in the twilight, and she was excited by the thought of it. She stepped closer and sat down on a rock, watching as he bathed. When he was through he walked out of the stream and wrapped the towel around him, picking up his pants. He walked past Anna to the shack. Again, she watched as he dried himself and put on a pair of clean pants, not the least bit interested in whether she was there or not.

"Are you hungry?" he asked, walking to the table.

"Yes. I brought some food."

Nathan nodded and sat down, eating in silence. He made no attempt to speak to Anna which completely bothered her. She couldn't understand it. Moreover, she didn't expect it. When Nathan was finished eating he walked over to the cot and lay down, stretching out on the flimsy makeshift bed. He looked over at Anna. "There's an extra blanket over here if you need it. I'm tired. I'm going to sleep." He turned over, his back to her.

Anna got up and walked over to him. "Aren't you even going to ask why I'm here?"

"No, why should I?"

Anna sat down on the edge of the cot, tentatively touching Nathan's bare back. "Nathan, I want to talk to you."

"About what?"

"About us."

Nathan turned over, his blue eyes seeking hers. "I didn't think there was anything more to talk about. I tried talking to you for over a month, Anna, but you didn't seem interested. I'm not going to waste my time where I don't belong."

"I was confused. I *am* confused."

"About what? About me or about Garrett?"

"I'm confused about both of you. Garrett has always been my friend. I was afraid I would lose that friendship once I married you. And you made me feel more loved than I ever thought was possible. You saved my life."

"So why are you confused?"

"Because I don't understand how you can still love me."

"What are you talking about?"

"I'm talking about what I was, what I had become."

Nathan sat up. "What the hell are you talking about?"

"I'm talking about the weeks I spent with Driscoll and that other man. You know the things they made me do. I couldn't remember them all but they started coming back. I don't know if I can live with those memories, Nathan." She looked at him, her large eyes pleading. "If I can't live with what I did, how can you?"

"Anna," Nathan said softly, pulling her to him. "Why are you doing this to yourself? You didn't do anything. You have nothing to be ashamed of. Driscoll and the captain took advantage of you. They used you. It wasn't your fault. The only feelings I have about that situation is hatred toward them because of what they forced you to do."

"Are you sure? Are you sure you won't remember what I was like when I was on the opium?" She shook her head. "God, I was awful. I'm ashamed to even remember."

"I'll never forget what you were like on that drug because it scared the hell out of me. I was afraid I was going to lose you forever. But I don't care that you were on it. I don't care that you were with Driscoll, and I don't care that you were with the captain. The only thing that matters to me now is that you're all right. You have to deal with your demons and not look back, Anna. It's a hard lesson to learn but it's an important one."

"Yes, Chin told me the same thing." She looked at him, nervously biting her bottom lip. "Have your feelings toward me changed?"

"Yes," he replied evenly.

"They have?" Anna could feel the fear in her rising. She had been too late. He had fallen out of love with her. "I understand." She started to stand up but Nathan took her hand.

"No, you don't understand. Sit back down here." He looked at her hand, bringing it to his lips and kissing it. "I was so damned angry with you when I came up here, I couldn't see clearly. I went out every day and shoveled and picked and carried rocks. I worked hard because I knew it would help me think clearly. And it did. I began to realize what you had been through. I couldn't imagine it myself because I didn't go through it, but I know it must've been hard for you. I knew that that's what was keeping you from me, not Garrett, and I knew that you had to work it out for yourself. I couldn't help you."

Anna squeezed Nathan's hand. "I want to work it out right now, Nathan. I want you to make love to me."

"Anna, that's not the way to do it."

"Don't you want to make love to me?"

"You know that I do but you have to be ready. Don't hurry it. We have all the time in the world. We know how good it can be between us. It will be that way again."

"Are you sure?"

"Yes, I'm sure." Nathan pulled Anna to him, kissing her head. "I still want you to marry me, Anna. But I want you to be sure this time before you answer."

Anna sat up and looked into Nathan's clear blue eyes, and there was no doubt anymore. She saw strength and love and support in his eyes, and she knew she wanted to be with him. "Yes, I do want to marry you. I do." Nathan put his arms around Anna and kissed her gently.

"Wait a minute." He got up and walked to the cupboard, taking out a scarf. He unwrapped the scarf and held a beautiful turquoise and silver necklace in his hand. He fastened it around Anna's neck.

"It's Sun Dancer's necklace," she said unevenly, her voice catching.

"Pa told me to give it to my wife someday. It looks good on you. Sun Dancer would approve."

"I love you, Nathan." Anna wrapped her arms around Nathan's neck, finally feeling the safety she had always sought.

"I love you, Anna. Since I found you, I have learned how to face my demons. I will go on from here. My future is with you."

Anna held Nathan's hands, kissing him softly. "And I will somehow find the courage to face my demons. I will not let them control me any longer. I will face my future with you."